THE NEXT
365
DAYS

THE NEXT
365
DAYS

A NOVEL

Blanka Lipińska

Translated by Filip Sporczyk

EMILY BESTLER BOOKS

— **ATRIA** —

New York • London • Toronto • Sydney • New Delhi

An Imprint of Simon & Schuster, Inc.
1230 Avenue of the Americas
New York, NY 10020

First Emily Bestler Books/Atria Paperback edition September 2022

EMILY BESTLER BOOKS / ATRIA PAPERBACK and colophon are trademarks of Simon & Schuster, Inc.

For information about special discounts for bulk purchases, please contact Simon & Schuster Special Sales at 1-866-506-1949 or business@simonandschuster.com.

The Simon & Schuster Speakers Bureau can bring authors to your live event. For more information or to book an event, contact the Simon & Schuster Speakers Bureau at 1-866-248-3049 or visit our website at www.simonspeakers.com.

Manufactured in the United States of America

1 3 5 7 9 10 8 6 4 2

Library of Congress Cataloging-in-Publication Data is available.

ISBN 978-1-6680-0531-6
ISBN 978-1-6680-0532-3 (ebook)

THE NEXT
365
DAYS

Cervical cancer doesn't hurt, but it WILL KILL YOU!
Get a cervical smear to live and enjoy sex for longer!

CHAPTER 1

Hot wind winnowed my hair as I drove my convertible down the promenade. Ariana Grande blared from the speakers. I couldn't think of a song more fitting for my current predicament than "Break Free." "If you want it, take it," sang the pop star, and I bobbed my head to each word, cranking up the volume.

It was my birthday. I was getting older and should probably be feeling depressed, but the truth was that I felt more alive than ever. As I stopped the car, waiting for the light to turn green, the chorus began. The bass boomed, and I couldn't have felt happier. I sang along.

"'This is the part when I say I don't want ya. I'm stronger than I've been before,'" I shouted with Ariana, waving my arms. A young man stopped his car next to mine. He sent me a flirtatious smile, tapping a hand on the steering wheel to the rhythm of the song. Aside from the loud music and my loud singing, what must have caught his eye was my outfit. Its scantiness, to be precise.

I wore a black bikini that perfectly complemented the color of my purple Plymouth Prowler. To be honest, there weren't many things that didn't complement that car. It was perfect. The beautiful, rare vehicle had been my birthday present. I suspected the gifts wouldn't stop coming anytime soon—that my man wouldn't stop showering me with presents—but I hoped against reason that this one had been the last.

It all began a month before. I would get something new each day. My thirtieth birthday required something special, and thirty gifts would apparently do the trick. I rolled my eyes and stepped on the accelerator as soon as the light turned green.

A few moments later, I parked the car, grabbed my bag, and headed to the beach. The weather was sweltering hot, and I intended to make the most of it. Reach my limits. Sunbathe until I'd had more than enough. Taking a sip of iced tea through a drinking straw, I plodded across the waterfront, relishing the feeling of the hot sand on my feet.

"Happy birthday, old girl!" my man shouted. I turned around and a geyser of Moët Rosé exploded in my face.

"The hell do you think you're doing?!" I screamed through bouts of laughter, trying to escape the fizzy stream. Without effect. He chased me with the bottle spewing out its pressurized content. When it was empty, he threw himself at me and toppled me to the ground.

"Happy birthday," he whispered. "I love you."

His tongue slid between my lips and started its dance. I moaned in pleasure, wrapping my arms around his neck and spreading my legs, as he took his place between them, hips slowly twisting.

He laced his fingers with mine and pinned my arms to the ground, pulling away his head and fixing me with an amused stare.

"I have something for you." He wiggled his eyebrows and got up, pulling me with him.

"What do you know," I muttered, rolling my eyes behind the dark barrier of my sunglasses. He reached out and took them off. His face grew serious.

"I'd like you to . . . ," he stammered as I watched on. He took a deep breath and knelt before me, extending his hands cupped around a small box. "Marry me," said Nacho, his lips spreading in a wide grin. "I wanted to say something smart and romantic, but most of all I wanted to say something that would convince you."

I inhaled, but he raised his hand. I said nothing.

"Before you say anything, Laura, please consider. A proposal isn't marriage. And marriage doesn't have to be forever." He prodded me gently with the little box.

"Remember, I don't want to make you do anything against your will. I'll never order you around. Say 'yes' only if you want it."

A silence descended on the both of us for a long while. He waited patiently for my reply. He got none. "If you refuse, though, I'll send Amelia after you."

I couldn't take my eyes off him. I was scared, worried, awestruck, and . . . happy.

If anyone had told me during last New Year's Eve that I would end up where I was, I would have burst out in laughter. I thought about it and laughed, but inwardly. And if a year ago, when Massimo had kidnapped me, anyone had suggested that I would find myself on Tenerife with that colorfully tattooed boy at my feet, I would have bet everything that such a thing was simply impossible. Well, impossible is nothing, as they say. The thought of what had happened eight months before was still chilling, but—thank God (or rather, Dr. Mendoza)—at least I could finally sleep. But after so much time and with that kind of company in bed, it really wasn't that surprising.

CHAPTER 2

When I opened my eyes for the first time after I had closed them in Fernando Matos's mansion, I saw the miles and miles of plastic tubes around me, piercing my skin and tunneling underneath it. There were what seemed like dozens of machines monitoring my life signs. Everything whirred, buzzed, beeped. I wanted to swallow, but I had a pipe stuck down my throat. I was afraid I'd throw up. My eyes glazed over. I was beginning to panic. Then, one of the machines blared with some kind of alarm. The door to the room swung open, and Massimo stormed in, panting. He sat down at my side and took my hand.

"My love." His eyes watered. "Thank God!"

His face was a mask of exhaustion—thinner than I remembered. The Man in Black took a deep breath and stroked my cheek. I completely forgot about the suffocating pipe in my throat. Tears rolled down my face, and he wiped each one off, keeping his lips pressed against the back of my hand. Suddenly, a group of nurses marched in and finally silenced the shrieking alarm.

Then the doctors arrived.

"You need to leave, Mr. Torricelli. We'll take good care of your wife," an elderly man dressed in a white doctor's coat said. When Massimo didn't react, he repeated the request.

The Man in Black pushed himself up and loomed over the older man. His expression was cold and his glare piercing and terrible.

"For the first time in two weeks, my wife has opened her eyes. If you think I'll leave, you are gravely mistaken," he growled. The doctor waved his arm dismissively. They quickly pulled the thick pipe out of my throat. It wasn't pleasant. Massimo really would do better if he didn't have to watch this. But here we were. A moment later, doctors of all types and specializations started coming and going, checking the readouts and jotting things down in their notebooks. Then there were the examinations.

The unending examinations.

Not even for a second did Massimo leave the room or let go of my hand. There were moments when I wanted him to go, but I was helpless. There was nothing in the world that could move him from his place at my side. Eventually, all the doctors left. I could barely speak, but I needed to know what had happened. Why was I here? I took a deep breath and started to talk, but my voice was a raspy horror.

"Shh. Don't speak," the Man in Black whispered, kissing the back of my hand again. "Before you start asking questions . . . probing . . ." He sighed and blinked away tears. "You saved me, Laura. You saved me just like in one of my visions, my darling."

He dropped his eyes. I didn't understand.

"But . . ."

He was trying to say more, but couldn't. The words just didn't come. That's when it dawned on me. I knew what he meant.

With shaky hands, I plowed through the sheets. Massimo tried catching my wrists, but he stopped, unwilling to fight me. He released his grip on my hands.

"Luca," I whispered, uncovering my bandaged abdomen. "Where is our son?"

My voice was barely a whisper, and each word caused me physical pain. I wanted to scream, jump to my feet and wail. I needed to ask him that one question. I needed him to tell me the truth.

He rose slowly, took the sheets in his hands, and gently covered my broken body. His eyes were dead. As he directed his cold stare at me again, I felt a wave of terror and despair.

"He's dead," Massimo said and turned away.

"The bullet hit too low. And he was still so small and completely defenseless. He didn't stand a chance." My husband's voice was rough and shaky. I couldn't name my own feelings then. Despair wasn't even close. It was as if somebody had ripped my heart out. The paroxysms of weeping made me breathless. I squeezed my eyes shut, trying to swallow the bile that rose in my throat. My child. My baby. My little son, who was a part of me and the man that I loved. Gone. The whole world stopped.

Massimo stood in perfect stillness for a long while. Finally, he wiped away his tears and turned back to me.

"At least you're alive." He tried to smile, but failed. "Get some sleep. The doctors say you need to rest." He stroked my hair and wiped away the tears from my cheeks. "We'll have other kids. A whole bunch of them. I promise you."

I couldn't contain my anguish at those words, and exploded with tears again.

The Man in Black looked resigned. His breathing was shallow, and I could see how helpless he felt. His hands balled into fists, and he left without so much as looking at me. A moment later, he returned with another physician.

"Laura, I will administer some sedatives now," said the doctor.

I couldn't speak, so just shook my head.

"But it is required. You need to rest. Enough emotions for one day," said the older man, shooting a critical glance at Massimo.

He squirted something from a syringe into one of the drips, and I immediately felt my eyelids growing heavy.

"I'll be here." Massimo sat on the bed and reached for my hand. I started dozing off. "I promise. I'll be here when you wake up." And he was there each and every time I woke up and opened my eyes before going under. He didn't leave me. Not even for a moment. He read to me, brought me movies, brushed my hair. Washed me. He did that when I was unconscious, too, shooing away the nurses each time they attempted to draw near me. I briefly wondered how he coped with the fact that the doctors that had operated on me were men.

From what Massimo told me, I had been shot in the kidney. It couldn't be saved. Fortunately, any healthy human has two of those, and living with a single kidney isn't impossible. Provided that the one you're left with works. During the operation, my heart gave out. It wasn't surprising in and of itself. What was, was that the surgeons managed to jump-start it again. Apparently, they unclogged one thing, sewed together another, cut out something else, and—all in all—that did it. The leading surgeon spoke to me at length about the procedure, pointing to various data and graphs on spreadsheets. My English wasn't good enough for me to understand the details, though. Truth be told, I didn't care much. What counted was that I was going to get out of the hospital soon. Each day I felt better. My body was healing quickly, but . . . my mind was another matter. I felt dead inside. The word "baby" disappeared from my lexicon, as did the name "Luca." A single mention of the child—or any child, for that matter—and I drowned in tears. I talked to Massimo, and he opened up to me more than ever before. The only topic he refused to comment on was New Year's Eve. And it was starting to get on my nerves. Two days before my planned discharge, I couldn't stand it anymore.

The Man in Black had just placed a tray of food before me and rolled up his sleeves.

"I won't eat," I said, crossing my arms. "We need to talk. And you can't refuse, saying I'm still too weak to hear it. I'm feeling great. I have the right to know what happened in Fernando Matos's mansion!"

Massimo put the spoon down, took a deep breath, and stood up. His nostrils flared.

"Why do you have to be so stubborn?" He shot me an angry glare, wiped his face with a hand, and took a step back. "All right, then. How much do you remember?" His voice was resigned.

I dug through the recesses of my memory, recalling Nacho. My heart skipped a beat. I swallowed loudly and exhaled slowly.

"I remember being beaten by that son of a bitch. Flavio." Massimo's jaw tightened.

"And then you came."

I closed my eyes, hoping this might help me recall something more.

"Then there was some commotion, and everybody left. We were alone."

I paused, hesitating.

"I walked toward you . . . I remember my head hurting badly . . . and then nothing."

I shrugged apologetically and looked at him.

He was fuming. This whole situation and my recollection must have made him feel guilty. And guilt wasn't something he was prepared to cope with. He paced around the room, balling his fists. His chest heaved.

"Flavio. He shot Fernando and then shot at Marcelo."

I stopped breathing.

"He missed," Massimo added, and I sighed with relief. He looked at me, surprised. I winced, pretending to be in pain. I placed a hand on my chest and nodded at him to continue.

"That bald motherfucker killed him. Or at least he thought so. Flavio fell and bled over everything. That's when you fainted."

He stopped for a moment, his fists balled so hard his knuckles went white.

"I wanted to catch you, but he got one more shot off."

My eyes bulged. I couldn't breathe or say anything. It must have looked bad. Massimo surged to the bed and put a hand on my cheek, quickly checking my vitals on the screen. I was in shock. How could Nacho shoot me? That was something I couldn't wrap my head around.

"See? This is why I didn't want to talk about it," Massimo growled as one of the machines chimed in alarm. A nurse barged into the room momentarily, followed by a couple of doctors. They fussed around me, but a moment later and another syringe emptied into my drip, and I was calm again. This time, it didn't put me under. I felt numb. I could see and understand everything, but couldn't really react. *I'm a lotus flower on the surface of a lake*, I thought dumbly as I let myself relax, watching Massimo explain what had happened to the physician. The man gestured wildly, shouting back at my husband. *Oh, Doc, you wouldn't have the balls to talk back to him if you knew who he is*, I thought, smiling faintly. The two men discussed something, and after a while Massimo backed down, nodding and dropping his head. A while later, we were alone.

"What happened next?" I asked, my words slurred.

The Man in Black thought for a while, watching me closely. I smiled at him with an expression of a junkie who'd just gotten his fix. He shook his head.

"Unfortunately, Flavio came to and shot you."

Flavio. It had been Flavio. I couldn't keep the smile off my face. Massimo must have downplayed it as an aftereffect of the medication the doctor had administered. He continued.

"Marcelo killed him. Massacred, more like. He emptied his entire clip at the man." He snorted derisively and shook his head. "I was tending to you when he did it. Domenico went to get help. The room was soundproof, so nobody outside heard anything. Marcelo brought a first-aid kit. Then the ambulance came. You lost a lot of blood." Massimo stood up again. "That's it."

"And now? What will happen now?" I asked, squinting to clear my vision.

"Now we go home." He smiled for the first time that day.

"I'm asking about the Spaniards. About your business," I added, reclining on the bed.

Massimo shot me a wary glance. He didn't answer for a long while. I fixed my eyes on his face.

"Am I safe or will someone else kidnap me?" I asked irritably.

"Let's just say I set things straight with Marcelo. The whole house was riddled with electronics. Cameras and recording devices." The Man in Black dropped his head and closed his eyes.

"I watched the recording and heard what Flavio said. I know the Matos family was framed. Fernando didn't know about what Flavio was intending. By kidnapping you, Marcelo made a big mistake." He opened his eyes and they flashed with fury. "But I know he saved your life and took care of you." He shook and growled. "I can't stand the thought of you . . ." He paused as I looked on, stupefied. "There will be no peace!" he roared then shot up, grabbed the chair he had been sitting on, and smashed it against the wall.

"My son is dead and my wife nearly so. All because of that man!" His breathing was quick and shallow. "When I watched the recording of that vile fucker torturing you . . . If I could, I would have killed him a thousand times for that!"

Massimo went down on his knees in the middle of the room, his back stooped.

"I can't stand the fact that I didn't protect you. That I allowed that bald bastard to take you and lead you to the place where that degenerate put his filthy hands on you."

"He didn't know," I whispered. "Nacho had no idea what they were planning."

Massimo's hate-filled glare pinned me into place.

"You defend him?" he growled, then shot up and jumped toward me. "You defend him after all he's done?"

He loomed over me, panting. His eyes were completely black.

I stared into them, feeling nothing. I didn't feel anger or hate or anything else. Strange. The drugs I had been given had washed away all my emotions. The only sign of what was happening in my head, under the surface, was the tears streaking down my cheeks.

"I just don't want you to have enemies. It always leads to me being hurt," I said and immediately regretted it. This was an accusation. Without intending it to sound like that, I had just told him that everything that had happened was his fault.

Massimo sighed and went quiet. He bit his lip. I could clearly see a silent plea for forgiveness in his eyes. He rose, turned his back on me, and went to the door.

"I'll go get you discharged," he whispered and left.

I wanted to call him, ask him to stay, apologize and tell him that I didn't mean it, but the words stuck in my throat. As the door closed, I lay there in silence, immobile, staring at the ceiling. Finally, I fell asleep.

———

My bladder woke me up. I had recently learned to appreciate this feeling and the fact that I could finally visit the restroom on my own. Each visit was an invariable source of exultation. My catheter had been removed, and the doctor had said that walking would do me good and that I should stretch my legs at least a couple of times each day, so I had developed a habit of taking short walks. Accompanied by my IV stand.

I took my time in the restroom, as lugging the five-foot pole with me everywhere wasn't exactly comfortable or easy. Especially since I had to manage on my own. Massimo was nowhere to be seen. The first day of my stay at the hospital, he had ordered the staff to bring in an additional bed, where he would sleep. Money talks, as they say, so it hadn't been a problem. If he had asked them for antique furniture and a piano, they'd have brought them in, too. The sheets on the second bed were untouched, which meant that Massimo had had some urgent business he'd had to take care of during the night. Business more urgent than taking care of me.

I wasn't sleepy anymore. I had slept through the day. I decided to go on an adventure and roam around the corridors on my own. Passing through the door, I latched on to the wall to keep myself upright. I stuck my head out and snorted in laughter as two tall security guards shot up to their feet at the sight of me. I waved them away and headed down the corridor, the IV pole trailing behind me. Both men followed me. I had another fit of laughter when I realized how ridiculous we must have looked. I, in my bright bathrobe and pink Emus on my feet, with tousled blond hair, leaning on the metal drip stand, followed by two burly guards in their black suits and with swept-back hair. I couldn't walk at anything even resembling a brisk pace, so our little procession moved slowly, in a stately manner.

After a moment, I had to sit down and regain my strength. My body was still too weak for such long treks. My companions stopped a couple of steps back. They moved their heads, looking for threats, but found nothing that could be seen as overtly dangerous, so they started talking. It was late in the night, but the corridor was far from empty. A nurse approached me and asked if everything was okay. I nodded and explained that I was just having a rest. She left.

After some time, I got up intending to return to my room, when I noticed a familiar figure down the hall. She was standing by a large window.

"Impossible," I whispered and headed the woman's way. "Amelia?"

She pulled away from the glass pane and looked at me, smiling weakly.

"What are you doing here?" I asked, surprised.

"Waiting," she replied, pointing her chin at something behind the glass.

I followed her with my eyes and saw a room filled with incubators. There were babies in each of them. So small. Some barely larger than an open palm. They looked like little dolls, just pierced with cables and tubes. Suddenly, I felt weak. *Luca*, I thought. *He would be tiny like that.* My eyes teared up, and I couldn't breathe. I squeezed my eyes shut and opened them again, turning my head toward Amelia. I took a good look at her. She was wearing a bathrobe. She was a patient, too.

"Pablo was born too early," she said, wiping her nose with the sleeve of her robe. There were wet streaks running down her cheeks.

"When I learned what happened to Father and . . ."

Her voice broke. I knew what she wanted to tell me. I reached out and wrapped my arm around her. Was I trying to cheer her up, or was that for my own sake? My bodyguards took a few steps back, giving us a bit of privacy. Amelia rested her head on my shoulder. She wept. I didn't know what she knew. Probably her brother had spared her from the gruesome details.

"I-I'm sorry for what happened to your husband," I stammered, the words leaving my mouth in a whisper. I wasn't sorry. I was happy that Nacho had shot him.

"He wasn't really my husband," she replied. "I just called him that. I wanted him to marry me."

She sniffed and straightened up.

"How are you feeling?" Her eyes were full of concern. She looked at my stomach.

"Laura!" The growl from behind us wasn't a good sign.

I spun around and saw Massimo, fuming, storming our way.

"I've got to go. I'll find you," I whispered, then let her go and headed back to my husband.

"What do you think you're doing?" he asked irritably and sat me down in a wheelchair. Then, in Italian, he berated the two ogres, who dropped their eyes meekly. We returned to my room.

Massimo took me in his arms and placed me on the bed, covering me with the comforter. He wouldn't be himself if he hadn't kept babbling about how irresponsible I was and how such carefree behavior would put me in danger.

"Who was that girl?" he asked, hanging his blazer on the back of a chair.

"Mother of one of the preemies," I replied, turning my head

away. "She's not sure if the baby'll make it." My voice broke. I knew he wouldn't press. Not when I talked about a child.

"Why did you even go to that ward?" he asked with reproach. I didn't respond. The only thing that broke the silence was my husband's heavy breathing.

"You should rest," he said finally.

"We're going home tomorrow."

It was a difficult night. I slept restlessly, dreaming about children, incubators, and pregnant women. I hoped that at least at home there would be something to keep my mind off the dark thoughts that plagued me. In the morning, I just couldn't wait for Massimo to leave me alone and go pester the doctors who were having a meeting about my discharge. They weren't too happy to hear that I was leaving already. My treatment wasn't finished. They did agree to let me go after they wrote a detailed treatment plan and made Massimo promise he'd stick to it no matter what. They were all Sicilians, though we were still on Tenerife.

I decided to use that bit of time to go see Amelia. I put on the comfy sweatpants and shirt Massimo had left me, grabbed a pair of shoes, and went to the door. I stuck my head out carefully. To my relief, there was nobody around. There was a brief moment where I felt unease. Maybe someone had been here, killed my guards, and was now coming for me. I quickly settled down, remembering where we were. I was safe. I headed down the corridor.

"I'm looking for my sister," I said, stopping at the reception desk at the maternity ward. An older nurse perched on a revolving stool behind the counter said something in Spanish, rolled her eyes, and went somewhere. A moment later, a younger woman took her place. She smiled.

"What can I help you with?" she asked in English.

"I'm looking for my sister. Amelia Matos. She's a patient here. Premature birth."

The woman glanced at her monitor and gave me the room number, pointing me in the right direction.

A moment later, I stopped at the door, ready to knock. *What the hell am I doing?* I thought. *I'm going to visit a girl whose man kidnapped and tortured me. Who was now dead. And I'm going to ask her how she feels?* This was just too surreal. I couldn't believe what I was about to do.

"Laura?" I heard someone behind me saying. I turned around. It was Amelia. She stood right next to me with a bottle of water in her hand.

"I came to check on you," I mumbled.

She opened the door and went in, pulling me along. The room was larger than mine. It had an adjoining living room and an additional bedroom. It was an apartment. The scent of lilies filled the air. There were hundreds of them everywhere.

"My brother brings me a fresh bouquet every day." She sighed and sat down. I felt paralyzed. Panicking, I looked around and took a step back.

"Don't worry. He's gone for today," she said, sending me a curious look. "He told me everything."

"What did he say?" I asked, sitting in the armchair facing Amelia.

She dropped her head. The woman looked like a shadow of herself. There was no sign of the beautiful, lively girl I had known.

"I know you weren't together and that my father ordered him to kidnap you. Marcelo was supposed to keep you comfortable and care for you."

She leaned in closer. "I'm not stupid, Laura. I know what Fernando Matos did for a living. I know who my family are. But I didn't know Flavio was in on it . . ." She paused, looked at my stomach, and shivered. "How is the baby . . . ," she started, but grew silent, seeing my eyes watering. She shut her eyes, and I saw the first tears flowing down her cheeks. "I'm so sorry," she whispered. "You lost your baby because of my family."

"Its not your fault, Amelia. You're not the one who should apologize," I said as calmly as I could. "We can both thank our men for that. You should thank yours for the fact that Pablo is now fighting for his life, and I should thank mine for my even being here in the first place." I had never spoken this way aloud. The bitterness in my words shocked me. This was the first time I'd voiced my resentment toward Massimo. I wasn't being entirely honest with Amelia. The only man fully responsible for all that had been Flavio . . . but I didn't want to bring her down even more.

"How is your baby doing?" I asked, stifling a sob. I wanted all the best for the kid and his mother, but the words didn't come lightly.

"I think he's getting better." She smiled. "My brother took care of everything, as you can see. He bribed or terrorized the doctors into submission. They treat me well. Pablo has the best care available, and he's getting stronger by the day." We talked for a few minutes more, but then I realized that if the Man in Black saw me here, there would be trouble.

"I need to go, Amelia. We're returning to Sicily today."

I pushed myself up with a quiet moan.

"Wait, Laura. There is one more thing . . ." I shot her a look. "Marcelo . . . I'd like to talk about my brother."

My eyes widened as Amelia started talking.

"I don't want you to hate him. I think he—"

"I have nothing against the man," I cut in, afraid of what she was about to say. "Seriously. Give him my best. I have to go now," I added and practically ran out of the room, placing a quick kiss on her cheek and giving her a brief hug.

In the corridor, I leaned against the wall, trying to slow my breathing. I felt nauseous, and there was a searing pain in my chest, but I couldn't hear my heart, which was a strange new sensation. There was none of that deafening thrum in my head that always accompanied my panic attacks. For a moment I considered returning to Amelia's room and asking her to finish what she was going to say, but I stopped myself. Instead, I headed toward my room.

CHAPTER 3

"**M**otherfuck!" exclaimed Olga, thundering into my bedroom and seeing me still in bed. "How long do I have to wait for you, bitch?!"

She threw herself at me, arms outstretched, but stopped halfway, remembering just how many stitches I had in me. She knelt on the bed instead, fixed me with a stare, tried her best to keep a straight face, and burst out crying.

"I was so afraid for you!" she cried. "When they kidnapped you, I wanted . . . I didn't know what . . . ," she sobbed uncontrollably.

I grabbed her hand and patted it gently as Olga snuggled against me and cried.

"I was supposed to stop *you* from crying, not the other way around." She wiped away her tears and raised her eyes to look at me.

"You're so thin," she moaned. "How are you feeling?"

"Not counting the pain after all the surgeries, the fact that I missed a month and that I lost my baby . . . I'm feeling great, thank you." She must have heard the sarcasm in my voice, as she dropped her head. For a long while, she kept quiet, thinking. Finally, she breathed in.

"Massimo didn't tell your parents." She grimaced. "Your mother is going batshit crazy with fear, and he's stringing her along. When they wanted to say goodbye to you when they were leaving, he told me to tell them . . . Can you imagine? He told me to lie to them! I told them that Massimo got you a surprise trip and staged a kidnapping." She raised her eyebrows.

"Pretty fucking crazy, right? His story was that he kidnapped you and took you to the Caribbean as a Christmas present. It's far, and the reception there is shit, so that's convenient. I fed that bullshit to your mother for three weeks straight. Each time she called. Sometimes she didn't believe me, so I wrote her on Facebook—as you, of course." Olga shrugged. "But she's not that stupid."

She lay down next to me and hid her face in her hands.

"Do you have any idea what that was like? Each lie led to two others. Each story was less believable than the last."

"So what did you end up with?" I asked.

"That you're doing business on Tenerife, and you lost your phone."

I shook my head, shooting her a glance. *And here we go again. I'll have to lie to my mother once more*, I thought.

"Give me your phone. Massimo didn't give me back my own."

"That's because I had it all along," she replied, fishing out my smartphone from the nightstand drawer. "When they took you, I found it in a corridor back at that hotel."

She sat up.

"You know what? I think I'm going to leave you alone now."

I nodded and took the phone from her, selecting "Mom" from the contacts list. Should I tell her the truth? Or should I lie? And if I lied, what should I tell her? After a moment of deliberation, I decided that honesty would simply be too cruel. Especially now, when everything was finally in order, and she was starting to really like my husband. I took a deep breath and dialed Mom's number.

"Laura!" My mother's shrill cry practically exploded my skull. "Why didn't you call earlier? I was so scared! Your father was worried too . . ."

"I'm okay," I lied, feeling tears pooling in my eyes. "We only just returned. I lost my phone."

"I don't get it. What's going on?" I knew she'd see through my deception at once. I also knew I had to tell her sooner or later.

"I had an accident . . ." I sighed. She said nothing. "I drove a car, and someone crashed into me and . . ."

My voice broke. Tears cascaded down my face.

"And . . ." I tried to finish the sentence again and failed. A great sob burst out of my mouth. "I lost the baby, Mommy!"

The terrible silence stretched. She was crying, too. I knew it.

"Oh, my sweet little girl," she whispered. She wouldn't be able to say anything more.

"Mommy, I . . ."

Neither of us was able to talk, so we stayed quiet and cried together. And though we were thousands of miles apart, I could feel her with me.

"I'll come," she said finally. "I'll be there with you."

"No, Mom. I have . . . We have to cope with this on our own. Massimo needs me more than ever now. And I him. I'll come to you as soon as I feel a bit better."

It took a long while to convince her that I'm really an adult and have a husband who I should support in this difficult time. In the end, she conceded defeat.

Our talk was cathartic, but at the same time, when we finally hung up, I felt exhausted. I fell asleep. A commotion from downstairs woke me up. The fireplace crackled with fire. I got up and headed to the door. I saw Massimo, tossing more wood into the fireplace. I closed my fingers on the railing and slowly descended the stairs. My husband was wearing suit trousers and a button-down black shirt. I stopped, and he raised his head and looked at me.

"Why did you get up?" he mumbled and took a step back, vaulting over the couch and staring into the fire. "You need to rest. Go back to bed."

"Not without you," I said, sitting down next to him.

"I can't sleep with you." Massimo grabbed the nearly empty bottle and poured himself another glass of amber liquor. "I could hurt you. And I've hurt you enough."

I sighed heavily and lifted his arm, squeezing myself in to snuggle, but he slid back.

"What happened on Tenerife?"

There was a hint of accusation in his voice and something else. Something I had never heard from him.

"Are you drunk?" I turned his head toward me.

His eyes stared into mine. There was anger in them.

"You didn't answer my question!" He raised his voice.

Thoughts traveled at the speed of light through my head. Especially one question: *Does he know?* Had someone told him what had happened at the beach house? How could he know I had a thing for Nacho?

"You didn't answer me, either."

I got up. Too fast. Pain flared through my side, and I grabbed the armrest of the couch to steady myself.

"But you don't have to say anything. You're hammered. I don't want to talk to you."

"You will!" he snapped, shooting up behind me.

"You're my goddamned wife and you will answer my questions!"

He flailed his arm, smashing the glass on the floor. Shards flew all over the room. I cringed. He loomed over me, his jaw tightening and palms balled into fists. I said nothing. I was scared. When I didn't respond, Massimo spun around and left.

There was glass everywhere. I sat down on the couch, afraid to walk barefoot through the room. A memory materialized in my head out of nowhere: Nacho collecting pieces of a broken plate so I didn't hurt myself. I recalled him lifting me up and carrying me away before brushing the pieces off the floor.

"Dear God," I whispered, afraid of what my mind was suggesting.

I curled on the couch, grabbing a blanket and pulling it over myself. I looked into the fire and quickly fell asleep. The next days, or weeks, looked exactly the same. I lay in bed, cried, thought about the past, and cried some more. Massimo worked, though I had no idea what he did exactly. I barely saw him. He would show up with doctors or during physio or examinations. He didn't sleep with me. I didn't even know where he slept. The mansion was so big and had so many bedrooms that it was futile to even start looking for him.

"This cannot go on, Laura," said Olga, sitting by me in the garden. "You're all right now. You're feeling well. And you're acting as if you were dying."

She hid her face in her hands.

"Enough of this! Massimo is always angry and keeps taking Domenico away. You're crying or lying around like a rag doll. What about me?"

I looked at her. She was fixing me with an expectant stare.

"Leave me alone," I muttered.

"No can do." She jumped to her feet and reached out a hand. "Get dressed. We're going out."

"I'll say this as gently as I can: fuck you."

My eyes wandered back to the calm sea. Olga was fuming. The heat of her fury was palpable.

"You egotistical bitch."

She stepped in front of me, blocking my view. And started yelling.

"You brought me here! You let me fall in love! I even got engaged! And now you're not there for me."

Her voice was raised, and her words pierced me to the core. Made me feel even worse.

I don't know how she managed that, but she dragged me all the way to the top floor of the mansion and made me put on a sweat suit. Then she dragged me back down and pushed me into a car.

We drove to a small, traditional Sicilian house in Taormina. Olga got out and sent me a glare. I didn't know what she expected.

"Get your fat ass out of the car," she growled. Despite the words, her voice wasn't angry anymore. It was full of concern.

"Tell me what we're doing here." I said when a security guard shut the car door behind me.

"We're getting treatment." She gestured to the building. "This is where you get better when you're feeling down. Marco Garbi is the best therapist in town."

I immediately spun around and grabbed the handle to get back in the car, but Olga was faster. She pulled me away.

"We can do it on our own or let your bossy brute of a husband find you some other fucked-up shrink who'll report right back to him."

She raised her brows and waited.

Resigned, I leaned against the car. I didn't know what to do to get better. And whether it even was worth it. Besides, physically I was all right.

"Why did I even get out of bed?"

I sighed but started walking to the door. The therapist turned out to be quite a man. I fully expected a shriveled-up old Sicilian with white, back-swept hair and thick glasses, who would make me lie down on an old-school settee. Marco, however, was nine years older than me, and the entire conversation took place by a kitchen counter. He didn't look like your typical therapist, either. He wore jeans, a T-shirt with a rock band logo, and sneakers. His hair was long and curly, tied in a ponytail. And he started with asking if I wanted a drink. At first this didn't seem too professional, but who was I to question his methods?

When he sat down, he told me he knew whose wife I was. And added that he didn't care. He told me that Massimo had no power here, in his house, and promised that he'd never tell him about anything that happened during our sessions.

Later, he asked me to recall the last year of my life. With details. As soon as I got to my "accident," he stopped me. I teared up and my voice broke whenever I started speaking about that. Then he asked me questions. What I wanted out of life, what my plans were before last New Year's Eve, what made me happy.

Truth be told, this wasn't what I had expected at all. We just talked. And it didn't change the way I felt.

"So? How was it?" Olga shot up to her feet when I left the therapy room.

"I don't know . . ." I shrugged. "How is he supposed to help me by just talking to me?"

We got into the car.

"Besides, he told me I'm not crazy or anything. Just that I need therapy to wrap my mind around everything." I rolled my eyes. "And he says I can lie in bed all day if I want to. It's just that I don't know if I really do want that . . ."

I paused, thinking. "That whole talk made me realize that my biggest problem is that I'm just so bored. He suggested that I find myself something to do. Something other than waiting for my old life to come back." I rested my head against the window.

"That's great, actually," said Olga, clasping her hands. "Because we're going to do stuff together. I'll get you back to your old self. You'll see."

She wrapped her arms around my neck before patting the driver on the shoulder.

"We're going home."

I stared at my friend with a silly face, wondering what she had meant.

When we stopped on the driveway, I saw about a dozen cars parked outside. *Are we having guests?* I thought and looked down at my outfit. The beige Victoria's Secret sweat suit was cute, but it wasn't exactly party attire. It would be okay if I was to meet with normal people, but it wouldn't do for my husband's business partners from all over the world. On the one hand, I couldn't care less, but on the other, I just didn't want anyone to see me like that.

We crossed the maze of corridors, praying silently that none of the numerous doors opened. Fortunately, we saw no one. Relieved, I slumped down into bed and was just about to wrap myself in the duvet when Olga pulled it off and tossed it to the ground.

"You got to be fucking kidding me if you're thinking I'm going to let you to rot in bed after I just waited an hour for that rocker boy to pull your head out of your ass. Now move it. We're going to dress you up and make you look presentable."

She squinted. Her arm shot out, and she grabbed me by the ankle and jerked roughly, pulling me toward her.

I latched on to the headboard and held on tightly. I screamed that I had had surgery and didn't want to dress up, but she didn't listen. When I didn't budge, Olga finally released me. For a moment I thought that would be the end, but she quickly moved her grip to my feet and started tickling. That was a low blow, and she knew it. My grip on the headboard lightened, and a moment later I was down on the floor, being dragged toward the closet.

"You cruel, treacherous, bitchy . . ," I growled.

"Yeah, yeah, I love you, too," Olga retorted, huffing and puffing as the pulled me across the room. "Now, let's get to work!" she said when we reached the changing room.

I stayed prone, crossing my arms and pouting. I had absolutely no desire to change, especially since my only outfit for the last couple of weeks had been my pajamas, and I had grown used to the comfort. At the same time, I knew Olga wasn't going to be dissuaded.

"Come on, please," she whispered, getting on her knees by my side. "I miss you."

That did it. My eyes watered.

I took her in my arms and hugged.

"Okay. I'll do my best."

She jumped with glee, but I raised an outstretched finger and said:

"But only if you don't expect too much enthusiasm on my part."

Olga jumped up and down, dancing and singing, crying out in joy, before heading to the shoe shelf.

"Givenchy boots," she said, lifting a beige shoe. "Before it's too hot I'm choosing those. You pick the rest."

I shook my head and got up, walking over to the hundreds of hangers. My head was empty of ideas. I needed inspiration. Those were my most beloved shoes, after all. I couldn't just pair them with anything.

"Let's go with something easy," I declared, reaching for a short A-line dress with long sleeves. It was the same exact color as the boots. I grabbed underwear from a drawer and went to the bathroom.

Inside, I stopped and faced the tall mirror, taking the first good look at myself for weeks. I looked terrible. Deathly pale, skeleton-thin, and with ugly, dark roots in my hair. I winced and turned around.

I took a shower, taking care to wash my hair, and shaved my legs. And all the other parts that needed shaving. Then, wrapped in a plush towel, I went to get some makeup. It took me a lot longer than it normally would. About two hours later, I was ready. Though that might have been a bit of an overstatement. Though I didn't look like a total and complete mess anymore, I wasn't exactly at my best, either.

When I returned to the bedroom, Olga was in my bed, watching TV.

"Hot diddly damn, girl, you're pretty!" she cried out, tossing the remote away. "I nearly forgot what a bombshell you are. But get yourself a hat, will you? You look like those broke bitches wearing sweatpants."

I rolled my eyes and went right back into the wardrobe to search for something to wear on my head. After a while I grabbed a light Prada handbag and was ready. I put on a pair of round Valentino sunglasses and headed to the door. I wanted my car, but I was told Massimo forbade me to leave the mansion on my own. We had to settle for the black SUV occupied by two security guards.

"Where are we going?" I asked.

"You'll see," Olga replied with a smirk.

About an hour later, the car stopped by the same hotel we had stayed in after I got back from my honeymoon. The same one I had escaped from to surprise my husband, only to find his twin brother fucking Anna on his office desk. I never thought I'd recall that particular situation with something approaching nostalgia and a smile on my face, but here I was, doing exactly that. I would have given much to live through that again instead of feeling what I was feeling now. Emptiness.

What happened next reminded me of those movies where they thaw out a frozen caveman and he springs back to life and has to be taught how to cope in the modern world. First, we had a meeting with a plastic surgeon about my scars. My body wasn't as flawless as it used to be. The doctor told me it was too early for radical procedures, but we could try some gentler treatments and cosmetics. Whatever was left could be removed with lasers.

Then it got a lot more pleasant: spa treatment, peelings, face masks, balms, massages. Then nails. Finally—the hairdresser. My stylist took a long while just standing there, stroking my hair, mumbling something in Italian. Then he shook his head and clicked his tongue. Finally, he said:

"What happened to you, girl?"

He crossed his arms.

"We had that beautiful hair of yours under our tender care for months. What happened? Where were you? A deserted island? That would have been the only place on Earth where people wouldn't run away screaming, seeing that mess."

He pinched a strand of hair between two fingers and released it with a disgusted grimace.

"I was away." I nodded. "When was the last time we saw each other? Christmas?"

He confirmed.

"At least it's longer now, right?"

He didn't seem to find my words funny. Wide wide eyes and shaking his head, the hairdresser sat down on his stool.

"What'll it be? Short and blond?"

I shook my head.

"I swear, I'm going to die, Laura!"

He clutched at his chest, leaning back on his stool. Meanwhile, I thought about my conversation with the therapist. Changes are good, he had told me.

"Now I want dark and long. Maybe extensions?"

He thought for a while, shaking his head and muttering under his breath. Then he jumped to his feet.

"Yes!" he cried out. "Long, dark, and with bangs!" He clapped his hands loudly. "Elena, wash it!"

I glanced sideways and saw Olga sitting in a chair by the wall. Her mouth was wide open.

"You'll be the end of me, Laura!" She took a sip of water. "Next time you sit there you'll want it all shaved off . . ."

Hours later, with my head and neck completely sore, I got up. Olga had to admit I had been right again. I looked mind-blowing. I stood hypnotized, watching my beautiful, long hair and perfect makeup peeking from beneath the long straight fringe. I couldn't believe I was so pretty again, after having spent the last months looking like something a dog threw up. I adjusted my dress and grabbed my hat, though I didn't need it anymore.

"I have a proposal. And since it's the weekend, you can't refuse." Olga raised a finger.

"And if you do, I'll plant a horse's head in your bed."

"I think I know what you have in mind . . ."

"Let's party!" she exclaimed, taking my hand and leading me back to the car. "Look at it like this: we're sexy, pretty, and dressed up to the nines. It would be a shame for all that to go to waste. You're breathtaking. Thin and so . . ."

"Sober. I haven't drank anything for months." I sighed.

"Just so. But think of it like this: it was supposed to happen. That day, the therapist, the changes. Everything is as it's supposed to be." Back at the car, the security guards didn't recognize me at first. I shrugged as they stood there, gawking, and walked past them into the SUV. It felt good. I was attractive again. Sexy and feminine. The last time I had felt like that was . . . with Nacho.

That thought made my stomach cramp. I swallowed, but the

weight in my stomach wasn't disappearing. I pictured that colorful, tattooed boy and his wide, white smile. I froze.

"What's going on, Laura? Are you okay?"

Olga jerked at my sleeve, but I didn't react, just stared right ahead.

"I'm okay, yes," I said finally, blinking. I felt dizzy.

"Okay, let's skip the party today."

"Now? When I'm pretty like this? No way."

I plastered a fake smile to my face and sent her a glance. I didn't want her to know. I wasn't ready to tell anyone yet. I had a husband, after all, and I loved him.

At least that's what I told myself when my mind showed me the same unwanted image.

"So when is the wedding?" I asked Olga to change the subject and focus on anything else.

"I don't know yet. We thought maybe May? But June or July work, too. It's not that simple."

Olga then started babbling about this and that, and I listened gladly, sharing her joy.

When we got out of the car, there were still some vehicles parked by the mansion. This time I didn't feel like hiding anymore. Strangely, I felt good. We entered the house, and what I immediately noticed was the complete stillness. There was nobody inside. Normally, there was the staff. This time, we were alone.

"I'm going to my room," Olga said. "Catch you in thirty minutes. Unless I don't find anything to wear. Then I'll come nick some of your stuff."

"Sure," I replied with a smile, already browsing through my things in my mind.

I walked down the corridor at a brisk pace, holding my bag in one hand and the hat in the other. As I passed the library, the door opened, and Massimo appeared. I stopped. He was standing with his back to me, speaking to some people inside. Then he turned around.

My heart hammered as he closed the door behind him. His eyes scanned me. I was left breathless. I couldn't speak. I was too nervous. It had been so long since he'd looked at me like that. Since he'd seen a woman in me. *His* woman. Despite it being dark in the corridor, I could clearly see his dilated pupils and hear his quickened breath. We stood there for an instant, looking at each other, until my brain started working again.

"You were having a meeting. I'm sorry," I whispered nonsensically, but what else was I going to say? He left the room on his own. I hadn't knocked at that door. *What the hell are you apologizing for, woman?* I thought. I took a step forward, but he barred my way. The pale light of the streetlamps shining through the window illuminated his face. He was composed, steady, and . . . horny. Massimo surged forward, wrapped his arms around me, and kissed me. His tongue forced its way between my lips. I moaned, completely surprised, as he leaned me against the wall, kissing, biting, placing a hand on my throat. His hands wandered around my body until he found the hem of my dress. Without breaking the kiss, he pulled it up and clamped his hands on my buttocks. Something like a growl rumbled in his throat as he clenched his hands on my skin, and then started pulling my panties down. His fingers caressed my skin, and I felt his crotch with my palm. His desire was clear. Suddenly enlivened by the fact that his manhood was pushing against me, I raised my hands and put them on the sides of his head, pulling at his hair. The Man in Black loved this subtle brutality. As soon as he felt it, his teeth bit into my lip. I moaned in pleasure and opened my eyes. He was smirking, his teeth still trailing a line along my lips.

That's when my panties dropped, sliding down my legs, only

stopping at my ankles. Massimo lifted me off the floor. I wrapped my legs around his hips as he carried me to the next door. We entered a room, and he slammed the door shut with a kick before propping me against the wall. His breathing was shallow and quick and his movements frantic. He was in a hurry. Keeping me in place with one arm, he unzipped his pants. His cock was ready. He whipped it out and impaled me. I felt it tearing through my insides. I'd missed it so much. I yelped and touched my forehead to his as our bodies connected in a passionate dance. His strokes were strong but slow, as if he was delighting in this moment. His teeth brushed against my lips. His tongue flitted inside my mouth. He entered me deeper and deeper with each push. An overwhelming orgasm was just around the corner. I hadn't felt Massimo inside me for so long. He was so close. He fucked me like there was no tomorrow, and I climbed higher and higher, slowly approaching the summit. Finally, a mountainous wave of ecstasy crashed over me, taking my breath away. I wanted to scream, but Massimo stifled it with another kiss. He came right after me. His skin was glistening with sweat. His arms and legs were trembling. For a moment longer, he kept me impaled. A few breaths later, I was back on the ground, with my back against the wall.

"You look . . . ," he whispered, trying to catch his breath.

"You're . . ." His chest heaved, and his mouth opened wider for air.

"I missed you, too," I said quietly and felt him smiling.

His lips touched mine again, and his tongue danced around mine before I could continue. His caress was gentle this time. Slow and sensual. There were voices outside. Massimo froze. He raised a finger to his mouth and returned to the kiss. The voices weren't quieting down, but the Man in Black disregarded them. His long, slender fingers slid down my body, touching my still-pulsating clitoris. I startled and then froze. After so long, his every touch was like a jolt of pain. Paralyzing. I moaned, and he pressed his lips against mine. Closer. Stifling any sound I might make. Back in the corridor we heard a door closing. The voices vanished. I sighed with relief and gave in to Massimo's caress. He slid two fingers inside me, while another rubbed at my most sensitive spot, sending me straight into space all over again.

"Fuck," he growled as the phone in his pocket started to vibrate. He pulled it out and glanced at the screen, sighing. "I have to take this."

He pressed the phone to his ear and talked to someone for a couple minutes. His other hand never wavered, staying between my legs.

"I need to go," he sighed, resigned. "But I'm not finished with you yet," he added.

The threat was also a promise. One that stoked the fire in my underbelly. For the last time he traced his tongue along my lips, before zipping up his pants.

We left the room, and Massimo bent down and picked up my panties from the floor. They were crumpled in the corner, in the darkness. Looking me in the eyes, he stuffed them into his pocket, took a deep breath, and opened the door to the library. There were people inside, talking animatedly.

The Man in Black left and closed the door behind him. I waited there, back against the wall, wondering what had just happened. It wasn't anything special. Having sex with my husband was normal. But after so long, I felt like it was August again, when he had taken me, kept me here, and made me fall in love with him. The next thought that came made me shiver. I wasn't pregnant anymore. But I could get pregnant again. The fear that washed through my entire body was paralyzing. The stream of thoughts and scenarios crashing through my head made my stomach cramp and my eyes water. I couldn't let that happen. Not again. Not when fate had already decided. I was agitated, dizzy. Standing here wouldn't change a thing, though. I headed toward my bedroom.

Inside, I opened my laptop and quickly searched for a solution on the web. There were as many websites with answers to my problem as there were pills for what I intended. For a moment I read articles about how they worked and how to get them, finally lying down on the bed, calming down. It wouldn't be hard to get my hands on what I needed.

"Well, shit. I can see you're not even close to ready," said Olga, walking the steps leading into my room. "I don't have a handbag yet, but you have absolutely nothing."

She passed me. I trailed her with my eyes.

She looked very attractive, wearing a very short white dress that was tight-fitting only right below her breasts. It was . . . girlish. And the lace it was made of gave her a look of innocence. My eyes wandered down. Yep. It was still good old Olga. She wore black leather thigh-high boots. The outfit seemed to convey a simple message: *I might be innocent, but hand me a whip and see what happens.* I slammed the laptop shut and followed my friend.

She rummaged through my handbags, and I started looking for something to wear. With my head between the hangers, I suddenly felt a pang of anxiety. I turned around and looked at Olga. She stood there, one eyebrow raised, and arms crossed on her chest.

"You fucked," she said matter-of-factly. "When did you do that?"

I rolled my eyes and went right back into the wardrobe.

"How would you know?" I asked, grabbing some things that I found fitting for today.

"Your lack of underwear, for starters."

I froze and glanced at the mirror on the opposite wall. Right.

When I had my arms raised, my short dress lifted, presenting my ass in all its glory. I lowered my arms and pulled the rim down.

"You panties weren't the only thing that exposed you." Olga sat back in the armchair, crossing her legs. "There's your hair and your lips. The former disheveled and the latter swollen and red after a kiss. Or a blow job. So. Tell me everything."

"Jesus Christ, there's nothing to talk about. We met in the corridor, and it just happened." I threw a hanger at her. "Now stop grinning like an idiot and help me out."

" 'We met in the corridor, and it just happened,' " she repeated, amused.

Half an hour later, I stood in the main door, watching Olga doing her best not to fall over on the stone driveway. *What a weird view*, I thought. Unfortunately, I was about to do the same. In my sky-high crystal-studded Louboutin stilettos I had even less chance to stay upright on the uneven ground than my friend. I hadn't want to overdress today, so I'd settled on a pair of boyfriend jeans and the plainest white tank top. To top it off, I'd grabbed a Dior blazer and a white Miu Miu clutch bag. I looked a bit like a teenager. But also a bit like a dirty whore who just pretended to be a good girl. And my new hair had nothing girlish about it.

CHAPTER 4

As we drove down the mountain toward Giardini Naxos, I realized that I hadn't told my husband that I was leaving. But he didn't exactly explain himself to me at all times, either. I stuffed my phone deeper into my microscopic bag. As soon as the Man in Black was finished with his business partners, he'd start looking for me, and it wouldn't take him long to see that I was gone. I rolled my eyes at the thought. Olga noticed.

"What's up?" she asked.

"I have something to ask of you," I replied in Polish, lowering my voice as if anyone could understand my mother tongue. "I'd like you to go to the clinic tomorrow and get me a prescription."

She frowned and grimaced at the same time, not understanding.

"I need a morning-after pill."

Olga's eyes widened in astonishment.

"What do you mean?" she asked, glancing around to check if anyone was listening in on us. "You have a husband!"

"But I want no more children with him," I said, dropping my head. "At least not yet."

I sent her a pleading look.

"Hair of the dog-style doesn't do it here, if you know what I mean. Besides, after all those surgeries, maybe I shouldn't get pregnant all over again."

I hadn't asked the doctors about that, but I really hoped it was true.

Olga went silent for a moment, studying me with her eyes, before inhaling and saying:

"I get it. And of course I'll do it for you. But just think about what's next. You can't keep sneaking out for pills each time you sleep with each other. Maybe I can grab you a prescription for some birth control, too?"

"That was the second thing I wanted to ask you." I hesitated. "But Massimo can't know. I'm not about to bring up the kid thing with him anytime soon . . ."

She nodded and reclined in her seat. The car stopped by a restaurant a moment later.

"Are you serious?" I asked, shooting Olga an annoyed look.

"Where were we supposed to go, Laura? All the best places are owned by the Torricellis. And Massimo knows you're out, doesn't he?"

She pinned me with a steady stare, and I dropped my eyes.

"He doesn't?!" she cried, only to burst out in laughter an instant later. "Well, then we're going to get in a fuckton of trouble. Now come on."

She stepped out of the car, crossed the sidewalk, and headed to the entrance. Imagining my husband's fit of rage improved my mood a little. Was I feeling satisfied with that act of disobedience?

"Wait for me," I called after my friend, wobbling on my crystal-studded high heels.

The first thing we ordered was a bottle of champagne. There was nothing to toast, but the lack of any special cause for celebration was a drinking occasion in itself. The manager practically carried us to the best table. He fussed over us a lot more than was strictly necessary. A waiter was stationed by our table, ready to cater to our every whim. Olga ordered him gone, saying that we didn't want any special treatment. We were just going to have dinner and move on to somewhere else.

When our bottle finally arrived, I couldn't help but feel giddy with excitement. This would be my first taste of any kind of alcohol for many months.

"To us," said Olga, grabbing a glass. "To shopping, going on trips, to life, to all that we have and all that's still ahead of us."

She winked and sipped. As soon as I felt the taste of my favorite beverage on my tongue, I downed the entire glass. Olga shook her head and reached out for the bottle to pour another one. Her hand hadn't even touch the cooler when the overeager manager appeared out of the blue to pour the champagne himself. *Great. We've got a nanny,* I thought and fixed the man with a glare.

A couple minutes later, I was having a plate of scallops in white wine sauce when the phone in my handbag started vibrating. It was one of two people: Mom or Massimo. I accepted the call without even glancing at the screen.

"Are you feeling better?"

The fork I was holding fell to the plate with a loud clink. Terrified, I jumped to my feet and sent Olga a panicked look. She looked at me quizzically.

"Where did you get my number?" I asked, practically running out of the restaurant.

"You're asking me that after I managed to kidnap you from a party secured by more than fifty guards?"

Nacho's laughter was like a nuclear explosion. I felt the alcohol suddenly go to my head, and my legs buckled under me.

"So, how are you feeling?" he asked again.

I plopped down on the nearest bench. One of my bodyguards jumped out of the black SUV parked a couple meters away. I raised my arm and waved at him, signaling that I was okay.

"Why are you calling?"

I tried and failed to slow down my breathing.

"Is it always this hard to get a straight answer out of you?"

Nacho sighed as I ignored his question once more.

"We were supposed to be friends. And friends sometimes call each other and talk about how they feel," he said. "So?"

"I dyed my hair," I said nonsensically.

"You look nice with dark hair. I'm just wondering how you managed to get it so long so fast . . ."

He broke off before muttering something in Spanish.

"How do you . . ." I managed before he hung up. I stared at the phone in my hand, analyzing our short conversation. I felt dizzy. If I raised my head, would Nacho be standing right in front of me? I stayed in place, huddled on that bench, for a long while, before I gathered the courage to look up. Slowly, I straightened up and looked around. There were people, cars, my security detail—nothing out of the ordinary. Something very close to disappointment took up residence in my head. My eyes finally wandered back to the restaurant entrance. Olga stood in the doorway, pouting, tapping her watch with a finger. I stood up and returned to my friend to finish my now-cold scallops.

"Who was that?" Olga asked as I downed a glass of still champagne.

Her fingers were tapping nervously on the table.

"Massimo," I said, avoiding her eyes.

"Why are you lying?"

"Because the truth would be too difficult to hear." I sighed. "Besides, I don't know what to tell you."

I picked up the fork and stuffed my mouth full of scallops, just so I didn't have to answer any more questions.

"What happened on the Canary Islands?" Olga asked, pouring two glasses of champagne and gesturing to the waiter to bring us another bottle.

Jesus Christ, how I hated that question. Each time I heard it, I felt guilty. Like I had done something bad. And it was hard to tell people who had been going out of their minds with fear for my well-being that I had actually had a lot of fun. Not counting the assassination attempts and all that had happened later, that is.

I raised my eyes and met Olga's stare.

"Not yet," I said quietly, gulping down more champagne. "Not today. I'm still getting all of that sorted out in my head. And you're asking the worst questions."

"Well, who would you rather talk to?"

She leaned over the table.

"You can't tell your mom, and judging by the way you're acting, Massimo wouldn't be happy to know, either. And when I see you flailing around, I'm pretty sure the best thing to do now would be to tell me everything. But I'm not going to make you. Don't talk if you don't want to."

She leaned back in her chair while I pondered her words. My eyes teared up.

"He was just so different," I whispered. "The guy that took me. Marcelo Nacho Matos." An unbidden smile appeared on my lips.

Olga blanched.

"I'll forget him," I added quickly. "I know it. But it's too soon."

"Fuck me," Olga stammered. "You and him . . ."

"No. It's not what you think. It's just that it wasn't as bad as everyone thinks."

I closed my eyes and recalled Tenerife. "I was free. Well, mostly. And he cared for me. Taught me. Protected me—"

I knew my dreamy voice wasn't appropriate. I just couldn't help it.

"Holy fucking hell, Laura! You're in love!" Olga cut in, eyes bulging.

I paused. Why wasn't I denying it? Was I really in love? There was no way to tell. Maybe it was just a fling. A crush. I had a husband whom I loved. A wonderful man. The best man I could imagine. But . . . was he really?

"You don't know what you're talking about," I snapped. And then smiled. And nodded. "He's just some guy. Besides, all of this is his fault." I raised my index finger. "I lost my baby. Then I went to the hospital for weeks and was bedridden even longer at home. And finally, my husband has grown distant and started treating me more like an enemy than his wife."

I raised my eyebrows, praying that Olga believed me. I needed to believe it myself.

"Oh, Laura." She sighed. "He just can't forgive himself for what had happened. He runs away because he feels guilty. For the baby. And even more, for you having to go through all this." She dropped her head. "Do you know that he wanted to send you back to Poland for good? So nobody could hurt you anymore. He was ready to give up what he loved the most. He wanted you to be safe."

Olga shook her head, sipping on her wine.

"One time I sneaked into the library and overheard him talking to Domenico. I'm learning that god-awful language, but I got next to nothing. Only that time I didn't really have to understand to know what he was saying."

She lifted her head. Her eyes were full of tears.

"He was crying, Laura. But . . . it was like hearing a dying beast. A wild, uncontrolled roar."

"When was that?" I asked, holding my breath.

"At night, just after you got back to Sicily," she said after a pause. "But enough of that. Let's get wasted."

I thought back to that night. That's when he had broken that glass and when I had started feeling lonely. That night had changed everything. It was then that my husband had started distancing himself from me.

We finished the second bottle and left the restaurant, swaying slightly. The place was crowded by that time. The manager opened the door to the car for us. The SUV was waiting right by the entrance, which naturally made us the point of attention of all the guests waiting in line. We looked like superstars. I would like to say "ladies," but we giggled like adolescents and staggered drunkenly. There was nothing ladylike in our behavior.

We settled in our seats, which wasn't that easy in our state, and Olga told the driver to go.

It was after midnight. A large crowd was waiting by the club. The place was another one of Massimo's businesses, so we didn't have to wait with the rest of the people. Holding each other, we jogged across the red carpet leading inside. Our security guards made way for us through the crowd. Finally, we took our seats in the VIP lounge. By that time I was pretty tipsy—verging on hammered. The tall bodyguards took places between us and the crowd, obscuring my view of the main door. Domenico had taken care of everything as soon as Olga had told him we were going to party. Among other things, he had made sure we wouldn't be able to talk to anyone.

The champagne arrived. Olga grabbed a glass and began dancing to the rhythm of the music. Our table was situated on the mezzanine level, and when she moved seductively by the handrail, the people downstairs had a great view of her underwear. I picked up my glass and joined her. I was so drunk that any attempt at dancing would surely end up in me falling down into the crowd below. So I occupied myself watching the people on the dance floor. Before long, I sensed that someone was watching me. My vision was blurred, so I closed one eye to see clearer. And then . . .

At the end of a long bar, there was Marcelo Nacho Matos, looking straight at me. I nearly threw up. I squeezed my eyes shut, only to open them a moment later. The place where I had seen Nacho a moment earlier was empty. I blinked, trying to find his clean-shaven head among the crowd, but he'd vanished. I went back to the sofa and downed the contents of my glass. I was hallucinating. There was no other explanation. Was that because of how long I hadn't had any alcohol? Maybe my brain was rebelling after I'd soaked it in booze following months of sobriety.

"I'm going to the restroom," I shouted to Olga over the booming music. She was coiling and curling seductively by the guardrail and waved a hand at me, leaning over the dance floor.

I told the security guards where I wanted to go. The man started barging through the crowd. That's when I saw him again. By the wall, next to a large statue, in the darkness. He was standing with his arms crossed on his chest and smiling that white smile of his. My stomach knotted, and my breath caught in my throat. If my heart had still been ill, I would have fainted. Instead, I stood my ground. I just couldn't breathe.

"Since when do you leave the mansion without my say-so?" I heard someone saying. It was Massimo. His voice broke through the din, freezing me to the core. He appeared out of nowhere and stopped right in front of me.

I raised my head. He stood rigid, his jaw clenched. I wanted to say something, but the only thing that came to my mind was to throw myself at him, wrapping my arms around his neck. And I did so, but my eyes scanned the hall for Nacho. The colorful boy had disappeared, and I felt a shiver running down my spine. Maybe the drugs and alcohol didn't mix that well?

I hung from Massimo's neck, thinking frantically. Would he lay into me? Curse me? Punish me? Or maybe he'd grab my hair and yank me off my feet to drag me back home. Nothing happened. I withdrew a step, only to notice that he was . . . smiling.

"I'm glad you're up from bed," he said, leaning in to my ear. "Come with me."

His fingers closed around my wrist, and he led me back to the VIP lounge. I turned my head around one more time, but there was nobody in the corner of the hall.

When we reached our table, I saw that Domenico had joined us, too. He and Olga were wrapped around each other in something that was a lot more than a simple kiss. He was sitting, and she straddled him on the couch. Their tongues flitted around each other faster than the machine-gun beat of the song. At least our lounge was out of eyesight. Otherwise people might start thinking we were filming a porn flick.

The Man in Black sat down, and a young waitress appeared instantly with a bottle of amber liquor and a covered silver platter. She placed it in front of him and left. I stood back, still dizzy, watching as Massimo sipped from his glass. He looked so nonchalant and so sensual, dressed all in black, reclining on the sofa. His eyes scanned me as he drank. He poured himself another one and downed half of it in one go. That was surprising. Massimo never drank that much before. I poked him with a finger, and he shoved aside, making space for me. I picked up my glass. The music boomed, and Domenico was practically fucking Olga right next to us.

Massimo leaned over the table and took the cover off the silver platter. I groaned, seeing the neatly arranged white lines. The Man in Black produced a bill, rolled it, and snorted one full line, sighing heavily with satisfaction. I didn't like what I was seeing, but he didn't seem to care. Instead, he downed his liquor and stared at me. My mood was quickly deteriorating. Was he doing that on purpose? Testing me? Or had he just turned into a junkie?

Thirty minutes later, the three of them were snorting coke from the platter, laughing and drinking. I'd had enough of this. I grabbed the bill, leaned over the table, and sniffed the white powder, too. Massimo's arms shot out and grabbed my wrists. He yanked me off my feet toward him, glaring at me angrily.

"You're all snorting this shit! Can't I have some, too?" I yelled.

A moment later, the disgustingly bitter substance started oozing down the back of my throat. My tongue immediately stiffened, and my saliva thickened.

"You must respect your new heart, Laura," Massimo growled.

I wasn't listening to him. I was too occupied with making him as angry as possible. My face contorted in a grimace, and I got up, stumbling. I considered my options. Nothing especially good came to my mind, so I flipped him off and headed out of the lounge. The large man standing in my way shot a glance at my husband and—to my astonishment—moved away, letting me through. I plowed through the crowd, ready for anything. Someone grabbed me by the elbow and pulled. I quickly found myself in a dark corridor. I jerked away and spun around, only to walk straight into the Man in Black, blocking the exit.

"Let me go," I said coldly. Massimo shook his head and leaned in closer.

His eyes were strange, numb. As if he weren't there at all. His fingers closed around my throat. He pushed me against the closing door. I was scared. Terrified. My eyes darted around the room. It was completely dark. The walls were lined with quilted leather. In the middle, there was a low platform and a dancing pole. There was an armchair by the opposite wall. Next to it, a small table with a couple of glasses and several bottles of alcohol. The Man in Black pressed a button on a panel built into the wall. Lights flashed, and music started pouring from hidden speakers.

"What happened on Tenerife?"

His clenched jaw made him look utterly ruthless.

I said nothing. I was too drunk to argue. He didn't budge, waiting for an answer. His fingers tightened their grip on my throat. When the silence stretched, he let me go. He took off his blazer and walked up to the armchair. I quickly grabbed the door handle, but the door was locked. Resigned, I pressed my forehead to the wall.

"You'll dance for me," said Massimo. I heard him tossing ice cubes into a glass. "And then you'll blow me."

I turned around. He was sitting in the armchair and unbuttoning his shirt.

"After I cum in your mouth, I'll fuck you," he added, taking a sip.

I stood still, watching him. I realized I had sobered up. I breathed in deeply. There was a growing feeling inside me. One that I hadn't known before. I couldn't understand it, but it felt so good—relaxed, happy. Elated. The feeling was akin to being in love, but not quite the same. Was that how cocaine worked? It suddenly dawned on me why Massimo loved it so much.

I pulled off my jacket and slowly walked to the pole. Since my surgery I had barely moved at all, so dancing was out of the question. I rubbed my back against the pole and slowly slid down, all the time keeping my eyes fixed on my man. My hips rocked slowly, and I curled my leg around the pole. I swung around quickly, licking my lips and sending the Man in Black a provocative, luscious look. My hand went to my shirt and slowly pulled it off. I threw it at him. Massimo fixed his eyes on my lace bra. He put down his glass and unzipped his pants, whipping out his enormous cock. He grabbed it in his right hand and started stroking. Slowly.

I moaned at the wet, hot feeling moving down my stomach. I undid the top button of my pants, and then another, slowly revealing my panties. Massimo bit on his lower lip. The movements of his hand were becoming faster. He leaned back his head and watched me from under half-closed eyelids.

I turned my back on him and bent over, keeping my legs straight and pulling my jeans down to my ankles. At least nobody had shot me in the back, and my body had kept its flexibility. That guaranteed my husband quite a stunning view. I held on to the pole and gracefully stepped out of the trousers. Now I only had my underwear and high heels on. Massimo's brow beaded with sweat. The tip of his manhood was swelling and darkening. Slowly, I descended the platform and stepped toward him. I bent down and slid my tongue into his mouth. He tasted bitter, but it didn't matter. I straddled him, my eyes locked on his, hooked a finger around the rim of my panties, and pulled them aside before slowly, patiently sliding Massimo's erect cock inside me. He moaned in ecstasy and closed his eyes. As if it was too much. His large, strong hands landed on my hips. He lifted me up and slid me back down onto himself. I sighed. My ass started moving to the beat of the music. The Man in Black was breathing quickly. His skin was wet with sweat. I froze, and then began unbuttoning his shirt. I could feel him growing impatient. Finally, I pushed myself up and then knelt between his legs.

"I love your taste," I said and slid his cock into my throat.

That proved to be too much for him. The glass he had grabbed an instant before fell to the ground, hitting the soft carpet, and Massimo's hands closed on the back of my head. He slammed his prick deeper in, thrusting fast and strong. The tip of his cock repeatedly hit the back of my throat. He roared, and his chest heaved. His sweat-beaded body shivered. That's when I felt the first drops of his cum on my tongue. A moment later, he shot his load, choking me. The sticky fluid trickled down my throat as he bellowed and thrusted uncontrollably. He was done, but the grip of his hands didn't lessen. His body went still as he looked into my teary eyes. I started choking, but he held me firmly for another couple seconds. Finally, he let me go. I collapsed to the floor.

"That hair makes you look like a whore."

Massimo got up and zipped up his pants. "*My* whore," he added, buttoning up his shirt and staring at me.

"I think you forgot something," I retorted, sliding my hand under my lace panties. "I was supposed to dance."

My fingers started moving. Very slowly.

"Then suck you off."

I slid the fabric aside so he could see what I was doing.

"And then you were supposed to fuck me."

I pulled the G-string down and kicked it off, before turning over and bending down, sticking my ass his way.

"All of that is yours."

That wasn't something he could ignore. He grabbed my hips and, before I could breathe in, impaled me. It wasn't gentle. His cock pistoned inside me quickly and brutally, and Massimo's hand gripped a fistful of my hair. My first orgasm came quickly, but with the booze and the coke, the Man in Black didn't even notice. He rammed me with the speed of a jackhammer. I came again and again, but still he wasn't stopping. After a full hour and what seemed like a dozen position changes, Massimo finally came, too, spilling his seed inside me.

Though I tried, I simply couldn't get up after that. Why had we had to leave home? It would have been a lot more convenient if he had fucked my brains out in bed or by the fireplace.

"Put some clothes on. We're going home," Massimo said, buttoning up his blazer.

I frowned, hearing the indifference in his voice, but I was in no position to argue. I gathered my things, and a couple minutes later we returned to the main hall of the club, into the booming music and the sweaty crowd. Domenico and Olga had already gone to the mansion. I envied them. The physical exertion had made me feel hungover already. My head was pounding, aching like it never had before. Leaving the black room was the last thing I remembered.

———

"You are so perfect," whispered Nacho, stroking my cheek.

His gentle hands smelled of the ocean as they trailed along my skin. He watched me with his happy green eyes before leaning in closer. His lips brushed against my nose, my cheeks, my chin and neck, finally touching my own lips. Slowly, without using his tongue, he caressed them. In the end, his tongue did slide between them. I was on my back, my hips gently undulating. My hand trailed down his spine, stopping on his rock-hard buttocks. He muttered silently, feeling my fingers, and I delighted in the heat of his body. He was calm, composed, his every movement and gesture filled to the brim with passion and affection.

"I want to be inside you," he whispered, looking into my eyes.

"I need to feel you, baby."

His lips rested on my brow as he moved his hips to hover above my slit. I breathed loudly, waiting for the thrust, but he only watched me. Waiting for permission.

"Make love to me," I said. He entered me, simultaneously pushing his tongue into my mouth.

"You're so wet." I heard that British accent I knew so well. I froze. "I forgot what a slut you become when you drink."

I opened my eyes reluctantly, feeling hundreds of needles pricking my eyeballs. The pulsating headache made me want to go right back to sleep, but I was too disoriented to know what was happening. I looked down and saw Massimo snuggling down between my legs, licking my pulsating clit.

"You're ready, aren't you?" he whispered, sliding his tongue inside me.

I moaned as he licked and sucked. It was only after a longer while that I realized why I was so turned on.

It had been a dream . . .

I slumped down, disappointed and numb, as my man did his best to satisfy me orally. I wasn't able to focus on what he was doing. Each time I closed my eyes, I saw the green-eyed surfer. It was torture. Normally, I would wait for the Man in Black's every touch. Now, I was praying for orgasm to come quickly. For Massimo to leave me alone. Minutes passed, but I wasn't any nearer to the climax.

"What's going on?" he asked, pulling away and knitting his brows.

I stared at him, looking for an explanation, but he wasn't the patient type. He waited a dozen seconds, pushed himself up and walked away from the bed, toward the wardrobe.

"I'm just so hungover," I muttered.

It wasn't exactly a lie. My head was pounding like crazy. I could have rushed after him and apologized, but what good would it do? Besides, knowing his stubbornness, he wouldn't have accepted it.

As Massimo disappeared down the stairs, I felt a jolt of pain in my sternum.

I recalled what he had told me last night.

"Massimo," I called. He stopped and turned around. "You told me that I wasn't respecting my new heart. What did you mean?"

He stopped, rooted to the spot, and sent me an icy glare.

"You had a heart transplant, Laura," he said coldly.

As soon as the words were out, he left.

I rolled over and covered myself with the sheets, mulling over what he'd said. I wanted to throw up. In the end, I didn't. I just fell asleep.

———

"You good?" asked Olga, sitting down in the bed and offering me a cup of hot tea with milk.

"I'm definitely not good. And I'm going to puke all over myself," I replied, sticking my head out from under the duvet.

"Something to drink," I groaned. "Massimo threw another hissy fit." I sipped the tea.

"Well, he and Domenico left about an hour ago, but don't ask me where they went. I don't have a clue."

I grew sad all of a sudden. We were finally starting to get by, but I just had to fuck it all up with that one stupid mistake.

"Why is he mad this time?" asked Olga, sliding into bed with me and drawing the curtains with a press of a button on the remote.

"Because I didn't orgasm."

I shook my head at how absurd this sounded.

"My head is killing me, I want to throw up, and he just had to be in the mood. He licked and fingered me for a while, and when I didn't come, he just threw a fit and left."

"Right," Olga muttered and switched on the TV.

The best thing about living with servants is that when you're hungover, you don't have to do anything by yourself. We stayed in bed all day, ordering food and watching movies. If not for the fact that my husband was mad at me again and wasn't returning my calls, I'd say the day was a success.

CHAPTER 5

The next morning, I woke up before noon and—to my great relief—realized that I had absolutely nothing to do, aside from my daily ritual, which consisted of staying in bed and feeling sorry for myself. I lay in my pajamas and watched TV, until it suddenly dawned on me that I really had nothing to feel down about. I'd made my peace with the loss of my baby. The thought of my son was still painful, but it was growing more distant—like an echo. My health was improving, and the aches I had been feeling after my surgeries had subsided to just a small nuisance. And it was spring on Sicily. The weather was warm and sunny, and I was a filthy rich wife of the island's greatest mob boss. Besides, I was growing bored.

Energized by those thoughts, I jumped out of bed and skipped to the bathroom. After taking a shower, brushing my long, fake hair, and applying some makeup, I went to the wardrobe, where I spent a long while rummaging through the hundreds of hangers. I hadn't been shopping for too long, but I didn't exactly need new stuff—most things in my collection still had their tags on. About an hour later, I finally settled on a pair of leather leggings and a loose, thigh-long Dolce & Gabbana sweater. I topped the outfit off with my favorite Givenchy boots and nodded in satisfaction, seeing myself in the mirror. My black attire gave me the air of mystery and sensuality. I looked just like I wanted to—like the mastermind behind a new clothing brand.

That had been the thought that had finally got me out of bed. I recalled the greatest present Massimo had bought me last Christmas. My own company. Now it was time to get it off the ground. I grabbed a black Celine Phantom bag, wrapped myself in a short black turtleneck La Mania poncho, and went out in search of Olga, who I needed to help me out with my master plan.

"Why are you still in bed?" I asked her, opening the door to her bedroom.

The look she sent me was worth the hour I'd spent preparing. She gawked, her eyes the size of satellite dishes. Her mouth was still open when I leaned nonchalantly against the door frame, waiting for her to come to her senses.

"Holy fuck," she said with her typical wit. "You look like a purebred bitch. Where are we going?"

"That's the problem. I need to go see Emi."

I took off my sunglasses.

"I wanted to ask you if you wanted to go with me." Normally, I would have just told her that we were going, but I remembered that Emi was Domenico's ex-girlfriend. I didn't want to push her.

Olga sat up, grimacing and sighing, but finally rose to her feet and replied, "Of course I'm going. Why would you even think I'd let you go on your own?"

Before my friend was ready, I managed to grow hot, take the outer layer of my clothes off, grow cold and put it on again, and repeat that process a couple times. When she emerged from her changing room, she was ready for war. A fashion battle. Her choice of attire was surprising. She looked . . . normal. Versace denim boyfriend jeans, a white T-shirt, and powder-pink Louboutin heels. To top it off, an ostentatious fur coat thrown over her shoulders and a set of golden necklaces around her neck.

"We going?" she asked, passing by. I burst into laughter.

In her shaded Prada glasses, she looked like Jennifer Lopez in *Love Don't Cost a Thing*. I grabbed my bag and followed.

I had called Emi earlier, explaining my intentions, so she wasn't surprised by our arrival. Massimo had asked her to help me out with my own business during the winter.

We entered her beautiful atelier. Olga called out, but there was nobody there. I poked her in the arm. Her loud exclamation felt out of line. The door on the opposite end of the room opened, revealing . . . God. We both stared dumbfounded at a man wearing loose black pants, as he headed toward a great mirror, barefoot and with a cup in his hand. With our mouths agape, we stood utterly still, trailing the muscular stud with our eyes. His long, black hair fell in disarray over his broad shoulders. He swept it back nonchalantly and looked at us. He smiled and took a sip from his mug, saying nothing. And we could only stare on, rooted to the spot.

"Hi." I heard Emi's jubilant voice and shook off the stupor. "I see you've already met Marco." The half-naked Adonis waved a hand at us.

"He's my new plaything," Emi said, slapping the man's ass. "Come, sit. Would you like some wine? This might take us a while."

I was taken aback by her cheery demeanor and the way she addressed Olga. The utter indifference to what had happened. Emi didn't seem to mind that Domenico had chosen my friend over her, but a brief glance at the long-haired godling allowed me to understand why.

After a few hours of talks, a brief lunch, and three bottles of champagne, Emi sat back in her plush armchair.

"You've chosen the designers from the art school," she said, "but there's still the question of the casting. You won't find it equally easy to work with all of them. I think our best option is to tell them to design something that would symbolize your brand."

She jotted something down on a piece of paper already covered with numerous scribbles.

"Then there are the shoe people. But I know you already have a vision on how to test them."

Emi smiled and nodded. She knew how much I loved shoes.

"We're going to meet with the sewing plants later this week. I'll teach you how to deal with them, how to check the quality of the seams, et cetera. We'll also need to go to the mainland and meet with the fabric manufacturers."

She picked up her glass.

"Are you aware of how much work that will be?" she asked with a smile.

"Are *you* aware how rich you'll become when it all comes together?"

"The only reason I'm doing this is my secret plan to buy myself my own island."

She raised an arm and high-fived me.

The following weeks were the most work-intensive time of my life. My therapist had been right—I simply had been bored before. Despite my depression being gone, I continued seeing him twice a week. Just to be sure. Have a chat.

I let myself be drawn in by my work. Working in an industry I knew next to nothing about quickly proved to be more satisfying than anything I had done before. Fashion was one thing, but creating my own company and making sure it was being profitable was another. The whole situation I found myself in had one enormous advantage—I was filthy rich already. Thanks to my husband's money, I could set the whole business up quickly, employ a lot of people, and completely disregard the costs.

Massimo seemed not to care. The more I tried to talk to him, complaining about the difficulties I was encountering, the less he wanted to listen. I could see the irritated glances he sent me between snorts of coke. He wasn't even trying to hide his addiction anymore. He'd drink, do cocaine, and sporadically fuck me. I hadn't known him like that before, though from what I heard from various stories, he had just got back to his old habits. One evening, I returned from my workshop completely drained. I was sure Massimo had left. Earlier that day, I had overheard him talking to Mario, who had been trying to convince the Man in Black to participate in some kind of business meeting. By that time I was used to us living separately. I would often talk about it with my therapist. He always said it would pass. That Massimo was just coping with his pain after losing our baby. That I had to respect his grieving. And he also thought that my husband was still afraid that me staying with him was simply too dangerous. And that meant that he had to constantly battle his own egotistical tendencies. Doctor Garbi's message was simple—if you want to get him back, let him go. That was the only way Massimo would return to me the same as he had been.

Thanks to my work, the problem of too much free time had disappeared. That night I was supposed to meet some people in Palermo.

I barged into the mansion, running down the corridor and nearly ramming some staff on my way. I had a plane to catch in an hour and a half. I had managed to do my hair back at the workshop, as my hairstylist was at my beck and call at all times. As for the dress . . . well, I was the owner of a clothing brand, wasn't I?

One of my designers, Elena, was a very talented young woman. I tended to favor her designs over others, but they were worth it. Simple, classic, delicate, and very feminine. She never overdid anything, preferring rather to add to her creations with accessories. I adored all her work—from basic shirts to dresses. Today was the day I was supposed to put on one of the latter.

Simple black bandeau top, flared from the waist down, with a black-and-white striped pattern. Spectacular. A circle dress that stayed light and breezy despite being so wide, it flowed and billowed as I walked. Only now I was running, clutching the thing in my fist, fully aware that I had next to no chance of making it in time.

At least my hairdresser had pinned my hair up high. If he had gone with the curls he had told me about, after I bathed, the coiffure would have looked like a haystack. As it was, my hair was tied in a beehive bun, so it was all right. I stepped out of my bright tunic and stormed into the wardrobe in nothing but my underwear, nearly toppling over the shoes I desperately tried to kick off my feet. I took off my panties and bra, before sprinting to the bathroom. I must have looked like a lunatic.

There was no time to dry myself with a towel. I applied lotion on my wet skin, quickly rubbing it in. Maybe it would absorb as I focused on my makeup. Then, with pinpoint precision, I nearly gouged my eye out with black eyeliner.

"This is a fucking joke," I muttered, sticking on fake lashes and glancing at my watch at the same time. *I'm goddamned Laura Torricelli! They should wait for me.* But here I was, frantically scrambling to finish on time.

I squeezed myself into the dress and went to look at myself in the mirror. That was the look I was going for. My skin was delicately tanned, and I had started to work out again, so I looked healthy and toned. The surgical scars were practically invisible. That laser might not have been the most pleasant of treatments, but it sure was efficient. Most of all, though, I finally felt like myself again. Even more! I was the best version of myself.

I grabbed a black crystal-studded clutch bag and packed a few things in it. I wouldn't be coming back from Palermo until the next day. The door downstairs slammed shut. My time was up.

"I'm upstairs," I called. "Grab the bag from the bedroom on your way up."

I hoped the driver would quickly do as I said. After a few pumps of perfume, I was ready. "I really hope we're not going to be late. I can't . . ."

I stopped. Froze, rooted to the spot. It wasn't the driver. It was Massimo. Wearing a gray tuxedo, he stood a couple steps away, facing me. He was silent. His jaw worked as he watched me. I knew that look, and I knew that I had neither the time nor the inclination to do what he wanted.

"I thought it was the driver," I said, trying to move past him. "I have a plane to catch."

"It's a private jet," he replied calmly, barring my way.

"I have a very important meeting with Mr. . . ."

With a burst of rage, the Man in Black grabbed me by the throat and slammed me into the wall. He assaulted me with his tongue. Licking and sucking, smothering me with his mouth, he continued. My need to rush out weakened.

"If I tell him to, he'll wait for you until next year," Massimo growled between kisses.

Tantalized by his unexpected attention, I submitted. Massimo's slender fingers unzipped my tight dress. The fabric flew to the floor. He lifted me into the air and carried me out to the terrace. It was late April. It wasn't hot outside, but it was pleasantly warm. The waves of the sea broke over the rocks on the shore, and a salty breeze gusted from the waterfront. It was like going back in time. The meeting, the company, and the negotiations suddenly felt insignificant. Massimo faced me, and his eyes were dark with desire.

Nothing else mattered. His hands clasped around my face as he clung to me in another kiss. I ran my fingers through his silky hair and drank in this extraordinary man's taste. My hands slid down his neck, reaching the first button of his shirt. They shook, fumbling with it. Quickly, his own hands tightened around my wrists, immobilizing them. Then he gripped me by the back of the neck with one hand and by the ass with the other, lifted me up, pulling me closer, and carried me toward the couch. He laid me down and looked me straight in the eyes. He raised two fingers and licked them before slamming them deep inside my snatch. Without any warning. I yelped, surprised. It wasn't unpleasant. He smiled faintly. Slowly, his wrist was picking up the pace, as his cold eyes trained on me. He was like a man possessed—there was no love or affection in his intense glare. His tongue licked my lips. I could see that he was aware that what his fingers were doing was equally pleasant and painful. He put them in his mouth, relishing the taste, before ramming them back in. My chest heaved, and I squirmed under his touch. Finally, Massimo decided I was ready. He rolled me over and impaled me with his cock. It was hard and thick. I came at once. A loud cry tore out of my throat. The Man in Black bit into my shoulder, as his hips thrusted even faster. He lifted my ass up and rose, straightening in a kneeling position behind me. Then he slapped my ass so hard, the blow echoed across the garden. I didn't care if anyone heard it. I could feel him inside me again, and that was what counted. Massimo fucked me with wild abandon. He slapped me again, on that same spot. I cried out, but he stifled my scream by sticking his fingers into my open mouth and then bending over and rubbing his wet hand against my pulsating clit.

"Harder," I gasped out, feeling another orgasm just out of reach. "Fuck me harder."

Massimo's teeth gritted above my ear. His hips slamming into my ass started pumping even more forcefully. His hands moved to my breasts and his fingers pinched my nipples. Pain mixed with pleasure, and cold sweat beaded on my skin. I trembled, feeling the finale was close. That's when he exploded, climaxing. He didn't slow down, just let out a great roar, hammering my ass with his hips until his legs buckled under him. His muscular body collapsed over me, and his hot breath on the back of my neck made my orgasm last longer than ever.

We lay like that for several minutes, until he just slid out of me, leaving a gaping emptiness. He zipped up his pants. I waited for his next step, but nothing came. He just stood there and watched me. Taking in the sight of my body, wracked with pleasure.

"You're so fragile," he whispered. "So beautiful . . . I don't deserve you."

My throat cramped. I hid my face in the cushion. Tears threatened to flood my eyes. When I lifted my head again and looked back, he was gone. I was alone. I sat up, suddenly angry. Sore. How could he just leave me? Without a word.

I wanted to cry again, but only for a moment. A feeling of strange calm washed over me. I wrapped myself in a blanket that hung conveniently from the backrest and walked over to the edge of the terrace. The black sea whispered to me invitingly, and the wind carried the scent of salt and water. The most beautiful smell in the world. I closed my eyes. Immediately, that most unwanted image appeared beneath my eyelids. I thought I had forgotten it, but no. It was Nacho, tending to the grill, wearing only his jeans. I wanted to open my eyes to make it go away. But it was so pleasant, so good . . . I couldn't explain it. Something was happening to me, but the tranquility and the happiness this memory filled me with made my tears go away. I sighed, dropping my eyes.

"Laura." It was my bodyguard. He waited in the doorway.

"Your car is waiting. Your plane, too."

I nodded and returned to the wardrobe. I had to grab my dress.

The sex was only one of the multitude of gifts my husband was showering me with, but it was quickly becoming less important. It was only something that happened. A minor perk of living here. My passion and my new clothing brand were on the forefront of what mattered.

———

"You should read that email, Laura," said Olga, using a sheet of paper as a fan.

It was May. The first heat waves had come. Fortunately—or unfortunately, depending on how you looked at it—I had no time to enjoy the weather. I rarely left my office. I walked over to Olga, leaned over the backrest of the chair she was sitting in, and looked at the computer screen.

"What's so important with this one?" I asked, reading the first sentences. "Holy shit!" I exclaimed an instant later, pushing my friend off her seat and plopping down in her place. It was an invitation to a fashion show in Lagos in Portugal. *How?* I thought. The message briefly explained what the whole deal was. The event was for European designers, new clothing brands, and textile manufacturers. *It's the perfect place for me and my company*, I thought, clapping my hands and jumping up and down.

"Olga!" I turned to my friend. "We're going to Portugal."

"You mean *you're* going there," she retorted. "I'm getting married in two months."

"So what?" I grimaced. "It's not like you have to do anything to prepare for that."

She wanted to say something, but I quickly raised my finger to shut her up.

"You even have your dress ready," I added, pointing to the spectacular white wedding dress showcased on a mannequin in the corner of the room. "There's really nothing you can say to wriggle out of this."

"If I don't fuck my man regularly, I won't be able to remain faithful. The men are super sexy in Portugal," she said with a laugh. "So I'll just fuck him twice a day until we go. Maybe that'll keep me in line."

"Oh, stop it. It's only one weekend. Besides, look at me. My husband barely fucks me at all, and when he does, it's only when *he's* in the mood," I said, shrugging. "But at least when he does . . ."

I nodded with a smile.

"Let me guess: you're talking about sex," Emi cut in, entering the room.

"Yes and no. We received an invitation to the fair in Lagos." I spun around in my happy dance.

"I know. I saw it. I can't go." She frowned and sat in her armchair.

"How sad," said Olga in Polish.

I fixed her with a glare.

"Quiet," I hissed and turned back to Emi. "You won't go with us?"

"Regrettably, I have plans for that weekend. Family meeting." I rolled my eyes.

"Have a good time, though."

"Party!" Olga cried out and hooted. I sent her a disdainful look and sat back down to look at the monitor, scanning through the rest of the messages.

The next two days came and went. I was too occupied with work and preparations for the fair to even notice the passage of time. Elena quickly made me a dress for the banquet that was to take place on Saturday, as well as some other less formal dresses for the other three days. I wanted everything to be earthy in color—neutral, without any patterns and embellishments. The young designer disregarded my guidelines and made a breathtaking, long, bloodred halter dress with deep cleavage and a pleated front.

"Tits," I said, putting it on. "You got to have tits for dresses like this one."

"Bullshit," Elena retorted, giggling and pinning the fabric with needles. "I'll show you something." She fished out some translucent adhesive patches from a drawer. "We'll stick those pads to you, so they don't move. They'll lift what needs lifting and make your boobs seem larger. That's going to be an illusion, but it'll do. Now lift your hands."

She was right. After the pads were applied, my breasts really did look a lot better. Delighted, I watched as the dress perfectly adhered to my skin and all the creases adapted to my curves. Despite my not being a fan of the color at first, it perfectly harmonized with the color of my hair, my eyes, and my tan. I looked like royalty.

"Everyone will stare at you," Elena said proudly. "And that's what it's all about. Just don't panic. I got the rest of the things like you wanted."

"You're a sassy one," I snorted, turning around and admiring my elegant look. "I'm your boss. You do as I say," I added, laughing, as she pinned me with another needle.

"Sure, why not? I can try that for a change." She took the last pin out of her mouth. "Now, take that dress off. I need to work on the details."

An hour later, I had packed my things in around thirty paper bags and was ready to go. At first, I tried lugging all that to the car on my own, but fifteen attempts in, I accepted defeat and called the driver, who was waiting downstairs. Seeing the crumpled and torn bags, he sent me an incredulous look and raised an eyebrow. Then he grabbed the bags. I shrugged and followed in his step.

My flight was in the evening. The event was starting Friday morning, and I didn't want to miss a thing. The plan was to get some sleep, dress up to the nines, and conquer Europe. Of course, as it often is with Olga, we were also planning to get absolutely wasted. Knowing that the weather in Lagos was especially good for outdoor parties, I wanted to have some fun. Didn't I deserve a bit of respite, after all? I'd booked a suite for the whole week. I even wanted to let Massimo know, but he was out. *Shame*, I thought, packing another bikini. Since the beginning of my fashion adventure, it had turned out I had some designing talent, too. The only thing I couldn't do was sew. I had a special fondness for designing lingerie and swimwear. Now, with three dozen sets, I zipped up the last travel bag.

"Are we moving?" Olga was leaning against the door frame, chewing an apple. "Or does some small country need to clothe its people?" She raised an eyebrow with a smirk. "Why do you need all this?"

I sat down, cross-legged, crossed my arms on my chest and glared at her.

"How many shoes did you take?"

She thought about it, looking at the ceiling.

"Seventeen. No, wait. Twenty-two. How about you?"

"Flip-flops included or not?"

"If I were to count flip-flops, I took thirty-one pairs." She snorted with laughter.

"Ha! Hypocrite." I showed her the middle finger.

"First of all, we're going to a party . . ."

"At least one." Olga laughed.

"At least one," I repeated. "And second, there's a chance we're going to stay the whole week. Maybe longer. And third, I won't carry all that around all the time, will I? I need to have a selection. Is that so bad?"

"The tragedy is that I actually have more luggage." Olga shook her head. "Does that jet of ours have a load limit?"

"I guess so, but I think our things won't be a problem." I beckoned her closer. "Now come here and sit down on that bag. I can't lock it."

Remembering my previous experiences with flying, I downed a couple glasses of wine and entered the plane already drunk. I didn't even manage to find a comfortable position before I fell asleep.

Semiconscious and hungover, I walked from the plane to a car and reclined in my seat. Olga was similarly wasted. We both hogged the water bottles perched on the armrest. It was still dark, and our drunkenness had dissipated. Sadly.

"My ass hurts," muttered Olga between two gulps of water.

"From the seat in the plane?" I asked. "It was pretty comfortable."

"From being thoroughly fucked. Domenico clearly didn't want me to think about sex for the whole week."

That piece of information sobered me up.

I straightened up.

"They were in the mansion? Both of them?" I opened my eyes wider, surprised.

"Yup. The whole time. But they went out in the evening."

She frowned. "Didn't he come to you?"

"No," I said, shaking my head. "That's it. Half of our marriage he's been acting like he hates me. He keeps disappearing for days, and I don't have a clue as to what he's doing. He doesn't take my calls, either."

I looked her in the eyes.

"I don't think this can get better," I whispered.

My eyes watered.

"Can we talk about it on the beach? Drinking cocktails?"

I nodded and wiped away the single tear that streaked down my cheek.

CHAPTER 6

I stretched out and reached out for the curtain remote. I didn't want to be blinded by the morning sun, so I only opened them a fraction. A stream of bright light spilled into the room through the narrow gap, letting my eyes adjust to the brightness. I looked around the apartment, shaking off the sleepiness. It was very stylish and modern, white and cold. Everything looked sterile. Only the red flowers located around the room warmed the interior a bit.

I heard knocking on the door.

"I'll open it."

Olga's shrill cry from the other room woke me up for good.

"It's breakfast. Move your ass, 'cause it's late."

Muttering curses and threats, I plodded to the bathroom.

"Cocoa," Olga announced, placing a mug in front of me.

"My savior," I mumbled and downed it. "God, that's good. When does the hairdresser come?"

"Should be here any minute."

Someone knocked on the door again. I rolled my eyes. I hated being in a hurry, but lately it had become the norm. Extending two fingers to show Olga how much time I needed, I went to have a shower.

Two hours and ten liters of iced tea later we were ready. I had my long, dark hair tied into a loose bun. That gave me the look of someone who had just gotten up from bed after some really good sex. I put on white high-waisted flaxen pants and a short shirt that revealed my toned stomach. Silver Tom Ford heels and a matching clutch bag I'd gotten from one of my own designers topped off the outfit. I put on sunglasses and waited in the doorway of Olga's bedroom.

"The car is already waiting," I said in a low voice, and my friend whistled.

"Let's go conquer the fashion world!" She rocked her hips and took my hand.

If I thought we would be the two best-looking people around, I had another thing coming. Pretty much all the other women were dressed up, and they all looked like *Vogue* models. Stylish hairdos, extravagant outfits, and meticulous makeup. The girl who had sent me the invitation showed us around, introducing us to various people with whom I exchanged brief greetings and business cards. My last name seemed to impress the Italians the most. That wasn't what I wanted. Their eyes all told me the same thing, as they exchanged looks: *Look, it's that gangster's bitch.* I paid them no mind. My husband had made my business possible, funding it at the start, but I'd climbed the ladder of success through my own resourcefulness. That thought gave me the strength to power through the day.

We watched a few shows, and I jotted down the names of three designers and realized it was past noon. Drained by the snobbish excesses of the fair, I took Olga with me and went out to breathe in some fresh air. The day was pleasantly warm, and the wide promenade stretching along the beach looked inviting.

"Let's go for a walk," I patted Olga on the back. She shrugged but followed me.

Massimo wouldn't be himself if he hadn't sent his security guards with us, so we were now trailed by troglodytes with pomaded hair. We strolled leisurely, talking about nothing in particular and rating sexy Portugese men, recalling the good old times. Olga salivated at the sight of some of the hunks we passed.

Eventually, we reached a place where a large crowd had amassed on the beach. Our interest piqued, we stopped and leaned against the low barrier. There was some party going on, or maybe a swimming competition down by the sea. I took my shoes off and sat down on the stone wall dividing the promenade from the sandy expanse. That's when I noticed the people in the water. They were sitting on their surfboards, waiting for the perfect wave. Some swam; others relaxed on the beach. It was a surfing competition. I felt my stomach knotting. My heart raced at the memory of Tenerife. I smiled, propping my chin on my knees, gently shaking my head. Suddenly, someone started talking through a loudspeaker.

"And now, our current champion, Marcelo Matos!" the speaker announced, and I stopped breathing.

I swallowed, but my throat was suddenly parched. Frozen in place, panicking, I combed the crowd with my eyes. And there he was. My colorful boy with his surfboard. His neon-bright wet suit reflecting the sun like a mirror. I felt dizzy. My fingers tingled. Olga was saying something, but I could hear nothing. I could only see *him*. Marcelo lowered his chest onto the board and paddled toward the waves. I needed to run. My muscles weren't responding to the signals my brain was sending, so I stayed in place, staring at him.

As he swam up the first wave, I felt as if someone had hit me in the head with something heavy. He was perfect. Simply perfect. His movements were dynamic and confident, and he had total control over his board. The whole ocean was his to command. The water listened to his every whim. *Jesus Christ*, I prayed, *let it be nothing more than a dream.* But no. It was really happening. It was over in a couple of minutes. The beach crowd cheered.

"Let's go," I barked, tripping on my own legs and toppling to the ground.

Olga stared at me with an idiotic expression before bursting out in laughter.

"What are you doing, you nitwit?"

She loomed over me, as I huddled behind the low wall, hiding.

"Is the guy in the neon wet suit out of the water yet?"

Olga glanced at the sea.

"He's coming out now." She clicked her tongue. "Hot stuff."

"Jesus Christ. Fucking hell," I muttered, rooted to the spot.

"What's going on?" she asked, now growing scared. She knelt by me.

"This . . . that is . . . ," I stammered. "That is Nacho."

Her eyes widened.

"That's the guy who took you?" She extended a finger in his direction, but I dragged her down.

"Why don't you wave a flag at him?" I hid my face in my hands.

"What is he doing?" I whispered quietly, though he couldn't hear me.

"He's talking with some girl. Hugging her and now kissing her. I'm so sorry."

I could clearly hear the sarcasm in her voice.

"What girl?"

My stomach cramped. What was happening to me? With the remainder of my strength, I pushed myself up and took a peek from over the low wall. There he was. Nacho with his arm around a good-looking blonde, who jumped up and down excitedly. She turned around, and I sighed with relief.

"It's Amelia. His sister."

I sat back down on the pavement. Olga sat next to me and went quiet, thinking.

"You know his sister?" She grimaced. "Maybe other members of the family, too?"

"We need to go," I whispered.

I spared a glance at my security guards. They seemed completely clueless. My thoughts quickly returned to the seemingly impossible coincidence.

Olga was glaring at me accusingly, but I had nothing good to say to her. She squinted, frowned, and then dropped her eyes, fiddling with a little stick she'd found on the ground.

"You slept with him," she said suddenly.

"No!" I cried in outrage.

"But you wanted to." I looked her in the eyes.

"Maybe . . . for an instant," I admitted, leaning my forehead against the wall. "Jesus, Olga, he's here."

I hid my face in my hands.

"You got that right."

She took a moment to think. Finally, she said, "Come on, he's not going to see us. He doesn't suspect you're here."

I prayed she was right. I slid my feet into my shoes and pushed myself up, scanning the beach with my eyes. He wasn't there. My friend grabbed me by the hand and pulled me along, keeping between me and the place where Nacho had been. We headed to the car.

I started breathing normally only when we were sitting safely in the back seat. I exhaled with relief, feeling streaks of cold sweat trickling down my spine. I must have looked really bad, as the guards started pestering me with questions and worried looks. It was just the stress and bad weather—at least that's what I told them before ordering the driver to get us out of there. As soon as the car accelerated, my eyes went to the window. I searched for him among the crowd. Just one more glance at him would be enough . . .

Suddenly, I heard loud honking. Our SUV stopped, tires screeching. I slammed my head on the back of the front seat. The driver was bellowing at the man behind the steering wheel of the cab that stopped in front of us. The man stepped outside his car and started gesticulating wildly. That's when I saw Nacho. My world stopped. I bit my lip and looked on as he walked to his own car. He bent down and reached for a cell phone from the glove compartment. For a few heartbeats, he scrolled through something before raising his head to look toward the two arguing men. That's when our eyes met, and I froze. His expression was that of complete and utter disbelief. I could see his chest starting to heave. And I? I couldn't look away. I simply stared at him. He started walking our way, but the black SUV we were in accelerated in that very moment and drove off. Nacho stopped midstride.

With slightly parted lips, I looked back at him and kept looking his way even when we left him behind us. He stood there with his arms hanging loose. A moment later, another car obscured the view.

"He saw me," I breathed. Olga didn't hear. "He knows I'm here."

God must be a mean, spiteful child if he'd brought me here, when my life had just begun to look normal. Nacho's presence meant that everything else lost sense. Nothing was important anymore. The demons of the past had come to claim their due.

———

"Well, now," said Olga, as the waiter brought us a bottle of champagne. "Let's get wasted, and then I want to hear the whole story. With details."

"If that's what you want to hear, let us get wasted indeed," I replied, stretching out a hand to grab a glass.

Two hours and multiple bottles of alcohol later, I'd told her everything. About the plate I had broken, about the way he had rescued me, about the beach house, learning to swim, the kiss, and Nacho shooting Flavio. Then I told her about everything else—my feelings and thoughts. Olga listened with a terrified expression.

"Let me say this," she said finally, her eyes glazed over with inebriation. "I may be wasted, but you have wasted your life." She nodded, grimacing. "Out of the frying pan into the fire. First a Sicilian macho, and then this tattooed Spaniard."

"Canarian." I wagged my glass at her, leaning back in my chair.

"Same thing," she retorted, waving a hand at me dismissively. The waiter misunderstood the gesture as a call. He appeared by our table, and she sent him a surprised look.

"What's this about?" she mumbled in Polish. I barked out a laugh.

"What a lady . . ." I couldn't stop chortling.

"We're just ladies out to have a good time. That's how we roll!"

Olga snorted in laughter, too, looking at the waiter, waiting for so much as a smile from him. He didn't seem to share our good spirits. "Another bottle of champagne! And some Alka-Seltzer."

She sent him away with a nod of the head.

"Laura," she said when the man was gone. "We have an important banquet tomorrow, but I can tell you already that we're going to look like shit that was left in water for too long. You know, like when a kid shits in the pool, and it floats for days before you fish it out."

I guffawed, but she lifted a finger, meaning she wasn't finished yet.

"But that's only one thing. The other is that I'm always horny when I'm drunk. So I'd like to fuck now, if you don't have any better ideas."

Olga leaned over the table and lost her balance, propping up on her elbows. The table shook, and the glasses clinked loudly.

I took a quick look around. Everyone was ogling us. That in itself was nothing out of the ordinary—we were being loud and obnoxious. I attempted to sit straighter, but the more I pushed into the backrest, the lower I slid.

"We need to get back to our room," I whispered. "But I don't think I'll be able to walk. Will you carry me?"

"Yes!" she exclaimed happily. "Right after you carry me."

At that moment the waiter brought us another bottle and opened it. He didn't even manage to tilt it over the first glass, when Olga shot up and grabbed it, plucking it out of his hand and launching herself toward the door. Though "launching herself" was a bit of an overstatement. For every two steps ahead, she stumbled one backward. After our long walk of shame through the restaurant, where the floor kept turning around chaotically, we finally reached the elevator. Despite our drunkenness, I realized just how difficult the next day was going to be. I groaned, thinking of the massive hangover that was coming.

We entered our apartment, or rather stumbled inside, toppling over after one of us tripped over the rug. *Jesus, I nearly hit my head on that chair,* I thought, hitting my hand on the coffee table standing right next to the chair. Olga was hysterical. She rolled on the floor until she found the door to her room. She crawled inside and waved a hand at me with a silly grin. I shot her a quick one-eyed glance, focusing on the bottle of champagne I now carried. I don't know how I'd managed to keep its contents inside. For a moment I opened the other eye, but that immediately made my vision swim, so I squeezed it shut again.

"We're going to die," I mumbled. "And start decomposing in this luxurious apartment."

I plodded deeper into the room barefoot, having taken my shoes off back at the restaurant.

"They're going to find us when our bodies start to stink," I continued, slurring the words. Finally reaching my bedroom, I collapsed on the bed and crawled under the comforter, letting out a satisfied purr.

"Nacho, love, be a darling and turn the lights off," I said to the silhouette of a man sitting in the armchair by the balcony.

"Hey there, bee." He got up and walked over to the bed.

"I'm so drunk I'm hallucinating," I said with a little laugh. "Or maybe I'm asleep already. And that would mean we're going to have sex."

I squirmed in the sheets with a grin, and he stood over me, grinning right back.

"You want to have sex with me?" he asked, lying down.

I moved over, making him more space.

"Mmm . . . ," I purred, my eyes still closed. "I dream about it. And in my dreams we always make love."

I tried pulling down my pants, but my fingers were too numb.

Nacho's slender fingers pulled the comforter off. He helped me with the button I was trying to undo, gently pulling my pants off and folding them neatly. I lifted my arms, signaling that it was time for my blouse. He found the zipper on my back and took it off. I rolled over, rubbing my ass on the mattress and inviting him to play with me. He put my folded clothes on a chest of drawers by the bed.

"Stay like that forever," I breathed. "I need you to be gentle today. I missed you."

His lips first touched my shoulder, before moving to the collarbone. It was the barest of touches, but the warmth of it made my entire body tingle. He took the comforter and covered me with it.

"Not today, bee," he said, planting a kiss on my forehead. "But soon."

I sighed, disappointed, and pushed my head into the soft pillows. I loved those dreams.

————

The hangover in the morning was excruciating. I threw up four times as soon as I opened my eyes. Judging by the sounds coming from the bathroom on the other side of the apartment, Olga felt much the same way. I took a shower and, hoping for some respite, swallowed a couple aspirin tablets I'd found in my luggage.

I walked up to the mirror and took a look at myself. Groaned at the sight.

If someone told me I looked bad, I'd take it as a compliment. I looked as if someone had ground me into a pulp, formed me into a burger, eaten me, and then shat me out. I tended to forget I wasn't eighteen anymore and that alcohol wasn't water you had to drink at least two liters of a day. On shaky legs, I returned to bed and lay down, waiting for the aspirin to act. Recalling the events of last night was difficult. I blacked out after we left the restaurant, where—by the way—we acted like complete bumpkins. Combing through the recesses of my memory to find something—anything—positive, such as safely returning to our rooms, quickly ended in failure.

Frustrated and angry at my own irresponsibility, I grabbed my phone to move the appointment with a hairdresser to a later hour. There was a message on the screen. A text from an unknown number. I hope you dreamed what you wanted.

I frowned, looking at the screen and thinking about what this message could mean. And then my mind pieced together the fractured memory of the Canarian sitting in the armchair by the balcony. My eyes shot to the left. The seat had been moved closer to the bed. My headache intensified. I glanced at the dresser. My things had been neatly folded and placed on top of it. The water I had drunk a moment before threatened to bubble all the way up my throat again. I shot up and sprinted to the bathroom. After painfully getting rid of the contents of my stomach, I returned to the bedroom. I was terrified. Something glittered on my white trousers, folded on the chest of drawers. A small surfboard key ring.

"It wasn't a dream," I breathed.

My legs folded beneath me, and I collapsed to my knees by the bed. "He was here."

I was so scared. A couple moments before, I had been sure I couldn't feel any worse. I had been wrong. Now I tried remembering what I had said. What I had done. My brain protected me from that knowledge. That memory remained off-limits. I was sprawled on the floor, looking up at the ceiling.

"You dead?" Olga asked, bending down above me. "Don't do this to me. Massimo will kill me if you die of alcohol poisoning."

"I want to die," I stammered, squeezing my eyes shut.

"I know. Me too. But what's better than dying? A big fried breakfast."

Olga lay down next to me, touching her head to mine.

"We need a ton of fried, fatty things. That'll get us up."

"I'm going to puke all over you."

"Bullshit. You don't have anything to puke with," she said, looking at me. "I ordered us breakfast already. And lots of iced tea."

We lay on our backs, keeping still, and I battled with my thoughts. Should I tell her what happened last night? Knocking on the door broke me out of my reverie. Neither of us so much as twitched to open it.

"Fuck me," Olga sighed.

"Yup," I agreed. "No chance I'm getting it. Besides, you're the one who wanted to eat. You go."

We took our time with the meal. Olga had ordered sausages, bacon, fried eggs, and pancakes. A fatty and sugary cholesterol bomb. I was so grateful that all meetings were taking place in the evening. Before we went to the banquet, we did absolutely nothing productive, spending our day on the terrace, sunbathing naked and drinking gallons of iced tea. The best quality of our apartment was the view on the ocean and the surfers. From the floor we were on, they looked like ants, but the knowledge that *he* might be there among them invigorated me.

How did he find me here? How did he get inside, and most important, why didn't he *do* anything? Last night I was as horny as it got. And open to all suggestions. All he'd have had to do was pull my panties down.

I recalled our argument back at the beach house, where he had told me the only thing he wanted was to fuck me. Back then, I hoped he had been lying. Today I was certain. I couldn't stop thinking about it. How could I get so drunk? The most infuriating thing was that he had finally been so close, and I hadn't done anything to keep him. Or maybe I had. I'd allowed him to undress me. See me practically naked.

"What are you thinking about?" Olga asked, raising a hand to shield her eyes from the sun. "You're wriggling on that sunbed like you want to fuck it."

"Because I do," I retorted.

At seven in the evening, a whole team of stylists left our apartment, and we stood in the living room, hydrated and filled with antihangover pills. Sending each other approving looks, we decided it was time to go. I wore my breathtaking red dress, and Olga had selected an off-white bandeau dress. Both outfits had been created by my designers. It wouldn't make any sense otherwise. The party was the last place that I could dazzle everyone with my talent—get the most influential people in the fashion industry to see me.

My phone vibrated. A voice from the speaker announced that our car was waiting. I hung up and glanced at the screen. The phone beeped. The battery was getting low. I didn't have a charger. Cursing inwardly, I stuffed the phone back into my small clutch bag.

We took the elevator downstairs and packed ourselves into the limo which took us to the banquet.

"I feel like having a beer," Olga muttered as I passed my invitation to the man standing in the entrance.

"A cold one," she added, shooting glances around.

"Sure. A mug of beer would look great with your dress," I said, looking her up and down. Her only response was to show me the middle finger. Then she practically ran toward the bar.

My Portuguese partner appeared from the crowd, grabbed me by the wrist, and pulled me into the swarming throng. That was unexpected. She didn't give so much attention to anyone else, though she had invited a couple other people aside from me. I pushed the thought away, but somewhere deep down I suspected that it might have something to do with my husband. There wasn't anything that a good bribe or threat couldn't do, I supposed.

Two hours later, I knew everyone worth knowing. Textile manufacturers, sewing plant owners, designers, and some stars—Karl Lagerfeld included. He voiced his approval of my dress. I could have either fainted or started jumping around like an overexcited teenager, but instead opted to retain a degree of dignity and just nodded in thanks.

As I was trying to build my fashion empire, Olga was chugging beers and chatting with a cute local boy behind the bar. The man was simply breathtaking. Whoever had gotten him the bartending job was a marketing genius. Regrettably, the fact that Olga hadn't been doing much else apart from standing at the counter meant that she was already pretty hammered.

"Laura, this is Nuno." She pointed a finger at the man, who nodded politely and smiled, presenting two extremely cute dimples in his cheeks. "If you don't take me away from here right now, Nuno—who finishes in about an hour—will fuck my brains out at the beach," she murmured in Polish. I knew it would end the way she had envisioned if I left her at the bar.

I smiled my most charming smile at the disappointed local boy as I pulled my friend away and headed to the exit. My bodyguards quickly noticed what I was doing and helped me discreetly stuff Olga into the back seat of the car. As soon as I left her there, she immediately changed her mind and stepped out.

"I'm going to get another drink," she slurred, staggering back to the banquet.

"Get inside the car, you piss-head!" I ordered, shoving her back into the vehicle.

Olga didn't comply. One of the bodyguards grabbed her and held her a couple inches above the ground, looking at me as Olga squirmed and tried breaking free. Resigned, I shook my head.

"Get in with her and hold her down. She might try escaping," I sighed. "I need to go back and talk to some people."

"Don Massimo prohibited us from leaving you unattended."

"Chill out, it's all right. I'm safe here."

I spread my arms, gesturing around to the beach, the palm trees and the calm sea.

"Get her home and then come back for me."

I turned around and went back into the hall, traced by a dozen pairs of eyes at least.

I mingled with the guests, who vied for my attention, and sipped on champagne. It wasn't a good night for drinking, but despite my hangover, the taste of Moët Rosé felt calming.

"Laura?" I heard a voice from behind. I turned around and saw

Amelia, making her way through the crowd. I felt a spike of pain in my chest. The champagne went straight to my head. I swayed. She took me in her arms and gave me a hug.

"I was looking at you for an hour, but wasn't sure it was you. Until your security guards showed up."

She grinned. "You look amazing."

"That is true . . ."

The sound of that other voice made me freeze. I stopped breathing.

"You do look amazing," said Nacho, appearing from behind his sister.

He looked equally good in a light gray suit, a white shirt, and a tie the same color as his suit. His clean-shaven head shined in the light, and his tanned skin made his green eyes stand out even more than usual. He stood there, stone-faced, with an arm around his sister's waist. She was saying something. I couldn't hear. The whole world disappeared when Nacho arrived. He was playing the cold, ruthless mob boss. I knew that act. He had hidden behind that facade the day I had been shot. Now, Amelia chattered excitedly, and the two of us stared into each other's eyes, fascinated.

"Nice tie," I managed finally, cutting Amelia short.

The girl froze, mouth agape. She frowned, realizing we were paying her no mind.

"I'm going to leave you alone now," she said and left.

The two of us kept still, looking at each other, keeping a safe distance. We needed no one's attention. My lips parted. I took a deep breath. Nacho swallowed loudly.

"Have a good sleep?" he asked after another minute of silence.

There were playful sparks in his eyes, but his expression remained impassive. My head swam at the memory of what had happened last night.

"I'm not feeling too good," I whispered, turning to the terrace door. My hand closed on a fistful of my dress as I headed to the exit, practically running. I went straight to the edge of the terrace, resting my arms on the guardrail. A heartbeat later, Nacho joined me. He plucked my bag out of my hand and gripped my wrist to check my pulse.

"I don't have a heart condition anymore," I breathed. "That's one of the advantages of getting out of Tenerife alive. I got a new heart."

"I know," he said curtly, looking at his watch.

"What do you mean, you know?"

I was genuinely surprised. I pulled my hand away, but he grabbed it again.

"Have you talked about it with your husband?" he asked, finally letting my hand go. He was standing with his back to the railing now.

I didn't feel like talking about my marital issues with him, especially that the fact that I had been seeing Massimo very rarely lately had nothing to do with this man. There was no chance I was going to tell him that.

"I'm talking to you now. I want to know your version of the story."

He sighed and dropped his eyes.

"I know . . . because I got you that heart."

He looked at me. My own eyes widened.

"Judging by your expression, you didn't know that. My physicians didn't think you'd survive, so . . ."

He paused, as if trying to hide something from me.

"So you have a new heart now," he finished, still keeping his expression serious.

"Should I know how I got the heart?" I asked uncertainly, taking his chin between my fingers and lifting it so he had to look at me.

His green eyes studied me closely. He wetted his lips with his tongue. Was he doing this on purpose? I forgot my question. The smell of spearmint chewing gum and his cologne was intoxicating. Nacho had one hand in his pocket. The other one held my bag. He looked straight at me. The world stopped. Everything was still. There were just the two of us.

"I missed you."

The sound of those words made my breath catch in my throat. My eyes watered.

"You were on Sicily," I whispered, recalling my earlier hallucinations.

"I was," he said. "Several times."

"Why?" I asked, already knowing the answer.

"Why did I miss you, why did I go or why did I want to see you?"

"Why are you doing this?"

I was tearing up. I needed to run away before he answered.

"I want more."

Finally, his handsome face split in a wide smile. He had been stifling it from the moment he first saw me that evening. Now, his brows raised, and his body relaxed.

"I want more of you. I want to teach you how to surf and show you how to catch octopuses. I want to ride motorbikes with you. And show you the snowy summit of Teide. I want . . ."

I lifted an arm. He stopped talking.

"I need to go," I said, turning around.

"I'll give you a ride," Nacho called after me.

"My security guards will do it."

"Your guards are chasing Olga around the hotel. They're rather occupied."

I spun around and was about to ask how he knew that, but I recalled that he knew everything. Even the size of my bra.

"Thank you, but I'll take a cab," I said and at the same time noticed the small clutch bag he was waving at me.

With an amused expression, he walked toward me and stopped a step away. He was a lot taller than me, even despite my high heels. I reached out for the bag, but he lifted it up, clicking his tongue and shaking his head.

"My car is waiting by the entrance. Come," he said and passed me by, walking to the door.

If not for the fact that I had my phone in that bag, I would have left then and there. But I couldn't. I was addicted to that phone. I followed Nacho at a safe distance until we left the building. His fingers closed around my wrist, and he led me back into the darkness. As his hand touched my skin, I shivered. He must have felt the same way, as he stopped and sent me a stunned look.

"Don't do it," I breathed. He released my wrist, but then his arm snaked around my waist. He pulled me toward him. I tilted my head back, making it easier for him to kiss me. We stood, touching each other, breathing quickly. Nacho looked into my eyes. He didn't do anything more. Only looked. I knew it was a terrible idea. I should run, leave the phone and return to my hotel. But I couldn't. He was here. He was real and standing right there—right in front ot me. The heat of his body washed over me.

"I lied," he whispered, "when I said I only wanted to fuck you."

"I know."

"I also lied when I said I wanted to be your friend."

I took a deep breath, afraid of what he'd say next. He released me and pressed a button on the key to his car.

The headlights flashed on. Nacho opened the passenger door, and waited. I stepped inside, waiting for him to join me. It was a strange, unusual car. A beautiful machine, but one from a different era. In the dim light of the streetlamps, I had only glimpsed the blue of its paint job and the two white stripes leading from the front to the back of the vehicle. I turned my head around, taking in the interior. *Now, that's a real car*, I thought, *not that high-tech spaceship crap.* It had three gauges and four switches in total. The wooden steering wheel didn't have any buttons. Perfect. The only disadvantage I could see was the lack of a roof.

"That is not the car we drove around in on Tenerife," I said when Nacho sat in the driver's seat and placed my bag on my knees.

"Surprisingly perceptive of you," he said with a grin. "Back there we had a Corvette Stingray. This is a Shelby Cobra. But I bet you can't tell those ugly fucking Ferraris apart."

He laughed ironically and turned the key in the ignition.

"A car has to have a soul. Price isn't everything." Guano Apes' "Lords of the Boards" boomed from the speakers as the engine roared.

The sound of the rock song made me jerk in my seat. Nacho laughed.

"I'll play us something more appropriate," he said happily, wiggling his eyebrows and pressing a button on the minimalistic dashboard. The song changed. The space inside the car was filled with the subtle sounds of Evanescence's "My Immortal." First the piano, then the singer's gentle and deep voice, as she sang about being tired and suffocated by her fears.

Each word of that song was so close to what I felt. Had Nacho chosen it on purpose, or was that only a coincidence?

My eyes watered as the vocalist sang and we slowly drove the empty streets of the town, leaving the beach behind us. "I've tried so hard to tell myself that you're gone. But though you're still with me, I've been alone . . ."

That was too much for me.

"Stop the car!" I cried, feeling like I was going to explode. "Stop the fucking car!"

I sobbed loudly, and Nacho parked the Shelby and sent me a terrified look.

"How could you?"

I opened the door and jumped out.

"How could you do this to me? I was happy! Everything was under control. He was perfect before you showed up . . ."

Nacho took me in his arms and pushed me against a wall. I didn't fight him. I couldn't. I didn't even defend myself when he slowly closed in. He stopped, doing nothing more. Waiting for my consent. I wasn't able to wait any longer. I grabbed his head and pressed my lips against his. Nacho's hands slowly moved up, past my hips, waist, and shoulders, finally reaching my face. He delicately bit my lips, caressed them, licked, until his tongue slipped past them and reached inside my mouth.

The song looped and reverberated anew. We froze, joined by the inevitable. Nacho was warm, gentle, and so sensual. His soft lips touched mine, not pulling away even for a second. His tongue danced with mine, leaving me breathless. It was so good, I forgot about everything.

And then a deafening silence descended. It brought us back to reality. The world crashed down on us. We both felt it. I closed my mouth. Nacho withdrew. He leaned his brow against my forehead and squeezed his eyes shut.

"I bought a house on Sicily to be closer to you," he whispered. "I watch over you. I can see what's going on, bee."

He lifted his head and kissed me on the forehead.

"When I called you for the first time, I was in the same restaurant as you. Back at the club I kept an eye on you. You were so drunk."

His lips trailed down my cheek. "I know when you order lunch at work. I know how little you eat. I know when you visit your therapist. And I know you and Torricelli aren't doing so well."

"Stop," I breathed as his lips neared to mine again. "Why are you doing this?"

I raised my eyes and pushed him away. He straightened up. I studied him. In the light of the streetlamps, his green eyes looked focused but happy. His beautiful face looked serene and gentle. A small smile appeared on his lips.

"I think I'm in love with you," he said and turned away, walking to the car. "Come."

He stopped by the passenger door and waited. My back was pressed against the stone wall. I was waiting, too. Waiting until I could walk again. My legs didn't want to listen to my brain. Not after what Nacho had said. It had seemed obvious before. I had suspected as much, especially after what he had tried to tell me when we stopped at Los Gigantes back on his island. I looked at him, and he met my eyes. Seconds passed. Maybe even minutes. The sound of my phone ringing brough me back to life. Nacho passed me the bag, and I stopped breathing. The screen was showing one word:

Massimo. I swallowed and was just about to take the call, when my phone chimed one last time and died.

"Shit," I hissed. "I'm going to be in so much trouble."

"I won't say that I'm worried that don Torricelli might blow a fuse."

Nacho's expression revealed his amusement as he looked at me.

"You'll charge it in no time."

He gave me his hand and helped me get in the car.

CHAPTER 7

We drove up to a gate, and Nacho pressed a button on a remote. With everything that had happened during the previous thirty minutes, I'd completely forgotten he was supposed to take me straight to my apartment.

"This isn't where I'm staying," I said, looking around the magnificent garden he was driving us through.

"Too bad for you."

The corners of his mouth twitched first, and then he grinned, presenting a set of perfectly white teeth.

"I have a charger for your phone," he added, killing the engine. "I also have wine, champagne, vodka, a bonfire, and some marshmallows. Be my guest."

He waited for me to step out of the car, but I didn't move from my seat.

"It's about five miles to the closest building." He laughed. "I seem to have kidnapped you again, my dear, so please . . . be my guest."

Nacho left, disappearing into the house.

I certainly didn't feel like he'd kidnapped me. That was only a joke, and if I pressed him, he'd take me back to my apartment.

But . . . wouldn't I rather stay? The thought of what might happen later in the night made a whole kaleidoscope of butterflies flutter in my stomach.

I felt fear, but also relief and desire. A desire that had been burning in me for months.

"God, give me strength," I breathed, stepping out of the Shelby and heading toward the entrance to the house.

It was very dark inside. A thin corridor quickly opened into a beautiful, spacious living room. It was illuminated by several lights hanging from the walls. Deeper inside there was an open kitchen with a large island and a plethora of knives, pans, and pots hanging above it. It was so big you could run around it and break a sweat. I went even farther inside, passing a stylish maritime-themed office. It was modestly furnished, but had an enormous window taking up one entire wall. In front of the window stood a dark, rectangular desk and a huge leather armchair.

"I do work sometimes," whispered Nacho. I felt his breath on my neck. "I'm the boss now, after Father died."

A glass of red wine appeared in front of me.

"I like my job. Or I liked it before," he continued, standing behind me. I drank in our closeness and the gentle tone of his voice.

"You get used to everything, especially if you don't treat it too seriously. If you view it as something like a sport."

"Killing and kidnapping people is sport to you?" I asked, standing in the doorway and keeping my eyes trained on the large desk.

"I love it when people tremble at the sound of my name."

His quiet voice and the words he was speaking made a shiver run down my spine.

"And now, instead of waiting on a roof with a sniper rifle or shooting people in the heads, looking them in the eyes, I'm sitting behind a desk and managing my father's empire." He sighed and wrapped his arms around my waist. "But you were never scared of me . . ."

Taken aback, I watched as his tattooed arm snaked across my stomach. Nacho must have changed clothes in the meantime. When we'd left the car, he had still been in his suit. I was afraid to turn around, thinking that he was completely naked. That I wouldn't be able to stop myself when I saw his toned body in all its glory.

"No. You do not scare me." I sipped my wine.

"Though I know you tried making me scared a few times."

I spun around and freed myself from his embrace.

He had pants on. His feet were bare. I studied his physique and saw that my scrutiny quickened his breath.

"I'll bring the world to its knees for you, baby."

His hand stroked my bare shoulder. His eyes followed the motion of his palm.

"I'll show you places you've never even dreamed about."

He leaned in closer and kissed the spot he had caressed.

"I want you to see the sunrise in Burma as we fly in a hot-air balloon."

His lips brushed against the skin of my neck.

"I want you to drink cocktails in Tokyo, watching the colorful lights of the city at night."

I closed my eyes as Nacho's lips touched my ear.

"I want you to make love to me on a surfboard off the shore of Australia. I will show you the world."

I took a step back. My will was weakening. Without a word, I passed through the door on the opposite side of the large living room and went out to the terrace. It bordered the beach. I took my shoes off and stepped onto the still-warm sand. My dress dragged behind me, leaving a streak of smoothed beach. I had no idea what I was doing. I was cheating on my husband with his greatest enemy and his worst nightmare. I might just as well stick a knife in his back and twist, watching him suffer. I sat down and listened to the steady rhythm of the waves, sipping my wine.

"You can run from me," Nacho said, joining me. "But we both know you can't run from your thoughts."

I didn't know how to answer. He was right. But at the same time I didn't want any changes in my life. Not now. Not when it had finally started to look normal. I thought about Massimo and suddenly realized something.

"Oh, God! My phone," I groaned, terrified. "His people will be here in a moment! I have a GPS chip implanted. Even if my phone is down, he knows where I am."

"No. Not here," Nacho replied calmly, even as I shot up in panic. "The house has jamming systems. Tracking devices, wiretaps, and all that shit can't see us here."

He turned his head, sending me a tender look.

"You disappeared, bee, and you can remain invisible for as long as you want."

I plopped down on the sand again, but inside my head, thoughts and emotions were spinning like a whirlwind. Part of me wanted to go back to my apartment. Another one dreamed of Nacho taking me then and there, on the beach. I shivered, feeling his closeness. My heart was racing, and my hands trembled at the thought of his warmth.

"I need to go," I whispered, squeezing my eyes shut.

"Are you sure?" he asked, rolling to his back and stretching.

"Jesus . . . you're doing this on purpose."

I put my glass down and propped myself on my hands, planning to get up again.

Nacho's arm shot out and pulled my arms from under me as he rolled me onto him. Sitting astride him now, I watched his joyful smile. He held me in a firm grip. I didn't defend myself or try escaping. He crossed his arms behind his head.

"I want to take you somewhere," he said, and his face brightened even more.

"My friend has a racing track not far from here. There are a couple of bikes there."

My eyes widened.

"I heard you like to ride and are quite good at it."

I nodded.

"That's great!"

He rolled us over. Now I was under him.

"I'm taking you to a race tomorrow. You can bring Olga. I'll bring Amelia. We'll spend some time together, get some lunch, maybe go for a swim."

"Are you serious?"

"Sure. Besides, I know you booked your apartment for the entire week. You have the time to spare."

I couldn't believe what he was saying. The notion of spending time together was enticing, but I knew I wouldn't be able to lose my security detail again. Those poor guys were probably having heart attacks. Massimo must have learned by now that he wouldn't be able to locate me.

"I need some time, Nacho. To think," I said. He grinned even wider.

"I'll tell you what conclusion you'll arrive at. Just wrap your legs around me, will you?"

Puzzled, I did as he asked. He sat up, lifting me from the ground. Now my most delicate spot was touching his bulging erection.

"At some point you will realized that your husband isn't the man you knew, but an imitation of who you wanted him to be. When you finally stop being reliant on him, you'll leave him. If you ask me, he can't even satisfy your most basic needs."

"Oh, really?"

I crossed my arms, trying to put some distance between the two of us. In response, Nacho lifted his hips slightly. I moaned quietly as his hard cock rubbed against my clit.

"Oh, really!" he said, grinning.

He wrapped one arm around my waist and grabbed the back of my neck with the other. Pressing my body against his, he thrusted with his hips.

"You want me, baby, but not because of my colorful tattoos and my money."

He thrusted again, and I threw back my head on instinct.

"You want me because you are in love with me. Same as I'm in love with you." Nacho's hips were ruthless. My hands flew to his face and started caressing it.

"I don't want to fuck you like your husband does. I don't want to dominate you."

His lips gently brushed against mine.

"I want you to yearn for my closeness. I want you to want me inside you. To want the two of us to be as close to each other as possible."

He kissed me slowly and delicately, and I didn't fight him.

"I will adore you. Each little fragment of your soul will be sacred to me. I will break you free from everything that takes your peace away."

Nacho's tongue slid inside my mouth and started its dance.

If anyone was watching, it would look like we were making love. My hips pressed against his. We stroked each other's faces. I felt an orgasmic wave rise in my stomach. Nacho felt it, too. I tried breaking free, but he held me in place.

"Don't fight me, my love."

His hand slid to the back of my head while the other rested on my buttock, pressing me harder against him.

"I want to bring you ecstasy. I want to give you everything you ever dreamed about." I climaxed. With a loud moan, I came, rubbing against the zipper of his pants. His soft tongue led me in a slow, gentle kiss. His open eyes glittered with what I saw was pure happiness and joy. Was it the fact that I hadn't had sex with my husband for weeks, or that I was with Nacho and one of my fantasies was being realized? I didn't care right then. It wasn't important what had made me come so hard.

"What are we doing?" I asked, sobering up. His hips stopped their motion, and his lips retreated.

"Ruining your dress."

His humor was contagious. I snorted in laughter.

"We've got a big problem now. My pants are ruined, too."

I rolled off him and noticed the dark stain on his trousers. He had orgasmed, too. It was . . . impossible. Mystical. He'd come with me, even though we hadn't even had sex.

"Last time I couldn't stop myself from coming was around primary school." Nacho laughed and lay back on the sand.

"I'm going back to my apartment," I said, smiling, and got up.

"I'll drive you." He jumped to his feet and started brushing the sand off himself.

"Not going to happen, Marcelo. I'll get a cab."

"Don't call me that," he said in a serious voice. I was sure he was trying to keep himself from smiling, though. "Besides, you have a great big stain on the front of your dress."

I glanced down and realized he was right. There was no telling if the stain was his seed or if I was that wet. I sighed, resigned, and headed to the door.

"Get me a hair dryer," I called, rubbing the stain with a moist cloth I'd found in the kitchen.

"I don't exactly use hair dryers," said Nacho, patting his bald head and laughing. "I'll give you some of Amelia's clothes," he added and disappeared into the living room.

I followed and saw him taking his pants off on the way toward the stairs. He wasn't wearing underwear. The sight of his tattooed buttocks was entrancing. I stifled a moan.

"I heard that," he called, vanishing upstairs.

Wearing slightly loose gray sweatpants, a white tank top, and pink Nike Air Maxes, I was waiting by the house for Nacho. None of my arguments had convinced him, even though I tried reasoning that he couldn't drive me to the hotel because the place was probably under surveillance. He finally agreed to drop me off a couple hundred yards from the place. I'd go the rest of the way on foot.

"Are you ready?" he asked, slapping my ass as he passed me. His forwardness was endearing—boyish and manly at the same time. I kept still, leaning against the door, but my eyes followed Nacho. My kidnapper wore a black tracksuit and looked very attractive.

As he went to the car and bent slightly to open the door, I noticed he was wearing a gun harness.

"Are we in danger?" I asked with concern, pointing to the leather straps.

"Nope."

He sent me a puzzled look, only noticing what I was looking at after a moment.

"Oh, this. I always carry a gun. Just a little quirk of mine."

He leaned his back against the car and looked at me. At my chest, to be precise.

"Sometimes I surprise even myself with my own ingenuity," he said with a smile.

"Your perky nipples will definitely make the drive a pleasant experience for me."

He wiggled his brows and grinned. I glanced down and saw that my nipples really were perfectly visible through the thin fabric of the tank top Nacho had given me. Last time I looked like that he had pounced on me. The difference was that last time I had been soaked through, and now the wetness was contained to my crotch.

"Hand over the sweatshirt," I ordered, stifling a laugh and holding an arm across my breasts.

We drove slowly, stealing glances at each other. We didn't talk. I was thinking about the future—about what I should do, and whether I would be able to focus on anything from that point on. I considered his proposal, wondering if we should meet the next day. I would love to spend another day with Nacho, but at the same time I was sure that Massimo would learn about that in no time. And then he would kill the both of us. If I told Olga about my plan to get together with Nacho, she would have died of a heart attack. Thoughts whirled in my head, and I couldn't decide. And I could already feel a headache coming. I turned left and looked at Nacho. He was driving topless. Two gigantic guns were strapped to his tattooed chest. He propped his head on his left hand, which in turn was propped against the car door. The right hand clutched the steering wheel. Once in a while he hummed along with the songs playing from the radio.

"Want me to kidnap you for real?" he asked all of a sudden, as we entered the part of town I knew. The car stopped.

"I was actually considering it," I replied, pulling the sweatshirt off. "That would make my decision a lot easier."

"That would mean I made the decision for you." He laughed.

"But on the other hand," I continued, "I would never get my past sorted out. I'd never have shut the doors that are still open."

I sighed, hiding my face in my hands. "I need to think about it. Get everything in order."

"I waited for you for months. And before that, my entire life. If you want me to, I'll wait years more."

"I can't meet you tomorrow. Or the day after. I need you to disappear for now."

"All right, babe." He sighed and planted a kiss on my brow. "I'll be close."

I got out of the car and started walking toward the apartment. My new heart suddenly flared with pain. It raced, pulsating. My eyes teared up. I wanted to twist around, but I knew that if I so much as glanced at Nacho, I'd go right back to him and tell him that yes, he should in fact kidnap me. My throat cramped. I prayed silently for God to grant me the strength to survive what was coming.

I entered the hotel and went straight to the elevator. My dress and my clutch were still in the car. Cursing quietly, I went back to the reception desk and asked the porter for another key to my apartment. On my way up, I could still smell the scent of the Canarian surfer on the air. It was everywhere: on my hair, my lips, my neck. It was torture. I missed him so much, I thought my heart would burst, even though we had parted no more than fifteen minutes before. *What is happening to me?* I thought, entering the apartment.

I wen to the chest of drawers, pulled my phone out of my pocket, and connected it to the charger.

"Where were you?" A familiar growl from behind me. The night lamp went on. "Answer me right now!" Massimo bellowed, rising from the armchair.

Shit . . .

My husband took a step closer. His expression could only mean trouble.

"Stop shouting. You'll wake Olga."

"She's so hammered not even a bomb would wake her. And she's with Domenico."

The Man in Black clamped his fingers on my shoulders. Painfully. "Where were you, Laura?"

His eyes flared with fury. His pupils dilated, and his jaw worked rhythmically. He was angry. Angrier than I had ever seen him, in fact.

"I needed to think," I said, meeting his eyes. "And since when do you care where I am or what I'm doing?" I shrugged off his hands. "Do I ask you where you are or who you spend time with when you leave for days on end? The last time I saw you was two weeks ago. When you stuck your dick in me and left me hanging." I was shouting now. A wave of anger surged inside me, spilling over. "I've had enough of this. Of you. Of how you started behaving half a year ago! I lost a baby! I was the one who needed surgery!"

My hand flew out faster than I could think. I slapped him in the face. "And you left me, you fucking bastard!"

Massimo stood rooted to the spot, his hands balled into fists. I could practically hear the frantic beating of his heart.

"If you think you can leave me, you're gravely mistaken." He grabbed the collar of my tank top with both hands and ripped it in two with one motion, before lunging forward and biting my nipple. I yelped, trying to defend myself, but he was stronger and shoved me over the bed.

"I'll remind you just what it is that you love in me," he growled and pulled his belt out. I tried to run, but he grabbed my ankle and pulled me toward him, straddling me and immobilizing me with his legs. Quickly and deftly, he wrapped the belt around my wrists and tied me to the headboard. I squirmed and screamed, thrashing to break free, but Massimo got up and slowly started taking my clothes off. Tears were rolling down my cheeks, and my wrists hurt. I was tied too tightly. He looked at me with satisfaction, and I could see the fury blazing in his eyes.

"Please, Massimo," I whispered.

"Where were you?" he repeated his question, unbuttoning his shirt.

"I went for a walk. I needed to think."

"You're lying."

His voice was composed again. Low. "I got scared."

He hung his shirt over the backrest of the armchair and pulled his pants down. They fell to the floor in a heap, revealing Massimo's bulging cock. He was ready. His muscular body was glistening with sweat. He was larger than I remembered, and more toned. His erection was massive. At any other time, I would have burned in ecstasy at the sight and explode like New Year's Eve fireworks before he even touched me. But not today. My thoughts revolved around the Canarian's tattooed body. He was probably still where I'd left him. Waiting. The window was open wide. A cool oceanic breeze gusted into the room. If I'd yelled his name, he would have heard me. He would have come for me. A river of tears flowed down my face, drowning out the thought. My body tensed as Massimo crawled over me.

"Open your mouth," he commanded, kneeling over my head. I shook my head.

"Come on, baby girl," he said with a mocking laugh. "I'll do what I want anyway. We both know that. So be a good girl and do as I say."

My mouth was clamped shut.

"I can see you're in the mood for some extremely rough fucking today."

He pinched my nose, cutting off my oxygen, and waited until I had to open my mouth to breathe in.

My vision swam. I was getting dizzy. My mouth opened a fraction to let some air in. Massimo thrusted with his hips and slammed his cock into my throat.

"Oh, yes, baby girl," he breathed, pushing harder. "Just like that."

I tried keeping still, but the inside of my mouth contorted around my husband's thick cock. Several minutes later, he got up and kissed me.

I tasted alcohol and the bitter tang of cocaine. He was drugged out of his mind and completely unpredictable. That scared me even more. The fear mixed with the trust that I had always had for him. He was my beloved husband, wasn't he? My defender. The man who had always adored me. But now, here I was, lying naked, strapped to the bed beneath him. Completely defenseless. Waiting for the pain to come.

His lips trailed down my neck, stopping at my breasts. He pinched and sucked my nipple. Hard. He bit it as his hand fondled the other. I squirmed, begging for him to stop, but he ignored me. I sobbed. He went lower, until he reached my thighs. They were pressed tightly together. With one strong motion, he pulled them apart. His tongue started playing with my snatch. He bit it. He finger-fucked me.

"Where's your vibrator?" he asked, raising his eyes to look at my face.

"I don't have one," I sobbed.

"You're lying again, Laura."

"I don't have one with me. I left it at home. In the drawer by our bed." I emphasized the word "our." Maybe that would work. I was wrong. His eyes filled with even greater anger, and he roared.

The Man in Black knelt between my legs, lifted them both up and placed them on his shoulders. Then he charged in with his throbbing cock, pushing himself inside me as deep as he was able. I cried out, feeling a ripping pain in my abdomen.

"So . . . how . . . ," he hissed through clenched teeth, fucking me hard. "How did you come?"

His hips were thrusting, hitting me, and I screamed, drowning the slapping sound out.

"Or, should I ask: Who helped you come?"

The frantic speed of his pistoning movement and the pain he was causing muddled my thoughts. I opened my teary eyes and looked straight at him. I hated this man with all my being. I hated what he was doing to me. But despite all that, I felt myself nearing another orgasm. I wanted none of it, but there was no way to stop the pleasure this unstable man was giving me. Soon enough, my body was wracked with ecstasy. In the throes of rapture, I let out a piercing shriek.

"Yes! Just like that!" the Man in Black roared, and I felt his cum spilling inside me. "You're mine!" He came. His fingers bit into my ankles, but I couldn't feel the pain anymore. The only thing that mattered was the enormous wave of orgasm crashing over me.

———

I was woken up by gentle kisses on the back of my neck. They cast away my dreams. Dreams of Nacho and his tenderness, in which the events of last night were just a nightmare. I sighed and opened my eyes a little, looking back. I saw my husband.

"Good morning," he purred with a smile. I nearly puked at the sound of his voice.

"How much did you drink last night?" I growled. His eyes grew serious. "And what were you on?"

I sat up and saw the look of shock on his face as he stared at my naked body marred by fresh bruises. My wrists were purple from the belt he had strapped me to the bed with. He hadn't untied me until just a few hours before. On my legs and stomach I bore the quickly blackening traces of his rough touch.

"Jesus Christ," he whispered, nervously studying the signs of his madness. I froze as he touched me. He felt it and retreated to the other side of the bed, hiding his face in his hands.

"Laura . . . darling."

He glanced back at my bruised skin, and his eyes teared up. I knew he hadn't been himself yesterday, but only this reaction made it certain. He really hadn't been in control during the night. I sighed heavily and covered myself, so he didn't have to watch how much he had hurt me.

"You and your twin have more in common than you think," I said with scorn.

"I'll stop drinking and I'll never take any drugs again," he said firmly, reaching out with a hand.

"Bullshit." I snorted. "You'll do it again."

Massimo shot out of bed, ran around it, and went down on his knees before me. He took my hand and kissed it.

"I'm sorry," he whispered. "So sorry . . ."

"I need to go to Poland," I hissed. He raised his eyes. There was fear in them. "Either you give me the space I need to think, or I leave you for good."

He opened his mouth, wanting to say something, but I stopped him with a raised hand.

"I'm one step from filing for divorce, Massimo. Our marriage died with our child. I'm trying to get everything sorted, and you're not making it any easier. Your grief must end, too."

I got up and passed him on my way to grab a bathrobe.

"Either you go to therapy, stop drinking, and return just the way you were a year ago, or we're done."

I walked over to him, wagging a finger.

"But if you try to control me when I'm in Poland, or send your goons after me, or come yourself, I swear to you I'll get a divorce and you'll never see me again."

I spun around and went to the bathroom. Standing by the mirror, I studied my face. I couldn't believe I had said all that. My own strength was terrifying. My assertiveness was surprising. I had nearly forgotten that I could be like that. Deep down in my heart, I knew the reasons for that. I knew what gave me the strength, but it was too painful to think about.

"You won't leave me. I won't allow it."

I raised my eyes and saw Massimo in the mirror. He was standing behind me. His voice was firm and commanding, and his eyes cold.

I shrugged off the bathrobe and let it crumple to the ground. Naked and bruised, I stood for him to see. He swallowed and sighed. Dropped his eyes.

"Look at me," I said. He didn't react.

"Look at me, Massimo! You can lock me up and rape me. You can do whatever you want. But you'll never have my heart."

I took a step forward. He took one back.

"I'm not leaving you. I'm just going away to get my head straight."

A long silence ensued. He watched me impassively, trying to keep his eyes from the fresh bruises. "The plane is yours. I promise you I won't follow you."

He spun around and left. I collapsed to the cold floor and started crying. I had no idea what to do, but at least the tears brought some respite.

———

It was afternoon when I emerged from my room. For several hours, I'd ignored Olga's attempts to get me out of bed. I didn't feel like explaining to her what happened or showing what my husband had done to me. She would have ripped him to shreds. At the same time, I was nearly certain that Domenico knew. He'd taken her out and kept her occupied so she didn't have time to pester me.

I put on a light long-sleeved tunic dress, a wide hat, sunglasses, and my favorite Isabel Marant sneakers, and left the room. I walked along the promenade, watching the ocean and thinking. What to do, how to behave? Leave Massimo or not? Organize my life from the ground up again? Each question was left without an answer. And each new one brought ten others. What if Nacho turns out to be a monster, too? I used to think my husband wasn't one, but his behavior the previous night had left me without faith or hope.

I noticed a small, gorgeous bistro on a corner. I went inside to have a snack, a sip of wine, and a moment to relax. A delightful old man took my order, and I reached for my phone. I wanted to call Mom and tell her I was coming home. I unlocked the screen only to see there was a message waiting for me. It said: Look to the right. I did. Tears immediately gathered in the corners of my eyes. Nacho was sitting at the table next to mine, looking straight at me. He wore a baseball cap, sunglasses, and a long-sleeved shirt. It hid his tattoos.

"Sit with your back to the street," he said, keeping still. "There's at least one car following you."

I rose slowly and moved, pretending that the sun was blinding me. I looked ahead but with the corner of my vision saw the car he had mentioned.

"Massimo is in Lagos," I whispered, keeping my eyes trained on the phone.

"I know. I realized that about an hour after I dropped you off."

"You promised me something, Nacho." I sighed and felt the tears streaking down my cheeks again.

"What happened, baby?"

His voice was full of concern. I didn't reply.

The elderly man walked over and placed a glass of wine on my table. I reached for it. The sleeve of my tunic slid up a little, revealing the purple weal on my wrist.

"What is this?" Nacho's voice suddenly changed. It was a growl now.

"What did that bastard do to you?"

I turned my head to him and saw his eyes. They were filled with murderous fury. He clenched his hand, breaking his sunglasses with a loud *crack*. Shards of glass flew to the ground.

"I will get up in a moment," he said. "I will kill your security guards, and then I'll go find that motherfucker and kill him, too."

He rose.

"Please don't," I muttered, taking a great gulp of wine.

"If you don't want me to do that, you'll get up, pay for your wine, and meet me two streets down the promenade. Go left, then turn onto a narrow street. The second on your right." I nodded at the waiter.

"But first drink your wine."

I walked across a narrow street, along a row of old houses. Suddenly, I felt someone grabbing me and pulling into a narrow doorway. It was Nacho. He rolled up my sleeve and studied my bruises. I dropped my head. He took my sunglasses off and looked me in the eyes.

"What happened, Laura?" he asked. I looked away. "Look at me, please."

There was desperation in his voice. Also anger. He tried hiding both of those things.

"He wanted to fuck . . . I . . . He asked me where I had been . . ." I started sobbing again. Nacho wrapped his hand around me and hugged me to his chest.

"I'm going to Poland tomorrow," I said. "I need to stay away from the both of you for a while."

He said nothing, keeping me in his embrace. His heart was racing. I raised my eyes and looked at him. He was focused. Cold. Serious. Completely absent.

"All right," he said finally, planting a quick kiss on my forehead. "Call me when you sort things out."

His arm released me, and I felt . . . hollow. Nacho passed through the door and didn't look back. I kept still for a long while, choking on tears. After some time, I returned to the hotel.

I was packing the last bag when Olga barged into my room. Her hair was in disarray.

"Have a spat again?" she asked, plopping down on the floor next to me.

"Why do you ask?"

I sent her a dispassionate look.

"Because Massimo booked the apartment below ours instead of sleeping with you. And Domenico and I are next door."

She pinned me with a stare.

"What's going on, Laura?"

"I'm going back to Poland," I muttered, zipping up the bag. "I need to get away from all this shit."

"Okay, I get it. But are you talking about Massimo, Nacho, or me?" She leaned back, resting her back against the wall and crossing her arms. "What about the company? What about everything you've been building all this time?"

"Nothing. I can manage it online. Besides, you and Emi will manage without me." I sighed. "I really need to go, Olga. This whole situation is too much for me. I need to talk to Mom. I haven't seen her since Christmas. And there are many more reasons."

"Okay, go," she said, getting up. "Just remember about my wedding."

I stopped by the door to Massimo's apartment, wondering if this was the right thing to do. Should I go in? In the end, reason and love won. I knocked and heard the lock turning. It was Domenico. He sighed deeply and gave me a weak smile, letting me inside.

"Where is he?" I asked, crossing my arms.

"In the gym," he nodded, pointing me in the right direction.

"I thought my room was big, but I see they always keep the best for the big boss."

I snorted ironically and passed through a series of rooms, realizing that my husband's apartment took up half of the entire hotel floor.

There were grunts and roars coming from behind a door. I knew those sounds. I passed through and saw Massimo pummeling one of the security guards with his fists. There was no cage this time. And no fight. The tall Italian stood in front of the Man in Black with boxing pads on his arms. My husband kept punching and kicking them with wild abandon. The other man barked things out, and Massimo followed the orders, switching hands and legs.

He didn't notice me, so I cleared my throat loudly. He stopped and said something to the large man, who threw the pads to the ground and left. The Man in Black grabbed a bottle of water and downed it before stepping closer to me.

If not for what had happened the night before, I would have thought his body was the sexiest thing in the world. His long legs bound in tight sports leggings looked more toned and longer than they really were, and his sweaty, heaving chest made me salivate. Massimo knew the effect he had on me. He pulled off his gloves and ran his fingers through his hair.

"Hi," he said, walking toward me.

"I wanted to . . ." I forgot what I was about to say.

"Yes?"

He stepped closer. Dangerously close. I inhaled his beautiful scent. I closed my eyes and felt exactly like I had several months before, when I had still wanted that man above all else.

"You wanted something, baby girl?" he asked again. I was rooted to the spot.

"I-I wanted to say goodbye," I stammered, opening my eyes.

He was leaning closer to me.

"No, please," I breathed, and his lips froze an inch from mine. I cowered.

"You're afraid of me." He slammed his empty water bottle against the wall. "Jesus, Laura, how can you . . ."

I rolled up my sleeve, revealing the bruise. He piped down.

"It isn't that you fucked me," I said calmly. "It's that you did it against my will."

"Jesus, I've done it about a hundred times against your will! That's where the fun comes from!" He took my face in his hands. "How many times have I fucked you after you told me to stop? Because you had just taken a shower, or because I would crumple your dress or ruin your hair . . . But then you always begged me to keep going."

"How many times did I tell you to keep going yesterday?"

The Man in Black bit his lip, but he withdrew a step.

"Exactly. You don't even remember what you did. You don't remember my tears. You don't remember my pain. How I begged you to stop."

I felt an explosion of fury inside.

"You raped me."

Here it was. I said it. I felt nauseous now.

Massimo stood immobile, breathing shallowly. He was angry and resigned. He looked wretched.

"I know there's no justification," he managed, dropping his head. "I want you to know that I called a therapist today."

My face must have contorted in the weirdest expression then.

"I'm beginning therapy as soon as I go back to Sicily," Massimo continued. "I'll quit drinking, and I'll never ever touch that white shit again. I'll do anything for you to feel safe with me again."

I took his hand, wanting to encourage him and show him my support.

"And then we'll have a daughter and I'll lose my mind with the two of you," he added with a laugh. I punched him in the stomach.

He was gorgeous at that moment. Smiling and almost relaxed. I knew it was just a mask.

"We'll see what comes next," I said, turning my back on him.

He grabbed me by the arm. More gently than usual. Then he pushed me to the wall. His face hovered right in front of mine, as if he was waiting for consent.

"I want to slide my tongue into your mouth. Taste you," he whispered, and I suddenly felt hot at the sound of his voice. "Let me kiss you, Laura. I promise I won't come to Poland, and I'll give you as much freedom as you need."

I swallowed loudly and exhaled slowly. The biggest problem was that my husband looked like a god, and I just couldn't say no to him.

"Please be . . . ," I began, but he didn't wait for me to finish. He pushed his tongue between my lips.

Strangely, he kept the kiss delicate and slow, full of affection. He was so gentle, as if he could break me with a touch. Slowly, his tongue brushed against mine.

"I love you," he whispered finally and kissed me on the brow.

CHAPTER 8

I wanted no bodyguards or drivers—none of that. But despite promising me that nobody would follow me, Massimo couldn't leave me completely alone. It just wasn't possible for him. I passed through the VIP terminal at the airport, and the first person I saw outside was Damian, grinning and leaning against his car.

"I can't believe it's you!" I cried out, greeting him with a great big hug.

"Hi there, babes," he said, lifting his sunglasses.

"I don't exactly know what's been happening out there for the last few months, but your hubby called Karol and asked that I keep an eye on you personally."

I laughed inwardly, as he opened the door to his Mercedes. It was clear why Massimo had done this. He wanted me to know he trusted me, and, knowing he couldn't renege on his promise, this was the only way to keep me at least a bit protected.

"Where are we going?" asked the Warrior, turning in his seat to look at me. "Let me just tell you this: I ain't going to wear a driver's cap."

"Take me home," I replied with a smile.

———

It wasn't far, so just a couple of minutes later he parked the car in the underground garage. I suggested we order some food and have a chat, and Damian happily agreed.

"I heard what happened," he said, putting his half-eaten KFC spicy wing on his plate. "You want to talk about it, or shall we pretend nothing's wrong?"

"That depends. How loyal do you have to be to Karol and my husband?"

"Not as loyal as to you," he replied immediately. "If you're asking if I'm here to grill you for intel, it's nothing like that. Your husband pays me a good buck, but you can't buy loyalty." He leaned back on the couch. "And you have it."

"Remember out last conversation? On Skype."

He nodded. "Yeah. Sure."

"That day, after we talked, I met a man who kidnapped me and changed my entire life."

Recounting the whole story took me a long time. I talked and Damian listened, laughing or shaking his head where appropriate. Finally, I reached the last forty-eight hours. Of course I skipped the details of what happened between me and Nacho in Lagos. I also left out what happened after that. How my husband raped me.

"Something seems off in this story,"

Damian said, pouring me another glass of wine and a cup of water for himself. "That Spanish guy."

"Canarian," I cut in.

"Yeah. That guy. You seem to care for him. And each time you talk about him, your eyes shine."

His words terrified me.

"See? I can see through you. And now you look like you're going to have a heart attack. So cut the bullshit and tell me everything."

I scratched my head, searching for a good explanation, but after practically chugging a bottle of wine and about a dozen sleeping pills to help me survive the flight, I wasn't exactly in my intellectual prime.

"He's why I'm here. Without Olga and Massimo." I sighed. "He's gotten into my head. And I let him."

"Don't you think he did that because you weren't as happy as you thought you were?"

He paused but kept his eyes trained on me. "Look at it like that: if you're sure of something, normally nobody can change your mind. Nothing can topple a solid foundation, especially when it comes to feelings." He lifted a finger, explaining, "But if there's even a shadow of a doubt, and the foundation isn't sound, all it takes is a gust of wind and everything tumbles like a house of cards."

"You're just saying that because you hate my husband."

"I couldn't care less about that fuck. This is about you." He paused, scratching his cheek. "Let's take us, for instance. You and I from years ago. I was an idiot, and I didn't take the risk . . . although that might be a bad example."

"It sure is," I agreed with a smile. "But I think I know what you're getting at."

———

The next morning, I was supposed to go to my parents' place, but as soon as I opened my eyes, I came up with a devilish idea. I skipped to the bathroom and prepared myself. An hour later, I rummaged through the cupboard, looking for the keys. It was May, and the weather in Poland was gorgeous. Everything was in bloom, waking to life—just like me. The intercom chimed. I told Damian I'd be with him shortly and grabbed my bag. I looked very good in off-white

Louis Vuitton ankle-high sneakers, white torn shorts, and a thin sweater that revealed most of my midriff. It was a bit girlish, but the idea I had had that morning wasn't exactly mature, either.

"Hi there, big man," I greeted Damian, looking for a comfortable position in the passenger seat.

"You look fucking amazing," he said, shooting me a glance. "To your parents' house?"

I shook my head.

"The Suzuki dealership." I grinned as his eyes widened.

"Protecting you means I have to make sure you're safe, you know . . . ," he muttered.

"To the Suzuki dealership!" I repeated, nodding my head vigorously.

———

I pointed to a GSX-R750, and the motorbike salesman nodded with appreciation.

"That one," I said, sitting on the bike and watching Damian fuming with anger.

"I can't tell you not to do it, Laura, but I'll have to call Karol, and he'll call Massimo," he said.

"Call him then!" I barked, leaning over the tank.

"One hundred and fifty horsepower at thirteen thousand RPMs," the young salesman prattled. "Top speed—"

"I can see what's written on the tag," I cut him short. "Do you have it in black?"

The guy's eyes bulged as I continued unfettered.

"And a racing suit. Also black. Dainese if you got it. I saw one that I liked somewhere here. And Sidi boots. With red stars on the sides. They're over there." I dismounted the motorcycle. "I'll show you the ones. The helmet will be the hardest to pick."

The poor man fussed around me, shooting glances at Damian, probably wondering if I was being serious and he'd score the best sales deal of the season.

When I had everything, I presented myself dressed in the tight-fitting racing suit, gloves, and boots. I had my new helmet tucked under my arm.

"Perfect," I said, glancing at the two dumbfounded men. "I'll take everything. Bring the bike to the entrance, please."

"Miss, there's just one problem." The salesman hesitated. "The bike must be registered for you to take it away. And the one you selected is brand-new, so . . ."

"What do you mean?" I snapped, narrowing my eyes.

"If you're in a hurry . . . We don't have a registered bike in black." He headed toward the door. "But we have a demo version. Same parameters, but it's red and black. And it's been used during test drives."

I pondered his words for a moment, biting my lip. Damian looked smug, thinking that my plan had just failed.

"Well, at least the red will go nicely with the stars on my boots. I'll take it."

I passed the salesman my credit card. Damian face-palmed.

"Get the papers in order."

I started the engine, and the motorcycle roared. I grinned wildly and put the helmet on, lifting the visor.

"He'll fire me," Damian groaned, dropping his head.

"Not going to happen. Besides, he'll be too furious to think about you. He'll want to kill *me*." I kicked the machine into gear, and it surged forward.

I hadn't felt power like that for a long while. I couldn't help feeling overexcited and a bit scared, too. I hadn't ridden for some time and needed to get used to handling that monster before I really started having fun.

I drove across Warsaw rather slowly, sensing my bodyguard's car behind my back and feeling the vibrations of my phone in my pocket. Massimo must have learned about my newest purchase already. I revved the engine. There was a lot of traffic on the streets, but after ten minutes or so I recalled why I loved riding bikes so much. The straight, wide road ahead challenged me to test the capabilities of my new motorcycle. As soon as there was some space, I gunned the machine and charged forward.

"You're a purebred bitch," I said, patting the bike with fondness as I parked it by my parents' house.

A moment later, a Mercedes S-Class arrived, tires screeching, and Damian stormed out.

"Do you have any idea how that man can fucking scream?" he called out, slamming the door shut. "I've been through hell!"

"Oh, so my husband called?" I asked with a smirk.

"Called? He was on the line the entire fucking time. Screaming at me in three goddamned languages."

"Right," I muttered. My pocket started vibrating again. The screen of my phone flashed with one word. *Massimo.*

"Good afternoon, dear husband," I said in fluent English.

"What the hell were you thinking? I'm coming to Poland!" he yelled into the receiver so loud I had to draw it away from my ear.

"Remember about our deal," I said. "If you come, I divorce you."

He piped down, and I continued, "Before I met you, I rode motorcycles and I intend to do so again. Why shouldn't I, after all?" I sighed. "Sometimes our relationship seems more dangerous than riding what's between my legs now."

"Laura!" the Man in Black growled.

"Am I wrong, though, don Torricelli? For twenty-nine years I was fine, and in the last year I've been shot, lost a child, been kidnapped—"

"That's a low blow, baby girl," he muttered.

"It's the truth. And stop taking it out on Damian. He was on your side in this," I said, winking at my ex. "Now, forgive me, but I'm sweating in this suit."

Silence.

"And stop freaking out. I'll come back safe and sound."

"If anything happens to you, I'll kill—"

"Who? Kill who this time?" I cut him short, irritated.

"Myself . . . I'm nothing without you." He went quiet and then hung up.

I stared at the black screen, admiring his self-control and negotiating skill.

"Done." I looked at Damian, who was waiting with his back propped against the car. "Now you can go back to the city. I'll stay here for a couple days."

"I'll be around. I booked a room at a hotel a mile away. Don't get mad, but I want to have my eye on you. You know how Massimo can get."

He shrugged, and I gave him the thumbs-up, accepting his reasoning. Damian brought my bags to the porch and left.

I turned the key in the ignition, and the engine of my motorcycle came alive. I revved it to the maximum. The demonic roar was so loud, my dad practically sprinted outside with a terrified expression.

"Now, envy me!" I called, getting off the bike and walking over to him to wrap my arms around his neck.

"Oh, darling!" He hugged me but quickly switched his attention to the machine. "You bought yourself a motorbike? You're having a midlife crisis or something? That's what your mom says. That you only buy things like that when you want to prove something . . ."

"Laura!"

Speaking of the devil. Klara Biel's shrill voice pierced my skull. Suddenly, I wanted to put my helmet back on.

"Darling, have you completely lost your mind?"

"Hi, Mom."

I unzipped the top of the racing suit and embraced my mother. "Before you start yelling, I wanted to tell you that my husband has already done so, but I managed to pacify him. So. Am I going to have to pacify you, too?"

"Honey," she pleaded. "Isn't it enough that your father keeps me on my toes all the time? Do you have to join him in his campaign to make me have a heart attack?"

Dad raised his eyebrows with amusement.

"Besides, what's this on your head?"

I ran my fingers through my hair, remembering that the last time they saw me, I had still been blond.

"I needed to change something after . . ." I swallowed. "It was a difficult time, Mom."

Klara's expression grew less severe as she recalled everything that had happened to me lately.

"Tom, bring us a bottle of wine from the fridge." She glanced at Dad, who was still giggling behind her back. "And you take off that horrible uniform. You'll get all sweaty."

"I already am."

Dad went to prepare the wine, and I took a shower and changed into a sweat suit before going to the garden and sitting on our soft couch.

"It's warm for this time of year. Why do you need a long-sleeved shirt?" Mom asked, pointing to my attire.

I rolled my eyes, thinking about what she'd say if she saw my bruised wrists. I quickly changed the subject.

"It's from my new collection. You like it?" I looked at her with a smile. "Did you check out the things I sent you?"

She nodded.

"And?"

"They're wonderful! I'm so proud of you. But I'm more interested in how you're feeling."

"I think I'm in love," I blurted out, and my mother practically choked on her wine.

"Excuse me?"

"I mean . . ."

I started telling her my story. She lit a cigarette with shaky hands.

"When we were on Tenerife, I met a man. One of Massimo's biggest competitors."

My subconscious was raging at what I was saying. I was spinning another lie.

"And Massimo didn't have much time for me, and Nacho had it in abundance. He taught me how to surf and took me hiking."

Jesus, what am I saying? I scolded myself.

"He introduced me to his family and, you know, made a really great impression . . . and he kissed me."

Mom had a fit of coughing then.

"It wouldn't be important if not for how Massimo changed after we lost our baby. He distanced himself from me. Started working around the clock. I don't think we'll ever be able to go back to how things were before."

I sighed. "It's exhausting."

"Baby," my mom started, putting out the cigarette, "I won't say 'I told you so,' but I tried telling you it was all happening too fast from the very beginning."

She poured us more wine.

"If you ask me, you got married because of the child."

Oh, how wrong you are, I thought.

"And the loss of the baby meant that the marriage lost its appeal." She shrugged. "So I'm not surprised that when you met someone intriguing, you took interest. What would you do if Massimo wasn't your husband but only a boyfriend? And you were in Poland, and not Sicily?"

"I'd have left him," I replied after a moment. "I wouldn't be able to live with a man who keeps ignoring me and treating me like I'm his enemy."

"Would you? Just like that?"

"Just like what?" I snapped. "I've been fighting for this marriage for months! And losing. How much time do I have to waste? In a few years, I'll suddenly realize I'm stuck with a man I don't really know."

My mother smiled sadly and nodded.

"So you see. You've answered your own question."

I was petrified. She made me say what I really felt. What I wanted and needed. It struck me that I had the right to feel everything that I was feeling. I could err. I could be wrong. But above all, I could do whatever made me happy.

"Let me give you some advice, dear. Something that has kept your father and me together for nearly thirty-five years."

I leaned in closer.

"You have to be selfish."

Shit, that's something new, I thought.

"If you put your happiness first, you will do everything for it to never end. So you will care for your relationship, provided that it gives you happiness. That it doesn't exhaust you. Remember—a woman who lives only to make her man happy is always miserable. You'll only feel held down. And that will make you complain. Men don't like women who complain."

"Yeah, and those who don't use makeup," I agreed.

"God forbid! Even if you're alone, you have to care about yourself. For your own sake," she said.

My mother was an expert when it came to that. She always had impeccable hair and makeup. Her whole demeanor said, *I have been born to shine.*

We got drunk that afternoon. I liked to do that with Mom. She got a lot funnier when she was drunk. And a lot less stuck-up.

The following days were similar. I went on walks with Dad, drank wine with Mom, and tried my best to get the telescope to work. Damian followed me everywhere, and Olga tried keeping the company afloat. We talked on Skype, selecting dress styles and discussing designs. And Massimo . . . he kept quiet. Apparently he had taken my ultimatum to heart. For the whole ten days I spent in Poland, he only called once. And that was the time he raked me over the coals for buying that motorcycle. I missed him, but I also missed Nacho. My mind was slipping into madness, it seemed, as I dreamed about the Man in Black and the colorful boy in turns. I was distraught. Torn in two. And I had no idea what to do. Finally, I decided to call my therapist.

"Hey," said Marco when I FaceTimed him.

"I nearly slept with Nacho," I blurted out, and he whistled in marvel. "But I didn't."

"Why?"

"I didn't want to cheat on my husband."

"Why?" he repeated.

"Because I think I love him."

"Aren't you sure? And, most of all, *who* did you refer to?" All conversations with Marco looked the same. I said something, he picked at the spiciest bit and led me to a solution that I had already known deep inside. With him, I always quickly got rid of all doubts.

And each time, I was the one to arrive at the final conclusions.

I decided to allow life to just happen. I would distance myself and observe its flow. There was no sense in trying to impact things. I needed everything to pan out on its own. I was ready to accept whatever fate had in store for me. Because, at least in theory, each resolution was good.

I asked Dad to go for a ride with me when the weekend came. Giddy with excitement, he pulled out his trusty chopper and donned his frilled leather outfit. We rode down the routes we knew, waving to other motorcyclists and enjoying the beautiful weather. I was at peace. Happy. And still without an answer.

We stopped at the main plaza in Kazimierz. I took my helmet off and shook my head to free my hair. It spilled over my shoulders. Everything played out like in the movies. The only thing that wasn't there was the slow motion. And I had clothes under the biking suit, instead of a sexy bra and a pair of gigantic boobs. Well, a modest black T-shirt would have to do.

The old marketplace was a favorite spot for bikers. The machines parked in a neat row provoked tourists to disregard the historical monuments all around them, instead snapping quick photos of the beautiful motorcycles.

"Like the old days," Dad said with a nostalgic smile, wrapping his arm around me. "Lemonade?"

He pointed his chin at our favorite bistro by the plaza. I nodded, and he led me there.

With his arm around me, we must have looked like a rich sponsor and his pretty mistress, but I didn't care about the snide looks of young men following us inside.

"How are you managing with Mom?" I asked, sipping on my beverage. "I can't stand her for more than two days in a row, and you've been together forever."

"Honeybun," he said with an affectionate smile, "I love her. So if I coped with her when she was pregnant with you, what's a little menopause?"

I burst out in laughter, picturing my pregnant mom berating Dad for nothing, and him bringing her all kinds of things she needed *right away*. I liked spending time with my father. He was unobtrusive and a good listener. But he was also an equally good talker. That meant I didn't have to keep up the conversation.

After an hour, we had skimmed over all subjects possible, from the horsepower of our bikes, to what alcohol we liked, to real estate investment strategies. Dad talked, and I listened. Then I talked, and he proved that I was wrong on all counts. He gave me business and personal advice.

"You know, honey, the main target in a business such as yours should be profit . . ."

The growl of an engine about five feet from us cut him short. We both looked toward the source of the sound. A beautiful yellow Hayabusa was driving up to the plaza. I moaned in envy, seeing the incredible bike. I had always dreamed of one, but I'd never had the chance to sit on one. The driver killed the engine and dismounted. Entranced, I stared at the yellow marvel. The man in the black suit took off his helmet, hung it on the handle, and turned our way. My heart practically exploded, and my body tensed. I stopped breathing as Nacho walked over.

"Laura." He greeted me with a grin, keeping his green eyes fixed on me and completely ignoring my dad.

"Jesus Christ," I whispered in Polish. Dad was dumbstruck.

"Nacho Matos," the Canarian introduced himself, extending a hand to my father. "Your daughter might need a moment to regain her wits. Do you mind if I sit?"

My jaw dropped. Nacho spoke Polish.

"Tomasz Biel. You two know each other?" dad asked, gesturing for Matos to sit.

"Jesus Christ," I repeated as Nacho took a seat, putting on sunglasses.

"We're friends, but I live pretty far away, so your daughter might be a bit surprised to see me."

Nacho glanced at me. I felt as if someone had hit my head with a baseball bat.

Disoriented, my dad looked at me and then at the intruder, who had managed to order himself an iced tea and recline comfortably in his seat.

"Beautiful bike you have there," father said, turning to look at the Hayabusa. "The lastest model?"

"Yup. Brand-new."

The two of them talked, while I felt the sudden need to jump to my feet and run. Run as long as my legs allowed. He was here, talking to my dad. I looked around. The black S-Class was parked on the other side of the plaza. I couldn't breathe.

"I'll be back," I barked, heading toward Damian.

I had no idea if he knew who Nacho was or what my husband had told him to do when he saw me with other men. I went for a bluff.

"Hey, Warrior," I said as he rolled down the window.

"Don't you want something to drink? Want me to get you anything?"

"I have everything I need right here." He nodded at the bottle of water by his side and chuckled. "Who's that guy?"

I turned around and glanced at our table. Both men were discussing something animatedly. The yellow bike, I guessed.

"Dad's buddy." I shrugged and sighed with relief. Damian seemed not to know who Nacho was.

"Nice bike he's got." He nodded in appreciation.

"Yeah, I like it, too," I agreed and spun around to get back to the table. "If you need anything, just give me a call."

I walked back to my chair. Dad got up, planted a kiss on my brow, and said:

"Your mother has gone ballistic. She probably thinks we're wet smears on a tree somewhere. I'd better go and calm her down."

He turned and shook Nacho's hand.

"It was nice to meet you. Remember about lubrication."

"Thanks, Tom. It's good advice. See you around."

Dad left, and I sat down, pinning Nacho with an angry glare.

"What the hell are you doing here? And how do you know my dad?"

Nacho reclined in his seat and took his glasses off.

"I'm testing the quality of Polish roads. I have some complaints." His grin was charming.

"And your dad? He's a great guy. I think he likes me."

"I asked you to give me time. Massimo got it. And you . . ."

"And the fact that he got it made it possible for me to travel to Poland. You have no guards with you, bee. Not counting that numbskull in the Mercedes."

He lifted his brows.

"Last time you left me and disappeared." My eyes teared up at the memory of him leaving me completely alone in that doorway.

Nacho sighed and dropped his head. His fists balled.

"I was afraid he'd punish you again. And I would have had to kill him then."

He raised his eyes. His stare was cold.

"And then I would have lost you . . ."

"Why are we talking in English?" I changed the subject. It wasn't a good time to talk about Massimo or me.

"When did you learn Polish?"

He leaned back and crossed his arms behind his head, smirking. Jesus, how I loved that smile.

"I know a lot of languages, but you already know that."

He looked at me closely. "You look gorgeous in this suit." He licked his lips, and I felt another slam of that baseball bat on the back of my head. How was I still conscious?

"Don't change the subject. When did you learn Polish?"

"I don't *really* know it," he admitted, leaning over the table. "I've been learning it for two years. I started taking a real interest in it around six months ago."

He sipped his iced tea and sent me a playful look. He was making fun of me.

"You're unbelievable."

I didn't want to give in, but it was stronger than me. I smiled back.

"Why did you come?" I asked, my voice growing less severe.

"I don't really know." He shrugged. "Maybe I wanted to watch you piss your husband off?" He was amused. "Or to see you start living your life. I'm proud of you, bee."

He leaned in closer. "You're fulfilling your needs. You're doing what you want, and you're looking happier by the day." He pulled back again and put on his glasses.

"Want to race?" he asked out of the blue, and I burst out laughing. I shook my head.

"You're joking, right? That beast of yours has to have at least seventy horsepower more than mine. Besides, if you had the limiter taken off, you can go twice as fast as me. Not to mention that you're probably a better driver."

Nacho smiled strangely, shaking his head slightly as he listened.

"You are a very impressive woman," he said in a low voice. "I've never met another girl who knows her way around a bike."

"You're pulling my leg," I replied, pretending to be offended.

"I've always dreamed about riding that beast of yours, so don't provoke me."

"That was easier than expected. You've just told me you've always dreamed about me." His lips were parted, and his eyes wide open.

That's when I realized how what I'd said might have sounded. I felt a tingling in my stomach. I raised my eyes, meeting his stare, and tried stemming the tide of desire that crashed over me. Oh, how I dreamed about him taking me on that yellow bike. Or at least about him taking me in his arms and kissing me. But most of all, I wanted him to kidnap me again. Take me with him and hide me from the world in that little beach house.

"Laura," he said when the silence stretched. "Come." He reached out with a hand and pulled me gently along. "Put on your helmet," he said. His own black helmet slid over his head, obscuring his eyes with the dark, reflective surface of the visor. Mounting his bike, he offered me a hand and helped me onto the vehicle.

I glanced at the nearby Mercedes. Damian, clearly disoriented, started the engine and was doing a U-turn. The four-cylinder monster beneath me woke to life with a growl. Nacho put my hands around his waist. As I hooked my fingers, the motorbike launched forward. I felt a fluttering in my stomach, the butterflies inside spinning in a frenzy as the Hayabusa rode along narrow streets to reach a straight, smooth road outside the small town. Turning my head back, I noticed Damian following us, overtaking other cars. The enormous S-Class had no chance to reach our nimble motorcycle. Half a minute later, we were alone. I pressed my head against Nacho's wide shoulders and drank in the experience. He slowed down, put a hand on my intertwined fingers, and squeezed, letting me know he knew I was there and was grateful for it.

A dozen miles more and he turned into a forest and stopped.

How he knew places like this, I didn't know, but he brought us to a house by the lake, hidden in the dense foliage. The engine growled one last time and then went quiet.

"Do you have your phone?" Nacho asked seriously, getting his helmet off.

"No. I left it in Dad's pannier," I replied, freeing my head, too.

"Are there any other transmitters on you?"

He turned my way. I shook my head.

"Good. Then the night is ours."

The sound of those words made me gasp. Fear mixed in with sudden arousal. I leaned on his strong shoulders and jumped off the bike, taking my gloves off.

Nacho dismounted the machine and hung his helmet on the handle before unzipping his suit. His tattooed torso was bare beneath it. I swallowed and watched him. He disentangled himself from the upper half of the overalls and turned to look at me. Without a word, he pulled the zipper of my suit down and slid his hands beneath the fabric, freeing me of the leather outfit. I could feel his minty breath on my shoulder. His touch sent electric jolts through my entire body.

"How is it, bee, that each time we touch, I feel like I'm being shot?"

I raised my eyes and met his stare. He was waiting.

His tanned skin was covered with a sheen of sweat, and his moist lips invited a kiss.

"I feel it, too," I breathed as we froze, inches from each other. "I'm scared . . ." I dropped my head.

"I'm here," he whispered, raising my chin with a finger.

"That's what I'm scared of."

His hand slid to my cheek. His thumb hooked under my jaw and raised my head a bit more. I was closing in on his lips. There was no sense in fighting. I didn't want to run or defend myself. My mother's words reverberated in my head like a mantra. *Be selfish. Do what makes you happy.* Nacho's lips flew past mine and pressed against the skin of my collarbone, then neck, then ear. My breathing quickened. I wanted more. His lips brushed against my cheek and nose. I was sure he'd kiss me next, but he froze.

"I would like to feed you," he said and grabbed my hand, lacing his fingers with mine.

We headed to the house.

God almighty, I moaned quietly. Food was the last thing I could think about now. My entire body yearned for him. With each brain cell, I *wanted* him to take me. But he only slid a key in the lock, turned it, opened the door for me, and gestured me to go inside. I took a look around. Heard the door lock again. Stopped breathing.

"Here you go," Nacho said, passing me a phone. "Call your parents. Tell them you won't be coming home for the night." He left me and disappeared down a corridor leading to the kitchen.

I stood rooted to the spot, thinking about my options. But most of all about how I'd explain to mother that I didn't intend to show up at dinner tonight. I turned and passed through the first door I saw. It led to the living room. The walls were olive green. There were brown leather couches in the room, perfectly harmonizing with the large fireplace and the deer antlers on the wall. There was also a large table surrounded by heavy wooden chairs with soft, burgundy cushions. The place was a luxurious cabin.

After a short talk with Mom and another million lies, I put the phone down on the stone kitchen counter and sat on a bar stool.

"I left the bitch on the main plaza."

Nacho spun around. There was a pan in his hand. He sent me a quizzical look.

"My bike," I explained. "I left it parked at the market in town."

"No," he replied with a smile.

"I never travel alone, bee. Maybe I'm not as ostentatious as Torricelli, but my people go where I go. Your bitch"—he snorted—"is in a parking lot near your parents' house."

He placed two large plates on the counter and arranged delicious-smelling shrimp on them. A moment later, he opened the oven and took out cheesy croutons. He added some olives and a bottle of wine.

"Eat," he said, digging in.

"How did you know I'd stay?" I asked, chewing the first bite of the delicious meal.

"I didn't. I still don't," he replied. "I can only hope."

He lifted his eyes, and I saw there was fear in them, too. Just like mine.

"What will you do to me if I stay?"

My tone was playful, but I did want to know. He smirked.

"I'll give you pleasure."

He froze with the fork midway to his mouth and looked at me. His smile vanished. The words slowly reached me.

"Oh," I stammered, shocked, and went quiet.

I didn't speak until we were finished eating. It was enough that we looked at each other. The air was thick with desire.

When I emptied my plate, Nacho took the dishes to the dishwasher and sipped his beer.

"Upstairs, in the first bedroom to the left," he said, sending me a calm look, "there is a bag on the bed. You can take a shower and change into the clothes I left there. I have to call Amelia. She's been trying to contact me for the past hour."

He passed through the kitchen, kissed my forehead, and went out to the terrace. I was speechless again. At how gentle he was, while at the same time being so manly and confident.

I hid my face in my hands, wondering what to do. Should I leave and take his bike? Run away? I didn't know where we were, though. How to find my way home. And, what was most important, there was no part of me that really wanted to run from Nacho again. I pushed myself to my feet and headed to the bedroom he had told me about.

Just as he had said, there was a bag on the bed there. It was filled with clothing that I remembered from his flat on Tenerife. There were no expensive clothes there. I grabbed a pair of pink cotton boxer shorts and a white tank top and went to the shower.

CHAPTER 9

"You get what you wanted?" Damian asked during our last evening together. We were having dinner at Karol's restaurant.

"No," I replied tersely, chewing my steak.

"And you're going back?"

"Yes. I decided that I won't do a thing. I'll let all my problems solve themselves."

"If you need anything, I'm here for you."

"I know. Thank you." I briefly pressed my head against his muscular shoulder. He wagged a finger at me in response.

It was eleven o'clock when I stepped aboard the miniature flying death trap they call a private jet. Slightly dazed with sleeping pills, I reclined in my seat and looked outside the window. I was calm, at peace, and totally in love. After my night with Nacho, I had a lot of things to think about. I missed the takeoff. This time I didn't sleep during the flight. Instead, I recalled the events of the night.

I left the bathroom and went downstairs dressed in clothes that resembled pajamas more than anything else.

By the stairs there was a coatrack. I found Nacho's sweatshirt there. It had his scent on it. I threw it on, inhaling. Slowly, I walked to the living room. He was there, lying on the couch with his legs resting on the low coffee table. For a while, I stood behind his back, watching the colorful paintings on his skin.

"I can feel you," he said and muted the TV he had on. "Every time you're close, my skin tingles." He shook his head, loosening up his neck muscles. "I can feel the ocean like that. Each time a good wave approaches, and I can't see it yet, I can feel that same excitement."

He took his legs off the coffee table, pushed himself up and turned around. I was standing by the wall with my legs crossed. My hair was tied in a loose bun. His sweatshirt was too big for me. Only the tips of my fingers reached the ends of its sleeves.

"You'll never be more beautiful than now," he breathed.

He walked over unhurriedly. I felt a wave of overpowering fear. Nacho's torso was bare. He had only a pair of thin, loose sweatpants on. His bare feet practically touched mine as he stopped an inch from me. We looked into each other's eyes, but neither of us knew what to do next.

"Come to me," he said quietly, slipping his hands over my buttocks and pulling me closer. Lifting me into the air.

I wrapped my legs around his hips and allowed him to carry me to the kitchen counter in a few long strides. His slender fingers trailed along my shoulders and then down my arms, taking the sweatshirt off. He took it slowly, closely observing my reactions. As if he didn't want to make any mistakes. His every gesture said, *I'll wait. Just say so.* But I didn't want him to stop. As the sweatshirt fell to the floor, Nacho closed in even more.

"I want to feel you," he said. His lips were just an inch away from mine. "Just feel you, bee."

Jesus Christ, I'll come before we even start, I thought frantically as his low voice vibrated in my head.

He hooked his thumbs under the hem of my top and started pulling it up, revealing my midriff, ribs, and then breasts. My breathing quickened. I was a bit panicked, but his gleeful green eyes pinned me with an intense stare, which calmed me right down. I lifted my hands from the cold counter and raised them above my head, allowing him to take my top off completely. As it hit the floor, Nacho was so close, I could feel his skin on mine. He didn't look down. He didn't need to see me. Only feel me. His hands slid under my ass again and lifted me up. I pressed myself against him.

"Oh, God," he breathed, taking my head and pulling it to the crook of his neck. "I can feel you."

He walked across the room, climbed the stairs, still carrying me, and entered a beautiful, dark bedroom.

There were multicolored blankets and pillows sprawled across the large, wooden bed. Nacho knelt and gently put me down, never pulling away, keeping our skin in contact. My heart was racing. My breath caught in my throat. Oh, how I had dreamed of him doing exactly that.

He spread my hands to the sides and laced his fingers with mine. His green eyes watched me. His tongue flicked out, licking his lips. I couldn't take it anymore. Lifting my head from the bed, I pressed my lips to his. Then I freed my hands and pressed them to the sides of his head, pulling him closer. I wanted him *now*, and I was greedy. But he kept it calm and slow, kissing me gently, sucking on my lower lip once in a while.

"That's not the pleasure I will give you tonight, Laura," he whispered, finally pulling away. I was struck silent.

"I want you to give yourself to me, thinking about *me* and no one else. Without the promise you made before God to another man."

As he said it, at first I wanted to slap him and just leave. It took me a while to get it. He didn't want to be my lover. He wanted to be the one I loved. I pressed my head into the pillow and sent him a resigned look.

He grabbed a blanket and covered us both. Then he pulled off his pants and slid back between my legs. I was disoriented. Wasn't that the complete opposite of what he had said?

"I won't make love to you tonight. I'll explore you." My hands slid down his back and stopped on his buttocks. He had boxers on.

"I won't take them off. You do the same," he said with a bright smile. "I'll learn your needs and desires, but I won't satisfy them yet."

He leaned in and kissed me again, this time picking up the pace. I moaned, surprised at the sudden change of tempo, and clawed his back with my fingers. My nails left red weals on it.

"I can see you like it rough, bee," he whispered and bit my lip. I rubbed against his throbbing erection.

"How rough do you like it?" he asked, suddenly pressing his cock against my clit.

"Very rough!" I cried out and threw my head back.

Our bodies undulated, intertwined. Nacho's hands pressed me against him. The only thing dividing us was our skin. We both panted. Our lips met time and time again, pulling away and exploring each other's shoulders, necks, and cheeks. The thrusting of his hips was getting faster and harder. I was going to explode any moment.

"Nacho," I whispered, and he slowed down and looked me in the eyes, checking if I was all right.

"What do you like?" I asked, licking my lips lasciviously, provocatively. "You like it rough, too?"

I grabbed his hips and pulled him closer with a strong jerk. "Deep?"

I pulled at him again. His eyes glazed.

I had never seen so much self-control in a man. It was turning me on, but at the same time . . . it was a challenge. My right hand released his buttock and slid beneath my cotton panties. Oh, God, I was so wet. The fabric was practically translucent on me. For a short while I played with myself, keeping my eyes on his. Then I pulled my fingers out and slid them into his mouth.

"Taste what you're missing out on."

Nacho closed his eyes and sucked, licking my fingers. He moaned.

Then, he pressed his lips to mine, and his hips resumed their thrusting. He made love to me—hard and passionate. Only . . . he wasn't inside me. Though, truth be told, he didn't really have to be. I could nearly feel him.

"Christ," he breathed and stopped, putting his face in the cook of my neck. "I dream of licking you whole. Caressing every inch of your sweet cunt. God, it smells good," he purred again and shivered. "I love it and hate it. The power you hold over me."

Suddenly, he pushed himself up and looked at me playfully.

"I need to go to the shower."

"But . . . you took one a moment ago." I narrowed my eyes.

"Yes, but I came," he said and smooched the tip of my nose, getting out of bed. "We'll both be sticky in a while."

I held him. Stopped him from going.

"So what?" I asked, lifting my brows and hooking my legs around his hips to hold him down. "Let's be nasty."

I grinned, and he froze. His expression was unreadable.

"Not going to happen, bee."

I screamed as he rose from the bed, lifting me up and walking across the room to the shower. He stopped and turned on the water. It was ice-cold. I cried out, getting off him. I tried running, but now he was the one to hold me in place. He laughed as I pummeled him with my fists.

"Let me go, you psycho!" I cried. At the same time, I couldn't stop laughing, even though the freezing water was taking my breath away.

"We both need to cool down."

That might not have been the worst idea. But in order for it to make sense, we showered with our backs turned to each other. I left first and wrapped myself in a bathrobe, glancing at his tattooed butt.

"I won't turn around when you're there," he said, tilting his head.

"You don't have to. That sight is even better than what you have in front," I said with a chuckle.

"Are you sure?"

Suddenly, he spun around, revealing his jaw-dropping erection.

I opened my mouth at the sight of the straightest and most beautiful cock I had ever seen. I had seen it once before, but then it had been dangling between Nacho's legs, and I had been doing my best not to look at it. This time there wasn't a power in the universe that could have made me take my eyes off this wonder. Its tip was pierced. I moaned and clamped my teeth shut. Nacho leaned against the wall and chuckled.

"You were saying?" he asked as I shook off my shock. "I think that in your mind you're already kneeling, aren't you?"

He wiped his bald head with a hand and came toward me.

We were close again. So close, I couldn't even see his manhood anymore. I frowned and pouted as he reached for a towel and wrapped it around his hips.

"Now, back to bed!" he barked with a laugh and pushed me back to the bedroom.

We did not make love that night. Nacho didn't even kiss me. We lay in bed together, talking, laughing, cuddling. I had on my tank top and underwear, and he kept his boxers on. The sun was up when

THE NEXT 365 DAYS

I fell asleep in Nacho's warm embrace. When I woke up, he made me breakfast and then drove me to the parking lot where his men had left my bitch. Before I put my helmet on, the Canarian took my face in his hands and kissed me so tenderly I wanted to cry.

"I'll always be close," he said, gunning the engine of his yellow monster.

He didn't ask what I was going to do. Where I was going. He asked me nothing at all, just gave me a chance to get to know him before leaving.

I went back home. On my way there, by the gate, I met Damian, who fumed, yelled, and bristled. I didn't give a damn.

"Did you call him?" I asked when he finally piped down.

"No. Your mother told me you were safe and that it wasn't any of my business where you were."

"She was right," I agreed and drove the bike up to the house.

Surprisingly, I didn't argue with my parents. Mom looked into my eyes and saw the happiness in them. She just sighed and shook her head. That wasn't like her. No questions? No demands for an explanation? Shocking.

"We're here, mistress," the captain of the private jet said, leaning over me.

"I must have dozed off." I stretched out and blinked away the dizziness.

Putting on my sunglasses I took the narrow stairs to the ground. I raised my eyes, squinting. Someone was waiting for me. Massimo.

My husband was standing there with his back to the car, smiling. In his thin, light gray suit and white shirt, he looked breathtaking. The warm wind gently ruffled his hair. I took a look at his strong, muscular arms hidden under the perfectly tailored jacket. He kept his hands in his pockets, looking confident. I felt my mouth dry up.

"Hi there, baby girl." The Man in Black's eyes skimmed across my body. He bit his lip.

We stood there for a while, watching each other, but neither of us decided to make the first move. I was completely disoriented. And him? His eyes held fear of what I'd do if he touched me.

"I'll take you home," Massimo said, opening the car door for me.

I cannot put into words how strange that felt. So official, emotionless. At least at first glance. He wanted to look distanced and wary. Even more than during the days after he had kidnapped me more than a year before. I stepped into the car, and he closed the door, taking the other seat. We were driven to the entrance to the terminal and crossed the hall, heading toward a Ferrari parked by the curb. *Those ugly fucking Ferraris.* I laughed inside, recalling Nacho's words. Approaching the supercar, I realized it wasn't a Ferrari at all. The door lifted up, instead of opening like in more traditional cars. Taken aback, I glanced at my husband. He was smirking.

"Is it new?" I asked, looking at the shiny black sports car.

"I was bored of the old ones," Massimo replied, shrugging. His smirk widened.

"Your boredom costs us a lot of money," I muttered, squeezing inside.

Massimo took the driver's seat and switched the ignition on with a button that would look more at home in a fighter jet. He stepped on the accelerator, and the Lamborghini Aventador lurched forward with a speed that pressed me deep into my seat. The Man in Black drove steadily. Focused. I could feel he was stealing glances of me once every minute or so. He didn't speak. Suddenly, I noticed that we overshot our turnoff and continued toward Messina. I swallowed loudly. I hadn't visited that house in more than six months. Since I'd first seen Nacho.

Massimo drove to the very door and parked the car. Did I want to even go inside?

"Why are we here?" I asked, turning his way. "I want to go to the mansion. See Olga and rest."

"Olga and Domenico are on Ibiza, partying. And I have the only key to the gate. So consider yourself kidnapped, " he said gleefully and opened the fancy door for me. "Leave your bag here. You won't need it."

He glanced at me.

"Especially the phone."

"What if I don't want to be kidnapped?" I asked, stepping out before he managed to offer me a hand.

"That's what makes for a good kidnapping."

His tone was icy. Frightening.

"It's all about keeping someone against their will, baby girl." He planted a delicate kiss on my forehead and entered the house.

I stomped my feet in frustration and cursed in Polish, but followed.

The interior looked different than I remembered. Without the great Christmas tree it was even more spectacular. Massimo tossed the keys on the kitchen counter and grabbed a bottle of wine.

"Someone's waiting for you."

He planted two glasses and, keeping his eyes trained on them, snatched a corkscrew from the tabletop.

"In the living room," he added with a little smile.

Curious, I went through the kitchen to the place that I had only associated with fucking before. And stopped suddenly. On a big pillow by the wooden table stood a . . . dog.

I yelped and rushed toward the beautiful little fur ball, which rolled over on its pillow as I approached. It was the most gorgeous little thing I had ever seen. It looked like a plushie. A small teddy bear. I took it in my arms and hugged it, practically crying with joy.

"You like it?" Massimo asked, offering me a glass filled with wine.

"Do I? It's wonderful! And so small. Barely larger than my hand."

"And completely dependent on you. Just like me." Massimo's words pierced my heart. "If you don't care for it, it will die. Same as me." He knelt before me and looked me in the eyes. "I will die without you. Those days . . ." He ran his fingers through his hair. "The hours, the minutes . . . I felt like . . ." His eyes teared up. "I can't live without you. I don't want to."

"That's pretty hypocritical, Massimo." I sighed, hugging the little dog. "You've been leaving me for days on end. A lot longer than I have been in Poland."

"That's it," he cut in and took my face in his hands. "It wasn't until you left me that I realized what I was losing. When I had no control over you. When I couldn't just have you, it struck me just how important you are to me. The most important thing in my life."

He released me and dropped his head. "I fucked it all up, Laura. But I promise you that I will make up each minute you were sad because of me."

I watched his resigned expression and his sad eyes. There was no trace of the man I had left. No brutality. No anger. Only sadness, affection, and love.

I put the little white dog down and sat down in Massimo's lap, hugging him. He pulled me closer, as if trying to hide from the world in my embrace. His arms tightened around me so hard, I felt his every muscle tense.

"Baby girl," he whispered. "I love you so much."

Tears rolled down my cheeks. I squeezed my eyes shut, and as soon as I did it, pictured Nacho. Silly, grinning Nacho, playing around in bed with me. I could see him kissing me and hugging me. I nearly threw up. What was I doing? Thank God the Canarian was so sensible—that he hadn't let me give myself to him.

I ran my fingers through Massimo's hair and pulled away his head.

"What's it called?" I asked, pointing to the white ball of fur. "The dog."

Massimo straightened up and smiled, taking the animal in his hands.

"It hasn't got a name yet. You can name it."

I fell to pieces. My big, strong man hugging that little creature, no larger than his hand.

"Givenchy," I said confidently. Massimo rolled his eyes. "Like my favorite shoe brand."

"Darling," he said gravely, handing me the dog.

"A dog's name should consist of two syllables. It's easier to call it this way."

"Why should I call it if it'll always be with me?" I asked, trying to hide my amusement. "But okay. Let's call it Prada. Like my favorite bag brand."

Massimo shook his head and sipped his wine.

"Mario Prada was a man, and that dog is a female."

"Olga had a female cat once and named it Andrew. So I can have a female dog and call her Prada."

I kissed the white fur ball, who started to wiggle excitedly in my hands.

"See? She likes the name."

Massimo sat on the rug, back propped against the wall, and watched me play with the newest member of our big, happy Mafia family. He took two calls in the meantime but never took his eyes off me. It was strange to see him for such a long time and to feel that nothing would be able to make him leave now. He was composed and relaxed.

"How's your therapy?" I asked after my second glass of wine. I immediately bit my tongue. Too many questions could make him angry.

"I'm not sure. You should ask my therapist." Massimo seemed unconcerned. "It has only been two weeks. Four consultations. So I wouldn't expect any miracles."

He stood up and went to the kitchen. A while later, he returned with two plates.

"Besides, you know . . . I've been doing my best to ruin many things for the last thirty years. It won't be so easy to get everything in order at once." He shrugged. "Maria made us seafood pasta."

He placed the plates on the table and handed me a fork. "Come and eat. I'll have to carry you if you get drunk."

"You said you wouldn't drink," I said, maybe with a bit too much accusation in my voice as he put his glass on the table.

"And I don't," he replied with a laugh. "It's cherry and grape juice. Want some?" I took his glass and sipped. He wasn't lying.

"I'm sorry." I felt stupid.

"Don't worry, baby girl. I promised you I won't drink or do drugs. It's not a steep price to get you back."

He looked at me with those big black eyes of his, eating his meal. "And remember: when I want something, I get it. It won't change now."

He straightened up and smirked. There he was. My Man in Black—strong, manly, confident, and composed.

I fidgeted on my chair. He noticed.

"Don't even think about it," he whispered. "Neither of us is ready for that. First, I have to get things in order. Only then will I take what's mine."

I felt a vortex of emotions, hearing those words.

"Which doesn't change the fact," he continued, "that I dream about slowly entering you, feeling your tight twat with my whole length."

I swallowed loudly.

I was lost in the darkness. Flailing and battling myself. On the one hand, I respected his decision and his self-control. On the other, he was challenging me.

"I'm wet," I blurted out. His fork hit the plate.

"You're cruel," he breathed, pushing away his unfinished pasta.

"Don't you want to taste me, darling?" I raised one brow playfully, provoking him.

Massimo sat immobile, pinning me with his black stare. His teeth bit into his lower lip.

"Get yourself freshened up. I need to work." He pushed his chair out, took my empty plate, and left. I was dumbstruck and impressed at the same time.

He had a lot more discipline than I had suspected. "Fucking hell," I cursed, pushing my chair back loudly. "Nobody wants to fuck me. Everyone's suddenly fucking celibate."

I took the tiny dog in my hands and went upstairs to our bedroom to wash myself after the day.

After taking a shower I changed into lace underwear and went in search of my workaholic husband. My choice of attire wasn't accidental. I knew what Massimo liked. There's nothing worse for a woman than a man who says he can't or won't take her. That makes her do stupid things only to show that man what his real desires and capabilities are.

Holding Prada in my arms, I passed through the rooms—the office and the guest bedrooms. He wasn't there. I finally went downstairs to the kitchen and put the dog on the counter, pouring myself another glass of wine. With the corner of my eye, I saw movement in the garden and froze. There were no security guards around, so it couldn't be Massimo's men on the terrace. I took the dog off the counter, afraid it would fall off if I left it on its own. Slowly, I headed to the window.

Outside, there was my husband. He was wearing loose trousers and nothing else. And he was waving a stick. His torso and hair were wet with sweat, and his every muscle was tense. What he was doing resembled fighting his own shadow. The stick in his hands acted as a sword. I passed through the door and my furry little friend sprinted toward Massimo.

"Prada!" I exclaimed, terrified that he might step on her.

The Man in Black froze, and when the dog ran over to him, he grabbed her and walked toward me.

"You won't have to call her?" he asked with a smirk, leaning on his stick.

I looked at him, captivated. Admiring his beautiful body. My libido was raging. Pushing me toward him.

"What is that?" I pointed to the stick, as he handed over the dog.

"This is called a 'jo.' A fighting implement."

He ran his fingers through his hair, and I inhaled his scent. It hit me like a ten-ton truck. "I returned to my training routine. It calms me down."

He flourished the wooden weapon.

"This is Jodo. A modern version of Japanese fencing. An art of self-defense. Look." He made a few more movements with the stick, assuming several very sexy poses. "It was created more than three hundred years ago, merging techniques of *kenjutsu*, or the way of the sword, *sojutsu*—"

I cut him off by greedily pressing my lips to his.

"I don't give a fuck," I breathed. He released the stick and took me in his arms.

"But you might take one," he replied, and I felt a wave of desire crash over me.

My husband. My cold and ruthless mob boss. My defender and the love of my life was back. He lifted me up, wrapping my legs around his hips, and headed to the door. Putting the dog in her bed and never breaking the kiss, he carried me to the bedroom.

We were completely engrossed in our lovemaking. Our hands explored each other's bodies, and our tongues flitted around each other at a breathtaking speed. As we reached our destination, Massimo sat on the bed with me perched on his knees. With one fluid movement, he pulled my blouse off before pressing his lips to my nipple and sucking. I balled my hand in his hair as he licked and bit my nipple.

"I can't," he gasped suddenly, pulling away. "I don't want to hurt you."

"But I can."

I slithered off his knees and pulled at his pants. Blinded by desire, I practically ripped them off him, before lowering myself to my knees and putting his erect cock into my mouth. Massimo let out a wild bellow as I hungrily pushed his throbbing manhood deep down my throat. His hands landed on my head.

"You need to tell me," he gasped out. "Tell me if it hurts. You have to . . ."

"Shut up, Massimo," I barked and thrust his prick into my mouth again.

I sucked him with delight, relishing every inch of his shaft. He controlled the tempo by holding my head, but it was a lot gentler than usual. He was reining himself in and keeping his wilder instincts at bay. I released his cock, pushed myself up and straddled his hips. My legs were tightly wrapped around him. I pulled away the lace panties and impaled myself on his rock-hard penis.

Massimo froze with his mouth open in a silent scream. He didn't move, only watched. His torso pumped air as his eyes—wide and full of desire—looked at me.

"I want to fuck," I breathed, grabbing his hair and pulling him closer.

"No," he growled.

Then, turning abruptly but staying inside me, he rolled us over, ending up on top. He kept still.

"Massimo!" I hurried him up angrily. His icy stare transfixed me.

"No," he repeated, but his hips pushed forward.

I threw my head back and moaned, feeling him brushing against all the most sensitive spots.

"Please, baby girl," he whispered, thrusting slowly.

"No, Massimo." I grabbed his ass and pulled him firmly toward me. "I'm asking you."

For a moment longer, he kept staring at me with sad, resigned eyes, wondering if he should listen. Then he assaulted me with his tongue. But his movements in my snatch were still slow and subtle. Practically undetectable. All the time, his tongue fucked my mouth with the speed of a machine gun. A couple seconds later, I suddenly felt his body tensing. Then, a geyser of cum exploded inside me. Massimo pulled away from me and hid his face in the crook of my neck. He shivered.

"You did it on purpose!" My voice was accusatory. It cut through the silence. "How could you?" I tried pushing him off me, but he was too heavy. I felt him shaking with laughter.

"Baby girl." He laughed and propped his head on his hands. "What can I do? That's just how much you turn me on."

I glared at him, furious, but soon enough his mirth proved contagious.

"I'll have to find myself a lover," I said, sticking out my tongue.

"A lover?" he asked, narrowing his eyes. "On this island?" He shook his head knowingly. "When you find one, let me know. I'd like to congratulate him for his bravery."

He burst out laughing, took me in his arms, and bent me over his shoulder. "I'll make it up to you. But first, we need a shower." He slapped my ass playfully and carried me to the bathroom.

Later, he really did make it up to me, licking my clit for an hour and giving me about a dozen orgasms.

CHAPTER 10

We spent the next few days alone, just the two of us. Walled off from the world, facing new challenges. Massimo did his best not to fuck me, and I did everything in my power to break through his resolve. He trained a lot. At times I was worried he'd hurt himself. Each time he nearly gave in, he immediately fled and got back to his Jodo routine. If that continued, he'd soon look like a bodybuilder. It was a beautiful warm evening. Perfect for some hot jacuzzi action.

"Oh, no you don't!" I cried out, putting Prada back into her bed and trying to pull Massimo's pants off.

"Let me go!" The Man in Black threw me to the couch with a laugh. "You'll hurt yourself."

He tried catching my flailing arms and finally succeeded, immobilizing me by pushing them between two pillows.

"Nacho, stop!" I exclaimed. As soon as my words were out, I clamped my mouth shut and froze, shocked.

Massimo's hands tightened around my wrists so hard, I winced in pain. He was crushing my bones.

"You're hurting me," I breathed, avoiding his eyes.

He released me and shot up, storming off to the kitchen to return a minute later with a vase in his hand. He smashed it on the wall.

"What did you say?!"

It was a shriek. A roar. The entire house shook with it. "What did you call me?" His fury was a red-hot conflagration. I imagined his clothes turning to ash on his skin.

"I-I'm sorry," I stammered, terrified.

"What happened on Tenerife?!"

I did not respond. Massimo leaped toward me and grabbed me by the shoulders. His fingers clawed into my skin as he lifted me from the ground.

"You better fucking tell me right now!" I looked him in the eyes.

"Nothing," I whispered. "Nothing happened on Tenerife." For a moment, he watched me closely. Finally, believing me, he put me down. I didn't usually lie, and that's what made my words plausible. Nothing had happened on Tenerife. But in Poland . . . A lot had happened in Poland, apparently. Since in moments of pure joy and happiness my mind was subconsciously reminded of the Canarian.

"Why that name?" Massimo asked in a terrifyingly calm voice, resting his hands on the mantelpiece of the fireplace.

"I don't know. I've dreamed a lot about New Year's Eve lately." My subconscious clapped its nonexistent hands at that masterful lie. "Maybe I subconsciously relive what had happened on the Canary Islands."

I sat down on the couch, hiding my face in my hands so Massimo couldn't see its expression.

"It's still in me . . ."

"Me too," he breathed and headed to the terrace.

I didn't want to go with him. I was too afraid. Of what I'd said or would say in the future. Everything was getting so good between us. And I'd fucked it up with a single word. I wondered what I should do, but there was no more strength in me. Not for another confrontation. I took the dog with me and went to the bedroom, lying down in my clothes. For a while, we played. Then I fell asleep.

Thin barking woke me up. I opened my eyes, but the light of the lamp blinded me.

"He fucked you." The sound of the words pierced through me like an icy stab. "Admit it, Laura."

I turned toward the sound and saw Massimo. Naked. With a glass filled with amber liquor in hand. He was sitting in a sofa chair by the table. An empty bottle stood on the tabletop.

"Did he do it the way you like it?"

The next question made my throat constrict.

"Did he enter all holes? Did you let him?"

The growl in his voice was so horrible, I quickly gathered the dog into my arms, huddling.

"Are you serious?" I asked.

I was silently praying for God to grant me the strength to survive what was coming.

"You insult me if you think—"

"I don't give a flying fuck what you have to say," the Man in Black barked sharply. He rose and took a few steps toward the bed. "And you won't give a fuck about *me* in a moment."

He downed his drink and put the glass on the table.

"After I rip your ass in two with my cock."

Scenes from Lagos flashed through my mind. I couldn't let that happen again. Holding the innocent white ball of fur, I launched myself at the door, ran through it, and slammed it shut in Massimo's face. I sprinted down the corridor, running as fast as I could. I could hear his steps behind me. Following me. Then, all of a sudden, the house shook with a great clangor. I didn't look back to see what it was. Practically flying down the stairs, I reached the kitchen. I grabbed the car keys from the counter and ran out of the house barefoot, jumping into the Lambo.

"Don't be afraid, little buddy," I cooed, more to reassure myself than the dog. I pressed the button, switching the engine on, and slammed my foot on the accelerator. The car launched itself ahead with shocking velocity. Something hit the window. I could clearly hear the crack. It was Massimo, half-mad with anger, trying to catch me. My eyes teared up, but I knew if he managed to drag me out of the car, he'd cause me as much pain as he was feeling himself. The gate was opening for me, but too slow. I shot terrified glances into the rearview mirror, patting the steering wheel nervously.

"Come on, you fucking piece of trash!" I screamed.

When the gap was barely wide enough, I shot through the gate in the black supercar, tires screeching.

I noticed something down on the floor. My bag. Thank God Massimo had told me to leave it here. I reached inside and fished out my cell phone. I'd had it connected to a power bank days before. The battery was barely clinging to life. I dialed Domenico and waited. Those were the longest three rings in my life.

"So. How are you two doing?"

His voice was happy and carefree. I could hear Olga shouting something in the background.

"He wants to do it again!" I cried in panic, though I could barely form the words. "I'm running away, but he's chasing after me. If he sends his people after me, they'll take me to him. And he'll do it again!"

Domenico went quiet. I knew why. My friend was with him. And she still thought my husband was the perfect man.

"Tell her I can't decide on which wine to pick for dinner."

Domenico kept silent.

"Tell her, goddamn it! And move away from her."

I heard him feigning amusement and repeating my words. Olga shut up.

"What's going on?" Domenico growled into the receiver.

"He got drunk again and tried . . ." I paused. "He tried . . ." I choked on tears.

"Where are you?"

"I'm driving the highway to Catania."

"Okay. Go to the airport. A plane is going to be waiting. Board it and I'll call off the men. If he's wasted, he'll have already called them."

I stopped breathing, nearly suffocating.

"Don't be scared, Laura. I'll get this sorted," Domenico said.

"Where am I going?" I cried out, sobbing.

"You'll come here. But for now, let me get everything prepared."

I drove like a madwoman, stepping on the accelerator with my bare foot. My tiny white companion mewled on the passenger seat. I put the dog on my knees. It took her no time at all to curl up into a ball and fall asleep.

When I finally boarded the plane, a stewardess brought me a blanket. I wrapped myself in it.

"Do we have vodka?" I asked, knowing full well how I looked: barefoot, wearing a sweat suit, and with completely no makeup on.

"Of course." She placed some disposable slippers at my feet.

"On the rocks with a splash of lemon," I said, and the girl nodded with a smile.

I didn't drink liquor, but it wasn't every day that my husband tried to rape me. When the glass appeared in front of me, I first took a couple of sedatives, which I found in my bag, and then downed the glass in three gulps.

———

"Want to tell me what happened?" asked Domenico when I opened my eyes again.

"Where am I?"

I pushed myself up on my elbows. I was on a mattress.

"Don't worry," he stood up from an armchair and walked over to the bed, holding me down.

He fixed me with a sad stare of his big, black eyes. I tried not to cry. I failed. Tears streaked down my face as I hugged him.

"I spoke to him during the night," Domenico snorted derisively. "Though that's an overstatement. From what I gathered, it's about Tenerife."

I wiped my eyes with the hem of the comforter.

"We fooled around, and I said the word 'Nacho.'"

I dropped my eyes and waited for the inevitable blow. It didn't come.

Domenico kept silent.

"I don't know why I said it. Seriously. Then I woke up at night and he was there. Naked, drunk, and on some drugs, I think. I thought I saw a baggie of cocaine on the table."

I lifted my eyes again, looking at Domenico. I couldn't hide my disappointment and pain.

"He was about to rape me again."

The tears stopped. The pain was changing into anger.

Domenico's expression didn't change. His eyes were fixed on me. He must have stopped breathing, too.

"Goddamn it," he muttered at last, grimacing. "I need to go

back to Sicily. I sent some guys over yesterday. Massimo has wrecked the house." He shook his head, disbelieving. "But he's the boss. The head of the family. We can't keep him anywhere against his will. When he sobers up, he'll come right here. And then . . ."

"And then I'll leave him," I finished for him. "It's over."

I got up and went to the window.

"It's really over. I want a divorce." My voice was composed and firm.

"You can't do this to him, Laura!"

"I can't? Just watch me." I stepped closer to him. "How do you imagine my life will look after all this? I had to run from my own husband. Barefoot. With my dog. At least I was fortunate enough that I could get away this time. The old bruises haven't even faded yet, and he was ready to give me some new ones."

I shook my head.

"There's no going back. You can tell him that!" I flailed my arms in Domenico's face. "Not his money, not his power, and not that fucking Mafia of yours will keep me at the side of a man who only uses me as a cum dumpster!"

"All right." Domenico sighed. "But I won't be able to stop him if he wants to see you. And you should tell him you're leaving him yourself."

"I will," I confirmed with a resolute nod. "I will tell him. When the right time comes. For now, I'm giving you reasons to keep him away from me."

"I don't know if this time it will be enough." He shook his head. "I think he won't fall for it twice. But we'll see."

He offered me a glass of water.

"Olga knows you're here because you had a spat. Tell her as much as you want. I won't come between you." He went to the door. "The villa is the property of the family. You'll have everything you need here. Olga's still asleep. Please do something so that she doesn't want to kill me after she wakes up and finds out I went away." He left.

I took a shower and found a dog cage downstairs. Prada was inside. I knelt and took my puppy out, thanking God she was still with me. I'd managed to take her with me, but what would have happened if I had left her?

"Oh, God, it's so cute!"

Olga's squeal brought me to my feet. I nearly choked the dog.

"Give it to me! Let me hold it! Please, please!" Olga stamped her feet like a little girl.

"God, you're so stupid."

I gave her the dog and sat at the table, watching as she smothered her with hugs.

"And now, don't even try to sell me any bullshit. Tell me what happened."

"I want a divorce." I sighed. "And before you start blabbering, let me tell you why."

Olga put the dog down and sat next to me.

"I went to Poland because Massimo . . ." And once again the word didn't want to pass my throat. "Back in Lagos . . ."

I stammered. "He was drunk and high. And I returned too late. And he . . ." I took a deep breath. "He raped me."

Olga blanched.

"I know how this sounds," I continued. "We're married, after all. We like it rough, but when it gets really brutal and happens against your will, it's rape. Nothing else. I still have some of the bruises." I shrugged. "Now I got back to Sicily, and everything was great for a moment. Until I called him 'Nacho' . . ."

"You're shitting me!" Olga cried out and then piped down immediately. "You're telling the truth? You really called him that?"

"Seriously? That's what got you going?"

"Well, you know . . . ," she tried, making a weird face. "I just don't understand how you can rape someone you're with. But yeah, I hear you. And I get it. But calling him that was a low blow."

"I know. I blurted it out. In Poland I had a great time with him . . ."

"What?!" Olga exclaimed again. I winced. "That Spaniard was in Poland?"

"Canarian," I muttered, resigned. "The story is longer than you think."

Olga sent me an incredulous look.

I sighed.

"All right, I'll tell you."

So I had to recount the entire tale once again. When I finished talking about the events of the previous night and took to justifying Domenico's abrupt departure, Olga interrupted me.

"The situation is this," she said. *Here it goes. Pure guesswork passed on as facts. Let's hear it.* "Your husband is an impulsive, aggressive, and unpredictable drug addict and an alcoholic . . ."

I nodded weakly.

". . . and Nacho is the seductive, gentle, tattooed kidnapper." She took a sip of her coffee. "Your story is pretty one-sided, don't you think? You don't want to be with Massimo anymore, and I can't blame you. But remember that he used to be different."

Olga's expression grew sad. She looked at me with concern.

"Remember how you came to my place and talked for hours about him? You were madly in love then, Laura. And you spoke of Massimo like he was God himself. Don't you forget that we only really know people when they're at their worst."

She was right. I didn't really know Nacho. I couldn't be sure his demons wouldn't change him in the future. For more than six months I hadn't suspected that my husband was even capable of hurting me. Not to mention this shit show.

"I can't take it anymore," I whispered, dropping my head to the glass tabletop. "I'm just too exhausted."

"The fuck you are. Look where we are." Olga spread her arms and turned around. "This is the party capital of the world. We have this great house, cars, a boat, Jet Skis . . . and no bodyguards at all." She lifted her index finger. "We're free, beautiful, and close enough to being thin for it to count."

"You mean you are." I laughed. "I'm so thin my butt bones are showing. And why is it exactly that we don't have any security?" I asked.

"Domenico is all the protection I need," Olga replied, raising an eyebrow. "Besides, he's not as overprotective as Massimo."

She inhaled to say something else, but that's when my phone vibrated.

"It's him." Shaking with fear, I glanced at Olga.

"So what? He's not going to jump out of that phone."

She silenced the chiming ringtone.

"He's just a guy. Dump him and forget him like any other. He won't be your last. And you can just ignore the phone."

"I fucking will!" I snapped, rejecting the call. "I need to go shopping. I only have my pajamas with me."

The phone vibrated once more. I rejected the call again.

"He's going to keep at it the whole day." I flattened myself on the table, resigned.

"I'm a wizard! I'll free you from what ails you!" Olga exclaimed, picked up the vibrating phone and switched it off.

"See?" She grinned and tossed the device back to the tabletop. "Now come. Let's get dressed and get out of here. We're on Ibiza, the weather is great, and the world's our oyster!"

She dragged me off of my chair, taking me with her and nearly knocking out my teeth on the edge of the table.

I had exactly zero pairs of briefs with me. Was that a problem? Not at all. I liked wearing no underwear anyway. But I had no shoes, and that was a catastrophe. Luckily, Olga wore the same size as I. Among hundreds of her hooker-style super-high heels, I finally managed to pick out a pair of white Giuseppe Zanotti platform heels. Sighing with relief, I grabbed a pair of high-waisted shorts that revealed most of my ass and a loose belly-button-length top. I topped off the outfit with a Prada handbag. I picked up my little dog and was ready to go.

"You look like Paris," Olga said with a smile. "Very celeb-like. And that dog . . ." She snorted with laughter.

"What was I supposed to do with the little fur ball? Leave her?" I frowned. "She'd be bored. And shopping is just the greatest, isn't it? Even dogs must love it." I grinned and pushed the door open.

Our villa was very different from the mansion in Taormina. Modern, sharp shapes, the ever-present glass and a sterile look—like a surgery room. There was no coziness about it. Everything was white, cold blue, and gray. A huge living room opened to an expansive terrace, divided by only a large wall of glass. Behind that, there was a steep slope leading straight down to the sea. On the front side of the villa lay a garden with palm trees and white gravel instead of grass. And a bloodred Aston Martin DBS Volante Cabrio was parked on the driveway.

"Don't look at me like that," Olga said as I rolled my eyes at the sight of her showy ride. "We have a Hummer, too. What would you rather take? This or the Waffle House on wheels?" She pointed her chin at the huge vehicle parked a dozen feet farther away. I walked to the passenger door of the red one.

"You know what the biggest advantage of this car is?" she asked as I made myself comfortable in the white leather seat. "Look." She pointed to the simple and elegant dashboard. "It's a *car*. Not a spaceship. Not an airplane with thousands of buttons everywhere. A ride for a woman."

I was astonished to see what brands had their boutiques on this small island. Everything I needed was at arm's reach. Any pricks of conscience I might have had at spending my husband's money evaporated like the smoke from Olga's cigarette.

We bought swimsuits, tunics, slippers, sunglasses, beach bags, shoes, and dresses. Victoria's Secret, Chanel, Christian Louboutin, Prada—where my tiny puppy peed a little—Balenciaga, and Dolce & Gabbana, where I bought one of every pair of jeans they had.

"It's not going to fit," said Olga, squeezing our things into the small trunk as a handsome young shop clerk was carrying out more bags. "We should have taken the tank."

"I might have gotten a little carried away." I shrugged.

"Oh, really? Here I was thinking this was some kind of revenge. As if Massimo cares how much you spend. He's not even going to notice that." She pushed her sunglasses up her nose. "It makes little sense, you know."

"What makes little sense is spending this much cash on clothes and shoes," I replied.

"Bullshit. It's not your money. Forget about it." Olga got into the car. "If you bought yourself a private jet, maybe he would have reacted. Not because of the money, though, but because a plane can be used to get away. That would piss him off."

We went back home and unpacked our bags, planned our day and finally went out to the terrace.

"I'm going on an adventure!" I yelled, rushing toward the beach. A couple of Jet Skis and a motorboat were moored in a small cove down the cliff.

"I can't remember you being this enthusiastic about anything," Olga said, throwing on a life jacket.

"Me neither, but it's great."

I gunned the Jet Ski's engine and zoomed out to the open sea. Olga followed.

We had fun, fooled around, cruising along the coast and watching half-naked people on the beaches. There were only a few things frowned upon on Ibiza—outmoded outfits, pale skin, and tan lines. There were only beautiful people around. And they were all high, hammered, and horny. They had the time of their lives, partying like there was no tomorrow. At some point we sailed out to the sea, stopping a few hundred yards from the beach, taking a moment to just enjoy the water. The Jet Skis rose and fell on the gentle waves. I wanted this moment to last forever.

"Hola!" We heard a man's voice. It was followed by a string of words I didn't understand.

"English, please," I called, screening my eyes from the sun with a raised hand.

A motorboat full of Spaniards was approaching.

"Oh, Christ," Olga breathed as six hotties in tight-fitting Speedos appeared on deck.

Their tanned, muscular bodies glistened with lotion, reflecting the light of the sun like mirrors. Their colorful briefs clung to their shapely buttocks. I licked my lips on instinct.

"Care to join us?" one of the men asked, leaning overboard.

"Never ever going to happen," Olga murmured under her breath, suddenly anxious.

"Sure!" I called out, grinning. "What exactly are we joining?"

"You numbskull," my friend berated me with her typical softness. "I'm about to get married."

"I'm not telling you to fuck them," I retorted, keeping my eyes trained on the Spaniard. "So?" I switched to English and sent him a seductive look.

"Ushuaïa hotel," he said. "Midnight. See you there."

The boat's engine growled, and the vessel sailed off. With a silly grin I turned to Olga. She revved her Jet Ski and came to me.

"Are you out of your fucking mind?" she cried as her arms shot out and pushed me off my vehicle. I fell into the water with a splash.

"What?" I scrambled back to my Jet Ski, still grinning. "We were supposed to have fun. Or did you mean you? I want in, too!"

"Domenico will kill me."

"See him anywhere?" I gestured with an extended arm. "No? Besides, he's too occupied getting his psycho brother in line. And you can always just tell him it was my fault."

I made a face and zoomed forward, leaving Olga behind.

———

I took a nap before dinner. When I came to, it was dark. I went down to the living room, where Olga and Prada were watching TV.

"Did you notice that each of our houses has Polish TV?"

"So what?" I asked, sitting next to them. My mind was still hazy after the nap. "I would be surprised if they didn't."

"And do you know how many houses we have?" Olga turned to look at me.

"No clue. But I don't really care."

I avoided her stare, instead looking at the screen.

"I know you don't believe what I said," I continued, "but I really want to leave Massimo."

"I get it. I just don't think he'll let you off this easily."

"Do we have booze?" I changed the subject, rolling to my back.

"Sure. Just say when."

"Right about now."

———

Two hours and a bottle of Moët Rosé later we were ready. I only knew Ibiza from stories and websites, but it was enough to know that too much was never enough in this place. And that the color of choice for practically everyone was white. So I went for white Balmain overalls and Louboutin heels. Though maybe "overalls" was a misleading term. The bottom looked more like a bikini mixed in with a thin strap of fabric that served as pants. The back made it seem I was topless. That went perfectly with my long, dark hair, which I had washed and straightened beforehand. Black eye makeup gave me a mysterious, ferocious appearance, but the skin-colored lipstick toned it all down. Olga selected a short, sequined cream-colored dress that barely kept her ass covered, at the same time completely revealing her back.

"The car is waiting," she called, packing her bag.

"I thought we didn't have bodyguards."

"We don't, but as soon as I told Domenico we were going out, he made me an ultimatum. I had to promise him we'd use cabs."

I nodded, respecting the man's concern and thoughtfulness.

"But nobody is supposed to keep tabs on us."

Olga glanced at me. "At least that's what I'm told."

Hundreds, or rather thousands, of people were crowding by the Ushuaïa, trying to get inside. We went straight to the VIP entrance. Olga talked briefly to the man standing guard, and a moment later another one led us inside, to a white lounge.

The crowd was immense. I had never seen anything like that. People literally filled every gap on the dance floor. I silently thanked God for my husband's money. Without it I'd have to mingle with the thronging partygoers. And I was claustrophobic. If I were to find myself in such a swarm, I'd get a panic attack in no time. We

ordered a preposterously expensive bottle of champagne and reclined on a soft sofa.

"I don't think we know each other . . ."

My heart stopped. The champagne I had poured into my mouth
now spurted out like a geyser, spraying the table.

"Hey, I'm Nacho," the Canarian said, walking over to Olga and
offering her a hand.

"Hey there, kiddo."

We both sat dumbstruck as Nacho took a seat next to us and
grinned.

"I told you I would be around."

A moment later, the six hunks we'd met in the sea joined us. I
nearly blacked out with excitement.

"You met these boys before, right?" Nacho smiled, gesturing to
the men. He waved at a waitress and soon the table was laden with
alcohol. "You smell amazing," he whispered in my ear, wrapping his
arm around my shoulders.

If anyone watched us, they would have concluded that we were
either stupid or were having strokes. Speechless and with our mouths
agape, Olga and I observed what was happening, trying to wrap our
heads around all this.

I turned to the Canarian.

"I would have asked what you're doing here, but your unexpected arrivals are starting to become rather less unexpected by the
day." I feigned seriousness and pretended displeasure. Nacho looked
as if it was the happiest day of his life. "Am I being followed?"

"You are," he said without changing his expression. I froze. "But
by my people. They protect you."

His eyes widened, and he wiggled his brows.

"If I may interject," Olga cut in. "We will be in serious trouble if what happens here gets out." She waved her arms at our table and the men. "When Domenico learns about this . . ."

"He's coming already," Nacho said with a smile. I had a heart attack. "Alone." I sighed with relief. "But he only just took off. We still have about two hours."

"Are you sure?" Olga cried, eyes bulging. "If he so much as sees me with these Spanish mobsters, he'll break the engagement." She grabbed her bag and jumped to her feet. "Let's go!"

"They're Canarian," Nacho corrected and grew serious.

"The car will take you wherever you want, but Laura is staying with me."

Olga opened her mouth to say something but didn't manage. Nacho stood up, took her hand, and kissed her on the palm.

"She'll be safe. Safer than with the Sicilians. It's a Spanish island, after all."

They eyed each other for a while as I wondered if I had a say in this at all.

Finally, I decided that I had nothing against this brief deprivation of liberty and kept my mouth shut. Olga softened up. Nacho grinned at her. She sat back down.

"I think I'll have a drink after all. I need booze," she muttered, keeping her eyes on the man. "How about you?"

She leaned closer to me, switching to Polish. "I know you're mad at Massimo for what he tried doing two days ago, but . . ."

"Jesus," I breathed, knowing that Nacho could understand her every word.

"What did he try to do?" he asked all of a sudden. The sound of our mother tongue in his mouth made Olga freeze.

"Holy fucking hell!" She sat back and downed a glass of champagne. "He speaks Polish." She sent me an incredulous look. I frowned, nodding.

"What did he want to do?" Nacho asked again, insistently. "I'm talking to you, bee."

I closed my eyes and hid my face in my hands. I didn't want to talk. Not about that.

"On the other hand, I think I better go. I need to . . . take a shower. Will you be okay?" Olga asked, trying to leave me. I didn't react. "Yeah, sure, you will. I'm out of here."

When I lifted my eyes again, she had already left. Two of Nacho's companions had also disappeared. I tried pretending that he wasn't there, but as soon as I peeked out from between my fingers, he took my chin in his fingers and turned my head toward him.

"Will you say anything?" he asked softly. His eyes were full of concern and furious at the same time.

There was only one way to make him stop. I reached out with both arms, placed my hands on his cheeks, and kissed him. His reaction was instantaneous. He wrapped his arms around my waist and pulled me closer, pressing his lips to mine. His tongue slid into my mouth. I opened it wider, giving my consent. He deepened the kiss before pulling away and touching his forehead to mine.

"Nice try, but no cigar," he said.

"Not today. Please." I sighed. "I want to get drunk, have fun, and not have to think about anything."

I looked him in the eyes. "Or, you know what? I want *you* to get drunk."

Nacho sent me a surprised look and kept his eyes on mine for a while.

"What?" He burst out laughing and crossed his arms behind his head.

"Why?"

"I'll explain some other time. But promise me that you'll get drunk." I sounded desperate. Pleading. It took him aback. He took a moment to think, before taking my hand.

"All right. But not here." He stood up and said a few words to his companions before leading me through the club.

He was practically running, making his way across the crowd. His fingers were laced with mine as he led me safely out. We exited the hotel and stepped into a Jeep parked by the street. Before, Nacho had always driven himself. Not this time.

"Where are you taking me?" I asked, trying to catch my breath.

"First, we're going to the Torricelli villa. And then I'll offer you your own garden of Eden. And me. Drunk."

I smiled and sat back. My plan was simple: I was going to get him so hammered that he wouldn't know what was going on. Then I would make him super mad and see how he behaved. That was going to be a risk, but as my mom liked to say, *The words of drunks are the thoughts of the sober.* And I desperately needed to know if I was repeating my mistake by trusting Nacho. Besides, the champagne had given me the strength to do it. I was ready. Like the yellow Power Ranger. At least.

"Here you go," Nacho said, handing me a bottle of water. "If I'm going to be drunk, you need to be sober. Because if both of us are drunk, we might do something we regret later."

I took the bottle and sipped.

I barged into the villa and passed Olga on my way to the bedroom. I grabbed some random things, squeezing them into a suitcase.

"What are you doing?" Olga asked, stopping in the door.

"Shit . . . it's too small. Hand me your suitcase."

I culled and sifted once again through my things.

I wasn't going out with Massimo. I wouldn't need Louboutin heels where I was going. I grabbed some swimwear, shorts, tunics, and dozens of other things as Olga placed her enormous suitcase before me.

"Are you sure you know what you're doing?" she asked with concern.

"I won't know until I do it."

I zipped the bag up. "Bye."

"What am I supposed to tell Domenico?" Olga called after me.

"That I left. I don't know. Improvise."

CHAPTER 11

The boat glided through the waves, but I paid no mind to what was happening outside.

Nacho was with me. My colorful boy had his arm wrapped around me. The night was gorgeous, and the slowly vanishing lights of the island made the dark, starry sky seem so close—just an arm's length away. After some time another dark shape appeared on the horizon.

"Where are we going?" I asked, brushing my lips against Nacho's ear.

"To Tagomago. A private island."

"How can an island be private?"

He laughed and placed a kiss on my brow. "You'll see."

As it turned out, the island was in fact private. It had a single house, or rather a mansion—beautiful, luxurious, and comfortable. We went inside, followed by the same man who had driven us to the shore and then steered the motorboat.

"Ivan," he introduced himself, putting my suitcase down. "I protect this kid." He nodded at Nacho, who was occupied switching the pool lights on. "And now I protect you, too. Marcelo told me what you expected of him tonight."

I stopped. He was protecting me *because* Nacho was going to get drunk?

"Mr. Matos doesn't drink much," Ivan added. "I've never seen him drunk since I've known him. And I've known him since he was a toddler."

That made sense. Ivan was around my dad's age. His salt-and-pepper hair and tanned skin made him seem older, but his bright blue eyes made it hard to notice the years in him. He wasn't big or particularly tall, but his shirt clung to his toned muscles, which suggested the man was physically fit.

"Here," he said, offering me a key ring with a small remote attached. It had just one button. "This is an anti-assault device. An alarm. You press the button, I hear a sound."

He pressed it, and a little black box he held in his other hand emitted a high-pitched shriek.

"That's enough." He switched off the device. "If anything happens, press the button. I'll be nearby. Good luck."

He spun around and left.

Standing alone in the half-light, I stared at the key ring, wondering if I'd have to use it. The memory of escaping the infuriated Massimo made my stomach cramp. But Nacho wasn't Massimo.

"Ready?" he asked, appearing with a bottle of tequila and a bowl of lemons. "Where are we doing it?" he asked with amusement, and I felt something akin to stage fright.

"I'm scared," I breathed.

Nacho placed the bowl and the bottle on a small table, before pulling me in closer and sitting me down in his lap.

"What are you afraid of, bee? Me?"

I shook my head.

"Yourself?"

I denied once more.

"So what?"

"I'm afraid of disappointment," I whispered.

"Yeah, that scares me, too. I've never been as drunk as you're expecting me to get. Come on."

I sat down by a low cocktail table by the pool, and Nacho left the bottle and the lemons with me and walked away. He returned a moment later with an alcohol-free beer for me and a saltshaker.

"Let's do this," he declared and downed the first shot, biting down on a quarter of a lemon. "Did Ivan give you the alarm?"

I nodded.

"Do you have it here?"

His eyes were smiling.

"Why would I need it?" I asked, turning the small remote in my hand.

"You wouldn't. But I thought that you might feel a bit safer with it. Since it was alcohol that put you in this position in the first place."

He downed another shot. "What was your friend talking about?"

I thought for a moment and finally stood up and walked to my suitcase. Nacho followed me, pouring himself another glass.

I'm on an island, and there's nothing aside from that house here, I thought. *Where would I run?*

I took a pair of shorts and a T-shirt and changed into them before returning and sitting right next to Nacho, facing him.

"I will tell you. Just not now. For now I'll keep watching you drink." We sat and talked. About me this time.

I told him about my family and why I hated cocaine. I spoke about my love for dancing and watched as Nacho's eyes were growing less and less green and more glazed over by the minute. His voice was becoming slower and a bit slurred. My stomach cramped.

Then he started singing. In Spanish. We were rapidly approaching the moment when I might need that remote.

Nacho was starting to sway. After some time, he rolled to his side, lying down on the couch. He fixed me with a stare, but it was semiconscious at best. And he started mumbling. It was time. I left him for a short while, saying that I needed to go fetch another water. Instead, I went to the kitchen, where his phone was. I switched on the camera and started recording.

"I'm sorry for what I'm about to do, Nacho, but I need to know how you'll react when I try to make you angry when you're drunk. I know it's despicable of me, but when you sober up, I'll tell you why I did it. Now, look at yourself."

I turned and faced the wasted Canarian.

"You said you didn't know what you looked like when drunk. Well, now you know." I smiled. "Remember that everything you hear next is a lie."

I walked back to the pool, helped Nacho sit up, and straddled him. He smelled of alcohol and chewing gum.

"Make love to me," I whispered and kissed him softly.

"I can't do that," he muttered, pulling away. "You talked me into drinking to use me."

I reached down to the zipper of his pants, but he grabbed my wrist.

"Don't do it, please," he spluttered. His head was swaying, and his eyelids were half-closed.

"I'll tell you what happened on Sicily. Would you like to hear it?"

His eyes snapped open and pinned me with an expectant stare.

"Talk," he growled, licking his lips.

"My husband fucked me so hard, I came every five minutes," I lied and thanked God Nacho wouldn't remember a thing of what I said here. "He took me like an animal, and I begged him for more."

His face grew rigid. He released my wrists. I felt his heart starting to race. I pulled away, dismounting him and glancing at the remote on the table. The Canarian was staring at me, waiting for the rest of the story.

"I gave myself to him, and he took me anyway he liked. I felt him with my entire body."

I reached down and put my hand between my legs, gently playing with myself.

"I can still feel his huge cock. You'll never be as good as him, Nacho. No man can compare to my husband."

I snorted derisively.

"You're all nobodies!" My arm shot out as I clasped my fingers around his chin, turning his head so that he looked straight at me. "You're nothing."

His jaw clenched. His eyes grew cold. He took a deep breath and dropped his head, propping his elbows on his knees. I waited, but he didn't react, only breathed quickly.

"That's it. I just wanted you to know this. That I fucked my husband."

"I understand," he whispered, raising his eyes.

My heart nearly broke. There was a tear rolling down his cheek. A single tear. He didn't wipe it off.

"Massimo is the love of my life. You were just a fling. I'm sorry."

The Canarian swayed, losing his balance as he got up. He couldn't keep himself upright, though, and collapsed back to the couch.

"Ivan will take you back," he said, closing his eyes. "I love you . . ."

He blacked out with an arm covering his face. I sat down by his side, feeling my own eyes watering. Nothing happened. He didn't do anything, even though I'd made him as miserable as I possibly could. He just clammed up and went to sleep. But the worst thing was that despite all I had said, he still told me he loved me . . .

———

"Ivan," I said, knocking at the security man's bedroom.

He opened at once.

"What's going on?"

"Nothing. Can you help me carry him to his bed?"

I smiled apologetically. Ivan shook his head and walked with me to the terrace.

He was surprisingly strong. He lifted Nacho up and took his lifeless-looking body to a bedroom.

"I'll take care of the rest. Thank you," I said as Ivan waved a hand at me dismissively and left.

I sat down at my colorful boy's side and broke down. I couldn't help myself. I sobbed, angry at myself. How could I be so selfish? I'd hurt a man who told me he loved me even though he was going through the worst thing he could imagine. I felt terrible. My own sick egoism had pushed me to do things I could never be proud of. It was revolting. Despicable. I took a shower and then went for my suitcase, which I lugged back to the room. I put on briefs. Nacho was curled up on the bed, wracked with shivers every so often. I knelt by him and started taking his pants off, all the way praying that he was wearing underwear. He wasn't. As soon as I unzipped his trousers, I saw the prize. *God, give me the strength to keep myself from using this beautiful man.*

I jerked his tattered jeans off and covered him with a comforter. The sight of his prick was making me think of stupid things. Things I definitely shouldn't do. At least not now. I went to the kitchen and grabbed a bottle of water from the fridge, carrying it back and putting it on the nightstand by Nacho. Then I slipped into bed and pressed myself to his sleeping form.

I was woken up by a sudden, overwhelming feeling of desire. My eyes opened to the shocking view of the glass wall of the room. The view from the bedroom was breathtaking. I could see Ibiza, the sea, and the beautiful sunrise. I inhaled and felt something . . . strange. Teeth biting my nipple. I lifted the comforter and met Nacho's eyes. His stare was semiconscious and very amused.

"I'm so wasted." He giggled. "And so horny." His lips brushed against the skin of my solar plexus and then moved to my other breast. He was on me, with his body positioned between my legs.

"But I'm still nimble as a cat," he continued and sucked on my nipple.

"Oh yeah?" I asked with a smile, trying to hide my arousal. "You call fumbling being nimble? You would have woken up a dead man."

He smirked and pushed himself up on his arms. His face hovered above mine.

"Do dead men wear briefs?"

His right hand lifted from the mattress. Between his fingers were my panties. He wiggled them around.

"So?"

His green eyes were glittering happily.

"You forget who I am, bee. As soon as this terrible inebriation passes, I will prove something to you."

He dived under the comforter. I froze, terrified of my own nakedness. Nacho must have felt my body petrifying. His head resurfaced.

"Did you get what you wanted?" he asked, growing serious. I was beginning to panic. Did he remember?

"I want to talk to you," I said, trying to clasp my legs together and push him off me.

His muscular tattooed arms slithered out from under the comforter and closed around me, pulling me down into darkness.

"You do?" he asked as his lips brushed against mine. The smell of his chewing gum was overpowering.

I clamped my teeth. I hadn't brushed my teeth yet. I felt him smiling. His left hand reached out for something. A moment later, he pushed that something into my mouth. It was gum. I started chewing, thanking God for Nacho's foresight.

"What do you want to talk about?" he asked, pressing his throbbing erection to my thigh. "Last night?"

He thrust forward, his knee brushing against my clit. I moaned.

"Maybe about how you love having sex with your husband?"

My eyes bulged, and my heart raced.

"Nacho . . . I . . . ," I stammered before his tongue slid into my mouth. He had never kissed me like that before. He was relentless. Tenacious. Something bad was happening. He wasn't like that normally. I twisted my head away, but he gripped my chin, turning it his way.

"If I was just a fling, I'd like you to remember me as the best fling of your life. And I'll make sure to see you off properly."

His words were tearing me apart. I had no idea how I found the strength to push him back, but I did. Nacho flew to the floor, wrapped in the comforter.

"I lied!" I cried out, curling up. "I wanted to test you!" My eyes were tearing up. I sobbed, freezing in a fetal position on the bed. "I needed to be sure that you wouldn't hurt me when you're drunk. I can't go through this again."

Nacho stood up, sat on the bed, covered me with the comforter, and then laid me down on his legs.

"What do you mean 'again'?" he asked. "Tell me what happened, Laura, or I'll go and find out myself. I don't know what's worse."

His arms wrapped around me. I could feel his heart hammering.

"Would you prefer to tell me now, on a deserted island, or later, with a gun in my hand?"

"Nothing happened. I ran."

He inhaled and said nothing.

"When I left Poland, I went to Sicily. And it was all right. He wanted to fix everything. I had to give him a chance. Otherwise I would never be sure if I did the right thing."

Nacho's breathing grew faster.

"But when we were fooling around, I called him Nacho . . ."

The Canarian's breathing stopped. He swallowed loudly.

"Then, at night, I woke up and he was there. He wanted . . . wanted . . . ," I stammered. "He wanted to show me who I belonged to. I took my dog and ran. And then Domenico brought me here."

I squirmed away and leaned my back against the headboard. There was fury in Nacho's eyes, and it was spiraling out of control. His body grew taut. Hard as steel.

"I need to go outside," he said coldly, through gritted teeth. His hand wrapped around his phone. He dialed a number and said: "Ivan, prepare the guns."

I felt the blood drain from my face.

Christ, he was going to kill Massimo.

"Please," I whispered.

"Get dressed and come with me. You don't have to take anything." Nacho stood up and put on his tattered jeans. He reached out for my hand. I put on my shorts and T-shirt, grabbed a pair of sneakers, and allowed him to lead me outside.

There was a foldable table by the main entrance with various types of guns arranged on top.

"You know what's the best thing about private islands?" Nacho asked and added, before I could respond: "They allow you to do anything you want."

He offered me a pair of binoculars. "Look there."

I directed it where he was pointing. Far away, I saw a human-shaped shooting target.

"Keep your eyes on it."

The Canarian selected a submachine gun from the weapons arrayed on the tabletop and positioned himself on a black mat he unrolled on the ground. He fiddled with the gun before unloading on the target. All bullets hit the cardboard head. Nacho pushed himself up and approached me.

"That's how I unwind." His eyes were cold and angry.

He swapped guns, reloaded, and shot a dozen more times at another shooting target—this one stood closer than the previous one. He repeated the whole process a few more times. I watched him, hypnotized, observing his silent anguish.

"Fuck!" he cried, putting another gun down. "It's not working! I'm going for a swim."

He stormed off into the house, only to reappear a minute later dressed in swimming trunks. He headed toward the shore.

For a moment, I remained by the table, disoriented. Then I went inside, found Nacho's cell phone, and dialed Olga.

"What's the situation?" I asked when she picked up after a long while.

"We're being hit by hurricane Massimo," she replied dryly. I could hear she was moving. Leaving the house. "How about you?"

"Christ, he's there?" I moaned.

"When Domenico refused to fetch you when he called during the night, Massimo got into his own plane and came here. He's wrecking the place as we speak. You're lucky you didn't take any of your stuff. There are transmitters in most of it." She lit a cigarette and took a drag. "Better not come here anytime soon. And don't call me anymore." She paused, inhaling the smoke. "God, it's all gone to shit," she added with amusement.

"You think this is funny?" I growled.

"Sure I do. If only you could see them now. The house is full of Massimo's goons and some weird equipment. They're planning something. They didn't even leave a table for me. I'm going hungry. Your hubby smashed all our plates. At least I found some Tupperware cups for my morning coffee."

"He can't take it out on you! Give me Massimo right now."

I said it firmly. Olga's reply was a long silence.

"Olga, can you hear me?"

"Are you sure? He's just coming over here."

"Give him the phone," I confirmed. I hear the Man in Black's bestial growl in the speaker. Then another silence.

"Where the fuck are you?"

I took a deep breath.

"I want a divorce."

Those words practically sucked the life out of me.

I sat on the floor.

Massimo said nothing, but I could imagine him blazing with fury. I thanked God Olga was the future wife of his brother. If she wasn't, he might have taken his anger out on her right away.

"Never!" he bellowed suddenly. "I'll find you and take you back to Sicily. And you'll never leave again!"

"If you keep shouting, I'll just hang up, and the only way we're going to talk again is through lawyers. Is that what you want?"

I rested my back against the wall.

"Let's do this like civilized people." I sighed.

"All right. Let's talk. But not over the phone." His voice was calm all of a sudden. I knew better. "I'm waiting for you in the villa."

"Not there," I said stiffly. "I'll only see you in public."

"You think you'll be safer that way?" he snorted mockingly. "I took you from the middle of the street before. But have it your way."

"I don't want to argue, Massimo," I breathed, dropping my

head. "I want us to part ways in peace. I loved you, and I used to be very happy with you. But this isn't going to work anymore."

I could hear his heavy breathing through the speaker. "I'm afraid of you. But not like in the beginning. Now I'm scared you'll . . ."

My voice broke as I lifted my head and saw Nacho, wet after his swim, standing on the other side of the room.

He was dripping water, and, judging by the size of the puddle at his feet, he had been here for some time. He walked over and plucked the phone from my hand, hanging up.

"Divorce?" he asked, putting it on the kitchen counter. I nodded.

"He's here," I whispered. "He came in the morning and wants to meet."

"Divorce?" he repeated, and his eyes sparked.

"I don't want to be with him anymore. But that doesn't mean I want to be with you." I laughed sadly.

Nacho knelt, facing me, and slid between my legs. He pulled me closer, wrapped one arm around my waist, and placed the other on the back of my neck. Fixing me with a long look, he leaned in closer. I knew what was going to happen. His salty lips closed in, stopping an inch from mine. I could smell his minty breath on the air. Suddenly, his face brightened in an expression of such joy as I had never seen before. His wide grin was the last thing I saw before his tongue rushed into my mouth. The kiss was so passionate, that I knew he had finally unleashed his desire. Nacho lifted me into the air and jumped to his feet. He laid me down on the cold kitchen counter, closed a fist over the fabric of my T-shirt, and pulled it off me with one swift motion. His hands landed on my breasts.

"Christ," he moaned as his hands explored my body.

"Make love to me," I breathed, wrapping my legs around his hips.

"Are you sure?" he asked, pulling away a fraction and looking me straight in the eyes.

I wasn't. Or was I? Nothing was clear anymore. But it wasn't that important. I was doing what I wanted. Not what others expected of me.

"And if I say no? Would that stop you?" He must have heard the amusement in my voice. "I'm not wearing underwear."

I bit my lip and nodded.

"Right, that's it. You brought this on yourself, bee."

He dragged me off the counter, pulling me toward himself, and closing me in the embrace of his strong hands. Then he carried me to the bedroom.

"Want the blinds up or down?" he asked as he gently put me on the mattress. His fingers were already unbuttoning my shorts.

"I don't give a damn! I could do this in the main plaza back in Warsaw for all I care," I said quickly, wriggling on the bed impatiently. "I've been waiting for this for six months."

Nacho laughed and tossed my shorts to the floor.

"I want to look at you." His green eyes scanned me inch by inch. I suddenly felt embarrassed. I closed my legs and started curling up.

"No need to be shy now," he said, dropping his swimming trunks. "I've seen you naked so many times nothing can surprise me anymore." He lifted his brows, taking a step closer.

"Oh, really?" I put my hand on his forehead as he leaned in, stopping him. "When?"

"The first night. I told you." He grabbed my wrist and pushed my arm away. "You didn't have underwear beneath your dress." He kissed my nipple. Softly. "When I pulled off your briefs in the morning . . . ," he continued as his lips sucked on the other one. "So, anything else to discuss, or can I taste you already?" He froze above me, growing serious. Pretending to be serious.

"I recorded a video on your phone. It's proof that everything I said to you was a lie."

"I know," he said, slowly sliding down. "I watched it before I woke you up. If you wanted to see my reaction, I wanted to see yours."

His tongue gently skimmed against my navel.

"And you'd never told me what happened on Sicily otherwise."

He chose this moment to touch his warm lips to my clitoris. He sucked at it delicately.

"Oh, Jesus," I breathed, pushing my head between two pillows. Nacho's parted lips closed around my snatch hungrily. He kissed it, and I grew wetter by the moment.

His tattooed hands swept up, crossing my belly and reaching my breasts. I didn't care what he was doing. The only thing that mattered was that I wanted him. When my impatience finally reached its limits, he parted his lips and rushed in with his tongue, straight at my clit.

The scream I let out then pierced the silence. Nacho began the sweet torture. He was calm and composed, but at the same time passionate. The way he licked me made jolts of electric energy run across my body—from my belly to my head and back again. I squirmed and held on to the sheets, encouraging him to continue. I didn't want it to end. There was not even a hint of roughness in his caress, but despite that, I was so aroused I couldn't breathe.

"Open your eyes," he said, pausing. When I finally managed to do it, I saw his face hovering above mine. "I want to see."

He pushed my legs apart with a knee.

"Look at me. Please," he whispered. I could feel him closing in. Our fingers laced as Nacho lifted his arms, stretching me on the bed.

"I will adore you."

His penis rubbed against my wet slit. I tried catching my breath.

"I will protect you."

The first inch slid inside. I was close to climaxing right away.

"And I will never hurt you willfully."

Nacho's hips thrust, fast and hard, and suddenly I felt him inside me. I moaned and twisted my head away, squeezing my eyes shut. It was too much for me.

"Look at me, bee," he whispered and started moving in and out of me. Slowly and surely.

I did as he told me. As soon as our eyes met, his thrusts picked up pace. He wasn't rushing, but his movements were precise and so passionate that I could feel him with every inch of my body.

Nacho's lips pressed against mine. His eyes were open and fixed on my own. He was making love to me! I lifted my hips, and he moaned, drilling deeper inside me. He dropped his head and kissed my chin, neck, and shoulders. Unable to last any longer immobilized like this, I freed my hands and clasped them on his tattooed buttocks. His arms wrapped themselves around me.

"I don't want to hurt you," he breathed. There was genuine concern in his voice.

"You won't." I tightened my grip on his ass, pulling him closer.

Something exploded in his eyes. They changed color to a sea-blue and went wild. His pace changed. He was thrusting faster. The whirlwind of pleasure inside me was gaining in strength. Nacho's cock slammed into me harder, charging in and withdrawing. The orgasmic tsunami was coming.

"That's what I want to see," he gasped, keeping his eyes on mine. "I want to see you come for me, bee."

It was like a blow to the head. I came immediately. Every muscle in my body tensed and froze. I was rigid as a pole, and the pulsating thrusts inside me were bringing me more and more pleasure. Nacho's green eyes hazed over. He was going to join me soon. That's when he detonated inside me with such force that I briefly thought he tore through me. The only sound coming out of his mouth was a frantic panting as he climaxed with me.

His hips slowed down, calming the tide. I wanted him to start over again. The last time I had had sex was Lagos, but then I hadn't derived any pleasure from it. This time . . . this was something else.

He collapsed, placing his head in the crook of my neck. I stroked his wet back.

"I couldn't last any longer," he whispered, biting on my ear. "I felt physical pain when I couldn't be inside you. So now I'm not going to leave."

He lifted himself.

"Hi there," he breathed, smooching the tip of my nose.

"Hey," I replied, a bit raspy.

"You know you'll have to pull out at some point, right?"

"I am Marcelo Nacho Matos! I do what I want. And since I already have what I want, nothing and nobody can make me do anything I don't want to."

He grinned and kissed me.

"Will you leave with me?" he asked all of a sudden, breaking the kiss.

I pushed my head into the pillow. Did I hear that right?

"Do we really have to talk about the future when your throbbing cock is still inside me?"

"That's what gives me an advantage."

He wiggled his hips with a grin. I moaned.

"So?"

"It's not fair," I whispered, trying to dig myself out of my ecstatic state. "All declarations made during sex have no power."

I froze. He sighed and pulled out, reclining next to me.

"Is this about him? You're still not sure?" Nacho fixed his stare on the ceiling. I glanced at him sadly.

"I need to meet him. Talk to him. Get this in order," I muttered, rolling to the side.

"You know he'll take you to Sicily? Lock you up somewhere. And before I find you, he'll do things to you . . ."

"He can't keep me forever."

Nacho laughed mockingly.

"You're so naive, bee. But if you're certain . . . I can't tell you what to do. I have no right. But please, at least accept my help. Let's do this my way. If he so much as tries taking you away, I'll kill him on the spot."

He laced the fingers of his right hand with mine. "I'm all yours now, and I cannot imagine the pain of losing you again."

"Okay," I acceded, closing my fist.

"Great. Now, let's not allow that sordid fuck to ruin our day. I have a few things for you."

"But I have to . . ."

"He'll wait a day." Nacho took my chin in his hands and kissed me again. "I'm very understanding and composed. I'm doing my best here. So please, bee, don't get carried away or I'll take a gun and go kill that bastard just so I never have to hear that you're afraid of him again."

He sighed heavily. "I know you're not telling me the whole truth. But that's your choice. I can't make you tell me."

"I just think that some things don't concern you. I can deal with them myself."

"Starting today, you don't have to deal with anything on your own, Laura," Nacho said and left for the bathroom.

CHAPTER 12

I sat blindfolded by the kitchen island. After I had confessed to knowing Spanish cuisine, I had been placed there and was awaiting my test.

"All right, let's start with something easy," said Nacho, feeding me a bite. "We'll do three tries. If you guess each one, you have one request. If I win and you guess wrong, you'll accept my one wish."

I nodded, chewing the meat. Because it definitely was some kind of meat. I swallowed and said:

"Insultingly easy. That's *chorizo*."

"Which is?" he asked, kissing my bare shoulder.

"You told me to guess what it was without elaborating," I snapped. "It's Spanish sausage."

He laughed and offered me another morsel.

"Jesus, that's how little you think of me? That's *jamon*—your aged ham." I chewed the delicious, salty meat with relish. "I can't wait to tell you what my wish is. You're going to lose and regret it!"

"Now something sweet," Nacho said with amusement. I opened my mouth. "I'd much rather stick something else into your pretty mouth," he added, laughing.

A second later, I smelled his minty breath and then his tongue gently slipped into my mouth.

"I won't let you go that easy," I mumbled, trying to push him away. "Give me the third sample."

I chewed on the next piece for a while, losing my confidence. I had no idea what that was. Smacking my lips, I chewed until there was no taste left. The thing had the tang of pineapple, strawberry, and mango. I frowned, trying to dredge up any recollection of what it might be.

"Who's going to regret losing now?" Nacho asked from behind me. "What was that, bee?"

"That's not fair," I said. "It was some kind of fruit."

"And its name?"

I said nothing.

"Do you give up?"

I tore the blindfold off and looked at him.

"I can even show it to you. If you don't recognize the taste, you've probably never seen it." He opened his palm. Inside, there was something that looked like a large green pinecone.

I turned the fruit, sniffed it, patted it and felt it from all sides, but Nacho was right—I'd never seen one before.

"It's a cherimoya," he said with a grin. "So. Will you act honorably and fulfill my one wish?" He crossed his arms, challenging me.

I thought for a moment. Recalling what had happened an hour before, I concluded that my failure would probably lead to some very intriguing consequences.

"All right, Marcelo. What do you wish?"

"Leave with me." My mouth opened. I wanted to protest, but Nacho raised a hand. "I'm not talking about you moving in with me forever. Just for some time."

His smile was disarming. I melted like the last icicle during a sunny spring day. There was one more thing I had in common with that icicle—looking at Nacho, I was so wet I nearly leaked water.

"That was a trick."

The Canarian nodded.

"You are a conniving, sneaky . . ."

". . . ruthless killer who now stands before a woman naked and offers her food only to steal some of her time for himself," he finished, spreading his arms. "That's me."

I wasn't going to say no, but decided to string him along a bit longer.

"You need to control me?" I stood up and walked to him, placing a hand on his tattooed chest. "Lock me up somewhere? Strap me with a transmitter?" I could see in his eyes that he thought I was being serious. Meanwhile, I was having fun at his expense. "Kidnap me and keep me against my will? Is that what you want?"

"Are you feeling kept against your will? Enslaved?" His leg jerked, kicking the legs out from under me. Before I hit the floor, he grabbed my wrist and delicately put me on the ground. "If yes, how does it feel?" He lay down on me.

His eyes narrowed. He saw through me.

He took my wrists and lifted my arms above my head, lacing his fingers with mine.

"Where's Ivan?" I asked, shivering as the cold of the marble floor pierced through my skin.

"On Ibiza or with the boys on the yacht. But I can check if you want. We're on our own here, bee," he whispered and bit my chin softly. "If you're used to having a lot of people around, you'll have to learn to live without them."

He turned my head and gently bit my ear. I moaned in pleasure. "I value solitude. I need it at work, where I have to stay focused. Meticulous. But ever since December I've been feeling different.

Like something was missing from my life." His legs pushed between mine, spreading my thighs. He entered me unexpectedly. I yelped. "Something kept distracting me. I lost my precision." Nacho's hips moved slowly, reaching a point very deep inside me. I moved under him, squirming lazily. "I started making mistakes . . . Should I continue?"

"Oh, yes, very interesting. Don't stop," I stammered. My body responded to his movements.

"Each day was torture." His tongue brushed against my lips. "I was going nowhere . . ." He picked up speed, and I moaned. "Are you sure I'm not boring you?"

"No. I'm waiting for the grand finale," I breathed, biting his lip.

"I killed a few people, made some money, but felt no pleasure."

I gasped, eagerly awaiting the conclusion of that story, though I didn't understand it.

"That's awful," I said. He impaled me deeper. My back arched.

"That's what I thought, too. So I started to look for the reason." Nachos hips pumped faster. I was beginning to drift away. "You're not listening to me."

"I am." I opened my eyes and took a deep breath. "So what's the ending?"

"I went in search of what I lost." His lips pressed against mine, and his tongue slid inside my mouth. The kiss was deep. He tasted me. "Finally, I found it. And now that I know what I needed, I'm not going to lose it again."

He went silent, but his hips only picked up the pace. Their movements were machinelike, measured and composed but incredibly fast. He made love to me again this time, and though he was gentle, I felt the great fierceness deep down inside him.

I tried freeing my hands, but he clenched his fingers around my wrists.

"I won't allow it to go away," he whispered, kissing me again.

"I'm coming," I moaned, feeling the orgasm waking down my stomach.

"I can feel it." He pulled away and watched the ecstasy take my breath away. "Jesus," he gasped out, joining me. He released my wrists. I put my hands on his buttocks and squeezed, my nails biting into his skin. I threw my head back impossibly far and cried out at the top of my lungs. I reached a high summit—one of the highest. And when Nacho's hips stopped, I fell into the abyss.

"The way you orgasm . . . ," he breathed, slowly picking up the pace again. "Makes me lose control."

"That's horrible," I whispered. My body was limp. My arms fell to the floor.

"If you keep making fun of me, I'll make you come so many times your legs will be too weak to surf."

"What?" I opened my eyes. "There are no waves around here."

"You're right. I just wanted to watch you paddle. And we'll start by practicing on a skateboard." His eyes glittered with boyish playfulness. "I want to see how you balance yourself."

"I can show you right here," I said, twisting my hips. "I'm a dancer, not a surfer."

"We'll see about that, too," Nacho replied with a laugh and took me in his arms.

———

I finished showering. At the same time, Nacho ended his telephone call. I closed the distance between us and hugged him from behind.

"You finished in me twice today. Aren't you afraid we're going to have a baby?"

"First of all, I know you're on the pill. If you'd like, I can even dredge up the name. I wrote it down," he said and turned to hug me back. "And second, guys my age don't worry about such things." He grinned, and I punched him in the chest.

"Even Massimo doesn't know I'm on contraceptives." I shook my head with resignation. "Is there anything you don't know about me?"

"I don't know what your feelings are for me," he replied, growing serious. "I don't know what's my place in your head." He paused, waiting for a reply to the unspoken question. There was none. "But I think you'll tell me in time if I'm in your head or in your heart," he said, planting a kiss on my brow. "Anyway. Ready for some action?" I nodded happily. "Then get your knickers on and let's go."

"Knickers? How about a wet suit?"

"You'll only wave your arms around, lying on your belly. I thought you wanted to get a tan," he said with a laugh.

"I told you, bee, there are no waves here. So put on your most revealing panties and let's be on our way."

Down on a small beach in a hidden cove, Nacho placed two boards on the sand and went through his stretching routine. I followed in his steps, doing what he told me with a smirk. I felt strangely comfortable, considering that I wore only a microscopic thong. At least God didn't give me boobs the size of watermelons . . . They might have smashed my teeth out with all the jumping and arm waving.

"All right, that's enough," Nacho said at some point. "Which one is your lead leg?"

I looked at him, baffled.

"What?" I had no idea what he was talking about.

"Do you snowboard?"

I nodded.

"Which leg do you keep in front?"

"The left one."

"Okay, so that's your lead leg. Now lie down."

He positioned me on the surfboard, pulling my legs so that, outstretched, they reached exactly to the end of the board. Next, he went to his own board, facing mine, and lay down.

"That's how you paddle," he said as his long, muscular arms began waving steadily. The tensing muscles of his shoulders attracted my entire attention. I may have started salivating.

"You're not listening to me," Nacho said with a chuckle.

"What?" I asked distractedly, turning my eyes to his face.

"You were saying?"

"I was telling you about the sharks." He narrowed his eyes playfully.

"What?!" I jumped to my feet. "What sharks?!"

"Lie back down and start listening." He laughed. Learning how to stand up on a surfboard was . . . strange, but I knew it would come in handy sooner or later. Nacho yelled at me frequently, bringing my attention back to the task at hand, but how could I focus on training when his sexy butt kept distracting me? I understood less than half of what he tried to teach me, but at least I caught some basics. You stood up in three phases. First, you extended your arms and pushed yourself up, then you brought up one leg—the trail leg—and finally you stood up. Simple, in theory.

In the water, it turned out that even paddling was difficult. After falling off my board several times, I was sure that if even the smallest wave appeared, I'd be doomed.

Thirty minutes in, I became an expert at waving my arms around. At more or less the same time, they became so sore, I was ready to give up. Splayed on my board, I watched my companion, who splashed around in the water with a silly grin. He was so carefree. So different from the ever-serious Massimo. Nacho was older than the Sicilian, but kept his childishness. With my face stuck to the surface of the board, I observed his antics and went back to the things we had been doing in the morning. On the one hand, I wanted that man so badly, the desire was practically seeping from me. On the other, I had a husband. Maybe not for much longer, and maybe I had already made a decision to leave him, but my situation was still a bit hazy. I was bursting with glee, but at the same time there was a hint of anxiety about everything I did. I kept asking myself if getting into another relationship with a man like that was a good idea.

"What are you thinking, bee?" Nacho asked, paddling closer.

His words hit me like a tennis ball volleyed by a pro straight into my face. "Nacho . . ." I began slowly, lifting myself up from the board. "I'm not ready for a relationship yet." His eyes grew somber. "I don't want to keep you from anything. I don't want commitment. And I definitely don't want to fall in love."

The shock and disappointment that bloomed on his face was like a bucket of cold water to me. I'd done it again—fucked up the most romantic moment. Created another problem. If everything was going well, and my heart took over from my brain, the brain suddenly rebelled and made me say things that ruined the atmosphere. And the words I had said were bullshit. Deep down in my heart, I felt that I simply *needed* to be with Nacho. The thought that after all that had happened I could leave him for months was breaking my heart.

The Canarian looked at me for a long while.

"I'll wait," he said and paddled toward the shore.

I sighed heavily and smacked myself in the head for being stupid like that. Then I followed.

I don't know if Nacho needed to blow off some steam or if he usually swam like that, but he reached the sand a long time before I did. He tossed the surfboard away into the sand, took off his wet swimming trunks, and wrapped himself in a towel. As he spun and looked over the water, I had my answer—he was fuming. There was no smile on his handsome face this time. His face tensed, and his eyes grew cold. I had no idea what to do. Maybe I should stay in the water? But I couldn't do that forever.

I swam to the beach and placed my board next to his, stopping before him and bravely meeting his gaze. I said nothing. What was there to say?

He reached out with his hand and took the strap of my thong, pulling at it. The knot untangled, but the wet fabric still clung to my skin. Nacho untied the knot on the other side, and the G-string flew to the ground. I didn't react. My mouth was open as I inhaled.

"Are you afraid of me?" he whispered, licking his lips and watching me.

"No," I replied without hesitation. "I've never been afraid of you."

"Do you want to be?" he asked. His eyes darkened. "Fear turns you on. I know it." His arm shot out, and his fingers tightened around my neck. A wave of heat crashed over me. "You'll only fall in love with me when I become terrifying?" He pushed me and tripped me. I fell to the sand. He lowered himself to me.

"I can be that," he growled.

Nacho's tongue brutally assaulted my mouth, sliding inside. I placed my hand on the back of his neck. He licked me, kissed me, and bit me. His massive arms crushed me in a viselike grip as he tore the towel from his hips.

"Tell me you don't want me," he whispered, fixing me with an intense stare of his emerald eyes. "Tell me you don't want me at your side." His hands clasped around my wrists and squeezed, immobilizing me. I moaned. "Tell me you won't follow if I leave." I said nothing. He waited for an instant, and then entered me. Without warning. "Tell me!" he screamed. His fat cock impaled me and took my wits away. I couldn't think. I couldn't speak. "That's what I thought." He laughed. He slid out and rolled me to my stomach. His legs pushed between mine, spreading. He closed his fist around a handful of my hair and pulled. I knelt before him. His grip on my ponytail was strong. I couldn't breathe. This gentle man had never acted this way before. He had never been so brutal. I was shocked. He kissed and bit my shoulders, my neck, and my back. We were alone on a deserted island, and he would fuck me on the beach. Salty water was still dripping from my hair when his hand reached down, touching my clit. His fingers rubbed my most sensitive spot, and I moaned, enthralled.

I felt his erect prick touching the entrance to my snatch, just brushing against it. I arched my back, sticking out my butt and moving closer. I was ready. I wanted him to start. Nacho kept still. Didn't move at all. And then, without a warning, he charged in, slamming his cock inside me and pulling at my hair at the same time.

His hips pistoned like crazy, slamming into my buttocks. He took his hand off my pussy and moved it to my side, tightening its grip on my ass. He fucked me just like I wanted. Expertly, steadily, rough, and loud. The sounds coming from my throat assured him that this hard fucking was just what I liked.

"So you don't want me?" he asked, stopping three seconds from an orgasm. "You don't want to fall in love with me?" He released my hair. "So you don't need that, either." His hips started retreating. I didn't let him.

"Are you kidding?" I gasped out as he smirked.

Pulled out a bit more.

Then he leaned over me, keeping just the tip of his penis inside me, his face hovering above my ear.

"Are you my girl?" he asked and simultaneously thrust forward with his hips, impaling me brutally. I let out a yelp. "Are you?" He slid out and rammed his cock back in.

"Yes!" I cried out. His hands closed on my buttocks as he started pumping with unbelievable speed.

We came together again. Nacho collapsed on me, pressing me into the soft sand.

"So we're a couple," he said, breathing heavily.

"You're impossible," I replied with a laugh when he moved to lie next to me. "I told you everything that I say when you're inside me doesn't count."

He rolled me to my side and threw his leg over me, at the same time pulling me toward him.

"Don't you want to be my girl?" he asked, disappointed, pouting.

"I do, but—"

"See? I'm not inside you now," he said happily, and before I could finish, he stuck his tongue into my mouth.

———

Sitting in the kitchen, I watched Nacho cook. Usually, when you get a villa, you also get your own chef, but this time, Nacho took things into his own hands. He didn't even allow me to help. When I tried, he pushed me over the kitchen counter and fucked me until I orgasmed for the fourth time that day.

"Tomorrow," he said, taking my plate after dinner, "we'll need a plan." I lifted my eyes, suddenly wary. "Massimo will try to kidnap you. He brought his private army with him. I could get more of my people, too, but I don't feel like engaging in a dick-measuring contest with that guy." I dropped my head and hid it in my hands. "Listen, baby girl . . ."

"Don't call me that!" I snapped, jumping to my feet. "Don't you *ever* . . . call me that again," I hissed, wagging a finger in his face.

My eyes teared up. I had that fight-or-flight instinct again. And I picked flight. I spun around and stormed out, stopping by the pool. My breath was quickened. That emotional overload was going to kill me. I couldn't even cry. My throat cramped.

"You don't have to see him," Nacho said, stopping behind me. "It was your decision. I only want to keep you safe. So please stop fighting. Talk to me."

I turned around and inhaled to start yelling again, but at the sight of him—barefoot, with his hands in the pockets of his torn jeans, looking at me so earnestly—I softened. My head dropped, and the lump in my throat vanished.

"Here's what we're going to do: We'll go to Ibiza tomorrow. You'll go to a restaurant I select and sit at the table I choose." Nacho took my cheeks and looked into my eyes. "It's very important, Laura. You need to do exactly what I tell you. Torricelli needs to sit at the right place, too. And that's about it." He didn't take his eyes off me for a while, finally reaching for his phone. "When the phone rings tomorrow, pick it up and turn the speaker on." He pushed it into my hand and hugged me to his warm, tattooed chest. "But if anything goes badly," he said, his voice suddenly braking, "remember that I'll find you and come for you."

"Nacho . . ." I raised my eyes and stroked his face with a hand. "I need to talk to him. I won't be able to continue without making this right."

"I get it, and as I said, I can't make you do anything. I can only make sure you're safe." He planted a kiss on my brow. "And as soon as we're done with that, I'm taking you to Tenerife. Amelia is preparing a welcome party." He rolled his eyes and smiled. "She's so happy you're coming."

Jesus, what was I going to tell my mom this time? That I felt like living in the Canary Islands for a change? With a guy I barely knew? I should probably also mention that I'd nearly died in his dad's house. And that the man who had shot me was my new lover's brother-in-law.

"Would you like to sleep alone tonight?" Nacho asked, feeling the tension in my body. I muttered in response, confirming. "There's a bedroom next to the one we slept in. I'll be there if you need me." He kissed my forehead and went back into the house.

———

Massimo sat down facing me, keeping his emotionless eyes trained on my face. He placed his hands on the table and waited. His jaw was clenched. That meant nothing good. His cold, dead eyes fixed me with a brooding stare.

"If you think you can just leave me, you're wrong," the Man in Black hissed through his teeth. "I'll tell you the same thing I said last time. Do you love your parents? Your brother? Do you want them to be safe? If yes, get your ass up and walk to the car like a good girl." He pointed his chin outside. I wanted to throw up.

"And what's next?" I growled. "You'll keep me locked up and rape me?" I stood up and propped my arms on the table. "I don't love you anymore. I love Nacho. You can fuck me however you want, but I'll always think only of him when you do it."

Overcome with deadly fury, Massimo bellowed and sprung to his feet. He gripped my neck and squeezed, ramming me into the wooden tabletop. All the glasses toppled and shattered. I twisted my head, looking frantically for some help. There was no one else around. "Jesus," I wailed. Massimo ripped my briefs off.

"Let's try you out," he growled, unzipping his pants with one hand and holding my wrists in a viselike grip with the other.

"No! I don't want to! No!" I screamed, thrashing to break free. "Please, no!"

"My love. My little girl," I heard a soft voice speaking into my ear. My eyes snapped open. "It was just a dream." Tattooed arms were around me, embracing me.

"Jesus," I breathed, feeling tears streaking down my face. "What if he threatens my family again?"

I looked at him pleadingly.

"Your family is already under my protection," he said calmly, stroking my hair. "My men have them under surveillance. Your brother works for Massimo and manages a couple companies, which he can't afford to lose. I think Jakub is safe. He's more than tripled the Torricellis' income since they made him CEO."

He shrugged. "But I have eyes on him, too. Just to be sure."

"Thank you," I whispered as he tucked me in. "Stay with me." I held his hand. He pressed his naked body to mine. "Would you like to make love to me?" I asked quietly, pushing out my butt and brushing against his hips.

"You have a weird way of coping with stress, bee. Sleep now," he said with a smile and snuggled up against me.

———

The next morning on Tagomago was beautiful. The sun rose and bathed the little island in golden light. And I couldn't find my place. Nacho went for a swim while I made us breakfast. Then I went to the shower. After that, I still had nothing to do. I even briefly considered doing some housework—just to stop myself from thinking. I wanted to get this over with.

For a moment, I felt a pang of sadness at the thought that I had no nice shoes with me. On second thought, though, I couldn't care less. I didn't have to dress up for my husband anymore. Back in the bedroom, I went to my suitcase and looked at the chaos inside.

"I can't do this without music," I muttered and switched the sound system on.

As "Run the Show" by Kat DeLuna and Busta Rhymes reverberated around me, I felt myself coming back to life. That's what I needed. More bass, rhythm, and music. Swirling to the music, I put on my navy-blue Dolce & Gabbana shorts, black Marc by Marc Jacobs sneakers, and a short gray stonewashed T-shirt with a skull motif. *It's going to kill him*, I thought, putting on gradient aviators and pirouetting.

And suddenly the booming music stopped, replaced with Nicole Scherzinger's velvety voice as she sang, "I'm done." I froze.

"I don't club dance," said Nacho, walking over. "But I loved how you shook your sweet little ass." He took my hand and kissed my palm before pulling me in and closing me in an embrace. I felt all my fears dissipate. The stress and everything I had been holding inside since waking up had vanished, too.

Jesus, does that man have a song for every occasion? I thought as I realized the song he picked was about me. "I don't wanna fall in love, just wanna have a little fun. But then you came and swept me up. . . ," Nicole sang. I knew that he knew. I knew that he felt what I kept inside. At the same time, I thought that as long as I didn't speak the words, I'd be safe. That the feelings I had for him wouldn't be real. Nacho swayed slowly, kissing my shoulders. One of his hands rested on the back of my neck and the other at the base of my back. Despite what he had told me, he could feel the rhythm perfectly. He might have lied when he had said he couldn't dance.

"Ready?" he asked, smiling triumphantly.

"No," I replied at once and went to the sound system. "Now

I'll play something for you." A steady beat filled the room. Nacho snorted with laughter, hearing "I Don't Need a Man" by the Pussycat Dolls.

"Seriously?" he asked with a frown as I wiggled my butt for him to see.

Some samba, some rumba, some hip-hop. Nacho watched me with an amused expression while I sang about needing no man.

"*Now* I'm ready," I said when the song ended.

"Now we're going to take a shower. Together. And I'm going to show you just why you do need a man."

———

I had to brush my hair again and redo my makeup. Luckily, I had taken my clothes off in advance, so I could still wear the outfit to the meeting. Nacho waited by the kitchen counter, sipping juice and talking over the phone. He wore loose, tattered denim trousers and a tight-fitting black T-shirt. I glanced in his direction from upstairs and couldn't help smiling. He had flip-flops on. A mobster and paid killer wearing flip-flops. He downed his juice and looked up at me, ending his call.

"Is the phone I gave you yesterday on? Is it fully charged? Do you have it in your bag?" he asked, putting on sunglasses.

"Yes. I checked twice. Listen, Nacho . . . ," I began, inhaling.

"You'll tell me on our way home, bee. Now come with me."

CHAPTER 13

I arrived at the place Nacho had chosen half an hour early. I needed to get there before Massimo if we were to sit at the right table. We didn't inform Massimo about the time and place of our meeting until a quarter before the appointed hour. That's how we had to do it. Otherwise, he'd have sent dozens of his goons our way, and I wouldn't even have reached the table before they'd have kidnapped me.

My heart was racing. I ordered a cocktail to calm my nerves. Cappuccino Grand Café, as the place was called, was normally empty at this hour.

Most people would be home, sleeping through the siesta or curing their hangovers. That day, it was nearly empty, too.

The restaurant was situated by the bay, overlooking a hill spattered with historic buildings, rising above an old port. All of a sudden, my phone vibrated. I jerked away, nearly falling from my chair. There was a message for me:

I can see you and practically hear your racing heart. Keep calm, bee.

"Keep calm. Sure thing. Easy for you to say," I muttered.

Another text came. I can speak Polish. My eyes bulged. He really could hear me.

I sipped my mojito, already calming down with the knowledge that Nacho was keeping everything under his control.

"Baby girl," I heard a voice. It cut through the air like a samurai sword—curt and sharp.

Fighting to keep conscious, I turned and saw my husband. He was wearing a black suit and a black shirt. He stopped by the table. I couldn't guess his mood—he had sunglasses on—but he must have been furious.

"Divorce?" he asked, sitting down and unbuttoning his blazer.

"Yes," I replied simply. His scent was already starting to prickle my nose.

"What's happening, Laura?" He put his glasses down and turned to look at me. "Is this your attempt at a manifesto? A test?" He frowned. "What the hell are you wearing? You're acting out like a teenager."

I said nothing. Here we were, talking, just as I had wanted, but I seemed to have nothing to say to him. A waiter brought us a coffee. I forced down the bile in my throat.

"I can't be with you anymore," I said. "I can't and I won't. You lied to me. And above all, you wanted to . . ." I paused, knowing that Nacho could hear us. "What happened in Messina was the final nail in the coffin, as they say. Our relationship is over." My voice was strong and composed.

"Can you blame me?" Massimo asked accusingly. "The way you called me . . . like that piece of shit who killed my son."

"I did. Was that a reason to get coked up?"

I took my glasses off so he could see the hate in my eyes. "You left me for close to six months and made me depressed because you couldn't cope with what happened to us." I leaned in closer. "Haven't you thought that I might need you? That we could go through this together?" My eyes watered. "I'm not going to continue like that," I said, reining in my emotions and putting the glasses back on. "I don't want the security guards, the constant fear, the control, and the transmitters. I don't want to be afraid each time you drink or do coke in your library. And I don't want to wake up in the night and have to check if you're there. Let me go. I want nothing from you."

"No." That curt refusal hit me like a truck. "And there are a few reasons why you'll stay with me. First, because I can't imagine any other man using something that belongs to me. And second, because I like to fuck you," he said with a mocking laugh. "Besides, I think everything can be settled. This is just another roadblock to ram through. Now finish your cocktail and get your things. We're going back to Sicily."

"*You're* going back. I'm staying," I countered, getting up. "If you don't sign the divorce papers—"

"What? What are you going to do, Laura?" Massimo stood up, looming over me. "I'm the head of the Torricelli family, and you're threatening me?" His arm shot out to grab me by the shoulder. That's when his cup exploded.

I fixed a terrified stare at the shards of porcelain on the table. My phone started vibrating. I accepted the call and put it on speaker.

"She is not threatening you," Nacho's voice said coldly. "I am. Now sit down, Massimo, or the next round hits your head."

The Man in Black was fuming. He kept still. A moment later, the sugar bowl detonated.

"Sit down!" the Canarian growled. Massimo took a seat.

"You're either very brave or very stupid to be shooting at me," he said impassively.

"I wasn't aiming at you. If I were, you'd be dead," Nacho replied. I could hear the smile in his voice. "Now let's cut to the chase. Laura will leave this restaurant in a moment and walk to the car parked by the entrance. And you, Massimo, will accept that she doesn't want to be with you anymore. And you'll let her go. If not, I'll prove to you just how many places on your island can serve as my firing positions."

"You employed a killer, darling." Massimo laughed. "My own wife." He smacked his lips, shaking his head. "Your have to know, Laura, that if you leave this place without me, there will be no coming back."

"Get up, bee, and walk to the gray Mercedes parked by the entrance. Ivan is waiting there for you."

"Won't you introduce yourself?" the Man in Black asked as I stood up. "So I know who I can thank for my newly acquired liberty."

"Marcelo Nacho Matos."

Those three words made Massimo's whole body tense like a bowstring before letting loose the arrow.

"Now everything makes sense," he said derisively. "You little whore! How could you do this to me?"

"Hold your horses, Torricelli, or I blast your brains out," Nacho growled. "Walk to the car *now*, Laura." My legs shook as I passed Massimo. Suddenly, he grabbed me, spun around, and obscured Nacho's view of him. His hands tightened on my shoulders. *Oh, God, I'm dead*, I thought.

"Look at your right shoulder, Massimo," Nacho said calmly. "There's more than one shooter."

The Man in Black glanced down. There was a red dot on his right shoulder. "I will kill you if you don't release her before I count to three. One . . ."

Massimo's eyes drilled holes in the dark surface of my sunglasses. He took them off.

"Two!" the Canarian kept counting. My husband watched me,

as if hypnotized. He leaned in and kissed me. I didn't even flinch. Jesus, the way he smelled! I couldn't help but recall all those months we had spent together. And all the beautiful moments.

"Three!" Massimo let me go. Barely able to keep upright, I staggered out.

"See you around, baby girl," he said, straightening his blazer and sitting back down.

I ran out. There was a car parked by the side of the street. Ivan was waiting for me there. I glanced back and saw Domenico with his back against a black SUV. He just shook his head sadly. I wanted to cry.

"Get in," Ivan said, opening the door for me. He took the driver's seat.

"Where is he?" I asked, my voice breaking.

"Take me to Nacho!" I couldn't breathe. A panic attack was coming.

"He has to stay where he is for a while longer. Play the little soldier boy."

The car took a turn into a narrow street and sped across the town.

"He's going to be all right," Ivan added.

"I hope so."

My heart was hammering, and a shiver went down my spine. I trembled. Even though it was sweltering hot outside, I felt cold. I curled up on the back seat.

"Are you okay, Laura?" Ivan asked. "I can take you to him, but I must ask him if it's at all possible this early."

"Give me the phone. I'll call him." Trying to block the tears coming to my eyes, I took the offered cell phone and nervously waited for Nacho to pick up. *Please, God, let him pick up*, I prayed silently.

"Ivan?" Nacho broke the deathly silence.

"I need you," I sobbed.

"Give me the driver."

I passed the phone to Ivan.

Ten minutes later, we parked by a narrow street in the historic old town. I sat up and swept away my tears, looking outside and waiting. Then, there he was, strolling calmly in those flip-flops and loose jeans of his. He had sunglasses on and a large bag thrown over his shoulder. Nacho opened the trunk, threw the package in, and joined me.

"I know now why I can't call you 'baby girl.'" He smiled broadly. "I promise you I won't."

With my back pressed into the seat, I stared at him without understanding.

"I hope nobody else ever calls you 'baby girl.' Come here." He spread his arms, and I launched myself at him, snuggling against his chest. "We did it, bee," Nacho whispered and kissed my head. "Now let's hope he's smarter than he is proud. I made him an offer he couldn't refuse," he laughed. "Though normally it's the Sicilians' style."

"How much did I cost you?" I asked, lifting my head.

"Too little," he said, pulling his glasses off. "You're worth a lot more, kiddo. Now, what were you going to tell me back home?" He pulled me closer.

"Nothing," I breathed. "Where are we going?"

"I need to go see the boys, and you need to go to one more place before we leave," Nacho replied and shook with laugher.

I sat in my seat and sent him a confused look as he grinned at me.

"What did you throw into the trunk?"

His face grew serious.

"A gun," he replied.

"Was that you who shot at the coffee cup?" He nodded his head.

"How could you know you'd hit?"

He laughed and slid closer to me to hug me again.

"Darling, if you'd shot guns for as long as I have, you'd be able to hit a grain of sugar from that distance. Besides, I wasn't really that far away. It was pretty easy. Before he came in, I watched through the scope the way your blood was pumping through the veins in your neck. I knew you were nervous."

"I want to be able to shoot like that, too," I said.

He tightened his embrace. "I think it's enough that I can do that."

The car stopped by a beautiful hair salon. I glanced at Nacho, surprised.

"Is this a cover for a Mafia meeting place?" I whispered furtively.

"No," he said, snorting with laughter. "It's a hair salon. I'll leave you here."

"How come?" I still didn't remember. Nacho gave me his hand and led me out of the car.

We went inside and were greeted by a gorgeous brunette who approached Nacho and smooched him on the cheek. She was simply breathtaking. Not too tall, and with tattoos covering her shoulders and cleavage. She stood a bit too close and smiled a bit too widely to my man. I did not like it one bit. Was I jealous? The realization was like a hit in the head. I cleared my throat and squeezed Nacho's hand, barging my way to the front.

"I'm Laura," I said, interrupting their chat.

"Yeah, I know. Hi," the girl answered with a beaming smile. "I'm Nina, and those are your extensions."

She pinched my fake hair between her fingers and shook her head in disgust.

"Give me an hour, Marcelo."

I was dumbstruck. My eyes darted from the girl to Nacho. I twisted around, facing him as he was preparing to leave.

"I will never interfere with what you do or who you are," he said, stroking my cheek. "But for crying out loud, that fake hair is just atrocious."

I burst out in laughter, finally realizing what we were doing here.

"I was planning to get rid of them anyway." I kissed him softly on the mouth. "They were part of my therapy. But I don't need them anymore. See you in an hour." I walked back to Nina, who was waiting for me by the barber chair.

After having all my extensions detached, to my surprise I found out that my own hair had grown fairly long. This was another time when a change in my life was about to be accompanied by a change of hairstyle. I asked Nina to brighten up my hair. In the meantime, Nacho called that he was going to be late, so we had time to effect some really spectacular changes.

"How much lighter?" she asked, standing behind me. There was a little bowl in her hands. She was stirring its contents.

"I want it chestnut-colored," I announced.

"From what you've said, you like to radically change hair colors pretty frequently. I can't guarantee that you won't leave here completely bald," she said and started applying the chemicals.

———

"Where's my woman?" Nacho cried out, entering the hair salon. All the other clients practically fainted at the sight of his toned, tattooed body. "Where is the lady of my heart?"

I watched him, paging through a newspaper and giggling quietly. He didn't even look my way.

"Wouldn't you like a new one instead?" I asked, putting the paper down. His mouth hung open in utter shock. "How long have you been together anyway? Maybe I'll could tempt you for a little fling?" I asked with a seductive smile, as I grabbed the fabric of his T-shirt and pulled him toward me.

"Dear madam," Nacho replied, wrapping his arm around me and fixing me with a delighted look. "My woman cannot be replaced. Besides, I have been waiting too long for her." His smile widened. "But I always wanted to know how a surfer kisses."

His soft tongue gracefully slid between my lips. He pulled away after a while and shot me another long look.

"Thanks, Nina." He waved at the tattooed girl and practically dragged me outside.

We got into his steel-colored G-Class Mercedes, and Nacho gunned the engine and accelerated.

"Are we in a hurry?" I asked, amused, trying to fasten my seat belt.

"Now we are," he replied shortly, keeping his eyes on the road.

We stepped out of the car straight to the concrete surface of the airport. My eyes were immediately drawn to our plane. It was even smaller than Massimo's—more a wheelbarrow with some wings strapped on than anything else. It was hard to imagine even being able to squeeze inside. I stopped and stared at the white-and-yellow flying death trap. Nacho must have lost his mind if he thought I was going to fly in this. Was there even a bed inside to take my mind off the fact that we were in the air? Doubts flew threw my mind. I reached for my bag instinctually, but there were no sedatives inside.

"I know you're afraid of flying," Nacho said, walking to the piece of junk he called a plane. "But this time you won't even know you're in the air."

He turned to me and halted.

"You'll sit in the front," he said and grinned. "And if you feel like it, you can even pilot." With that, he spun around and entered the small craft through an even smaller door.

I raised my brows, looking at the metal shell before me. *He'll let me pilot it*, I thought. *Fucking hell, is he going to drive this thing by himself?* I was torn. On the one hand, I had to admit I was curious. I also felt pretty close to invincible after all that had happened earlier. But on the other, the fear and the incoming panic attack were very clear signals that I should probably turn tail and run.

"Christ," I muttered and tightened my grip on the bag as I set out to the plane.

I didn't even look around the interior. It was enough that I had to keep my wits together. There was no time to take in the cramped cabin. I took a left turn and found myself in another small compartment—more akin to a cage than a luxury jet.

"I'm dying," I announced, taking my seat next to Nacho. He had just put on a pair of headphones and was now flicking millions of switches on the dashboard. "I'm having a heart attack. A panic attack. A general attack!"

He leaned in and kissed me. And just like that, his soft lips made me forget where I was. I forgot my own name, my house address, the name of my best friend from high school.

"It's going to be fun," Nacho said and pulled away. "Put on your headphones and prepare for something better than . . ." He paused, sending me a curious look and smirking. "Well, I was going to say sex, but there's nothing better than sex with me, so . . ."

He shrugged apologetically. The device over my head chimed with a sound.

A man's voice was saying something that I couldn't understand, and the Canarian replied. He turned some knobs, touched some buttons, looked at some gauges, and all the time I just watched him, completely entranced. Was there anything that this man couldn't do?

"What's that?" I asked, pointing to one of the gauges.

"Catapult," he replied curtly. "If you press that red button next to it when we're in the air, you'll catapult me out into the sky."

At first, I just wanted to nod, but suddenly my dazed brain registered what he had said. Was the sly bastard making fun of me?

"I wish you could have seen your face just now," Nacho said and chuckled. "This is the fuel gauge, darling. Now, let's check if the rudder and foil flaps are okay."

After I was made to look like a complete idiot, I decided to keep any questions to myself and just watch my man expertly prepare the craft for takeoff. *My man*, I repeated to myself, watching Nacho. I hadn't even properly left the previous one, and I already had a new lover. I shook my head, turning to look through the windshield. My mother would have told me what she thought about that. She'd start with: *That's not how I raised you!* Then she'd add: *Just think about what you're doing, child.* And she'd conclude with a: *But that's your life you're wasting.* In other words, she wouldn't have been of any help whatsoever. I sighed, thinking about the conversation that I'd have to have with her. Sooner or later.

The engines burred. I went a little sick. It didn't matter if I could look out the windshield or had a luxurious passenger cabin around me—the only thing I could think about was the fear gripping my heart.

"I can't do it, Nacho," I whined. "Please let me out of here." I was growing hysterical.

"I need you to keep updating me on the values you see on that monitor," he replied, pointing to a screen. "Whatever shows up there. Can you do that?" He glanced at me with concern.

Nonsensical sets of numbers were appearing on and vanishing from the screen. I focused on my task, reading them out loud. Suddenly, I felt the plane lifting into the air.

"Oh, Jesus . . . Nacho," I stammered, trying to catch my breath.

"The numbers," he repeated. I went back to reciting.

Fifteen minutes into the flight, I felt Nacho's eyes on me. I turned my head and saw him facing me and beaming. His brown aviators lifted a fraction on his nose as it wrinkled when he grinned. "You can stop. It's not as if you can get out now."

I looked outside. There were clouds . . . below us. And the sun above us. Nothing but absolute nothingness.

I was still feeling a bit nauseous, but the endless expanse of blue around added a new feeling to the range I was experiencing—bliss. Suddenly, I wasn't afraid anymore.

"Want to know what I'm thinking?" I asked. He bobbed his head, keeping his face still. "I'm thinking that you've never allowed me to taste you before." His lips stretched into a thin line as he clenched his jaw. I threw my head back and closed my eyes. "I'd like to see you come. I want to give you pleasure."

"Seriously? That's what you thought about seeing those clouds?" he asked, surprised. "I'm beginning to worry about you, bee. Do you know that clouds are just collections of water droplets or small shards of ice—"

"Don't change the subject." I cut him short, keeping my eyes shut. "I'd like to suck you off, Nacho."

"Jesus, woman," he muttered. "And you're telling me this now? When we're thousands of feet above the ground?"

He licked his lips, and I glanced at his zipper.

"I can see you like my idea. Judging by your reaction," I said and went back to enjoying the trip.

CHAPTER 14

We landed at Tenerife's southern airport, where the world's most extravagant car was parked by the entrance to the terminal. Nacho opened the door for me, and as I was about to get inside, he wrapped his arms around me and pushed me against the car. It wasn't especially rough—more like firm and horny.

"I've been hard since you told me you wanted to taste me," he said with a smile and rubbed his crotch against my leg. Then he planted a quick, soft kiss on the tip of my nose and released me.

He was nothing if not a master of provocation. I froze with one leg inside the car and wondered if I should blow him right away, on the parking lot.

"I want to suck you off," I whispered in his ear before stepping inside. The triumphant smile disappeared from Nacho's face.

"Then it's going to have to wait," he replied, shutting the door and marching around the black car. "I told you Amelia was preparing a welcome party. And I don't think you'll need much lovemaking afterward." He grinned and put on his shades.

"Want to bet?" I asked as we headed out, tires screeching.

Nacho's hearty laughter sliced through the air. He didn't have to respond. I knew he accepted the challenge.

———

The car stopped in an underground garage below the apartment. I felt strange. Anxious. I was about to step out, but my legs refused to cooperate. I felt as if I had gone back in time. The difference was that when I had been here last time—six months before—I had still been pregnant. And married. And happy. But had that ever been the truth? I had been pregnant—that's for sure. And I was still married. But had I ever felt really happy with Massimo? My brain was receiving conflicting signals. On the one hand, I regretted having to end my relationship with Massimo this way, but on the other, the man now sitting next to me was the fulfilment of all my dreams. And then there was another thing. What if I was just trying so hard to convince myself that I loved him that I'd started believing in my own lie? Maybe this was just curiosity. Attraction. A simple crush. And that would mean that I had wrecked my marriage and the genuine feelings between me and my husband.

"If you don't want to be here, I'll take you to a hotel," Nacho said cheerlessly. "I know that what happened before is still very painful, Laura, but—"

"It's not," I cut him short and stepped out. "Shall we?"

I didn't feel like reminiscing. And my head was already aching from the crowding thoughts. I needed a drink, some fun, and no thinking. At the same time, I realized that I was about to face all my demons on this island.

I passed the door to the apartment, and . . . it felt like coming home. Everything was exactly as I'd had left it. The difference was that this time, I wanted to be here.

Nacho acted as if we'd been living here together for months.

He tossed his bag to the floor and went to the kitchen. He grabbed a bottle of beer from the fridge and dialed a number on his phone. Was he giving me time to acclimate or was he just laid-back and casual, not needing to keep up appearances for my sake? I wasn't going to interrupt him and ask, so I went upstairs to my bedroom instead.

I opened the wardrobe. It was empty. *Just great*, I thought bitterly. Where was my suitcase? Nacho hadn't taken it with us to the car, but I had seen it back at the plane. What was I going to do without even a single set of underwear?

"You're in the wrong bedroom," said the Canarian as he joined me after some time. He wrapped his arms around me, standing behind me. "It's the first door to the right. By the stairs."

He kissed me on the back of the neck and left without another word.

I turned around and followed him. Opening the door to his room, I noticed the changes. The room looked nothing like it had before. All the furniture was different, the white walls had turned gray, and the bed now had a neat set of columns. It was still modern and stylish, but the metal poles sticking out from every corner were a portent of the wild times to come.

"Your things are in the wardrobe," Nacho opened the door, revealing another room. "Amelia bought you some more stuff. She told me that if I did that, you'd wear nothing but shorts and flip-flops." He shrugged.

"If you need—"

"Do you want to tie me up?" I asked. Nacho's head turned toward me, and he fixed me with an intense stare. "Why would you need those columns otherwise? And why did you change the décor?" I narrowed my eyes with suspicion and took a step in his direction.

"I threatened you with a gun here," he replied, dropping his head. "I didn't want it to remind you of that. If you'd like, we'll move. I've never invested in real estate, but I looked for some other places, and there are a couple at—"

I interrupted him again, pressing my lips to his. My tongue slid inside his mouth and caressed it. Nacho bent his knees, lowering himself to my height, and cupped my cheeks.

"Yes," he breathed. "I want to tie you up. So you never run away." He smiled charmingly, jumping onto the bed. "And there are extendable speakers in those columns. I'm not planning an orgy, but I do like a good sound system. It's going to come in handy when I play movies for you at night." He smooched me on the nose. "Or music. And speaking of music . . ."

He turned his back on me and walked over to a tablet perched on a modern wall cabinet. "I'd love to see you dance for me." He pressed a button, and long, black speakers slid out of the metal columns. The entire room filled with the clear, crisp sound of "Cry Me a River" by Justin Timberlake. I laughed out loud. I hadn't heard that one in a long while.

Nacho smiled. As soon as the beat came on, he started dancing, mimicking the singer. My jaw dropped. I watched him fool around, twisting and spinning across the room. He grabbed a baseball cap from the wardrobe and started singing. I was entranced, surprised, and amused in equal measure. At one point, he skipped over to me and put his hands on my hips, inviting me to dance. And he was good at it. He glided fluidly across the floor, and I followed. I had suspected he was a good dancer as far back as Ibiza, but I never thought he'd be that good.

"You liar," I whispered to his ear when the song ended and the first notes of another one resonated. "You told me you couldn't dance."

"I told you I couldn't *club* dance." He laughed and took off his shirt, flexing his muscles. "But we surfers have excellent balance."

He winked and went out, heading to the bathroom and swaying his hips.

I was about to follow him, but that would end in thirty minutes of petting and lead to another hour of fucking in the shower. I stayed where I was.

I was supposed to show myself to Nacho's friends as his girlfriend for the first time. And he was the head of a mob family. That was no joke. I headed to my side of the wardrobe and rummaged through the dozens of hangers. With a sigh of relief, I discovered that there were lots of wearable things in there. There were no colorful T-shirts and denim trousers, but instead dresses, tunics, and breathtakingly beautiful shoes.

"Thank you, Amelia," I breathed, carrying clothes out. Suddenly, something occurred to me: if Nacho is going to wear those shorts of his again, I'll look like an idiot at his side. I plopped down on the rug and stared dumbly ahead.

"Did she do a good job?" the Canarian asked, passing me by and drying his head with a towel.

Oh, God almighty, I thought as his naked, tattooed buttocks swung in front of me, maybe a dozen inches away from my face. I was impressed by my own self-control when I kept still and just looked on as Nacho took a pair of gray linen pants off a hanger.

"Did Amelia do a good job with your clothes?" he repeated when I didn't say anything. I nodded numbly. "Good. It's nothing official, but you know . . . since I'm the boss I can't always dress like an eighteen-year-old."

He pulled the pants on, and I sighed with relief. What the eyes don't see, as they say. Meanwhile, Nacho grabbed a dark blue shirt and rolled its sleeves up. The color of the lining was the same as the trousers. He looked amazing with that tan and the clean shave and the tattoos. The outfit was rounded off by a pair of dark blue loafers and a wristwatch.

"You look like you're having a stroke, honey."

He walked over to me and wiped the corner of my mouth with the hem of his shirt. "You're salivating." He laughed and took me in his arms, lifting me up. "Now, off to the bathroom!" he ordered, then slapped me on the butt and pushed me toward the door. I shook my head but went. As was my custom, I took a cold shower, making sure the water didn't touch my hair. Nina had layered my hair slightly, creating a very sexy, messy hairstyle. Facing the mirror, I discovered that the cabinets in the bathroom were filled with cosmetics. I quietly thanked Amelia again. I did my lashes and then dusted some gold-flecked powder on my cheeks. It was a fresh, natural, and clean look. Nacho wasn't in the bedroom when I returned. I was glad, as that meant I could pick my outfit without any interruptions. I went with a short, bare-back, sand-colored slip dress and a pair of sandals with a strap fastened around the ankle. To top it off, I selected a small dark blue clutch bag and a wide gold bracelet. And that was that. I was ready.

Taking the stairs to the lower floor, I saw Nacho bent over his laptop. He heard me and shut the monitor, turned to face me and froze. My dress wasn't especially tight-fitting. It flowed gracefully as I walked.

"You'll be mine forever," Nacho said, his lips spreading in a smile.

"We'll see about that," I replied, nonchalantly throwing my hair back.

He laughed and closed the distance between us, lifting me up and helping me down the last couple of steps. He watched me, his eyes slightly narrowed, before he skimmed my lips with his tongue.

"Let's go." He took the car key and laced his fingers with mine, heading toward the door.

"You had alcohol," I snapped. "And now you're going to drive?"

"It was one small beer, bee, but if it helps, I can ride shotgun."

"What if the police stop us?" My voice was a bit too bitchy.

"You know what?" he asked, as the tip of his nose trailed a line across my cheek. "If you'd like, I can get us a police escort. Would that make you happy?" He lifted his eyebrows with a smile. "I'll say this once more: I am Marcelo Nacho Matos, and this is my island. And now, if there are no more questions, let's go, or Amelia will kill us." He laughed. "Oh, and by the way, speaking of phones." He plucked a white iPhone from his pocket and passed it to me. "This is your new one. I've copied the contacts and unlisted the number. But that was the only thing I was able to retrieve. Your clothes, your computer, and whatever you left on Sicily is still there." He shrugged apologetically.

"Those were only things," I said, pocketing the phone. "I've other worries," I added.

Nacho froze and leaned in closer. "What worries?"

He knitted his brows. "What do you worry about?"

I sighed. "Olga. Her marriage. My divorce. My company." I shook my head. "Want me to keep going?"

"I have solutions for most of those worries already," Nacho said, pressing his lips to my forehead. "The only thing I can't plan for is your visit to Olga's wedding, but we'll talk about that later. Now come on."

When we headed up the driveway of the Matos family residence, I felt my stomach cramping painfully. I hadn't thought I'd react this badly to seeing this place again. It wasn't surprising that we were going to visit that house, but as soon as we reached our destination, I had to fight to to keep the contents of my stomach down. The images of that horrid day flew before my eyes. But it was just a place. A building. Nothing special.

"Darling." The Canarian's voice broke me out of my reverie.

"You look like you're having a stroke again." The car stopped, and Nacho took my hand.

"I'm all right . . . it's just this place," I paused, scanning the palace with my eyes. "I remember him hitting me . . ."

"Fuck," Nacho growled, startling me. "I think about it every day. Every day I want to kill myself for what I made you go through."

His face went cold and rigid, and his eyes filled with burning hatred.

"I'll protect you from anyone and everyone, bee. I promise. Just please forgive me for that." He dropped his head. "It's neither the place nor the time for that conversation, but we'll have to talk about that at some point."

"Laura!" Amelia's cry broke through the awkward silence that fell on us when Nacho finished.

"I don't want empty words. I've heard enough as it is," I said, getting out. The gorgeous blonde launched herself at me and closed me in a big hug.

"Hi there, brat." I kissed her. "You look amazing," I added, pulling away.

"You too!" Amelia replied and took her brother by the hand. "Are you officially a couple now? Do I finally have a sister? Does Pablo have an auntie?"

We both kept silent, glancing at each other.

"I know what Marcelo thinks, but I'm interested in what you have to say. Are you lying to me again?"

I wondered for a while, before taking Nacho's hand and placing a long, passionate kiss on his lips. He looked straight at me, and once more the world stopped existing. Hypnotized by each other, we kept still for a long while.

"We'll try our best," I said, keeping my eyes on him. "But no results guaranteed." I raised my brows, signaling to Nacho that my response was directed at him, not his sister.

"You guys are super in love with each other!" Amelia chittered, clasping her hands. "But enough of that. Let's drink. And Ivan wants to speak to you, Marcelo. As soon as you find a moment." She took me with her to the entrance.

We passed the main door, and—to my surprise—the mansion looked different. I'd only been here for a short while, but you don't forget a place you're taken to for torture. We walked down a long corridor. Nacho was right behind me, strolling nonchalantly with his hands in his pockets and a wide smile on his face. I let go of his sister's hand and wrapped my arm around his waist.

"You've changed the décor?" I kept thinking it had been less modern last time.

"Everything," he replied with a chuckle. "The entire house has been renovated, even though you've seen only a small part of it. We did it right after the accident." He nodded at Amelia, who was still blissfully unaware that her fiancé had been my torturer. And that there had never been any accident, only an attempt to kill me. "I ordered the whole house rebuilt from the floor up. It was getting old, and, to be honest, I didn't have too many good memories from here, either."

"Marcelo is the boss now," Amelia chimed in. "And the family will finally enter a new era!"

"Please don't keep your head occupied with what we're entering and why, Amelia," Nacho berated her in a serious voice. She only rolled her eyes in response. "Better focus on raising your son. Where is he, by the way?"

"In his room with the babysitters, cats, and dogs." She glanced at me. "Marcelo thinks that children should be raised with animals."

Judging by her expression, she didn't share her brother's views on child-rearing. "But he's the boss," she added and grinned.

"That I am!" he boomed, pressing me closer to himself. "And don't either of you forget that!"

We reached the end of the tangle of corridors and went out to the back garden. The centerpiece was an enormous, three-level pool that descended toward the rocky slope. Around it there were wooden, canopied gazebos, sunbeds, and sofa chairs. Farther out, there were four large sofas arranged in a rectangle around a large bonfire. Next to those, a long, backlit bar and a grand table for at least thirty people. Only there were a lot more people than that. Most of them were men, but there were some women among them, too—they lounged in the water or lazily sipped on their drinks. Everyone was young and laid-back, and didn't look like gangsters at all.

"*Hola!*" Nacho called out, raising his arms. Everyone looked at us.

The crowd exploded in cheers, applause, and whistles. The Canarian pressed me closer to his side with one arm and waved his other at the guests. They piped down. The music did, too. Amelia offered her brother a microphone, which she had taken from the DJ.

"I'm going to speak English, as the love of my life has only just started learning Spanish," Nacho began. I dropped my eyes shyly.

"Thank you for coming to this ass end of nowhere, but I hope all the alcohol will make the long trip up to you." The guests cheered. "Those who still need more will get some to take away. And now I would like to introduce to you . . . Laura! I'm sorry, ladies: from now on I'm officially taken. Thank you for your attention. Have a good night," Nacho finished and tossed the mic to one of his buddies before kissing me deeply. The entire crowd raised their glasses, and I heard another round of applause.

I was so embarrassed. The ostentation was completely unnecessary, but at the same time it seemed natural. That was Nacho's style.

Who was I to complain? The kiss lasted for a long while, and most people stopped looking at us after the first few seconds. Nacho's tongue flitted in my mouth. The music went back on, and the party continued.

"Was that necessary?" I asked when he pulled away.

"You look way too good today," he said. "I needed to mark my turf, so to speak, or else some of those guys would start hitting on you, and I'd have to kill them."

He grinned, and I rolled my eyes.

"They don't look dangerous." I shrugged, scanning the crowd.

"Because not all of them are. Some are just surfers. Others are Amelia's friends. Only a small group are my men."

"But they all know who you are?" I asked, biting my lip. Nacho nodded. "So no man will speak to me?" He shrugged with a sly smirk.

"Only as much as courtesy dictates. Or if they're gay." He pulled me toward Amelia, who was kicking her heels impatiently. "Let's get something to drink."

I watched Nacho in his natural habitat and was relieved to see he behaved the same among his friends as he did with me. He didn't pretend or act. Instead, he smiled, laughed, joked, and fooled around. Soon after, I started telling apart his partners from his friends. It was no easy task, though. The Canarian liked to surround himself with people like himself. The surfers wore their hair long, had tattoos, and were tanned. The employees and partners were either taller and more muscular or were gaunt and ratty. Other than that, they all looked suspiciously . . . normal. Just relaxed people that liked to have fun.

Nacho sipped a beer, while I downed glass after glass of my favorite champagne. I didn't want to get wasted, especially now that I didn't have Olga who normally kept me from doing the stupidest things that came to my mind. Thinking of her made me sad. Amelia was great friend material, but she was no Olga. I decided to call her and walked away.

"What's going on?" Nacho asked, wrapping his arm around my waist and pressing his lips to my ear.

"I need to talk to Olga," I said.

"Invite her here." That short sentence made the flurry of butterflies in my stomach all take flight. "As long as Domenico lets her go, I can arrange everything tomorrow."

He kissed me on the head and released me. I didn't walk away. I was rooted to the spot.

And boom! I was in love. If I had doubted before, now I knew that I loved this man. He stood there, talking to his friends. And I couldn't move. Something broke inside me. I grabbed him by the shirt and broke into his conversation, pulling him strongly toward myself and kissing him passionately. The men he had been talking to just a second before went silent and then all burst into laughter as I deepened the kiss. Nacho's hand fell and landed on my ass. The other one touched the back of my neck. This man was perfect. Ideal. And all mine.

"Thank you," I whispered in his ear. His eyes sparkled with joy.

"What was I saying?" he asked, turning his head to his buddies. He slapped me softly on the butt, and I was off. I went into the house and took a seat on a couch in the main hall, fishing out my phone and dialing Olga.

"Hey," I said when she picked up. The silence that followed lasted for a couple long seconds.

"Are you all right?" she asked.

"Yes! Why wouldn't I be?"

"Fuck, Laura." She sighed. "When Massimo returned to the villa, we barely escaped with our lives. Domenico told me what happened. That Nacho of yours is one crazy son of a bitch. I get it, but shooting the head of the Sicilian Mafia?"

I heard her moving somewhere.

"Come on, he didn't exactly shoot *Massimo*. He shot a sugar bowl." I paused and then burst out laughing. "He just wanted to scare him a little bit. And I think he managed it."

"The only thing he managed was to piss Massimo off," she replied, raising her voice. "Okay, I'm out of the house. I'm not sure if they're listening. Tell me everything."

"Will you come here?"

Olga was dumbstruck.

"I'm on Tenerife."

Olga breathed in.

"I promise I won't get you into anything this time. Please, come." I sounded pathetic, even though I didn't feel that way. But only pity could make her ask Domenico to let her go.

"Do you know I'm supposed to get married in two weeks? Remember that?" she asked. She was torn. I could tell.

"Sure I do. Shouldn't you spend some time with your maid of honor? And we still need to talk about my company. Though I'm not sure it's mine anymore. Anyway, we should plan ahead, and we can't do that over the phone. Domenico will get it." I grimaced, hearing my own words. If I were in his place, I would never have let Olga go.

"Jesus, Laura, you're impossible." I could imagine her shaking her head now. "All right, I'll talk to him tomorrow."

I hesitated for a moment, wondering if I should ask what I was thinking. Finally, my curiosity prevailed.

"How's he dealing with it?" I suddenly felt guilty.

"Massimo? I don't know, to be honest. After he unloaded a full clip into a Jet Ski, making it explode, he vanished. Even Domenico said 'fuck it' and stayed with me. We went back to Sicily, and Massimo stayed on Ibiza. I'll tell you everything when I come. I can see Domenico wants something from me. I doubt I'll leave here without sucking him off."

"I love you." I laughed.

"I love you, too, bitch. Call me tomorrow or send me your number. I'll call you back after I talk to him."

Returning to the garden, I heard another round of applause. I went out and saw Nacho standing on the scene, gesturing for the crowd to quiet down.

"You make me do this every time," he chuckled. "But all right, since you've come such a long way, I'll play for you. But just one song."

Play? Did he play an instrument? I stopped on the marble terrace and watched. The Canarian quickly caught sight of me and fixed me with his emerald stare.

"At the risk of sounding a bit trite," he started, dropping his eyes shyly, "I'll start with reminding you of a book. *Fifty Shades of Grey*. It's since been turned into a movie. A silly story of a bossy asshole addicted to sex and control. But every one of us knows someone like that, so I'd wager it's a story based on real events."

Nacho's eyes drilled holes in me. "I know, for instance, that I know at least one such guy. But such is life. You can't get rid of all Italians, can you?" I shook my head with a little smile. The crowd roared with laughter.

"Sorry, Marco. We're tight." Nacho pointed at one of his friends, who waved back with a hand. "But back to music." Amelia walked on the scene and handed Nacho a violin. "There's this guy named Robert Mendoza. He came up with a violin version of 'Love Me Like You Do.' Now, witness my sentimental side." Nacho grabbed the instrument and propped it on his shoulder. The guests applauded.

The DJ put on a subtle backing track, and Nacho began his

concert. His eyes were still on me. My jaw dropped to the ground. That man really could do anything. He gently glided through the sounds. I could see he was putting his heart in it. His fingers deftly slid along the strings, and the bow danced in his right hand. I felt my body melting. Nacho's strong, muscular arms held the wooden instrument with such delicacy. His face was serene.

At some point—I don't know when—my feet took me through the crowd. I needed my man's touch right now.

He kept playing and tracing me with his eyes as I approached. The violin was attached to the speakers with a cord, so he couldn't meet me halfway. But I didn't care. I also didn't care that around a hundred people I didn't know were staring at me as if I were a witch and they wanted to burn me at the stake. I walked across the garden, led by his eyes, as all the heads turned my way. Finally, I reached the scene and stopped two feet ahead of Nacho. He turned to face me but didn't stop playing. I was ensorcelled. Enthralled and hypnotized. Completely dazed. The music rose as the song reached the chorus. I grinned. That was everything I could do. I was so happy. My man played for me, and even if every other girl present thought the same, I *knew* it. Nacho played the last few notes, put the violin and the bow down, and waited. As did everyone else. I threw myself at him, wrapping my legs around his hips. He pressed me close to him, and the crowd exploded in applause. I suspected that my short dress was rather revealing and that my butt was there for all to see, but when Nacho kissed me like that, I wouldn't care even if I was completely naked.

"You can play the violin," I whispered. My expression was blissful. I smiled widely as he held me in his arms. "What else can you do? Or should I ask: What can't you do?"

"I can't make you love me." His big, green eyes fixed me with an attentive look. "And I can't curb my erection when you're wrapped around me like that." He grinned and I grinned back. "I need to put you down. Everyone's watching, and I suspect they won't miss my bulging dick." He let me find my footing and lifted an arm to wave at the crowd. The concert was over. The DJ played the next track, and the guests returned to partying.

"Come on." I took Nacho's arm and led him back to the house and then through the labyrinthine corridors. The whole time he laughed.

"Know where you're going?" he asked when we turned another corner.

"I have no idea, but I definitely know what I want to do," I replied, glancing around.

Nacho closed his arms around me and halted before throwing me over his shoulder and walking back. I didn't defend myself. He was trying to make it easier, after all. He knew where to go. He carried me up the monumental staircase to the second floor, where he opened one of the doors and kicked it shut behind us before putting me down on the ground and pushing me against a wall.

"I want to make love to you," he said, lifting my arms above my head.

His lips pressed against mine, caressing my skin, all the time keeping my wrists in his grip.

I was turned on, but the alcohol in my veins pushed me in a direction other than submission.

I knew he was going to be tender and gentle, but what I needed was something completely different. My dark side needed appeasing. I bit his lower lip. Hard. He hissed, paused, and pulled away.

"We're not going to make love," I said with confidence, freeing my hands.

"No?" he asked with amusement, allowing me to push him away until his back touched the closed door.

"No." I started unbuttoning his shirt.

It was dark in the room, but I knew what I was doing and what was in front of me. I didn't need to see it. His tattooed chest heaved as his breathing quickened. My hands trailed across his skin, lower and lower. I could feel him breathe in and out. The smell of his chewing gum was overpowering. Some women feel pheromones, others love the scent of cologne, while I was apparently turned on by the smell of mint. I slid the shirt off his shoulders and traced a line on his skin with my lips. He smelled of the ocean, the sun, and himself. I bit his nipple softly. A sound emerged from his throat. I had never heard it before. It was something of a growl, but also a sigh. He liked what I was doing. I increased the pressure and sucked. Nacho's hands moved to the back of my neck.

"Don't provoke me, bee. Please."

His barely audible voice was a warning.

I slowly moved to his other nipple, ignoring him, and bit into his skin even harder. Nacho let out another sound. This time it might have meant he was getting annoyed. His grip on my neck tightened. I went lower, my teeth brushing against his skin, until I knelt. His long fingers were still on the back of my neck as I slowly unzipped his pants.

"I want to suck you off," I breathed, gripping the fabric of his pants and pulling them down.

"You're so dirty," he whispered.

"Not yet," I replied and slid his cock down my throat.

The sound that filled the air was one of relief. Nacho's low voice made it clear that he was aroused and very, very pleased. I didn't pay any mind to the fingers digging into my skin and hungrily sucked his dick. Hard, deep, and fast. I couldn't wait until I could taste him. Nacho wasn't helping me. On the contrary, he was making it harder, trying to slow down my mouth. The fact that he was resisting added to the alcohol in my blood woke something violent in me. I grabbed the hands on the back of my neck and pushed them away, slamming them against the door. That's where he was supposed to keep them. Then I took his manhood in my right hand, right at the base, and squeezed, at the same time licking the tip.

"Don't move, Marcelo," I growled and swallowed him whole again.

"I love the sound of my name when you say it." He sighed.

I fucked him with my mouth, feeling him squirm against the door. The first trickles of sweat were running down his stomach. He muttered in Spanish, Polish, and what I supposed was German, and I relished the sweet torture I was subjecting him to. My free hand slid behind him, and my nails bit into the skin of his rock-hard buttock. He cried out and slammed a fist into the wooden door, which shook under the blow. I picked up the pace. Nacho's open mouth gasped for air.

Suddenly, the lights went on. Disoriented, I stopped with his prick in my mouth, and looked up.

Nacho's emerald eyes were trained on me. His arm swung down from the switch.

"I need to see you," he whispered. "I just need to."

I didn't care what he needed. Like a first-rate hooker, I continued sucking him off. I licked, bit, and sent him the most lascivious looks I could muster. His hands tried moving away from the door, but every time they did so, I stopped until he put them back against the surface of the wood. When I was sure I'd feel the first drops of his cum on my tongue, Nacho shot out with his arms, lightning-fast, and jerked me up.

"I need to be inside you," he breathed, his eyes wide and wild.

"Don't move," I growled. I closed my hands on his neck and slammed his head against the door.

"No," he hissed, gripping my neck in return and tightening the hold.

We held each other as our stares met. Our breathing was fast and shallow. The Canarian took a step forward. Despite my resistance, he pushed me deeper into the room. I moved back step by step, unaware of what was behind me, until my butt touched something soft. Nacho released my neck and moved his hands to my shoulders before shoving me back. I toppled to a large, soft bed. Before my back really touched the mattress, he grabbed my thighs and pulled me toward him, tore off his shirt, and went down on his knees, pressing his lips to my moist snatch. I yelped, trying to push his head back. His mouth greedily devoured my throbbing, sensitive clit. He hadn't taken my panties off, instead pulling them aside to push deeper inside me. I squirmed and clawed at his neck, but he only doubled his efforts.

"I want to taste you," I moaned as his slender fingers slid inside me.

"And you will. I promise." He pulled back for a short while before diving right back in.

His tongue moved expertly, seeking out spots so sensitive that I was at the verge of climaxing after a minute. Then, unexpectedly, he stopped before rolling me over and pulling the thong down my legs. It was surprising. He hadn't been so quick-tempered before—he had never used any kind of force with me, with the exception of that one time at the beach. My dress flew to the floor. I was left with only my shoes. Nacho pressed himself to my bare back and laced his fingers with mine, lifting my arms above my head. My knees were on the floor, but my chest pushed against the soft mattress. Nacho spread my legs with his own, and his teeth bit into the back of my neck.

"Do you know who I am, Laura?" he asked in a low, cold voice.

"I do," I whispered, my face pushed into the comforter.

"So why do you keep prodding? Do you want me to prove that I can take you by force?"

"I want . . ." My voice was muffled, and Nacho's heavy breathing practically drowned it out.

His hand closed around a strand of my hair. He rose a fraction, wrapping it around his wrist, and pulled my head back. I cried out as he impaled me in one swift motion. It wasn't him. Or, at least, I hadn't known him like that before. This was so much like my husband, the image of Massimo flashed in front of my eyes. I wanted to make him stop, but my voice caught in my throat. Nacho kept fucking me roughly, slapping my ass with his free hand without stopping or releasing my hair. The slaps kept on coming. Pain mixed with pleasure as I couldn't decide what I really felt. He was doing it just the way I liked it, but my eyes teared up at the same time at the memory of what I had gone through with Massimo.

Suddenly, Nacho let my head go, as if sensing that there was something wrong. He rolled me to my back and pulled me up, laying me gently down on the mattress. He cupped my face and kissed me. Softly and passionately at the same time. I felt his manhood sliding inside me again, but slower this time. Tenderly.

"What do you really want?" he asked, keeping the steady undulating motion of his hips. "I can be whoever you want, but I need to know you trust me. That you'll tell me when you've had enough. I don't want to hurt you." His lips brushed against my nose, my cheeks, and my eyes. "I adore you. If you want to feel pain, I'll give it to you, but you have to know I'm doing it out of love. I love you . . ." His lips found mine, and I tasted the mint on his saliva again. "Now come for me."

The calm emerald eyes flared with fire, and I felt his cock growing inside me.

He laced our fingers again and raised my arms above my head. His movements became faster and more forceful. He knew I was on the brink. I didn't know how, but he always sensed when I was about to have an orgasm. Those green eyes of his . . . The tattoos. The tenderness and the ability to turn into a rough brute, even despite himself . . . It all turned me on. Nacho lowered his head and bit my lip. I moaned. He bit it harder and then moved to do the same with my neck and my shoulder. I writhed beneath him as his prick picked up the pace and started racing.

"Come on, bee. Come for me," he breathed, and a bright smile illuminated his face.

I climbed higher and higher, losing control over my body, nearing the climax.

"Oh, Jesus, Nacho," I gasped out as the orgasm finally hit me, crashing over my entire body and taking away my breath.

The Canarian took my face in his hands and kissed me deeply, wildly. I tried breathing in, but I couldn't. His kiss was taking my air away. It was over—the wave had passed. But no. Nacho accelerated his thrusts again, and another orgasmic tsunami washed over me. My body arched, and my muscles tensed. I cried out into his mouth, coming harder than I ever had before.

"That should be enough," he said finally, his lips stretching in a satisfied smirk. He slowed down, calming both our bodies in the process.

My head dropped to the pillow. It was fortunate that I hadn't picked a more elaborate hairstyle earlier, or I would have looked like roadkill by now.

"I'm not finished yet," he said, kissing me on the nose. "but I wanted you to catch a breath. Come to me."

He lay down alongside me, his feet next to my head, and beckoned me with a finger.

"Finish what you started."

Sixty-nine? Now? I was barely able to think straight . . .

I glanced at him in surprise and alarm and didn't move. His

arms shot out and closed around my hips as he sat me down on his face. His tongue slipped between my labia, finding its way to my clit without pause. Nacho moaned as I dropped my head, swallowing his throbbing erect cock. The caress of his tongue and the sight of his tattooed body spun the maelstrom inside me anew. Propped on one elbow, I tightened my grip on his shaft and started pumping, fucking him with my mouth and my hand. My movements were quick and jerky—chaotic—but the Canarian tensed and moaned. I silently congratulated him on his ability to concentrate on two things at a time—even with his prick deep in my throat he didn't stop pleasuring me with his tongue.

And then, after just a few heartbeats, I finally got what I had been waiting for. A stream of his hot semen spurted down my throat. He tasted sweet. Delicious. He came with a loud cry. His mouth released my pussy and his teeth bit into the skin on the inside of my thigh. I swallowed every drop, listening to the rhythm of his body. The only thing I regretted was not being able to see his green eyes as he came. I licked his shaft and stroked it until I felt the teeth on my leg releasing their grip.

"Satisfied?" Nacho asked, panting. "Did the lady of my heart finally get what she wanted?"

I lifted myself up and straddled him, wiping my lips with a finger. He was grinning. I smiled back.

"Now I am." I widened my smile, running my hand along one of his tattoos. "I waited long enough."

"I waited longer," he replied, wrapping his arms around me and pressing me to his chest. "I really want to make you happy, kiddo. But sometimes I'm afraid I might hurt you and you'll run away. Leave me."

I lifted my head and sent him a puzzled look. There was concern and fear in his eyes. He was . . . sad.

"Are you talking about Massimo?"

He dropped his eyes and played with my hair.

"Nacho. With him it was something else—"

"You've never told me what happened."

I sighed heavily as he looked at me.

"Because I know you don't really want to know. And I don't want to talk about it." I wanted to get up, but he held me tight.

"Where do you think you're going?" he asked, a bit too loud. "I'm not letting you go as long as you're sad or angry. And that's how it's going to be from now on. So stop resisting. Tell me."

His arms tightened around me when I didn't respond. "Bee . . ."

"You're making me talk about something I would rather not even think about. And right after we had sex . . ."

Nacho waited, tensing, fixing me with his eyes.

"Let me go, Nacho!" I hissed, upset with his stubbornness. I jerked away, but his grip was steel.

"Goddamn it, Marcelo!" I cried out, pushing away.

Surprised, he let me go. I jumped to my feet and grabbed my dress. The Canarian rolled to the side and propped his head on an elbow. He was still waiting for a reply. He looked at me somberly. To be honest, I didn't know why I was so angry with him. He was just concerned. But I didn't feel like talking about it. Or thinking about it, for that matter.

I put on my dress and pulled up my panties.

"Shall we go?" I asked, tidying my hair in the mirror.

"No," he replied matter-of-factly, rising from the bed. He passed by me and picked up his pants from the floor.

"We will talk now." He turned and fixed me with a cold stare.

"Now!" he snapped. For a while, I had forgotten that I was dealing with a ruthless killer.

"You won't make me talk. And I'm drunk. I don't want to talk with you after I've been drinking."

"You're not drunk anymore," he said, zipping up his trousers. "You've sobered up. I'm listening."

I halted, rooted to the spot, unable to believe what I was hearing. My gentle, tender lover was now a domineering, relentless mob boss. I narrowed my eyes, considering my options. He had a right to know the truth. He was worried for me. But at the same time, he was making me do something I didn't want to do.

"Marcelo . . ."

"Don't call me that," he growled. "You only call me that when you're angry at me. And you don't have anything to be angry about now."

I sighed, gritted my teeth, and headed toward the door. It was locked. I turned around and frowned, crossing my arms. Nacho wasn't even looking at me. I tapped my foot, and the sound of my heel hitting the floor echoed throughout the room. Even this didn't make him look my way. I took a few steps forward and faced Nacho. He was composed, serious, focused, and concerned. He looked at me, waiting.

"So?" he asked, lifting his brows.

"He raped me!" I snapped. "There! Satisfied now?" My cry reverberated across the entire house. "He fucked me in all holes! As punishment. Is that what you wanted to hear?" A cascade of unwanted tears flew down my cheeks.

The Canarian stood up and closed the distance between us, raising his arms to embrace me, but I lifted my hand to stop him. I was shivering hysterically. The last thing I wanted was for someone to touch me.

Nacho stopped a foot away and balled his fists. He said nothing. I was sobbing, choking on tears. He was choking on sudden fury. His chest was rising and falling quickly, as if he had just run a marathon. We stood like that, ensnared by our emotions. How was it possible that a paltry five minutes before, we had been grinning at each other after the best sex in our lives?

"Come." Nacho grabbed my wrist and dragged me to the door. "There's a lock in each room. You have to press a switch to exit." He pointed to a small button on the top of the door frame.

We left the room, and Nacho led me down the corridor. I was barely keeping up with his quick stride. I pulled my hand from his grip and bent down to take my shoes off, unbuckling them. Nacho crouched beside me and took them in his hand.

We passed people on our way. They were trying to stop us, have conversations, but the Canarian simply ignored them all, pushing ahead. We went two floors down, and my claustrophobia kicked in—the narrow corridor under the mansion made my head swim and my breath catch in my throat. I stopped, leaned against the wall, and dropped my eyes. Looking at the floor was supposed to calm me down. Nacho glanced at me and, seeing this wasn't another of my furious outbursts, grabbed me, lifted me up, and threw me over his shoulder. We went through a door, and he put me down. I raised my head and froze. It was a shooting range.

Nacho walked up to one of the shooting booths and handed me a pair of headphones. Next, he reached to a tall cabinet on the wall. I was lost for words. The ten-foot-tall stretch of reinforced concrete was covered with guns. I had never seen so many at once. There were machine guns, pistols, and even some things that resembled cannons—just bite-sized.

"I want one, too," I said, stretching out an arm.

Nacho watched me for a moment, considering my words. Finally, he took a pistol from the rack.

"This is a .22 Hämmerli X-ESSE. It's a good weapon. And good-looking. You should like it." He reached out a hand in which he held a gun with a raspberry-colored handle. "Semiautomatic. Backsight with vertical and horizontal control."

He reloaded the gun. "The clip has ten rounds. It's loaded. Here." He handed me the weapon. I grabbed it and thumbed the safety off before walking straight to the shooting stand.

I looked back, glancing at Nacho, positioned myself, and took off the headphones. I wanted to look like a pro. Nacho's face brightened, seeing me engaging in his passion. He pulled out another gun from the cabinet and readied himself.

"Whenever you're ready," he said, rolling the targets to the right distance.

I took a deep breath, and another one, visualizing the scene I had told Nacho about before. The night in Portugal. I'm walking back to the apartment after kissing Nacho for the first time. I see Massimo—drunk. He sees me. I felt a jolt of pain in my chest. My eyes watered. And then I was overcome by fury. Another deep breath, and I unloaded the entire clip at the piece of paper ahead, as if massacring the cardboard target could erase the pain from my mind.

"Clip," I snapped, nodding my head. "More rounds."

Nacho looked surprised, but did as I'd ordered, placing a box in front of me.

With shaking hands, I loaded the gun and shot ten more times at the target. Then I repeated the whole process another time.

"That's enough, bee," Nacho whispered. The touch of his hand brought me back to reality. His hands deftly plucked the gun from my own. "I see you needed this more than I did. Come now. I'll put you to bed."

I dropped my head and allowed him to carry me back to the bedroom.

———

Curled up in bed, I waited for Nacho to finish showering. I hadn't spoken to him in an hour. He'd washed me, changed my clothes, put me in bed. All that time, I'd just stared ahead numbly. Just like when he had first saved my life and taken me to the beach house.

"Laura," he said, sitting on the bed. "I know this is difficult for you, but I want to end it once and for all. I want to kill Massimo. But only if you allow me," he added in a deadly serious voice. "I've only ever executed people for money before. It was never personal. But this time it is. I want to take his life."

He placed hands on both sides of my head and leaned over me. "Just say yes, and the man who hurt you will disappear forever."

"No," I whispered and turned away. "If someone kills him, it's me." I pressed my face into the pillow and squeezed my eyes shut. "I had more than one chance and enough reasons. But I don't want to become what he is. And I don't want to live with a man who reminds me of him," I breathed.

A silence followed. The Canarian rose and walked away, closing the door behind him. And I fell asleep.

CHAPTER 15

I woke up with a headache, but it wasn't caused by a hangover but rather by the emotional overload I had experienced the night before. I took a look around, realizing I had slept alone. "Here we go," I muttered, grabbing a bottle of water from the nightstand.

I could finally see the entire room now in daylight. It was furnished in a modern style—a lot of rectangular shapes, mirrors, and dozens of photos. Glass mixed in with wood, metal, leather, and stone. A huge window made of a single pane of glass overlooked the ocean and the gorgeous, steep cliff. Two large gray sofas stood facing the window, as if the landscape outside were meant to be a substitute for television.

I got up and walked closer to take in the breathtaking view. And my breath was taken away indeed. Down in the garden stood Nacho. With a toddler in his arms. He hugged the child and played with it. And he wore only his loose, tattered jeans, and nothing else. Lying on a sunbed, he allowed Pablo to climb his torso and reach for his ears and nose, putting his little hands into Nacho's mouth.

"Jesus," I breathed, leaning against the window frame.

Nacho was so beautiful. He was perfect. And the sight of him with the child melted my heart, making me want the man even more. I thought about last night's events, putting my forehead to the cold glass. I had been so stupid . . . I always am when I drink. When the alcohol had evaporated, everything looked different. I felt embarrassed. *Why do I always kick up a fuss when the only thing he wants is for me to be safe?* I thought. Why did I have to keep comparing him to the man he hated the most?

I took a super-fast shower and put on Nacho's T-shirt before sprinting downstairs. I passed the door to the garden and slid on a pair of shades that I had found on a table in the hallway. The Canarian didn't see me. He was sitting with his back to the door, but as soon as I went out, he turned his head and looked straight at me. I slowed down and walked toward him, dropping my head in remorse.

"I can feel you," he said, then got up from the sunbed and kissed my forehead. "Meet Pablo, the kid who turned my world upside down."

The small blond-haired boy reached out his hands to me. On instinct, I took him in my arms. He snuggled against me, grabbing my still-wet hair.

"Oh, wow," Nacho blurted out as I kissed the little angel. "I want to have kids with you." The smile on his face was brighter than the sun.

"Stop it." I turned my back on him and went to the food-laden table. "I need to deal with my divorce, confront Olga, and talk my man out of killing my husband first." I sat Pablo in his high chair and raised my finger, continuing: "And let me be clear about something—"

"You said 'my man,'" Nacho cut me short, wrapping his arms around me. "Does this mean we're officially a couple now?" He took off my sunglasses to look me in the eyes.

"You're officially the lover of a married woman," I replied with a snort of laughter.

"He was never your husband. But I will be," he countered, grinning and putting my shades back on. "And . . . I'm sorry," he added, kissing my brow and sighing heavily. "I shouldn't have pressed yesterday."

"It was the last time," I said seriously, pulling away. I lifted a finger once more. "Marcelo Nacho Matos. It's the last time I allow you to sleep without me. Or I divorce you before you even ask for my hand." I smirked. Nacho's expression grew taut.

"So do you accept?" he asked.

"Jesus, what now?" I was puzzled.

"My proposal, of course!"

"Oh, please, Nacho. Let me get a divorce first, seriously. Get to know you a little better. Ask me another day." His face saddened. "For now, I'm starving. Where's Amelia?"

"You don't want to be with me?" he asked.

"Listen up, you tattooed brat—I want to get to know you, fall in love with you, and then let's see what happens. Is that okay?" I was getting annoyed now, but only slightly.

"I already know you're in love with me," Nacho declared, and his customary grin returned to his face. "And by the way, you look mega-sexy in my T-shirt. I want you to only wear my things from now on." He smooched the top of my head, slid his hands down the sleeves of the T-shirt, and cupped my breasts.

"You're touching her tits in front of my son?" Amelia's voice shot through the air like a whip crack. Nacho withdrew his hands and propped them on the headrest of my chair. "Poor Pablo," she said with a chuckle. "And poor Pablo's mom. Nobody touches her tits anymore."

She sent her brother a provocative glance, and Nacho wagged a finger at her.

"Don't you push me!" he growled. Astonishingly, he seemed serious. "Go play with the kid or something. But don't even dare look at a man or I'll have to kill him."

Amelia rolled her eyes and grabbed a bottle to feed Pablo.

"You wouldn't hurt a fly, Marcelo."

She stuck out her tongue and took her son in her arms. "That whole gang nonsense has gone to your head." She snorted with laughter. The Canarian took a deep breath, preparing to respond, but my hand on his thigh stopped him in his tracks. He helped himself to some scrambled eggs and, shooting angry glances at Amelia, ate them.

"You're too controlling," I said in Polish, sipping tea with milk.

"I'm not. I just don't want her to fall in love with another idiot," he said, putting his fork down. "She should focus on the kid now. And herself, too. And renovating the mansion. Not seeking thrills. She's been through a lot and should take some time to heal."

"You're so sexy when you're domineering like that," I bit my lips and leaned in closer. "I'd like to blow you right now. Slide under the table and suck you off." My hand on his thigh tightened its grip. His dick jerked awake, lifting the fabric of his pants.

"You're being indecent, Laura," Nacho cut me short, trying to keep a smile from stretching his lips. "We have a tight schedule today, so stop thinking about that. Eat up."

"I can see that something else is tight today." I grinned and clasped my hand around the tip of his erect cock.

"You're doing it again. *And* speaking Polish so I couldn't understand." Amelia rolled her eyes. "Bunch of perverts. I'm super hungover, and my libido is off the charts, so . . ."

"Enough!" Nacho slammed his fist on the table. I pulled away, shocked. "I saw that fucker hitting on you yesterday. I swear that if not for the fact that his father is a business partner of mine, I would have skinned him alive already."

"You're a bit irritable today, aren't you?" Amelia, unfazed, kept feeding Pablo. "I might have kissed him once or twice a couple years back, and you're still kicking up a fuss about it. Come on, Pablo. Your uncle's a bit too angry today to keep up a civilized conversation."

She passed by the table and leaned over so that Nacho could kiss the little boy on his head. Amelia winked at her brother and left.

"I don't like it when you're like that," I said, turning to Nacho.

"Don't be silly." He reached for a piece of bread, keeping his eyes on the table. "You love me when I'm like that. And now, since she's gone, you can drop under the table." He grinned, but as I immediately pulled away my chair and did as he had told me, the grin faded. "You're going to do this as I'm eating?" he asked, surprised, as I unzipped his pants.

"Why not? I'll keep it quick," I replied, sliding his manhood into my mouth.

And I did, though a staff member nearly interrupted us twice. I was lucky in that Nacho—when required—could sit perfectly still and focus on more than one thing at a time. The staff member hadn't even passed through the door when the Canarian shooed him away. He finished his scrambled eggs stiffly, and when he did that, I told him to at least have some juice. He choked on it a couple times, but we happily reached the end. After I was done, I sat back in my chair to finish my breakfast.

"You're impossible." Nacho sighed with his eyes closed, throwing his head back.

"What are we going to do today?" I asked as if nothing had happened.

"Fuck," he replied without a moment's pause.

"Excuse me?"

"We're going to Teide." He laughed and put on his shades. "And then we're going to fuck. Now, I have to deal with a thing. You call Olga and ask her if she spoke to Domenico."

Nacho put his hands on the edge of the table and pulled away with his chair to get up. That's when the employee who had tried interrupting us before appeared in the doorway again. He walked closer, hearing no complaint this time. There was a large package in his hands. Nacho looked at him, and the man said a few words in Spanish, handing over the box. The Canarian's eyes darted from the package to me and back again.

"This is for you," he said solemnly. He looked anxious. "I don't know where it came from, but I do know who sent it. Let me open it, bee." He looked me in the eyes and froze, waiting for my decision. I shook my head.

"It's not as if he wants to kill me, Nacho," I said, reaching for the package and placing it before me on the table to rip the paper open. "He's not a psychopath," I added, tossing away the outer layer. Inside, there was a Givenchy box. "Shoes?" I muttered with surprise and took the cover off.

The sight of what was inside made my stomach churn. I jumped away from the table and threw up on the grass, falling to my knees. My breath caught in my throat, and I trembled, practically convulsing. I felt dizzy, and my head swam as I regurgitated my breakfast. Nacho knelt at my side, holding my hair. When I couldn't vomit anymore, he offered me a napkin and a glass of water.

"Not a psychopath, you say?" He lifted me from the ground and sat me down on a chair pulled away from the table and turned around so I couldn't look at the package. "I told you I should have opened it. Fuck!" he growled, hitting his fists on the table.

I shivered, mouth agape, unable to wrap my head around what I had seen in the box. My little dog. My lovely little white fur ball.

How can a man be so cruel? How can anyone treat a defenseless animal like that? My eyes teared up.

I heard Nacho ripping more paper. I glanced his way, unsure what I was going to see. There was a letter in his hand.

"Goddamn it," he hissed through clenched teeth and crumpled it. I reached out for it. For a moment, he just looked at me, finally sticking the paper into my outstretched hand.

" 'You did the same to me . . . ,' " I read. That short text and the massacred body in the box made me puke all over again.

"Laura." Nacho's strong hands lifted me from the ground. "I'll take you to the bedroom and call a doctor."

I didn't resist when he carried me back inside the house and tucked me into bed before pressing a button on a remote to close the blinds. The room went dark. Small lamps by the bed switched on.

"I don't need a doctor," I sobbed, rolling to the side and trying to wipe the tears from my cheeks. "I'm okay. I think . . ."

I pressed my head into the pillow and looked at Nacho. He sat by my side, softly stroking my hair. "What the hell was that?" I asked, suddenly furious. "Aren't you supposed to send your enemies a horse's head instead of a cut-up dog?"

The Canarian snorted and shook his head. There was a bitter smile on his lips.

"In my world, there's the ocean, the calm, and the board." He sighed. "Nothing else. Let me repeat what I said yesterday. I can off him."

"No!" My raised voice made Nacho drop his head immediately. "But that animal was harmless and innocent. I just can't believe he could be so cruel."

"I thought you knew who you were dealing with. After he raped you." He regretted the words. I could see that. "Christ . . . I'm sorry."

I kept still for a moment, shocked into silence, before launching myself out of the bed and storming off to the wardrobe. Nacho followed me.

"Honey . . . ," he tried, but I raised my hand to shut him up.

"Laura . . . ," he stammered as I put on shorts and a T-shirt. "Wait a minute, girl!" He grabbed me by the shoulders, but I jerked away.

"Get. The. Fuck. Away. From. Me," I growled.

"And don't touch me or I'll fucking lose it," I snapped. "Why the fuck did I even tell you about what happened?!" I couldn't stop myself now. I couldn't believe he'd brought this up. "You'll keep talking about it now. Thanks, Nacho."

I put on sneakers and grabbed a bag. "Give me a car," I barked.

"You don't know the island, darling. You shouldn't drive."

"Give me the goddamned fucking keys!" I shrieked.

Nacho took a deep breath and gritted his teeth. He went to the door, and I followed, putting on sunglasses.

A moment later, we were in the garage, which was filled with various cars. Nacho keyed in a code on a cabinet and glance at me.

"Big or small one?" he asked.

"I don't care," I growled, stomping my feet impatiently.

"All right, come on. I'll set your GPS so you can find the house later." He took a set of car keys and headed deeper into the expansive garage, finally opening the door to an enormous black Cadillac Escalade. "Home One will be the apartment. Home Two is the mansion. Need anything else?"

Nacho's face was impassive. My fury was slowly turning into despair.

What was I thinking? Maybe that he'd try to control me and stop me, keeping me in the house by force. Or that he'd just fuck my brains out so I could forget the last thirty minutes. But if I didn't know what I wanted myself, how could he?

"Call Ivan if you need assistance."

He stepped out and left me with the car.

"Fucking shit," I muttered, taking a seat in the SUV. I started the massive engine and nearly rammed the other cars as I drove out of the garage. A moment later, I passed the driveway.

It was a strange feeling, knowing that nobody was following me, protecting me, or keeping their eye on me. I wasn't feeling threatened, but the image that had been haunting me since breakfast was still in the back of my head. I drove up, following signs to Teide. I needed to be alone now, and the volcano seemed like the perfect spot for that.

The drive took a little more than half an hour, but finally I pierced the clouds and found myself a parking spot with a view of the snowy summit. The air was crisp and clear, and the view itself breathtaking: an empty, stony wasteland covered in tufts of snow, and a gigantic crater in the middle of the island.

I leaned back in the driver's seat and dialed Olga.

"Do you have any fucking idea what Massimo did?!" I exclaimed the moment she picked up.

"You're on speaker. Domenico is here."

"Good! Can you tell your psycho of a brother to stop?" Silence. I closed my eyes. They were watering all over again. "He sent me a dismembered dog in a shoe box."

"Goddamn it," Domenico muttered, and Olga cried out. "I can't control him, Laura. I don't even know where he is. He left and vanished."

"I need Olga now, Domenico." I sighed. Another silence followed. "What happened today . . . Jesus, everything that's happened in the last couple days . . . I need Olga here or I'll go mad." I started sobbing uncontrollably.

"Do you know what you're asking for?" Domenico asked softly.

I could practically see his expression. "If Massimo discovers I allowed it, he'll fly off the handle."

"The fuck do I care?!" Olga snapped suddenly. "My friend needs me, Domenico, so I'm going! Be happy I even asked for your opinion. But your brother? I couldn't fucking care less!" I pictured her flailing her arms in Domenico's face.

"Do I even have a say in this?" The Sicilian sighed heavily. "I'll get her on a plane tomorrow. So tell your . . ." He paused and cleared his throat. "Tell Marcelo our plane is going to land on Tenerife. Just remember, Laura—she already has a fiancé and doesn't need another 'adventure.'"

Olga's laughter drowned him out. I heard her kissing him.

"Right then, bitch, off I go to fuck my future husband. I see he needs to hump any stupid ideas out of my head." They both said bye and hung up.

My anger dissolved. In its place came sadness. I had had my first real argument with Nacho. Or, to stick to the truth, I'd thrown a temper tantrum. It was entirely one-sided. I dialed his number and put the phone to my ear. He wasn't picking up. Was he this mad at me? I started the engine, selected Home Two, and accelerated.

I parked by the mansion and went inside in search of Nacho. The house was big and labyrinthine, so it took me no time to get lost. I called Amelia. A short chat yielded some valuable information as to the topography of the building. Five minutes later, I was saved.

"Where is your brother?" I asked Amelia as she led me down a corridor.

"You had an argument." She sighed, rolling her eyes. "That's what I thought when he stomped around the house, cursing, and you were nowhere to be seen. I think he might be at the beach house."

I halted.

A series of wonderful memories flitted through my head. The moments we had spent on the beach were the main reasons I had decided to come to Tenerife again.

"Can you set it in my GPS?" I asked, biting my lip.

"Sure thing."

Ten minutes later, I was driving away from the Matos residence again, this time downslope. The GPS said the trip would take more than an hour. I had ample time for thinking and planning what I intended to say and do when I met Nacho. Regrettably, nothing came to my mind. Was I supposed to apologize? What for? Truth be told, I had more reason to keep being angry at him, but at the same time, I had lost the confrontation by running away. As always. That was my coping mechanism, it seemed. Driving the enormous truck, I promised myself I'd never run again. And not just from Nacho. From anything. I decided that I had had my fair share of escapes already. It was time to face my demons.

When, after a long time, I finally reached the sandy stretch of land, my heart started racing. The last time I had been here, I was terrified. Then I had felt excruciating anguish at having to leave this little piece of paradise. This was where the daring kidnapper had kissed me first, and where I had fallen in love with him. Everything was exactly like I remembered: the wooden house, the grill on the porch, the beach, and the endless ocean. When I noticed his bike parked by a palm tree, I was sure Nacho was somewhere close. I went to the door and grabbed the handle, taking a few deep breaths. I should just go inside, not expecting an apology and not intending to give one. Just walk inside and see what happened next. I breathed out and passed the door.

He wasn't there. His phone was on the table, next to a half-empty beer bottle. I sipped it and gagged. It was warm. And since it was, it had probably been standing there for a while. I sighed and went outside to sit on the stairs, wondering when Nacho would be back. That's when it dawned on me: since we were in the middle of nowhere, and I planned to make up with my man, I should probably surprise him.

I went back inside and took a shower. Then, wrapped in nothing but a blanket, I sat back down on the porch. I leaned my head against the railing and watched the sea. The waves were big today. Was Nacho all right? He was an expert surfer, and it wasn't like he suddenly decided to get drowned just to spite me. I shook my head and waited. Minutes passed. Then hours. I fell asleep.

I felt wet hands pull away the blanket I had wrapped myself in. Startled and still half-asleep, I tried getting up. The hands held me down and laid me on the floor. I could see it was dark already and sighed with relief as the familiar scent of minty chewing gum reached my nostrils.

"I waited for you," I breathed as Nacho's tongue brushed against my neck.

"I like that about you," he replied and slowly slid his tongue into my mouth.

I moaned, putting my hands on his buttocks and discovering that he was completely naked. Splayed on the blanket, I pulled him closer. He was wet and salty. His muscles were taut. He must have been surfing for hours.

"I'm sorry, bee," he whispered, pulling away. "Sometimes I act stupid. But I'll learn."

"I won't run away ever again." I fully opened my eyes, staring at the dark silhouette looming above me. "Sometimes I just need to think, and I think best when I'm alone." I shrugged.

"You don't say." He grinned. "We have more in common than I thought." He kissed me again. "You'll chafe your back if we make love here," he added.

"I hope that won't be the only thing that's chafing me after we're done."

I pulled him closer.

"Knees?" he asked, rolling me over and lifting my ass. "Or . . ." He paused, stroking my buttock with a hand. ". . . we do it standing up and thus save your delicate body." Suddenly, he jerked me up. I yelped, surprised. He pushed me against a wooden column supporting the roof and spread my legs with a knee.

"You're so tiny." I could hear him smile as he kissed the back of my neck. "But we'll handle that. Wait for me." He slapped my butt and went inside, returning a moment later with some kind of a wooden platform. He planted me on top of it.

"A beer crate?" I smiled, looking down. "How creative."

"A wine crate. I ordered the cellar filled with your favorite vintage." He kissed my shoulder as his hands cupped my breasts. "I stocked the fridge . . ." I felt the hard shaft of his cock on my buttock. "The bathroom . . ."

"Why would we need wine in the bathroom?" I breathed as his fingers slid down my stomach, reaching my clitoris.

"I stocked the bathroom with cosmetics, the wardrobe with clothes, and got a high-speed Internet connection so we don't have to move out." His teeth bit into my shoulder. I inhaled through clenched teeth. "I also bought you a present, but you'll only get it when you're good and stick your little ass out for me." He pressed the base of my back with his hand. "Grab on to that," he said, taking my hand and putting it on a post.

His hand traced a line from the tips of my fingers, up my arm, and then down my shoulder and my back, to finally land on my hip.

"You have such a nice ass," he breathed, spreading my butt cheeks. "Each time I enter you, I fight not to come immediately," he added, and his cock slowly slid inside me.

Nacho moaned and tightened his grip on my hips. My hand closed on the wooden post. The slow movement of his hips and the depth he reached inside made me swoon. He picked up the pace and I squirmed, crying out with each thrust. His strong hands kept me up, clasping harder with each second. After a while, Nacho started pumping so fast the lovemaking quickly turned into a rough fuck. The passionate grunts carrying from our throats drowned out the sound of the waves splashing on the beach. The clapping of our hips ripped through the air. Nacho was very domineering. At the same time, he was tender and loving, careful and composed. I couldn't keep the orgasm at bay anymore.

"I need to see you," he gasped out when I was only seconds from what I had been waiting for.

He grabbed me, lifted me into the air, and carried me inside the living room, illuminated with pale light. He put me down on the couch by the fireplace and knelt behind me, pulling me closer and sliding inside me again. His right hand clasped around the back of my neck, and the left landed on my hip. His eyes were focused on my face. He went back to fucking.

"Oh, Jesus," I breathed, pressing my head between two pillows. "Harder!" I lifted my hips, pushing my ass back and impaling myself on his prick. The orgasm came immediately.

I cried out so loud, I drowned out all other sound.

Nacho leaned over me, pressing his torso to my back and stifled my scream with his tongue. A moment later, he came, too. Our lips joined in a passionate kiss. I don't know how long it lasted, but I lost my breath.

When he did pull away, he was still inside me. I tried opening my eyes, though I was semiconscious with bliss.

"Sleep now, bee," he breathed and gently carried me to the bed-room.

CHAPTER 16

I shifted impatiently from foot to foot, waiting by the car at the VIP terminal. It was sweltering hot outside. I had only shorts, flip-flops, and a skimpy top on, but still I was melting in the heat. A pair of tattooed arms wrapped around me. I rested my head on Nacho's shoulder. We hadn't slept much last night, and he'd taken me to the beach for a surfing lesson in the morning, so I was understandably exhausted. His lips brushed against my cheek, finding my mouth. With my head tilted, I kissed my man passionately, like a teenager in love.

"You called me here to watch you drool over that guy?" asked Olga, leaving the terminal.

I spun to face her, pulling away from Nacho. Olga looked breathtaking. She wore wide-legged linen trousers, a revealing top of the same color, and pointed stilettos. Her hair was tied in a tall, elegant bun, and she held a Chanel bag in her hand. I was rooted to the spot, wrapped in Nacho's arms.

"I called you here because we need to talk," I said finally and stepped forward to hug her. "Good to see you," I added as she kissed me on the cheek.

"I'm used to being dragged all over the world by now, so no worries." She released me and reached out a hand to greet the Canarian. "Hi there, Marcelo. Or Nacho? What should I call you?"

"Whatever you like," he said and pulled her close, smooching her on the cheek. "I'm happy to see you here, on my island. Thank you for coming."

"As if I had a choice." Olga pointed her chin at me. "She's the all-time champion of emotional blackmail. Besides, I'm getting married soon and we need to discuss the details."

Nacho sighed heavily and opened the door to the car for us.

We spent the afternoon together. I wanted Olga to get to know Nacho, so she could better understand my decision. We drank wine on the beach, watching him surf, then we had lunch in a gorgeous little bistro in the middle of nowhere, and finally we drove back to the mansion.

Nacho showed Olga to her room, kissed me on the brow, and told us it was time he did some work. I was left with my friend. I loved that about him—the fact that he gave me space and respected my needs. Allowed me to live my own life.

I was surprised and happy to discover that he had prepared a pajama party for us. We were going to spend the whole night together, the two of us. The room had been decorated with balloons with the logos of the best fashion brands, and two cute Chanel sweat suits were waiting for us on the beds. He probably hadn't picked them by himself—they were just too nice. Bottles of pink champagne were sticking out from coolers and the low coffee table bent under snacks. Colorful muffins, cotton candy, seafood, tartlets—this looked like a birthday party for a little princess. He had even ordered a jukebox and a karaoke set brought in. And if that wasn't enough, there was a jacuzzi on the terrace adjoining the bedroom, flanked by two massage tables, and a call button that would summon masseurs.

Olga stood in the middle of all this, scratching her head in disbelief.

"When he was surfing earlier today, I thought you were with him for the sex," she said after a while. "Then, when he told us about his adventures in the Caribbean and I nearly died of laughter, I thought it was because he was a kid in a grown man's body."

She looked around, gesturing widely. "But now I'm just lost for words. He might be perfect, Laura. There has to be something wrong with him."

Olga nodded knowingly.

"Yeah. Like the fact that he is the head of a Mafia family. And a paid killer." I raised a finger. "Or that his butt is covered in tattoos." I laughed as Olga's eyes widened.

"You're kidding me! Why'd you tell me that?"

"Anyway, I really haven't noticed a dark side to Nacho yet. He pampers me like a baby and at the same time gives me as much freedom as I need. I have no security detail trailing me, or at least I don't know about any. I can ride bikes and surf. If I wanted to base jump, he'd let me do it, too. He never tells me I can't do something. Never makes me do things, either. And he's only rough with his sister." I shrugged. "But she doesn't even care, so it's not harmful."

"But Massimo also used to be like that at first." Olga sent me a keen stare.

I sighed and handed her a pink sweat suit.

"Not really. Massimo used to be great, but he's also been domineering and imperious. And it's not like I'm saying I didn't have it good with him. It was nearly perfect until New Year's Eve. But however you see it, he made me do most things. I had no say in anything. The marriage, the baby, each trip . . . Whatever we did, it was always his decision." I sat down in a sofa chair and grabbed a glass.

"Now I'm free, and my man treats me like a queen and makes me feel like I'm sixteen again."

"Just like Domenico and me." Olga changed and sat down, too. "He's taking it badly. You leaving, his brother disappearing . . . Now he and Mario are taking care of business. The house is empty. Haunted." She shook her head. "I'm thinking of moving out. Domenico doesn't seem to have anything against that, so . . ." She paused, hesitating, and sipped on her wine.

"How's the company doing?" I asked.

"Good, actually. Emi takes care of everything. The collection is nearly done. All according to your guidelines. No changes on that front, but we do need to think about the future."

I nodded.

"Better tell me what's the deal with my wedding," Olga said suddenly. The thought of going back to Sicily made me want to retch. "You're my maid of honor. And Massimo was supposed to be the best man . . ."

"I don't know." I dropped my head.

"You can't do this to me!" Olga growled, lifting it by the hair. "Tell your Canarian to think of something. I don't care how, but you're coming. And Massimo might not even be back by that time. Domenico tells me he's doing a tour of Mexican brothels. Maybe he'll die of some STD."

She raised her brows with a grin.

I felt a jolt of pain in my heart. I hadn't thought of Massimo and other women before. Maybe it was a bit hypocritical of me, but I felt jealous, thinking of that now.

"Let's drink up," I said, raising my glass.

"Nuh-uh! Let's get wasted!"

Two hours and four bottles in, we were so hammered we weren't able to stand on our own two legs to change the song on the jukebox. The damned thing was jammed. So instead, we lay on the soft rug, rolling around and laughing—talking about the good old times. The conversation was rather simple, as neither of us really listened, but we both prattled over each other. At some point, Olga grabbed the edge of the table, trying to pull herself up. The whole thing toppled to the ground, along with the lamp and everything on it. The crash of broken glass sobered us up a bit, but not enough to get us on our feet. We stayed on the ground, cackling.

In an instant, the door slammed open, and Nacho barged in. He only had his sweatpants on, and there were guns in both of his hands. We froze at that sight. He looked down and saw the state we were in and grinned. "I can see you're having a good time, girls."

We made an attempt at making serious expressions, but, surrounded with bottles and bits of food, we looked far from dignified. Giggling, we watched Nacho as he wrapped some cotton candy around his finger.

"Need some help getting up?" he asked, amused, and we nodded.

First, he went for Olga, lifting her up and carrying her to bed without breaking a sweat. Then, he returned for me, hugged me closely, and sat on the other bed without releasing me from his embrace.

"What's up with you two?" He placed a kiss on my brow and glanced at Olga. "You're going to be so hungover tomorrow, you know?"

"I think I'm gonna throw up," my friend muttered.

"Would you like me to carry you to the bathroom or will a bucket suffice?" Nacho grinned and tucked me in.

"Bucket," Olga spluttered, rolling to the side.

Nacho brought everything she could have needed: a bucket, some water, and a towel. Seeing that she had fallen asleep in the meantime, he sat on my bed and brushed the hair away from my forehead.

"You okay?" he asked. I nodded, afraid that if I opened my mouth, I'd throw up, too.

"Next time I'll get you juices and vegetables." He kissed me on the tip of my nose. "I see you two like to party hard."

I don't know how long he stayed there, watching me, but when I went under, I could still feel his hand stroking my hair.

———

"I think I'd like to die now." Olga's voice woke me up. At the same time, I felt the blow of a sledgehammer on my temple.

"Oh, fuck me," I moaned, reaching out for a bottle of water. "This was such a bad idea."

"A bucket? How nice," Olga said, surprised. "Oh, I seem to have barfed in it," she added. I snorted with laughter, but as soon as I did so, the sledgehammer smashed into my head again.

"Nacho brought it in for you," I said, trying to keep still. "Remember?"

She groaned and shook her head slowly.

"I think we wrecked something," she muttered.

I looked at the ruin of the table, the lamp, and part of the buffet. "We ruined something, all right. And Nacho came in to rescue us, guns blazing. And he did rescue us, but not like that. He carried us to bed."

"How nice of him," Olga whispered and took a gulp of her water. "Is there a baby monitor by my bed? Your man was listening in on us." I looked the way she pointed and realized she was right.

"You know what? I think that if he really wanted to spy on us, we'd never know."

It took us an hour to crawl out of bed. We wanted to shower but decided against it. With our shades on and still wearing the pink sweat suits, we headed downstairs to the garden. The sight of

Nacho with Pablo in his arms melted both our hearts. He was pacing around the patio with the boy sleeping, snuggled against his chest, with a phone in hand. Olga and I sighed, and Nacho turned and smiled.

"I think I'm in love, Laura," said Olga, salivating a bit.

"I know, right?" I sighed. "With that kid, he's just impossible."

Swaying on our feet, we headed to the table. Nacho finished his call and put Pablo gently on a couch standing in the shade of a tree, a couple feet away.

"He's finally asleep," he said and kissed me on the top of the head, showing us to our seats.

There were plates prepared for us. They had pills on them. And some green goo in glasses.

"I suggest you drink up." He slid two chairs out. "Unless you prefer an IV?"

He laughed and smooched me again as I took a seat. "Those are electrolytes and glucose mixed in with something awful." A grin split his face. "But the doctor said it'll fix you up."

"What's this?" asked Olga, putting the baby monitor next to her glass.

Nacho rounded the table and sat facing us.

"This is Pablo's baby monitor." He tried and failed to keep a straight face. "You fell from your bed three times, Olga. And each time I heard a commotion from your room I ran to check up on you. So after the umpteenth time I decided to make my life easier and planted that monitor there so I would know if you were okay and asleep." He laughed.

"Fucking hell, what an embarrassment." Olga groaned, swallowing a bunch of pills.

"It wasn't so bad. You know what was more embarrassing? That time you two tried leaving that restaurant back in Lagos." He reclined in his chair and crossed his arms behind his head. "I really wanted to help back then, but I couldn't. After all, I was still just a dream." He winked at me, and I chuckled.

"You saw that? God . . ." My friend had sunglasses on, but I could imagine she was rolling her eyes.

"The behavior of your friend tells me a lot about yourself," he said to Olga, keeping his eyes on me. "But you're young and like to party. It's nothing bad. And the sight of a hot girl in a pink sweat suit throwing up like there's no tomorrow was kind of funny, I have to admit."

Olga grabbed a pancake and threw it at Nacho.

"I like him," she said in Polish, glancing at me. "I really like him."

"Thanks," Nacho replied in Polish, and Olga face-palmed, suddenly recalling that Nacho could understand us.

"And I like you, too," he added. "Now, bottoms up, ladies. That green goo isn't going to drink itself." He laughed and pointed a thumb at the house. "The bucket is over there, if you need it."

———

Olga stayed for another few days. She met Amelia and immediately fell in love with her. We covered for her when she drank wine with us, and when one time Nacho discovered that, I distracted him with a quick blow job at the shooting range. Amelia might have been an adult and technically could do whatever she wanted, but Nacho treated her like a child and banned her from most fun activities. I learned how to surf, but Olga complained that the wet suit was too small, and the board too big and heavy. So she tried it once and never repeated the experience. While I played in the water, she accompanied Amelia and Pablo. I had everything I could ever want: my best friend, the sun, and a man who took up more and more space in my heart by the day. I couldn't tell him that, of course. If he got too complacent, he'd stop sucking up to me. And then everything would change.

The last evening, we were having dinner in one of the restaurants by the shore. Amelia stayed with Pablo, but I knew that it was really Nacho who had sent her away. He wanted to talk. We finished our dessert, and he sighed heavily.

"All right. Let's talk about what happens in a week's time," he said humorlessly, putting his napkin down. "I won't lie, I'd prefer if Laura didn't go to Sicily. But I can't tell her not to." I placed a hand on his thigh and sent him a grateful look. "I'd like to discuss her safety with Domenico. I can't imagine her going without my men. At least eight people. And no alcohol." He breathed in and looked at me. "I understand it's your wedding, but I want her to be as safe as possible. You'll have a party here afterward. Or anywhere else in the world, for that matter. Just not there." His voice remained soft and composed, but he wouldn't take no for an answer.

"Why can't you go with us and protect her as one of my guests?" Olga asked, putting her glass down.

"It's not that simple." He sighed and wiped down his face. "We're criminal organizations, but we have a code. And the rules are sacrosanct. I work with many other families who also do business with Massimo. My presence on Sicily would be seen as too ostentatious. And disrespectful to the Torricelli clan. The other groups wouldn't take it as me caring for my woman, but as an act of war." He shrugged. "It's bad enough I took his wife away. They won't overlook that. So dial Domenico, please, and ask him if we can talk about security measures."

Olga did as he asked and handed the phone to Nacho, who excused himself and walked toward the beach.

"You told him that Massimo probably won't show up at the wedding?" she asked, sipping wine.

"Yes, but it did little to calm him. And it's not as if we're sure. Even Domenico doesn't know if his brother would be back in time. And Nacho likes to play it safe."

Around twenty minutes later, the Canarian returned and gave Olga her phone.

"Your battery is nearly dead," he said and waved at a waiter before ordering another beer. "So, this is how it's going to play out. You'll take my plane to Sicily, Laura. I can't pilot this time. You'll stay at a house I bought and be under the protection of several dozen men. Though that's nothing when compared with Torricelli's army." He took my hand and looked me in the eyes. "Darling, I know this is going to sound bad, but you can't eat or drink anything during the wedding. You can only try what your security personnel offer you."

He glanced at Olga. "I trust Domenico and know he won't do anything, but his people may have other orders. And we don't want all hell to break loose. Please understand me."

I put my hand on his back and kissed him on the temple.

This was costing him a lot.

"I'd like you to return to Tenerife on Sunday morning. Let's just get through Saturday and everything will be okay." He smiled.

"All right," Olga chimed in. "But can she help out with the prep-arations?"

"Yes, but I told Domenico it would have to be on neutral ground. Not in the mansion. It's a compromise. We all need to make conces-sions." He sent Olga a stark look.

"And it's all my fault," I said.

"I just had to change my life and ruin everything for everyone else while I was at it. Maybe we should . . ."

"Don't you dare!" Olga snapped, raising a hand. "You'll be safe. I'll make sure of that. If something happens to you, I'll become a widow right after I marry Domenico. I'll kill him if he lets something happen to you." She nodded with finality. "Now get that waiter over here and let's have another bottle."

I wasn't happy. I felt guilty. Even alcohol wouldn't be able to soothe me. The two people most important to me were now sitting across the table and talking, and the only thing I wanted was to burst out crying. Nacho felt my mind was somewhere else. He decided to make me feel better. When his numerous customary tricks failed, he got up and left the table without a word. We both followed him with our eyes.

He walked to the small stage and the waiter passed him a violin. I couldn't help myself and grinned widely. He saw it and winked at me.

"No shit! He's going to play?" Olga asked, dumbstruck.

The first sounds of his music reached our ears. The other guests grew silent. "All of Me" by John Legend. Nacho was trying to tell me something with a song again. This time it was a declaration of love. Olga sat hypnotized, and my man played for me, keeping his eyes fixed on mine. When it was time for the chorus and the notes climbed higher, my eyes watered. I couldn't control them. Instead, I allowed the tears to flow freely. He saw it and knew they weren't tears of sadness. Keeping his eyes on me, he caressed me with the beautiful sounds, until he reached the end of the song. Despite it lasting a good few minutes, I felt it was decidedly too short. The song slowed down and faded away to silence. People started clapping their hands, and the Canarian bowed and returned the violin to the waiter, patting the man on the back.

"'Cause all of me loves all of you." Nacho repeated the first line of the chorus and kissed me.

We stayed this way for a minute, ignoring Olga, who was sitting with her jaw slack, before Nacho took a seat at his chair.

"More wine, Olga?" he asked, lifting the bottle.

My friend nodded dumbly, her mouth agape.

———

The next day, Olga and I said our farewells as if we were never to see each other again. Standing on the tarmac at the airport, we both cried. Nacho had to drag me away back into the terminal. When finally he succeeded, he wrapped his arm around me and led me to his extravagant car.

"I have to leave for Cairo," he said. "I'd like you to go with me."

"Why would you go there?"

"A commission," he said matter-of-factly.

"Oh."

"We won't stay long. Two days, tops." He closed the door and started the engine.

"Two days to kill a man?" I was baffled. He smiled.

"Darling, the preparations always take longer than the act itself. But I only go there to keep an eye out so that nothing goes wrong and then to pull the trigger." He paused for a while.

"Although this time I think I'll also press some buttons," he added, grinning.

"I don't get how you can smile at the thought of killing another human being," I said, shaking my head.

Nacho drove off the road and stopped the car. I sent him a startled look.

"Don't ask questions if you don't want to know the answers." His eyes were kind, and there was a slight smile on his lips. "And best not to try to understand it. It doesn't make sense. It's just my job. I go where they want me and do what they tell me. I'll just say this: these are not good men."

I nodded.

"So. Want to go for a swim?"

My eyes widened in surprise at the sudden change of subject, and I breathed in, calming myself down. The sight of dead men was nothing new to me at that point, but at the same time, I couldn't just let it go. What was I supposed to do? I had known for ages that Nacho was far from innocent.

I startled myself, realizing what I was thinking about. But living among men like Massimo and Nacho for so long had changed my point of view.

On the way, I quickly realized we were driving to our beach house.

The ocean was very turbulent, but Nacho decided I'd cope with the taller waves. I was still swimming on a board twice as large as his, but I trusted him when he said it wasn't time for a small one yet. I loved his lessons, but what I loved even more was simply watching him surf. After what he had told me back in the car, however, I wasn't in a good frame of mind, but as soon as I relaxed a bit and took in the magnificent view, I paddled toward the breaking waves. I spun and waited, watching the ocean. Finally, there it was—the perfect wave. I burst into motion and stood up on my board. Nacho was shouting something. I couldn't hear him over the crash of the waves but was too happy to be keeping my balance to care. Suddenly, the incoming wave broke right behind me, collapsing onto my head and back and pushing me under. I kicked out with my feet, trying my best to swim to the surface, but the leash strapped to my ankle had knotted, limiting my range. I couldn't move. The waves kept on coming, dragging me back and forth underwater. I lost my orientation. Which way was up? I panicked and started thrashing until I felt the board hit my head. My ears rang, and my eyes teared up. Out of the blue, a pair of strong arms appeared from the darkness. They grabbed me in a tight lock and lifted me up, throwing me over the board. Nacho leaned over me and detached the strap that had been constraining me. Meanwhile, my yellow board floated toward the shoreline.

"Are you all right?" he asked, panting. He scanned me with his eyes, terrified. "You have to keep track of where the line is. It can knot and tangle."

"You don't say," I gasped out, spitting out a mouthful of salty water.

"I think it's enough for today. Come on. I'll feed you." He laid me down on his board and started swimming to the shore, dragging me.

"I'm not that hungry. I just had a drink."

Nacho slapped me on the butt playfully, as I calmed my breathing. I felt safe with him.

He started the grill and focused on preparing his usual set of delicacies, wearing the same clothes he had that first night, many months ago. I watched his bare torso and the buttocks revealed by the loose tattered jeans.

"I remember you saying that you only wanted to fuck me."

He turned my way.

"Why?"

"What was I supposed to say?" he asked, shrugging. "I was falling in love with you and hoped that if I hurt you, you'd distance yourself from me. This way, I wouldn't end up ruining our lives. And you called me names when you left."

He kissed me on the nose. "That was the first time a woman said no to me. I didn't really know how to react." He stood up and took a sip of beer.

"Hey, we haven't talked about your past yet," I said, lifting my brows. "Let's hear it, Mr. Matos. What was your love life before?"

"I think something is burning on the grill," he said quickly and practically ran toward the barbeque.

"Oh, no you don't!" I shot up and followed him. "You won't leave me with nothing. Now talk."

I smacked him on the butt and crossed my arms, waiting.

"I've never been in a relationship, if you really want to know."

I pressed against his back as he pretended to flip the food on the grill. "I told you back in December. I always wanted a woman unlike any other. And I found one." He turned around, then kissed my forehead and held me like that for a long while. "We need to talk about what happened. You know when."

"There's nothing to talk about, Nacho. Everything was an accident. If you need to know if I blame you, the answer is no. This is how it was meant to be."

I went quiet for some time, listening to the beating of Nacho's heart.

"Do I regret losing my baby?" I continued. "I don't even know what it is to be a mother. The only thing I'm certain of is that everything in life happens for a reason. And since we don't have a time machine, it makes no sense to think about what-ifs." I climbed to my toes and kissed his chin. "I can tell you what I feel now."

Nacho's eyes widened.

"I'm happy, and I wouldn't change anything. I like spending time with you. I feel safe and . . ." I paused, careful not to say too much.

"And?" he prompted.

"And I think this time the fish really is burning." I kissed the colorful tattooed skin on his torso and went inside to refill my glass.

We ate in silence, stealing glances at each other and smiling. There was no need for words. Gestures sufficed. When he fed me, delicately brushing his fingers against my lips, shivers went down both our spines. It was magical, romantic, and completely new to me. I put the fork down and realized I had downed a whole bottle of wine. I felt a little dizzy but not yet drunk, so I decided to get another one. Nacho shot up, took my hand, and led me to the beach instead. Curious, I didn't resist, following him into the darkness, listening to the waves crashing on the sand.

It was completely dark outside the radius of the house's lights. Nacho released my hand and reached down for his zipper. He threw off his trousers and turned to me without a word, taking off my top before kneeling to pull down my briefs. I was left completely naked. He took my hand again and led me to the water. It was warm, soft, and black as the night. It was scary, but he was there and knew what he was doing. Wrapping his arm around my waist, he lifted me up and walked deeper in. When the water reached his shoulder blades, Nacho stopped and kept still for a long while, listening to the water.

"I want to spend the rest of my life with you, bee," he said and interrupted me as I was about to cut in. "I know what you're going to say. But I wanted you to know this. You don't have to say anything," he added quietly, pulling me closer. His lips hovered an inch away from mine. His minty breath was overpowering. "I can feel you, Laura." His tongue slid into my mouth. I pressed myself even closer to him, wrapping my legs around his hips. "The two things I really love . . . the ocean and you."

Nacho's hand cupped my butt as he entered me.

"Mine," I whispered as he caressed me with another kiss.

The water we were standing in made my body feel weightless. He could do as he pleased. He slid deeper inside, passionately, and I felt him with each molecule of my body. I threw my head back and looked into the sky. It was full of stars. Nothing could compare to this moment. It was perfect: him inside me, the warmth, the soft touch of the water . . .

Nacho pulled away a fraction, laid me down on the surface of the ocean, and slowly, steadily touched my breasts and then fingered my clitoris. He pinched my nipples softly, looking into my eyes, making me burn with desire.

As I was nearing a blissful orgasm, he turned me over with one quick motion and impaled me again with his bulging erection. I sat over him now. Such a position would be impossible were we out of the water. With one hand, he gripped my breast. The other one drew slow circles around my sweet spot. His teeth bit into the back of my neck, my shoulders, my arms. His hips undulated with the waves. I felt the coming explosion down inside me as my insides, prodded by his manhood, started to rhythmically tighten around him. I moaned and rested my head on Nacho's shoulder. He knew—or rather felt—what was coming. His pace quickened.

"Relax now," he whispered to my ear. "Let me bring you ecstasy." Those words did it. I bit my nails into the arm holding my breast and orgasmed.

"I need to see you," Nacho breathed when I was nearly done, and rolled me over again, facing me.

He moaned, kissing me hungrily. Swayed by emotions and turned on as much as it was humanly possible, I came again. This time, he joined me, spilling his hot seed inside me.

We kept still then, looking into each other's eyes. I wanted time to stop forever. So that there would be no wedding, no Massimo, no Mafia, and nothing that could ruin what was between me and this man in this moment.

Keeping me in his strong arms, Nacho turned around and slowly walked back to the beach.

"No," I breathed, hugging him closer. He stopped.

"I don't want to go back to life. Let's stay here. I want nothing else. If we stay here, time will stop. Nothing else will happen."

Nacho pulled his head away and looked me in the eyes. His gaze pierced through me, reaching my soul.

"I'll be with you, bee. Don't be afraid." He pressed me closer and left the ocean.

Putting me down on the ground back at the porch, he wrapped a towel around me and took my hands in his. Next, we took a shower, rinsing the salty water off our skin. After that, Nacho gave me one of his T-shirts and tucked me into bed and lay on top of me, his warmth familiar and comforting. He fell asleep with his head snuggled in my hair.

———

I stretched out and reached out with a hand to hug my man, but his half of the bed was empty. Startled, I snapped open my eyes and looked around. There was a phone on his pillow and a card saying, *Call me.* I grabbed the phone and dialed Nacho.

He picked up at once.

"Get dressed and come to the beach," he said.

I didn't feel like getting out of bed already, but that commanding tone of voice . . . I stretched out once more and got up. I brushed my teeth and put on shorts and a white T-shirt (no bra) and a pair of Converse sneakers. Why would I need anything more? I was comfortable here. This was our hideaway—I could just as well have stayed naked. With my hair tied into a messy bun, making sure that some strands fell over my face, I put on sunglasses and went outside.

Nacho was standing by the house, next to two black horses. I smiled.

"You steal those?" I asked with a chuckle and walked over to him. He kissed me.

"Storm and Lightning are their names. They're ours."

"Ours?" I repeated, surprised. Nacho grinned. "Do we have more?"

"I'm sure there are some . . ." He paused, thinking. "There's exactly twenty-three more. Twenty-five in total, but there will be even more."

He patted the animal, and it snuggled its head against his torso. "These are Friesian horses. Cold-blooded Dutch animals. Very strong. Historically, they were used as cavalry horses. They're great for carriages, but we'll ride them today. Now come on."

My huge black horse had a long mane and a beautiful, thick tail. It looked like an enormous fairy-tale pony.

"How did you know I could ride?" I asked, taking the reins.

"I felt it in your movements," he replied, raising his eyebrows with amusement.

I put my leg into the stirrup and bounded off the ground, sitting in the saddle. Nacho bobbed his head, watching me. I was surprised I hadn't needed any help getting on the horse. I hadn't ridden for a long time, but it's probably like riding bikes—you don't forget how to do it. I clicked my tongue and jerked on the reins, making the horse trot in place and turn around.

"Want to check if I can do rising trot?"

I snapped the reins, cried out, and the horse launched itself forward in a canter.

The beach was completely empty and very wide. Mine to do as I pleased. I turned around and looked on as Nacho mounted his horse with a grin and followed me. I didn't intend to race him, so I reined the horse in and slowed it down to a trot. Nacho quickly reached us.

"Well, well," he said with a fond smile. "I didn't know you could do that."

"You thought this would be another thing you could teach me?"

"If I'm to be honest, yes." He nodded and laughed. "But I can see it's you who will have to teach me a few tricks."

We rode slowly along the wet beach. I didn't even know what time it was, though it must have been early. It wasn't hot yet, and the sun was still low over the horizon.

"I was about ten years old when Dad first took me to a stud

farm." I smiled at the memory. "My mom was hysterical, of course. She didn't like seeing me anywhere near horses. I was too small and they were too big, she said. I could get hurt. But Dad ignored her, as usual, and kept taking me there to train. So I can ride. I don't have many opportunities to do it, though." I patted the black mare. "Do you breed them?"

"They relax me," Nacho replied with a calm smile. "Mother used to love them. It was exactly the other way round with my parents. She taught me how to ride. After she passed away, I couldn't bring myself to visit the farm for a long time, but when Father declared that he was going to sell the horses, I promised to take care of them. It later turned out it was a rather lucrative business and even the big boss himself warmed to the thought of having horses."

He sighed and shook off the memory. "So you see, my beautiful, we have a few ponies to ride on." Nacho flashed one of his spectacular grins and shot forward in a gallop.

He wasn't a man who kept things to himself. You asked him anything, and he answered. There were some emotions inside him, however, that he kept hidden. Those two natures—the two souls within him—intrigued me. He really was the most extraordinary man I had ever met. I smiled, satisfied that he was mine, and followed.

CHAPTER 17

We spent three days in Cairo. I thanked God we didn't have to stay longer. I had never experienced sweltering heat like that. Nacho had to "work," so I had a lot of time to myself. Egypt was the first time Nacho didn't allow me my freedom—I had to take Ivan with me wherever I went. He wasn't the talkative type, but at least he replied patiently to my many questions. We saw the pyramids, but my claustrophobia didn't allow me to go inside. We went to a mosque, to the Egyptian Museum, and shopping, of course. Poor Ivan kept very calm and impressively patient. I rewarded his stoicism with an afternoon at the pool.

Having spent some time in Cairo and its vicinity, I became convinced that Egypt wasn't a country friendly to women like me—the word "women" being the key here. The religious traditions of the locals restricted women's rights too much. A lot of things were prohibited. I couldn't believe just how much I couldn't do. It was very difficult to accept.

The worst thing in this surprising country and its unfamiliar culture was the institution of the "guardians of morality." According to the law, you risk the death penalty for sleeping with someone else's spouse. That was frightening, to say the least. I had a lover, after all. The feeling of being threatened at each step followed me wherever I went. The first day, Nacho spent a full hour begging me to cover my shoulders and knees to at least try to blend in with the crowd. I only listened so he'd stop nagging. But he was Christian. If he were Muslim, he could have hit me for insubordination. It wouldn't be a problem if we stayed in a tourist town, but the capital had its customs. At least the weather was pleasant. It was hot and sunny, and the sky was blue and cloudless. After a day in the sun, I had a wonderful tan. The water in the Four Seasons hotel pool was pleasantly chilly, and the staff didn't seem to mind that I liked to sunbathe topless. The dress that was waiting for me on Sicily was so revealing that I simply couldn't wear a top—I needed to avoid tan lines.

That didn't seem to convince Ivan, who called Nacho immediately after I stripped. I told him to keep to his business and promised him an action-packed night, then returned to my sunbathing. It was good to know that Nacho wouldn't show up out of the blue, shaking with fury and commanding me to put something on.

———

When we finally returned to Tenerife, I realized it was nearly time to leave again. I had two days. The prospect of seeing everything that I had left behind filled me with dread. On the other hand, if I was able to nick some baubles from my wardrobe, the whole trip might be worthwhile. Olga had promised that she'd at least pack the things I had brought from Poland.

Nacho couldn't settle down on Friday morning. He paced around the apartment nervously. I had never seen him stressed out like that before. He slammed the fridge door, yelled at people, and at one point stormed out, only to come back in a minute later. I tried staying out of his way. I packed my small suitcase, took it downstairs, and left it by the wall.

"Fucking shit!" Nacho bellowed and stopped pacing, fixing me with a glare. I raised an eyebrow, keeping my calm.

"I'm not going to let you go. I shot that man a couple weeks ago, and now I'm supposed to let you go to his island? Not going to happen."

I shook my head, observing his fury.

"Olga will understand. She'll forgive you. I can't track that fucker!" he complained and took a deep breath to continue.

"Darling," I cut in, taking his hands in mine. "She doesn't have any other friends. I'm her maid of honor. Nothing is going to happen. Don't worry. We have everything under control. I'll stay at your house with your men. We'll spend her bachelorette party drinking wine in our bedroom. And the next day we'll dress up, she'll marry Domenico, and I'll be back. Okay?"

He sighed, dropping his arms limply. His helplessness melted my heart. My eyes teared up. There was no way to help him. I couldn't let my friend down.

"I'm going to be all right, Nacho, okay?" I lifted his chin, making him look me in the eyes. "I talked to Olga and Domenico. Massimo has vanished. Domenico's trusted people will protect us. And your guys will, too. Please stop worrying." I pressed myself to him and forced my tongue into his mouth. He was in no mood for that. He hadn't touched me for two full days. I didn't care and didn't intend to leave without a good fuck. I spun him round and shoved him against the wall, grabbing his wrists. Just like he used to do with me. His eyes were full of surprise as I slid down, reaching for his zipper.

"I don't want to," he groaned, trying to stop me.

"I know," I replied. "But your cock seems to disagree." I poked his growing penis.

He bent down and wrapped his strong arms around me, lifting me into the air. Holding me by the elbows, Nacho carried me through the room to the kitchen.

He laid me down on the island. Roughly. With a single, fast motion, he unbuttoned my shorts, tore them off, and threw them aside. With one hand, he pulled me closer to him, freeing his bulging cock with the other.

"You've done it now," he hissed, smiling.

"I hope so," I retorted and bit my lip, waiting for him to impale me.

This time, Nacho was not gentle. As I'd hoped he wouldn't be. I felt his frustration and anger—all his boiling, turbulent emotions. He was passionate, brutal, relentless. Perfect. He took me on the kitchen counter, fucking me in all possible positions, but underneath it all there was tenderness and love. He listened and felt me. His every movement was for me. There was no pain and no uncontrolled aggression. Only his own feelings he wanted me to experience. Was it right for me to provoke him to such roughness? Maybe not, but since he could act like that, it was probably a part of him in the first place. Some time later, we stood on the tarmac of the airport, embracing each other. I didn't want him to let me go, and he didn't seem to want that, either. The takeoff was delayed. Nacho cupped my cheeks, looking into my eyes and kissing me every so often. He said nothing. He didn't have to. I knew perfectly well what was happening in his head.

"I'll be back in two days," I whispered.

"Listen to me, bee . . . ," he began and paused. His voice froze me in place. "If something goes bad . . ."

I put a finger to his lips, silencing him.

"I know." I stuck my tongue into his mouth, and he lifted me in the air without breaking the kiss. "Remember—I'm yours," I said as he finally released me. Walking to the plane, I knew that if I so much as glanced back, the trip would be off. And Olga would kill me.

I swallowed a tranquilizer pill and took a deep breath, stepping inside the flying death trap. I tried my best to stop thinking about the flight, and . . . I succeeded. My thoughts returned to the man I'd left on the tarmac. He looked sad. Or maybe angry. With his hands in his pockets and a white tight-fitting T-shirt clinging to his muscular body, he'd looked breathtaking. I'd wanted to jump right back out of the plane. I don't think I had ever wanted anything so badly. To just run and throw myself into his arms. Forget about everything. And I'd nearly done it. If it were about anyone else, I would have. But it was Olga's wedding. She had always been there for me. This was my chance to pay her back.

A flight attendant walked over with a glass of champagne, which I snagged from the platter and downed. Mixing drugs and alcohol wasn't the best idea, but I didn't care.

When I left the terminal, the sun was setting on Sicily. I got into a car. It was probably armored. Another one stood in front of it and two more behind. Even the president of the USA didn't have this much security. My phone rang as soon as I switched it on. I talked to Nacho the whole drive. We spoke about nothing in particular, just chatting, so I didn't have to think about where I was. The sight of the smoky summit of Mount Etna brought me back to reality, though. There were moments when the nervousness took my breath away. Fortunately, the cars took a turn off the highway before we reached Taormina and drove up the slope of the volcano, finally parking by a tall wall. My eyes bulged. It was a fortress. The building was so unlike anything else Nacho owned.

"What is this castle?" I asked as Nacho was prattling on about his surfing adventures.

"Oh, so you're there." He laughed. "I know it's a bit too much like a military base, but at least it's defensible. My people know what they're doing, and they know the terrain. You'll be safer than in a bunker there." His voice grew serious. "Is Ivan driving?"

I confirmed.

"Listen to me, bee—do as he says at all times. He knows his job."

"Come on! Don't be paranoid, baldie," I joked.

"Baldie?" He burst out in laughter. "I'll grow my hair long, and you'll see just how awful I can look. Now. Go get some dinner. You haven't eaten anything since breakfast. Apart from my dick, of course."

I heard his amusement and giggled in delight that his humor was back.

"I spoke to Domenico," Nacho continued. "Olga will be there in an hour. The whole residence is at your disposal. Have a good time."

I pocketed the phone, thinking about how perfect my Nacho was. Ivan opened the door. The house was huge. It had two floors and was surrounded with a gorgeous garden. Neatly trimmed bushes lined little alleyways meandering among rich vegetation. I wasn't sure if this was the safest place on Earth, but since a paid killer had vouched for it, who was I to disagree? What was most surprising about the house was that it stuck out like a sore thumb. It was nothing like its surroundings. It was modern and angular, and had dozens of terraces without any kind of railings. They reminded me of open drawers. A blindingly white spaceship of a home.

All the men stepped out of their vehicles. I felt cornered. There were dozens of them. More and more showed up, poking their heads out from around corners. There were some inside the house, too, and on the walls, patrolling. A veritable army. Was all this really necessary? I guessed so. After all, I knew who could appear out of nowhere and take me.

"Don't be afraid," Ivan told me. "Sometimes Marcelo likes to overdo it." He chortled and led me inside.

Just as I had suspected, the house had a very modern interior. Glass, metal, and angular shapes everywhere. There was a grand living room with a high ceiling downstairs. It had a white marble floor and a shallow pool right next to the sofa. Then a twelve-person table and some round poufs. The view from the large glass wall was beautiful—I could see the slope of the volcano and the terrace. On the right, there was a spacious kitchen. Right. My man loved to cook, and he only wanted the very best quality. The fireplace was a gigantic rectangular hole in the wall. With the press of a button, it started a pillar of fire. I had my thoughts about what it could really be used for, so with growing trepidation, I decided to leave it alone. I went upstairs. On the second floor there was a large open space with glass walls. *No privacy*, I thought. It was then that Ivan pressed a button and all the walls turned milky white. The furniture in each bedroom consisted of a single bed and a TV. Each bedroom also had its own bathroom and wardrobe.

Led by my caretaker, I reached the end of the corridor. He opened a door, revealing a beautiful, cozy, and comfortable Scandinavian-décor bedroom. A large, white wooden bed stood in the middle. Right next to it were two soft, cream-colored armchairs on a fuzzy rug. This had to be the main bedroom.

Pictures of Amelia, Pablo, and Nacho stood on the dresser. And then . . . a picture of me. Intrigued, I took it in my hand. I didn't know that picture. I was blond and . . . pregnant. This had to be a frame from a video. I sat down, looking at the photo of Nacho.

"We seem to have cameras at the house," I muttered to myself. That wasn't surprising. I placed the photo by my bed, so Nacho's green eyes were the first thing I saw every morning.

It was strange to be on Sicily but have your heart back on Tenerife. If several months back someone had told me that I would be where I was now, I'd never have believed it.

"Let's get fucked up!" I heard Olga's voice from outside.

"Greetings, bitch!" She beamed, hugging me. I felt a sudden calmness fall over me.

"I'm joking, of course. We can't get wasted, but we can take a sip or two. I need to look like a million dollars tomorrow."

"I do know that," I said with a smile, leading her to the house. "Nacho took good care of us."

"How're things?" I asked, wrapping my arm around Olga's shoulders as we walked to the terrace.

"Everything's perfect. I don't even have to do anything. I have people for everything." She stopped at the edge. "By the way, why are there so many? Do we need all that? They patted me down before we left. Didn't look in my ass, but that's about the only place they missed."

I shrugged apologetically.

We didn't get drunk that evening, only sipped on the champagne. We talked about nothing in particular, mainly reminiscing about the previous year and wondering how our lives had changed in that time. When Olga talked about Domenico, I felt her confidence. She loved him. In her weird way. They understood each other, fooled around like buddies, argued like an old couple, and fucked like new lovers. They were perfect for each other. He was seemingly soft and conciliatory, but whenever she went over the top, he immediately transformed into a furious, crazy bastard. And that made her love him even more. Their love was undeniable.

On Saturday morning, we went to the hotel where we were supposed to get ready for the ceremony. Sitting in the barber chair, I sipped from a water bottle Ivan had given me. We'd also brought juice, iced tea, and a whole crate of other stuff. Nacho hadn't called me at all until morning, when his sweet laughter woke me up. He'd reminded me that it was just another day until we would see each other again. If he could, he would never hang up the phone, but he wanted me to feel as free as it was possible. So instead of calling me, he pestered Ivan. The poor man picked up his phone every fifteen minutes, and I could see his jaw working each time he had to assure his boss that everything was going smoothly. He had probably never seen Nacho this paranoid, but the Canarian hadn't exactly been used to leaving things to chance before. He was a perfectionist and preferred to keep awake for two full days instead of letting anything go wrong.

"Jesus fucking Christ, Laura, I'm asking you for the third time!" Olga's voice got my attention. The makeup artist nearly gouged my eye out with his brush as I snapped my head back to look at her.

"Stop yelling at me," I growled. "What do you want?"

"Isn't this bun too tall? And too smooth?"

She rubbed at her hair, trying to arrange it better. "It doesn't look good, does it? We need something else. I look terrible. I'm going to wash it all off and start all over. It makes no sense! I don't want to get married after all!" she complained, panicking. She shook me, her hands clenched around my shoulders.

"Why would I want to lose my freedom? There's so many guys on this planet. And he'll get me pregnant sooner or later . . ." She was spewing out words like machine gun bullets, and her face grew deathly pale.

I raised an arm and slapped her in the face. Hard. She piped down at once, glaring. The staff went absolutely silent. All eyes were on me.

"Enough?" I asked calmly.

"Yeah. Thanks," she replied in a whisper, sitting back down and taking a deep breath. "Yeah, let's just lower the bun, and it's going to be okay."

An hour later, Emi herself put Olga's dress on her. That was strange, to say the least, considering that Olga had taken away her man. I was relieved to see that my disappearance had helped them make up, and now the two were inseparable. Emi finished, and I scanned Olga with my eyes. She looked gorgeous. I could barely keep myself from bursting out in tears. Her long, light gray train slinked behind her. The dress style itself wasn't very unique—it was just your typical wedding dress, bare-shouldered and loose from the waist down. But those crystals . . . The bright stones were formed in lines that flourished, meandered, and shone, creating an image spun of light on the fabric. Most were on and around the breasts, and they gradually faded the lower you looked. Around the feet, there were none left, which created an ombré effect. A beautiful and elegant gradient. The whole thing must have practically weighed over two hundred pounds, but Olga didn't care. She wanted to look like a princess, and that was that. She'd even insisted on a tiara, which had elicited a bout of laughter from me. I didn't press the matter, though. It was her wedding. At first, she'd even considered a Russian tzarina-style crown, but I managed to talk her out of it. We narrowly avoided making her look like a freak.

The whole outfit would look vintage and classy and would have taken my breath away, if not for that abominable tiara. I loved wedding dresses in colors other than white. And this one was simply spectacular. Multilayered and very unusual, despite its ostensible simplicity.

"I'm going to puke," Olga said, tightening her grip on my wrists.

Without changing my impassive expression, I reached for the cooler, which had been emptied a while before, and stuck it under her chin.

"Do it," I said, nodding.

"Oh, come the fuck on, you're spoiling it for me," she snapped, pulling away. "I need compassion, not a fucking bucket," she muttered.

"We both know the moment I show any emotion you'll go ballistic." I rolled my eyes and followed her.

———

There were cars parked by the entrance. Two filled with my guards and another three with Torricellis inside. One of them was to take us to church, and the remaining ones were reserved for the goons. Domenico agreed for our driver to be one of the Canarians, but at the same time decided that the bodyguard inside the car had to be from Sicily. Now all those burly mobsters were glaring at one another, trying to come to terms with the situation.

Madonna della Rocca church. I nearly fainted as we ascended the slope. I had only good memories from this place, but I simply didn't want to think about my own wedding. I'd known Olga's ceremony would take place there, but knowing and seeing are two very different things.

Mario, Massimo's consigliere, greeted me with a weak smile and kissed me on the cheek.

"It's good to see you, Laura," he said. "Though things have changed since you left."

I didn't really know how to respond to that, so I just stood and watched the breathtaking panorama spreading before my eyes. It was going to be over soon. We waited by the church until Olga's dad joined her. When everything was ready, I turned to Olga and gave her one last hug.

"I love you," I whispered in her ear. Her eyes watered. "It's going to be okay. You'll see." She nodded, and I took the arm offered by an older Sicilian and allowed him to lead me inside the church.

We passed the gate and halted at the altar, where Domenico was already waiting. He was beaming. He kissed me on the cheek and grinned even wider. I took a look around the minuscule house of worship and a feeling of déjà vu filled me. The same dour mobster faces, the same atmosphere. The only difference was Olga's sobbing mother, who just couldn't keep it together.

Suddenly, "This I Love" by Guns N' Roses played from the speakers. I was sure Olga was drowning in tears at that point. I smiled at the thought of her nervousness right now and looked back toward the entrance. Seeing her enter the church, Domenico nearly fainted himself. Without waiting to be led the whole length of the nave by her father, Olga ran straight at him and pressed her lips to his. Her dad just waved a hand, resigned, and joined his wife, who was by that time bleating like a goat. The young couple ignored everything and everyone, kissing with wild abandon. If not for the fact that the song ended, they would have continued.

Finally, panting, they faced the altar. The priest wagged a finger at both of them. He was just about to begin the ceremony when Massimo appeared in the door.

My legs buckled. Shivering, I collapsed to my seat. Mario grabbed my elbow, and Olga sent a terrified, disoriented look at the Man in Black. He looked breathtaking. He wore a black tuxedo and a white shirt. They looked perfect with his tanned skin. He looked relaxed, calm, and composed.

"This seems to be my place," Massimo said as Mario took a step back, leaving me right next to my husband.

"Hey there, baby girl."

The sound of those words made me want to run, puke, and die at the same time. I couldn't breathe. My heart was racing like crazy. All the blood drained from my face. He was right next to me. And his smell. Oh, God, how wonderful he smelled. I closed my eyes, trying to calm my breath. Finally, Domenico and Olga faced the altar, and the priest began.

"You look wonderful," Massimo whispered, leaning in a bit, taking my hand, and resting it on his forearm. A jolt of electricity went through our bodies as he touched me. I pulled my hand away quickly and lowered it so he couldn't try that trick again.

My chest, wrapped in a tight-fitting, deep-cleavage dress, was rising and falling at a dangerous pace. I couldn't stand straight. I also couldn't ignore my husband. I was certain of one thing—if I showed any sign of weakness, he would use it against me.

The thirty minutes or so we spent in the church seemed to last for an eternity, and I prayed for it all to end. Nacho would already know about Massimo's return. He was most likely going crazy with dread and rage. My security guards stayed outside. I had no way of knowing what was happening to them. And what would happen in the near future.

I stole a glance at the Man in Black. He was focused, composed, listening to the sermon with his fingers laced on his abdomen. This was a mask, and I knew it. He would glance at me every so often. How could he be so beautiful? Hadn't he been partying somewhere? Wrecking his body with drugs? But no. He looked like he had gone through a total metamorphosis. From a hero to a god. His neatly trimmed stubble reminded me of the moments when I had delighted in the rough feeling of it on my skin. His hair was longer than usual and combed back. He must have been preparing for this occasion for a long time.

"Like what you see?" Massimo asked suddenly, looking at me. I desperately wanted to stop ogling him, but I couldn't. I was frozen. "He's never going to turn you on like this," he added in a whisper and turned his head to the altar.

I needed to escape this place. My head dropped. I breathed in, feeling a pain in my solar plexus.

Finally, mercifully, the ceremony ended. Just like last time, all the guests went straight to the party, and we walked over to the chapel to sign the necessary papers. Massimo was beaming. He kissed and congratulated the newlyweds while I kept my distance.

"You fucking liar," I hissed at Domenico when it was my turn. I closed my fingers over his elbow, making sure my nails bit into his skin. "You told me he wasn't going to be here."

"I told you he'd disappeared. I can't ban him from my wedding." Domenico put his hands on my shoulders and looked me in the eyes. "Everything is going as planned. Nothing has changed. Please calm down . . ."

"I'd like to introduce you to Eve," I heard Massimo saying. Turning around, I saw him standing next to a beautiful, dark-eyed woman. She was smiling charmingly, pressing against his arm. A jolt of pure envy pierced my heart.

I had left *him*, not the other way round. I had no right to be angry with him, but there I was, fuming at that disrespect. The gorgeous girl with long, black hair offered me a hand and introduced herself. I must have looked pathetic. Completely shocked and literally speechless. Eve wasn't tall, but she looked a lot like me otherwise. Petite, very elegant and subtle. Well, okay. She didn't look like me at all.

"We met in Brazil and—"

"And I fell in love with this wonderful man," she finished the sentence for Massimo. Both Olga and I rolled our eyes.

I spun on my heel, unable to cope with all the emotions that were accumulating inside me, and went to sign the documents.

"At least that's over," Olga said, walking over. "He has a woman, you have a man. Now get the divorce over with and everyone lives happily ever after."

"Oh, fuck off," I snapped. "He found her in, like, three weeks. And I'm his goddamned wife."

"Isn't that a bit hypocritical?" She grew serious. "This should be great news to you. Now there's a chance everything will end up like you wanted. So sign that shit and let's go."

"But how is that . . ." I paused, realizing the stupidity of what I was going to say.

"Listen to me, Laura," Olga said firmly. "You've got to decide. It's either the surfer or your husband. You can't have both. And I won't tell you which one to pick, because I'd pick the latter. I want you here with me, after all. It's your life. Do whatever makes you happy."

She nodded.

I went out and stopped by Ivan, waiting for Olga and Domenico to finish their photo shoot. After a while, Ivan gave me his phone. I took a few deep breaths and put it to my ear.

"How are you feeling, kiddo?" Nacho asked, his voice filled with worry.

"Everything's fine, honey," I breathed, moving a bit to the side. "He's here."

"I fucking know that," he growled. "Laura, please do as I told you."

"He's with a woman. I think he might have backed down finally," I said, trying to make my voice sound impassive.

That's when my eyes caught Massimo leading that woman to the car. He opened the door for her and kissed her on the top of her head as she stepped in. I balled my fists. He walked around the car and gracefully slid inside, pausing for a moment to look straight at me. The phone nearly fell from my hand. I opened my mouth, trying to take in a deep breath. The confident smirk that blossomed on Massimo's lips took the breath away from me.

"Laura!" The voice from the speaker brought me back to reality. I turned my head away from Massimo and looked over to the sea.

"What's going on, bee? Talk to me."

"It's nothing. I just got distracted." I dropped my eyes and waited for the Ferrari's engine to roar and the car to drive off. "I just want to be back with you," I added. The sound I had been waiting for echoed across the small plaza. "Olga's coming. I'll call you on my way to the airport." I returned to Ivan and gave him his phone back.

"He's pretending," the man said. "Torricelli. He's faking it, Laura. Watch out for him."

I didn't have the slightest idea what he was on about, so I just nodded so he left me alone and entered the car. My head was pounding, and the dress was beginning to chafe. Each hairpin in my elaborate bun was now seemingly intent on scratching a hole in my scalp. And I was furious. Dangerously so.

"I need a drink," I snapped. "Where's the alcohol?"

"Marcelo said no alcohol," Ivan replied without emotion.

"I don't fucking care what Marcelo said! Where's the alcohol?"

"We don't have any," he said. I rested my head against the window and looked out, battling my own thoughts.

There were dozens of security guards at the door to the mansion. the driveway was lined with armored cars and policemen. Domenico and Olga hadn't wanted their party to take place in a hotel. They'd gone for a garden party instead. A huge tent had been erected in the garden by the sea. It was beautifully decorated. I was waiting patiently for the newlyweds, standing still. Suddenly, I felt someone's eyes on me. I knew that feeling intimately and was sure of who I'd see if I was to turn around. Lifting the hem of my dress slightly, I slowly spun around and halted. He was just a few inches behind me. Massimo—towering over me with his hands in his pockets. His dark, cold eyes were drilling holes in me. He bit his lip. I knew that look and that expression. I thought about the taste of his lips. He took a step forward and stopped just an inch before me.

Ivan cleared his throat and closed in, trailed by five other men.

"Call your dogs off," Massimo growled, sending them an icy look. "I have more than a hundred men here." He smirked. "Domenico and Olga decided to take a detour to fuck, so we have a while for ourselves." He offered me an arm, and I took it without thinking. "There's only one exit from the mansion, and you're blocking it," he added, addressing Ivan.

The old security guard took a step back, sending me a warning look. I allowed Massimo to lead me deeper into the garden. He was radiating heat, and his smell was overpowering. His muscles tensed below the fabric of his suit. We walked in silence. I felt as if I had gone back in time.

"The company is yours," Massimo said finally. "It was never mine. I didn't want it. You can move it to the Canary Islands and continue your work there." Why was he talking about the company first? And why was he so calm? "I don't want to talk about the divorce today. We'll speak about it after the wedding party. You're staying for a few days, aren't you?" He stopped and turned to look at me. My knees buckled.

"I'm going back to Tenerife after midnight," I stammered.

"Pity. I want to get this done, so since you're in such a hurry, we'll deal with the divorce later."

There was a beautiful gazebo in the shadow of a thicket of palm trees and bushes. He led me there. I sat down, and Massimo took a seat next to me. We looked out to the sea, but the only thing I could think of was his sudden transformation.

"You saved my life, baby girl, only to kill me later," he said with so much sadness, I had to drop my eyes. "But that allowed me to come back to life again. I found Eve, stopped doing drugs, and even made a few lucrative business deals." His eyes sparked with unexpected joy. "You might say you saved me from myself, Laura."

"I'm glad, but what you did to the dog . . ." I paused, suddenly feeling sick. "I didn't think you capable of such cruelty." My voice broke.

"Excuse me? What are you talking about? I sent it to Tenerife right after you left."

"I fucking know that. I got it in pieces, you bastard," I snapped.

"What?!" Massimo jumped to his feet with a shocked expression. "I personally sent a man with the dog safe and sound. I wanted it to remind you of me. I wanted you to hurt. But . . ."

"You didn't kill Prada?" This was getting too much for me. "I got a massacred dog crammed into a shoe box. And a card."

"Baby girl," Massimo knelt before me, taking my hands in his. "I may be a monster, but why would I hurt a dog the size of a coffee mug? Do you really think I would be capable of that?" He lifted his brows and waited, before putting his hand to his mouth and thinking about something a little longer. "Matos, you son of a bitch," he said finally and laughed bitterly. "I could have suspected that. You'd pay any price." He shook his head. "Do you know what he told me when you left the restaurant back on Ibiza? That he'd pay any price to prove how unworthy I was of the love you had for me." I felt dizzy all over again, but willed myself to keep listening. Massimo laughed again. "I underestimated him."

My ears rang, and my breath caught in my throat. Nacho? My colorful, gentle boy had hurt that tiny, defenseless creature? I couldn't believe that.

The Man in Black saw how torn I was. He pulled a phone from his pocket and dialed a number, saying a few words and ending the call. A few minutes later, a tall, burly man appeared in the gazebo.

"Sergio," said Massimo, "what did you do with the dog I told you to take to Tenerife?"

"I took it to the Matos residence, as you ordered."

The man shot a glance at me, clearly disoriented. "Marcelo Matos said Laura wasn't there and that he'd take it."

"Thank you, Sergio. That will be all," Massimo said and propped his arms on the balustrade. The man left us.

"Laura!" I heard Olga's cry in the distance. "Come on."

I stood up too fast and swayed, still dizzy. Massimo shot across the gazebo and held me.

"Everything all right?" he asked with concern, looking me in the eyes.

"Nothing's all right!"

I tore free and stormed off.

We positioned ourselves by the entrance to the huge tent. Massimo offered me his arm. He didn't make me take it. Didn't ask. He just offered it and waited. I took it, and the four of us headed into the crowd gathered inside. People cried out and applauded. Then Domenico made a speech. We looked like one big happy family. The men stood on the sides while Olga and I smiled for everyone. Keeping up the appearance of happiness cost me a lot. The applause died down, and the Sicilians led us to a table situated on a low pedestal halfway down the tent. On our way, I grabbed a glass of champagne from a tray held by a waiter and downed it in one gulp. Olga sent me a surprised look, and Ivan stepped closer. I halted him with a gesture and shooed him away. He didn't resist. Another waiter offered me another glass, and I drank that, too. Alcohol calmed my nerves. That's what any alcoholic would say. I relished the taste in my mouth.

A while later, Domenico took Olga's hand and went to the dance floor for the first dance.

I waved at the waiter again, ordering another champagne.

"You'll get drunk," Massimo said, leaning in.

"That's what I intend to do," I retorted. "Don't you worry about me. Go play with your Eve."

The Man in Black laughed out loud, grabbed my wrist, and stood me up before leading me to the dance floor. "I'll keep you company instead."

We passed my six bodyguards. Ivan shook his head, seeing Massimo pressing me against himself. I didn't give a fuck. I was so incredibly furious at the whole Canarian gang, I could send them off without another thought.

"Tango," Massimo whispered, kissing me on the crook of my neck. "Your dress has the perfect fly, you know."

"I'm wearing panties," I said, licking my lips lasciviously.

"We can give it our best this time."

The alcohol I had drunk and the anger inside me made this the best tango I had performed in my entire life. Massimo led me expertly, holding me firmly in his arms. After the dance, everyone applauded us—the newlyweds included. We both bowed and returned to our table.

"A call for you, miss," Ivan said, approaching with a phone.

"I'm not in a mood to talk," I blurted out. "Tell him that . . ." I paused, searching for a fitting response. "You know what? Give that to me. I'll tell him myself."

I grabbed the cell, shot up to my feet, and stomped outside.

"What's the matter, bee?" Nacho asked.

"Pay any price?" I screamed. "You said you'd pay any price? How could you, you fucking bastard?! You already had me! I was already in love with you! But you wanted me to hate the man I left for you. Wasn't my love enough?" I dropped to my haunches, fighting to keep myself from throwing up after drinking that much champagne in such a short time. "You killed my dog only to make Massimo look bad! How could you?" Tears streaked down my cheeks. Suddenly, I felt hands on my shoulders. I launched myself to my feet.

Startled, Ivan took a step back, staring.

"That does it, Nacho!" I yelled into the receiver and smashed the phone on the cobblestones. "I don't need you anymore," I growled at the bodyguard. He inhaled, wanting to say something.

That's when I swayed on my feet and felt the champagne rising in my throat. I spun around and threw up over the neatly trimmed lawn.

I didn't notice Massimo and his men approaching. The Sicilian wrapped his arms around me and held me up.

"I believe you're free to go now, gentlemen. You won't be needed here anymore," he said, sending Ivan an icy glare.

The men stood immobile for another while, looking at each other. Finally, the outnumbered Canarians admitted defeat and withdrew. I heard the slams of the car doors, and then two dark SUVs drove off, engines roaring.

"Oh, baby girl," Massimo whispered, offering me a handkerchief. "I'll take you home."

"Take Eve," I snapped.

"My wife is more important." He laughed. "And I don't remember having any other wife."

I didn't fight. I had no strength left.

CHAPTER 18

The sound of a phone ringing woke me up. Huddled against a pair of strong arms, I smiled. It was all over. I opened my eyes. The arm wrapped around me, pressing me against a wide, strong bare chest, had no tattoos. I immediately snapped wide awake, realizing where I was, and launched myself up. A huge hand shot out from under the comforter and held me down.

"It's for you," I heard a voice. A phone appeared in my vision. The screen said *Olga.*

"Congratulations on your wedding," I mumbled, completely disoriented.

"Oh, good. You're alive," she said. "You two disappeared so suddenly, I thought you left without saying goodbye and fucked off to God knows where. After you and Massimo ran so early, I presume you've made your choice? I'm glad you're coming back . . ." She prattled on, excited.

"You're interrupting something here. Go take care of your husband," Massimo cut in with a chuckle and took away the phone, ending the call. "I've missed you," he said slithering onto me. His giant cock rubbed against me. "I love fucking you when you're drunk. You have no inhibitions at all, baby girl." He kissed me, and I tried recalling the events of last night. I failed.

Suddenly, it dawned on me that we were naked. And I hurt all over. I hid my face in my hands.

"Hey, baby girl." Massimo pulled away my hands and looked me in the eyes. "I'm your husband. What happened wasn't anything bad."

He held my wrists tightly, making it impossible for me to hide again. "Let's just forget the last few weeks, shall we? I was an ass. You had every right to run away . . ." He paused. "Have a little taste of freedom. But everything is going to be okay now. I'll take care of it."

"Massimo, please," I groaned, trying to free myself from under him. "I need to go to the restroom."

The Man in Black rolled back, releasing me. Wrapped in a bedsheet, I crossed the room. Why was I ashamed? He must have fucked me in all conceivable positions for the last couple of hours. But that didn't matter. I just felt troubled.

What was I doing? I looked into the mirror at my smudged makeup and hair in disarray. I was disgusted with myself. The last thing I remembered was speaking to Nacho, and then . . . blackness. So . . . what had I done? Nothing good, I feared. I sighed and turned the water on to take a shower.

Standing in a stream of hot water and trying to rein in my raging headache, I was considering my options.

Should I return to my husband? Talk to Nacho? Or maybe leave the both of them and finally take care of myself? If there was one thing I had learned during that last year, it was that men made my life a complete shit show.

I went to the wardrobe, glancing at Massimo—still naked— talking over the phone, leaning against a door frame. That sexy butt . . . the most beautiful ass on the planet. I went to my side of the wardrobe and rummaged through the drawers for some underwear and a T-shirt.

That's when I noticed the shoe drawer. It had always been very tidy, and all my shoes arranged according to color. All aside from the long boots, which had always been packed into their elegant boxes.

My breath caught in my throat at the sight of a pair of Givenchy boots lying on the floor. They weren't in their box. And Olga had assured me she had never been to our apartment. The door had always been kept locked, and only Massimo had the key. I stared at the boots on the floor by the drawer, until I felt his eyes on me.

"Well," he said, "I didn't think you'd come here this early."

I spun on my heel and saw the Man in Black closing in on me. He had a bathrobe belt stretched between his hands.

"It doesn't matter." He shrugged. "You were only supposed to send those numbskulls off and come here. I told you I wouldn't allow you to leave me. That I'd take you home and never let you out again."

I slapped him, ducking and running, but he grabbed me by the scruff of the neck and slammed me into the floor, quickly tying my arms. Then he sat on my back, satisfied with himself. With one hand he held both my wrists above my head, while the other softly caressed the skin on my cheek.

"My little baby girl. So naive," he purred, smirking. "You really believed Eve was important to me? And that I'd give you the divorce?" He pressed his lips against mine. I spat in his face. "Oh, I see we're being feisty now." He licked my spittle off his lips and lifted me up roughly. "We'll discuss the new rules when I return from my meeting. Meanwhile, you'll just . . . lie here." He tossed me to the bed and straddled me again. "I've been thinking long and hard how to discredit that tattooed fuck." He reached up to the headboard and pulled out a thick chain. "See what I have here? I ordered another set installed in our room. I know you like to play with it." He smiled, dangling a blindfold in my eyes. I thrashed, trying to break free, but he was too strong.

After a while, I was strapped to all four columns of the bed, and Massimo was calmly getting dressed, glancing at my naked body.

"I love that view," he said, raising his brows. "I'd fuck you right away, but I need to explain to Domenico and Olga that we're back together and that they won't be seeing you for some time. I'll keep bringing you breakfast in bed and all that. Like the good husband I am."

He pulled on a black shirt. "We don't want them poking their noses into our affairs, do we? Because if they do, I might stop playing nice. Now lie there and keep quiet. I'll be back in no time." He narrowed his eyes, staring at a point between my legs.

I heard the door closing. My eyes watered. *Oh, dear God, what have I done?* Inebriated, I believed in his story. In that little show he had prepared for me. In his lies. In the biggest lie of all—that the best, most gentle man I had ever known was capable of hurting my dog. I couldn't move. Sobbing and wailing, furious with myself, I was beginning to surrender to panic. I had cheated on Nacho, yelled at him, sent his men away, and let myself get caught. Now he must think I was back with Massimo. There was no chance he'd come and rescue me. Olga and Domenico would believe anything Massimo would say to them. Especially that I'd picked up that damned phone and acted envious the day before, back at the church. Not to mention hugging my husband and dancing that tango and taking long walks with him around the garden . . . I slammed my head into the pillow. It was the only part of my body I could still move. That motherfucker hadn't even covered me when he left, so I was splayed over the bed like some kind of sex doll, waiting for my lord and master.

———

"See, darling?" Massimo said when he returned, fixing my crotch with a lustful stare. "We're together again. Your friend is happy as a clam, my brother has breathed a sigh of relief, and you've generally made everyone happy by returning of your own free will." He covered me with the comforter. "A doctor is going to be here anytime. He's going to administer your IV. You need to eat up."

"An IV? Why would I need an IV?" I asked. "Let me go!"

"Don't be absurd," he said, wagging a finger at me. "A future mother like you needs to remain calm and composed at all times."

He left before I could respond. "I gave you some sedatives yesterday," Massimo called from the bathroom. "I need to keep you healthy so you grow strong and can have another baby."

I stared into the ceiling, panicking. If I had ever felt kept somewhere against my will or locked up, it was nothing when compared to what I was going through now. The thought of Massimo getting me pregnant, that I'd never be with my colorful boy again or return to what I had left on Tenerife, made me cry again. A great sob wracked my body.

The Man in Black returned to the room and sat at the edge of the bed.

"Why are you crying, baby girl?"

Oh, Jesus, was he being serious? I felt empty. Lethargic. As if I was asleep, or maybe comatose, but could still see everything. I couldn't speak, move and for a while even breathe.

There was a knock at the door. The physician came inside. What struck me was that he wasn't even a bit surprised at the state I was in. He must have seen worse in this house.

"The good doctor will now administer some more sedatives. You'll sleep, and when you wake up, everything will be better. You'll see," Massimo said, stroking my cheek, and left.

I sent the physician a pleading look. He didn't react, setting up the IV. Then he gave me a shot. I blacked out.

Each subsequent day looked the same. The difference was that I woke up without the restraints. That didn't matter, though. The drugs Massimo kept giving me made me too weak to get out of bed. My husband fed me, washed me . . . and fucked me. All the time, I couldn't move. The most horrifying thing was that he didn't even mind that I just lay there immobile. I often cried when he did it. After around a week, I grew distant, and only stared numbly at the wall.

Sometimes I closed my eyes. Thinking of Nacho. That's when it felt good. But I didn't want Massimo to think I smiled because of him, so I just switched off.

Each day, I prayed to die.

———

One day, I woke up feeling uncharacteristically fresh and strong. My head wasn't as heavy as it had been for the past weeks. I got out of bed. This in itself was a miracle. I sat on the edge of the mattress and waited for the world to stop spinning.

"Nice to see you in good spirits," the Man in Black said, walking out of the wardrobe. He planted a kiss on the top of my head.

"Domenico and Olga went for their honeymoon. They'll be gone for two weeks."

"They've been here all this time?" I asked, disoriented.

"Of course. But they thought you were in Messina. We live there, remember?"

"How do you imagine this works, Massimo?" I asked. I was starting to think logically for the first time since the wedding. "What will you threaten me with now?" I narrowed my eyes as he came to a standstill in front of me, buttoning up his blazer.

"Nothing," he replied, shrugging. "I've threatened you before with killing your parents, and despite that, you fell in love with me within three weeks. Do you think you won't be able to love me again? I haven't changed, baby girl . . ."

"But I have," I said. "I love Nacho. Not you. I think about him when you stick your dick inside me. I dream of him when I sleep and imagine him when I wake up. You may have my body, Massimo, but my heart is on Tenerife." I turned around and got up, walking across the room toward the bathroom. "And I'd rather kill myself than give birth to a baby that would have to live with you."

That was too much for him. He grabbed my neck and squeezed, slamming me against the wall. The fury in his eyes made them look like two bottomless pits. A bead of sweat formed on his brow. After a week of lying in bed, I really was weak. All I could do was wait, my feet dangling in the air.

"Laura!" he hissed and set me down.

"You can't forbid me from killing myself," I said as my eyes teared up. His hands loosened their grip. "It's the only choice I still have. And that's pisses you off, doesn't it? That you can't control it. Don't count on me staying alive much longer, then."

Massimo's expression changed into one of sheer despair and sorrow. He pulled away, fixing me with a stare. He understood now.

"I loved you once, Massimo. I was happy with you," I was saying, counting on any positive reaction. "But we lost each other at some point." I shrugged and slid down the wall, crumpling in a messy heap on the floor. "You can keep me here and keep doing all those horrible things, but at some point you'll lose interest in a sex doll. You'll want more. And I won't give it to you. How long do you want to fuck someone who doesn't react?" He didn't respond. "This isn't even about the sex anymore. Why do you need me? You can have any woman on Earth. Eve, for example."

"Eve is a hooker," he growled. "She was supposed to play a role."

"Did you kill our dog?" I asked, trying to catch him off guard with the change of subject.

"Yes." His eyes grew cold again. "I kill people all the time and look them in the eyes as I do it. What was a stupid mutt compared to that?"

I shook my head in disbelief. I didn't know that man at all. The memory of our first months seemed one big lie. How could I miss that he'd just been faking everything? The man standing in front of me now was a monster. A tyrant. How had he been able to pretend he loved me for so long? Or maybe . . . it was me. I just didn't want to see the truth.

"I'll tell you how the next weeks are going to play out now." Massimo took a step closer and picked me up from the ground.

"You can do whatever you want, but one of my men will follow you wherever you go. The quay and anything outside the residence are off-limits. And since you're planning to take your own life, which I cannot allow, the man following you will be trained in CPR and will bring you back." He rolled down his sleeves and pinned me with his black eyes, sighing and cupping my cheek. He kissed me on the mouth softly. "Something died in me on New Year's Eve. Forgive me." With that, he left.

I stayed in the room, dazed, completely taken aback by his changing moods. One minute, he wanted to kill me, then he wanted me scared, and another I could nearly see the man I had loved. I took a shower and got myself in order, pulling on shorts and a T-shirt. I went back to bed, switched the TV on, and started planning. The mansion didn't hold any secrets from me by that time. I knew it in and out. The garden and the grounds outside, too. If Nacho could take me in the middle of the night, I would be able to escape on my own.

I ordered breakfast to the room, checking if Massimo hadn't been lying and would send one of his troglodytes after me. I ate and felt a bit better. In slightly better spirits, I went out in search of something that could help me. The only route outside was the terrace, but it was the third floor. I glanced down and decided that falling from such height would end in death or at least lasting injury. That way was out of the question.

I rummaged through the apartment and found nothing of use. And suddenly, something dawned on me. If he could pretend, I could, too. Maybe it would take some time, but there at least was a chance that in a month or two I'd be able to find a moment when he'd let his guard down. However . . . would Nacho wait that long? Would he want to even listen to me after I'd cut him off and accused him of terrible things? Or maybe I had nowhere to run. Another wave of tears flooded my eyes. I rolled up in the duvet and pressed my head into the pillow, waiting for sleep to come.

I woke up in the evening. If not for the fact that I would have preferred to never regain consciousness, I'd probably have been angry at myself for sleeping through the day. Massimo was sitting in the armchair with his eyes fixed on me. Back in the day it had been normal, especially when he returned from business and waited for me to open my eyes to surprise me.

"Hi," I whispered in a coarse voice. It was supposed to sound affectionate. "What's the time?"

"I was just about to wake you up. Dinner is going to be served in a moment. I'd like you to eat with me."

"All right, let me just get myself in order," I replied meekly.

"I want to talk," he added, pushing himself up. "See you in an hour in the garden."

He wanted to talk . . . What was there still to talk about? I had my instructions. I rolled my eyes and went to the bathroom.

Dinner was the perfect time to start making my plan reality. Even if Nacho wouldn't wait, I'd run back home or even farther. At least I'd be free. Later, I'd tell Olga. She'd tell Domenico, and maybe he'd be able to do something about it. And if not, I'd disappear.

I dug through the wardrobe, looking for a black, nearly translucent dress. The one I'd had on during my first dinner with Massimo. Of course, the outfit wouldn't be complete without red lace underwear. I applied some makeup—red lipstick and dark eye shadow—tied my hair in a smooth bun, and slid my feet into a pair of stilettos. I looked amazing. Simply perfect. Just like my husband liked me. Well, maybe besides the fact that I had been drugged for the past couple of days and now had the unmistakable charm of a drug addict.

I took a deep breath and headed downstairs. Just past the door I nearly walked into the largest man I had ever seen. My jaw dropped. I hadn't known people could grow to such sizes. I passed the ogre and started walking. He followed.

"My husband told you to follow me?" I asked without turning back.

"Yes," the ogre rumbled.

"Where is he?"

"In the garden. Waiting for you."

Good. I picked up my pace. The sound of my stilettos on the marble floor was an omen of the coming cataclysm. If Torricelli wanted to play, I'd play him like a fiddle.

The air outside was hot. I hadn't left the air-conditioned villa for a long time and had nearly forgotten just how warm the weather on Sicily could be even after sundown.

I slowed down, knowing that Massimo could probably hear me

approaching, even though he had his back turned on me. Candles were lit on the long table. Their shimmering glow softly illuminated the beautifully set table. My husband rose and turned to look at me. He froze.

"Good evening," I said, passing him by.

He followed and pulled a chair out for me. I took my seat, and a waiter appeared out of nowhere to pour me a glass of champagne. Massimo narrowed his eyes and gracefully sat down next to me. I might have hated that man with all my heart, but I couldn't help but notice that he looked breathtaking. His off-white linen pants, a shirt of the same color with the top few buttons undone, the sleeves rolled up, and a silver rosary around his neck. What hypocrisy. A man so ruthless and cruel and evil carrying a holy symbol.

"You're very provocative, baby girl," he said in a low voice. "Just like before . . . Do you intend to tease me now, too?"

"I'm just refreshing your memory," I replied, raising my brows, and skewered a piece of meat.

I wasn't hungry at all, but my new role required me to act normal, so I made myself chew the morsel.

"I have a proposal for you, baby girl," he said, reclining in his seat. "Give me one night with you. But the way you were before. Then I'll set you free."

My eyes widened, and I dropped my fork.

He was being serious.

"I . . . don't understand," I stammered.

"I'd like to feel that you're mine one last time. After that, if you want, you can leave." He reached out for a glass and took a sip. "I can't keep you locked up. I don't want to. You know why? Because the truth is you are not, and have never been, my salvation. You were never in my visions after I got shot. I just saw you that day."

I narrowed my eyes, startled.

"Croatia. Five years ago."

He leaned in closer. I froze. Martin and I had been on vacation in Croatia five years previous. My heart started hammering.

"You lied? How typical . . ."

I blurted out nonsensically, hoping that he was bluffing and that this piece of information was just something his people had dredged out from somewhere.

"No. I found out by accident."

He crossed his legs and sat back. "When we lost the baby. I didn't know how to live with that. Mario tried his best to bring me back. The organization needed me. Especially after Fernando was shot and all families started looking at me suspiciously. That's when Mario came up with hypnosis."

I gaped at him, even more confused.

"I know this sounds stupid, but I didn't care anymore. He could have killed me for all I cared." Massimo shrugged. "The therapy was effective. On one of the sessions, I just saw it. Saw you. The real you."

"How do you know it isn't just another projection?" I asked, annoyed. As if I *wanted* to be this man's salvation after all that had transpired. I rolled my eyes at the sound of my own voice. But his words were just so absurd, I had to listen to the end.

"Are you sad?" he asked.

I looked at him impassively and snorted with derision.

"My heart broke, too, baby girl. I understand now that it hadn't been fate that brought us together. Just coincidence. Forgive me. You were at a party in one of the hotels, dancing with another girl. Martin was there, too. We left a meeting and were standing on a terrace one floor above you. You didn't see us." He sipped his wine and glanced at me. "It was the weekend. You were wearing a white dress."

I pressed my back against the backrest, trying to calm my breathing. I remembered that day. It had been a few days before my birthday. But how could he know that? How could he remember something after so many years? The shocked expression didn't leave my face.

"There's something called 'regression' in hypnosis. It allows you to go back to any point in your life. We needed to go back to my death." He leaned in closer. "After I saw you, I was dead. Do you understand?" I kept my eyes trained on him, frozen in terror. Was this just another one of his games? Or was this finally the truth?

"Why are you telling me this?"

"To explain why I don't care about you anymore. You were just a phantom. The last image I saw before I was shot. A memory. Nothing special." He shrugged. "I'll set you free because I don't need you anymore. But before that happens, I want to take you. I want to feel you. As my wife. One last time. Not out of compulsion. I don't want to make you do anything you don't want to. It has to be your decision. After that, you'll be free. The choice is yours."

I couldn't believe what he was saying.

"What guarantee do I get that this isn't another one of your games?"

"I'll sign the divorce papers and send away the entire staff." He slid an envelope across the table, closer to me. "The papers are here." Then he took out his phone and dialed a number, saying: "Mario, take everyone to Messina."

Then the Man in Black rose to his feet and offered me a hand. "Let's take a walk."

I put down a napkin I had been holding and took his hand, feeling a shiver run down my spine. Massimo led me across the garden until we reached the driveway. His men were boarding their huge, black SUVs. I watched the scene in astonishment. Mario was the last to leave. He nodded at me and stepped inside a black Mercedes. They left the two of us alone.

"I still don't know if this is a trick," I shook my head.

"Let's find out."

Massimo led me inside the house and walked through the entire residence, showing me various nooks and crannies. I followed barefoot, with my shoes in hand. It took us an hour to tour the entire estate. It was deserted.

We walked back to the table. Massimo poured us more champagne and then came to a halt, sending me an expectant look.

"All right." I ripped open the envelope, looking inside. "Let's assume I agree. What do you expect of me?"

I scanned through the documents. They were written in Polish. He wasn't lying. I didn't understand everything, but it looked like my husband for once wouldn't renege on his word.

"I want the woman who loved me. For one night." He dropped his eyes, staring into the glass he was turning in his fingers. "I want to feel you kiss me passionately. I want you to fuck me like you need me." He sighed deeply. "Are you able to remember how it felt when I still brought you pleasure?"

I swallowed, thinking, and then put the papers down and looked at him. He really was serious. I considered his proposal. The thought of having sex with him was paralyzing and terrifying. But, on the other hand . . . I had done so many things with this man—maybe one more night wouldn't hurt. Just a few hours and I'd be off. I would leave this place once and for all. But first, that one last time. Hundreds of memories, an inhuman exertion. But freedom awaited. I looked at Massimo, wondering if I was strong enough. If my acting skills were good enough to play that last part. He was a beautiful man, but the only thing I felt was revulsion. The hate that burned inside me was a lot more likely to make me kill him in the act than continue pretending to be his loving wife. Finally, reason overcame heart. Cold calculation won over emotion. *You can do it*, I said to myself.

"Okay," I said. "But no binding, no drugs, and no chains. And no alcohol."

"All right." Massimo nodded and reached out with a hand. "But we do it where I want." I got up and put my shoes on. He led me into the house. My heart was pounding as we walked through the maze of corridors. I knew which room would be the first. And I wanted to throw up at the thought of what was coming.

———

Massimo closed the door to the library behind us and walked to the fireplace. I was so nervous, I had to consciously keep myself from puking. I was shivering. I felt like a whore, a hooker that had to please her most hated customer.

The Man in Black gently cupped my cheeks and leaned in, waiting for consent. My lips were parted, and my breath dried the skin on them with every exhalation. My tongue flicked out to moisten them, and that was Massimo's cue. He pushed his tongue into my mouth. I felt a jolt of electrical energy coursing through our joined bodies. It was a strange feeling. I hated this man with all my heart, after all. I returned the kiss, fighting down the bile in my throat, as he pushed in deeper, mistaking my response for approval. With a swift motion, Massimo turned me around, kissing the back of my neck, and ran his hand down my thigh and then up again, stopping on the lace surface of my underwear.

"I love it," he breathed, touching the fabric. I felt goose bumps. "This is my drug."

He faced me again and kissed me passionately. His long fingers slid into me, spreading my labia and pressing against my clitoris. I moaned theatrically and felt him smiling. I pretended that he was turning me on like before. He rubbed against my sweet spot, and I kissed him.

"I need to feel you," he whispered, lowering me onto the soft couch.

With a quick motion, he unzipped his pants, fell over me, and skewered me with his prick. I cried out, pressing my head into the pillow, as Massimo closed his hands over my hips and started fucking me fast and rough. I squirmed and scratched his back with my nails. His cold eyes were focused on my face. My own eyes glazed over. His silhouette blurred. I squeezed my eyes shut, unable to take this anymore. Then I saw Nacho. Smiling, amused, covered in tattoos. My colorful boy, who treated me like a goddess. I felt a pain in my abdomen. I was doing my best to keep the act up, but I didn't want to open my eyes again. If I did, a stream of tears would be released. And then the plan would crumble to pieces. Massimo's hard cock was ripping me apart. It was torture.

"I can't," I sobbed and burst out in tears.

Massimo froze with a shocked expression. For an instant, he didn't move, but then suddenly he pulled out, stood up, and zipped up his pants.

"Go to sleep, then," he hissed. I brought my legs together and curled up. "Our agreement is off." He turned his back on me and went to the desk.

I was barely able to get up from the couch. My legs buckled under me. I traveled the labyrinth of corridors and went back to our apartment. In the wardrobe, I tore my dress off and changed into a T-shirt and a pair of cotton briefs before staggering to bed and wrapping myself in the duvet, sobbing. I was so ashamed. I hated myself. How stupid and naive I'd been to think that this man had any honor. I lay in bed, sobbing and thinking about all the ways I could kill myself. Which one would be the most painless? I closed my eyes.

Suddenly, a large, strong hand clamped over my mouth. I cried out, but it stifled the sound.

"Be quiet, bee." The words made me go rigid. Another wave of tears came—stronger than the one before. But those weren't tears of despair. They meant hope.

The hand slid off my face. I could breathe again, and immediately pressed myself against my savior. He was here, with me! I could smell the mint on his breath as I hugged him closely.

"I'm sorry, I'm sorry, I'm sorry," I repeated frantically. His chest was heaving.

"Later," he whispered. "We need to go now."

I couldn't let him go. Not now, when I finally had him at my side, when his every breath was proof that he was really here. That this wasn't a dream. He tried pulling away, but there was no force that could split us apart now. I held Nacho with all my strength.

"Laura, he can come back at any time."

"All his men went to Messina," I stammered. "We're alone."

"No, we're not," he replied. I froze.

"His entire army is waiting about a mile outside the mansion. We have literal minutes before they return. He's lied to you again."

I lifted my head, trying to see through the darkness.

"Did you hear everything?" I asked. The thought of him knowing what had happened made my heart break in a million little pieces.

"It's not important now. Get dressed right away." He lifted himself from the bed and gently pushed me toward the wardrobe.

I didn't switch the lights on, reaching for my shorts and a pair of sneakers. Then I ran back to the bedroom, afraid that if I wasn't quick enough, he'd disappear.

The Canarian's hand grabbed me as I passed the door. He pulled me into the bathroom and locked the door behind us. The pale light inside finally allowed me to see him. He wore military attire, like a Navy SEAL. His face was covered in black paint. There was a submachine gun strapped to his back and another two guns on his chest. He took one out of its holster and handed it to me.

"You need to go through the main door. The rest is locked." He thumbed the safety off. "If you see anyone, shoot. Don't think. Just shoot. Understood? It's the only way we leave here alive and return home."

"Home." I repeated the word, feeling another stream of tears cascade down my cheeks.

"Don't waste time crying, Laura. I'll be right behind you. Nobody is going to shoot you." He kissed me, and the touch of his warm lips stopped the tears.

I nodded and headed to the stairs, opened the door, and took a look around. There was nobody there. With my shoulder sliding along the wall, I moved down the corridor, listening to the sound of footsteps from behind. There was nothing. I was about to turn around and return to the apartment when I recalled Nacho's words. He'd told me he'd be right behind me. Reassured, I continued ahead, squeezing the gun in my hands, fearing I'd have to use it.

I went one floor down and breathed a sigh of relief. There was nobody in the house. Slowly and soundlessly, I took the stairs down before launching myself into a run to the main door. I was a couple feet from freedom.

That's when the door to the library opened and a beam of lights spilled over the corridor. Massimo materialized before me. I extended my arms, aiming the gun at him. He was lost for words, frozen, glaring at me angrily.

"I can't believe it," he finally managed. "We both know you wouldn't dare." He made a step toward me. I pulled the trigger. The silencer wheezed. A flowerpot just to Massimo's side exploded into a thousand pieces.

The Man in Black stopped.

"Don't move," I hissed. "I have enough reasons to kill you as it is. I don't need another one. You're a sick, evil bastard, and I hate you," I said with conviction, though my arms were shaking so badly, I wouldn't hit him if he were a thousand feet tall. "I'm leaving you. If you want to live, get back into the motherfucking library and lock the door behind you." Massimo laughed, putting his hands into his pockets.

"I taught you how to shoot," he said with something like pride in his voice. "You won't kill me. You're too weak." He took another step forward. I closed my eyes, preparing to shoot him.

"She won't," I heard Nacho's voice behind me. "But I can."

The barrel of his gun appeared from the darkness. His strong hand moved me to the side.

"I've waited for this moment so long, Massimo," Nacho said, stepping in front of me. "I warned you on Ibiza that I'd fulfill my promise."

Massimo stopped, rooted to the spot. His hate was palpable. Nacho gave me his hand and pulled me to the front again.

"Get inside," he said, pointing the Man in Black to the library. "Run to the driveway, Laura. Ivan is waiting there for you. Don't look back. Just run."

My heart was racing, but my legs didn't want to listen to my brain. I froze. The last thing I wanted was to leave him here.

"N-Nacho . . . ," I stammered.

"We'll talk at home," he barked, keeping his eyes on Masimo, and pushed me toward the hall.

I took a step, but something still wasn't allowing me to leave.

"The last week was perfect," the Man in Black said, looking straight at me. "I haven't fucked this much for ages. I love that little ass of yours." He leaned causally against the door frame.

"Run, Laura," Nacho growled.

"I fucked her like an animal. She was unconscious. Strapped to a bed. But when she woke up, she begged for more," Massimo was saying. He laughed ominously. "We both know you won't get out of here alive, Matos."

That was enough. I shot out and slammed Massimo on the jaw with the handle of my gun. He fell, stunned. Blood poured down his face. I slammed the door shut.

"Either we go together, or I stay," I cried, grabbing Nacho's wrist.

He burst into motion, sprinting to the door and pulling me with him. A few seconds later, I heard the library door open with a loud bang. We were already on the stairway when the first shot came. Marcelo kept running. I needed to keep up. We were right in front of the main entrance, when Mario suddenly appeared in our way.

Before Nacho managed to raise his gun, Mario aimed his own firearm at us. The only thing I could see was the dark abyss of its barrel.

"Please," I sobbed. The old man sent me an icy look. "I don't want to be here. I can't take it anymore . . ." My voice broke and tears streaked down my cheeks. I heard Massimo's steps behind us. "He's a monster. I'm terrified!"

The only two sounds were Nacho's breathing and Massimo's steps closing in. And then Mario lowered his gun, sighed deeply, and moved out of our way.

"None of this would have happened if his father had lived," he said and retreated into the darkness.

Nacho grabbed my wrist again. We rushed outside. Ivan joined us and threw me roughly over his shoulder before racing to the quay.

CHAPTER 19

I slowly opened my eyes, afraid of what I would see. The memory of last night was fresh in my head, but only until the moment we boarded the boat. After that, I remembered nothing. Maybe something went wrong, and I was back in Massimo's room? I inhaled and looked around. Tears blurred my vision.

It was our hideaway—the beach house. Rays of sun were illuminating the room through half-closed blinds, and the wonderful smell of the ocean spilled inside.

I turned my head and saw Nacho. He was sitting in the armchair by the bed. He leaned forward, propping his head on his hands, watching me without a word.

"I'm sorry," I whispered.

"I have a proposal for you," he said so gravely my heart nearly stopped. "Let's not talk about it ever again. I can only suspect what you went through. If you still don't want me to kill him, just don't talk to me about it." He straightened up, swallowed loudly, and knitted his brow. "Unless you've changed your mind."

"If I had changed it, I would have shot the bastard in the face yesterday," I sighed, sitting up. "Everything that happened on Sicily was my fault, Nacho. It was my own stupidity."

He sent me a curious look.

"I believed Massimo's lies and brought danger upon you. But he planned it so good . . . I'll understand if you don't want to be with me anymore."

"You told me you were in love with me," he replied.

"What?" I asked, dumbfounded.

"After Olga's wedding, when you screamed at me through the phone. You told me you were in love with me."

His eyes sparked with amusement.

I dropped my head, lacing my fingers. What was I to say? My wall had just fallen. And the man sitting in front of me was stripping me of the lies I had been feeding myself for months. I didn't want to love him. I was afraid of it. But I was even more scared that he might discover the truth.

"Bee," Nacho said, sitting next to me on the bed.

He lifted my chin with a finger.

"I was drunk and drugged," I blurted out.

The Canarian raised his brows, fixing me with a stare of his emerald eyes.

"So you were lying?" The corners of his mouth lifted a fraction.

"Christ," I breathed, trying to avoid his eyes. He held my chin firmly, making me look into his eyes again.

"So?"

"I'm trying to apologize for acting like an idiot, and you're asking me if I'm in love with you?" He nodded with a grin.

"You're the idiot if you haven't noticed what I feel for you yet."

I was starting to smile, too.

"Of course I've noticed. I just want you to finally say it." He cupped my cheek.

"Marcelo Nacho Matos," I said seriously, "for a long time . . . at least for the last couple of weeks I've been . . ." I paused, and he waited with bated breath.

". . . totally and completely, blindly in love with you."

The grin that appeared on his face was the brightest and widest I had ever seen.

"But that's not all. Each day I fall more in love with you." I shrugged. "I can't help it. It's your fault."

The tattooed hands closed around my ankles and pulled me down onto the bed.

Nacho hung above me, propped on his arms, looking me in the eyes.

"I want you so bad," he breathed, brushing my lips with his. "But first, you need to see a doctor. I'm afraid you might be too exhausted."

The memories of the last days flew through my mind with the speed of a hurricane. I tried stopping the tears but couldn't. The more I thought about it, the more I felt guilty. And the worst came last. Massimo had been doing all that for a reason. And I was off the pill. My face contorted in an expression of terror. Nacho pulled away immediately.

"What's going on?

"Oh, God," I sobbed, hiding my face in my hands.

"Talk to me, kiddo," he pulled my hands away.

"I might be pregnant, Nacho," I said, seeing my words cause him physical pain.

He gritted his teeth and dropped his head, getting up and walking out. I stayed in bed a moment longer, the chaotic thoughts still thrashing around my head, when he came back, wearing colorful swimming trunks.

"I'm going for a swim," he said and headed to the door. He slammed it so hard, it practically splintered.

Will this ever end? I thought and shook my head, covering myself with the comforter. I couldn't hide from my own thoughts, though, and there was one question that kept appearing in my mind . . . What if I was . . . No. It was unthinkable. I'd do anything to sever my ties from that monster.

I reached for the phone Nacho had left and searched the web for a solution. Fortunately, it turned out there was something I could use. And it wasn't invasive at all. There were some pills that should do the job. I sighed with relief and put the phone back down. God loved me after all. Maybe he didn't give me the best luck, but at least I was smart enough to cope.

Now to calm Nacho down. I went to the wardrobe and changed, putting on a very revealing G-string and a surfing shirt. I brushed my teeth, tied my hair in a tall bun, and grabbed a surfboard, carrying it to the sea.

The ocean was stormy, as if mirroring the mood of that godling that was now cutting through the waves on his board—focused and sexy as hell. I strapped the leash to my ankle and paddled toward him.

Reaching the spot where the waves were breaking, I straddled the board and waited. Nacho had to see me, but I wanted it to be his decision to swim closer. He didn't make me wait long. Several minutes later, he was right by my side, watching me with a composed expression.

"I'm sorry," I said again. He rolled his eyes.

"Would you stop already?" There was annoyance in his eyes now. "I don't want to think about this anymore. Each time you apologize it just reminds me of what happened."

"We need to talk, Marcelo."

"Don't fucking call me Marcelo!" he screamed, startling me.

I suddenly grew angry but didn't want an argument. To keep my composure, I started paddling back to shore.

"I'm sorry, bee," he called out, but I didn't stop.

I reached the beach and threw the board to the sand before rushing back home. I came to a halt in the kitchen, propping my arms over the counter. My chest heaved. I cursed. That's when his strong arms turned me around and pushed me against the cold surface of the fridge.

"When you hung up on me," Nacho said, touching his forehead to mine, "I felt my world crashing down on me. I couldn't breathe. I couldn't think straight. Then, when Ivan called me and told me what had happened, I was terrified. He said you were drunk and on some drugs. You didn't want to listen to reason. And that Torricelli took you away. I thought you went back to him. Left me." I raised my eyebrows, shocked. "Don't look at me like that," Nacho said, pulling away a bit. "You thought I cut up your dog. I flew to Sicily, but that house of his is a fucking fortress. And the army he got just to keep me away complicated things. It took me a while to prepare everything. Besides, Domenico and Olga's behavior fooled me. They were calm and acted normally. I had doubts. I hesitated. Until they left and I overheard one of Massimo's phone calls. Then everything became clear. I cobbled together a plan to rescue you."

"Did you hear our conversation in the garden?" I asked. Nacho said nothing, looking at his feet. "Did you?"

"I did," he replied in a whisper.

"Nacho." I cupped his cheeks and kissed him softly. "It was the only way for me to break free. You know I didn't do it for pleasure." I looked into his eyes, but they were empty. "I'm scared," I whispered. "I'm scared that you'll distance yourself after that. You'd be right to." I turned around, rubbing my temples. "I'd understand if you did."

I took a step toward the bedroom, but he reached out to me. He took me in his arms and hugged me, lifting me into the air. I wrapped my legs around his hips.

"So are you in love or not?" he asked seriously, passing through the door.

"How many times do I have to say it?" I sent him an irritated look.

"As many as it takes for it to turn into 'I love you,'" he replied and lay me down on a wide sunbed behind the house. "I'll make love to you now, if you allow me."

His lips stretched into a smile, and he kissed me.

"I've been dreaming of it for days." I tore off my wet shirt. "There wasn't a time you weren't with me." I put my hands on his hairless head and pulled him in.

His warm, minty tongue caressed my own, and his tattooed hands reached for his swimming trunks. He pulled them off without breaking the kiss. With the corner of my eye, I could see how ready he was.

"You're that glad to see me?" I asked playfully, raising an eyebrow. Nacho straightened up, looming over me.

"Open your mouth, please," he said with a smile and grabbed his thick cock with his right hand.

I lay back comfortably and did as he asked. Nacho knelt over my head and made me slide a few inches down. When my head touched the soft surface of the sunbed, he closed in and allowed me to kiss the hard tip of his manhood. I wanted to slide it deeper, but he withdrew.

"Slowly," he breathed and closed in again, gently putting his hard cock on my tongue. "Can I push in deeper?" he asked with a charming smile. I nodded. He slid in an inch. I started sucking. "A bit more?" He was waiting for consent. His breath quickened.

I clasped my hands on his buttocks and pulled him closer, making his penis push down my throat.

"Keep your beautiful hands right where they are now," he said, propping his arms on the headrest. He pushed harder with every moment.

His scent and taste and the sight of him above me were turning me on so bad, I thought my head would explode. My nails bit into his tattooed buttocks. Nacho hissed and shot me a look from under half-closed eyelids. He thrust with his hips, sliding his cock all the way down, and stopped. I tried swallowing, but his manhood was blocking its way. I couldn't breathe.

"Use your nose, bee," he said with a chuckle, seeing me choking on his prick. "And don't move."

Gracefully, he twisted around, keeping his cock down my throat, and a moment later, his tongue was tracing a line down my stomach, aiming between my thighs. Even doing a sixty-nine, his dick was simply too long. I kept choking on it. I recalled the first time I'd given him a blow job. This was like that, but he was on top now.

His slender fingers hooked around my G-string and started to slowly slide it off. I couldn't wait for his tongue to start its dance in me, but as I was completely immobilized, the only way I could express my desire was by sucking him harder. I worked him like a maniac, putting all my skill and strength into it. That didn't seem to impress Nacho. He kept his composure and pulled down my panties.

When the wet piece of fabric finally flew to the ground, the Canarian spread my thighs as far as they would go and pressed his lips to my clitoris. My cry was stifled by the penis in my mouth. Nacho was greedy. His tongue slid into every crevice of my wet pussy, and his teeth briefly brushed against my clit. Oh, God, how wonderful it was. His lips were perfect. As if made for pleasuring a woman.

He licked two fingers and pushed them inside me. Dazed by that, I raised my hips. With his free hand, Nacho pressed me down. With the other, he assaulted me ruthlessly. I could feel that whirlwind of ecstasy I was so addicted to starting to spin inside me. Everything around me blurred. Nothing else mattered. Nothing. My man was giving me pure bliss, and that was the only thing I wanted to focus on. The orgasm was just around the corner when the movement between my legs stopped. Nacho got up and faced me.

"You're getting distracted," he said with a disarming smile, licking his lips.

"If you don't get back to what you were doing, I swear I'm going to get violent." He laughed and dismounted me. I sighed with disappointment. "Nacho!" I protested as he took his place between my legs.

"I'm going to come soon," he breathed, entering me. I threw my head back and opened my mouth. No sound came out of it. "And so are you. But you know I need to see you." He kissed me and burst into motion, fucking me with the speed of a machine gun.

His one leg was propped in the sand. The other one was bent at the knee and on the sunbed. He lifted my leg by the ankle and threw it over his shoulder, pushing inside me even deeper. His lips kissed my foot and my calf. His green eyes were focused on my face, full of desire and love.

And that's when his cock found that special spot that took me over the edge. I orgasmed, taking his head into my hands and kissing him as deeply as I could. Nacho's hips kept hammering, and after an instant, I felt him spilling inside me with a warm wave. We clung to each other, overwhelmed with orgasms, and our bodies became one. A while later, we came to our senses. Our movements grew slower and then came to a standstill. The Canarian collapsed onto me, kissing my collarbone and then putting his head on my chest.

"I missed you," he whispered.

"I know. I missed you, too." I stroked his back, slowly calming my breathing.

"I have a gift for you. It's back at the residence." He pushed himself up and pulled out of me. His eyes sparked with good humor. "Of course, we can stay here if you want."

"I do," I replied, pulling him in and relishing in the sound of the waves crashing over the beach.

———

We spent a few days in our hideaway. Nacho didn't work. He didn't do much aside from fussing over me. He cooked, made love to me, taught me surfing, and played violin. We sunbathed, talked, and fooled around like kids. Several times, he brought the horses. Once, after I asked really nicely, he took me to the stud farm. I watched him tend to the animals, brushing them and talking to them. They nuzzled their heads to him, feeling his love for them and in turn trying to show him their gratefulness.

Eventually, there came a day when I woke up alone and found Nacho in the kitchen, sitting by the counter. As soon as his eyes found mine, I knew our retreat into paradise was finished. I wasn't angry and didn't hold it against him. He had his obligations, after all.

We went for a swim for the last time, and then I got dressed and walked to Nacho's amazing car.

We drove back to the mansion, where he helped me out of the vehicle. The boyish grin on his face told me he was up to something.

"The gift," he said, "is waiting for you in our bedroom." He lifted his brows. "But you don't know which room *is* our bedroom, do you? Let me show you. Before my sister discovers you're here and steals you from me."

He pulled me with him past the large door and entered the

building. I tried to take in all the characteristic spots so I wouldn't get lost and registered the location of our bedroom. The other rooms were of no interest to me.

We took the stairs to the second floor, and then to the third and the fourth. The Matos family mansion was impressive, but what I saw in the attic was simply breathtaking.

The entire wall was made of glass and overlooked the cliff and the ocean. Incredible. The room was enormous. It must have been at least three thousand square feet. The walls were lined with wood, and so was the ceiling. Huge off-white sofas connected to one another, forming a square. Inside it stood a large, shiny, white coffee table. Tall black floor lamps loomed over the couches. A table with six chairs stood farther back, and a vase filled with gorgeous white lilies was perched on top. Finally, a mezzanine with a gigantic bed overlooked the whole floor. I spun around and saw a frosted glass wall, behind which there was a bathroom. Thank God the restroom was behind a solid wall.

I calmed down a bit, looking around the gorgeous apartment, and heard a strange noise. I peeked out from around the frosted glass wall and froze. Nacho was leading a small white bull terrier my way.

"This is the gift," he said, grinning. "My replacement for times of loneliness. Your defender and friend."

He raised his brows. I didn't move. "I know it might not be a small, fuzzy ball of fur, but bull terriers have their uses, too." He sat on the floor beside the dog, which immediately climbed onto his legs and started licking Nacho's face. "Come on, say something. Don't you like it? I thought this might be a good way to get to know each other. By taking care of a pet we're equally responsible for." He frowned, waiting for my reaction. I stared at them with my mouth agape. My heart was racing.

I walked over and plopped down next to them. The goofy white pup waddled toward me hesitantly. First, it licked my hand, and then it launched itself into the air and salivated all over my face.

"Is it a she or a he?" I asked, pushing away the white piglet.

"A he, of course," Nacho replied indignantly. "A big, strong, angry . . ." The dog interrupted him, climbing over his torso, wagging his tail, and licking Nacho's face. "Okay, maybe not yet, but he will be." Resigned, Nacho toppled the pet and scratched its belly.

"Dogs often become like their owners, you know?" I wiggled my eyebrows. "But hold on. What's the occasion, anyway?"

"Good question! You see, my dear"—Nacho jumped to his feet and pulled me up—"in exactly thirty days you are going to celebrate your thirtieth birthday." He grinned as I rolled my eyes. "This year has been a life-changing one for you. And I intend for it to end like a fairy tale instead of a nightmare." He kissed me on the top of my head and embraced me. "Now let's go see Amelia. She can't wait to talk to you."

———

We sat at the table, eating lunch. Everyone was laughing and joking around. I couldn't stop thinking about what Nacho had said. My three hundred and sixty-five days were about to pass. I couldn't believe they had flown so fast. I recalled the day when I had been kidnapped, or rather the night I had woken up. The memory made me smile, albeit sadly. I couldn't even suspect this would all end this way. I recalled the first time I saw Massimo. That beautiful, dangerous, tyrannical man. Then shopping in Taormina and all those attempts he had made to control me. And my resistance. All those things now seemed so innocent. The departure from Rome and the run-in in the club that had nearly cost me my life. I looked at the Canarian, who was explaining something to his friends. That day at the Nostro I hadn't even known that someone had just entwined my fate with that of the greatest man on Earth. I picked at my jamon, thinking about how happy I felt after that. When I first made love to the Man in Black before he disappeared. And the baby. I recalled my baby. That particular memory was especially painful. Instinctively, I put my hands to my belly. What if I had another baby inside me now? A shiver went down my spine, chilling me despite the weather being hot and sunny.

Nacho's hand tightened on mine.

"What's going on, kiddo? You're having a stroke again," he whispered, kissing my temple.

"I'm not feeling so well," I replied, not even looking at him. "I think being brought back to reality is a bit harder than I anticipated. I'm going to go lie down for a while." I kissed his head and excused myself.

I headed to our new bedroom, took Nacho's phone and dialed Olga. I knew her honeymoon was about to end. I shouldn't ruin it for her, but I really needed my friend now. I tried dialing her ten times, quickly disconnecting, unable to decide. Finally, resigned, I went to take a shower.

For the following days, I fought my inner demons. On the one hand, I wanted to get this over with—go see a doctor and take the pill. On the other one, I was so afraid that I just couldn't make myself do that. Nacho had either forgotten about our conversation, or pretended to have done so. Either way, we didn't talk about it anymore.

When I finally gathered the strength to do it, I made an appointment. Keeping it secret from my man. Dressed in shorts and a T-shirt, I went down to the driveway, where my Escalade was already waiting. The phone in my bag vibrated.

"What the hell happened this time?" Olga asked as soon as I picked up. "That bastard practically dragged Domenico out of the plane, and they both disappeared. I'm at home, but everything's locked up. Where are you? Have you been arguing again?" I said nothing, unable to believe she had been kept out of the loop this whole time.

"Things have gone a bit . . . awry." I said, stepping into the car. "Massimo and I—we didn't make up. He planned it all and kidnapped me again."

"What?!" Her cry was deafening. "God-fucking-damn it! That guy . . . Tell me everything."

I did tell her everything, skipping only the part when my husband had raped me repeatedly. The guilt would have killed Olga.

"That conniving bastard." She sighed. "He told us you made up, Laura. During the wedding, I was pretty surprised. You know, when you went ballistic on Nacho over the phone. And then, when you got into his Ferrari, you looked like you wanted to fuck him then and there. What was I supposed to think? And then you picked up the phone, and later he came downstairs, beaming . . . I thought everything went back to normal. Remember saying that Nacho might have only been a crush?"

I did.

"So I thought that you realized that was the case when you saw Eve. The wedding, Taormina, the church, all the memories . . . You know."

"All right, shut up already," I cut her short. "Tell me this: Was Mario with Massimo?"

"Yeah," she replied. That made me sigh with relief. "Why do you ask?"

"I didn't tell you the most important thing. It was Mario who allowed us to escape. I was afraid Massimo would kill him."

"Well, he didn't. At least not yet. But I'll ask Domenico how things are. I'll let you know. How's Nacho?"

"Good, mostly," I said. "Well, the knowledge that his girlfriend got drunk and fucked another guy didn't seem to make him too happy, but he gets it. I was drugged. But still, I did cheat on him."

"Bullshit!" Olga cried out. "Don't you even think that. I know what's gonna happen now. You'll crawl into bed and start mulling things over, coming up with more unnecessary problems." Her resigned tone broke my heart. "Listen. Do something. Start working on your company again. Call Emi. There's a lot to get in order."

"For now I'm going to see a doctor." A silence followed. "I might be pregnant. With him."

"Oh, shit," Olga breathed. "Well, at least your kid is going to have a cousin."

I jerked up, shocked, hitting my head on the headrest.

"I'm pregnant, Laura."

"Jesus Christ." My eyes watered. "Why didn't you tell me?"

"I only just found out. On the Seychelles."

"I'm so happy for you, darling," I sobbed.

"Me too, but I wanted to tell you eye to eye. I thought you'd be waiting here for me."

I suddenly felt guilty. "Olga, I need to get rid of it. I don't want anything to connect me to that psycho."

"Think about it, babe. But first go find out if there even is anything to worry about. And call me."

Someone knocked on the window, startling me. I dropped the phone. Nacho was outside, staring in with his brows raised. I picked the phone up and said bye to Olga. Then I rolled the window down.

"Hey there, kiddo. Where are you going?" he asked.

Did I hear mistrust in his voice? Maybe I just imagined it. I glanced down and saw our nameless dog at his feet.

"A little shopping. I want to buy something for our little monster. And just, you know, for a drive."

"Is everything okay?" Nacho leaned against the door, putting his chin on the edge of the glass, looking at me with concern.

"I spoke to Olga."

He raised his head.

"They returned from their honeymoon . . ."

"And?" he prompted.

"And they had a great time, but back home things are . . . not that good." I shrugged. "But at least she's happy, relaxed, and in love. Just like me."

I smooched Nacho on the nose. "Now, I'm off. Unless you want to come with me?" I asked, smiling.

I hoped he didn't.

"I need to see Ivan. We're going to Russia next week. And remember, our dog is a powerful male. A killer. An alpha!" He kissed me and then grinned. "So no pink, no ribbons, no colorful little bones."

He flexed his biceps. "Power! Skulls and guns!"

"You're so stupid." I burst out in laughter and put on sunglasses.

"And don't forget to let me know what the doctor said," Nacho called out, leaving. I froze.

Goddamn it . . . I slammed my head into the steering wheel. He knew. He had known from the beginning. He had just been waiting for me to tell him, and instead of doing that, I'd lied. I squeezed my eyes shut and took a deep breath. I was wrecking my relationship. And before I could even start calling it one. Angry at myself, I gunned the engine and left the mansion.

CHAPTER 20

I sat on a soft couch in the waiting room of a private clinic, nervously picking at my nails. I was so stressed, I might have started pulling my hair out. The doctor took a blood sample and told me I'd have to wait two hours for the results. I was too upset to drive around and couldn't think about anything besides my current predicament, so I just sat there waiting, numbly staring at the wall.

"Laura Torricelli." My body tensed at the sound of my name.

"The first thing I'm going to do tomorrow is change my name back," I muttered, walking into the doctor's office.

The young physician scanned the results, sighed, and shook his head. Then he glanced at his computer screen and finally took off his glasses, laced his fingers, and said:

"The test results are conclusive. You are pregnant."

My ears rang. My heart was hammering like crazy, and my stomach cramped painfully. The doctor must have noticed the effect of his words. He called a nurse. The two of them led me to a couch and elevated my legs. I wanted to die. The doctor was saying something, but the only thing I heard was my own blood pumping in my head.

Fifteen minutes later, I was feeling well enough to sit up and continue my conversation with the physician.

"I need to get rid of it," I said firmly. The man widened his eyes. "As fast as possible. I read about those pills I could take—"

"Get rid of it?" he repeated. "Mrs. Torricelli, you should talk with the baby's father first. Or a psychologist. I wholeheartedly recommend thinking about it."

"Doctor!" I snapped, interrupting him. "I will get rid of that baby with or without your help. Only with regard to the surgery I had earlier this year, I think it would be safer to do it under your supervision."

"What you're asking me is illegal in this country."

"Let me assuage your fears," I cut in again. "The child is a result of rape. I don't want to have anything in common with the rapist. And before you tell me I should call the police, it's not possible. Will you help me or not?"

The young doctor fell silent and thought. "All right. Return tomorrow. You'll have to stay for a day or two. We'll administer the medication and do a procedure if it proves necessary." I nodded in thanks and left.

———

I took a seat in my huge car and burst out crying. I spasmed and sobbed and the waves of emotion rolling over me was like the ocean. As soon as one crashed and faded, another came. This continued until I was completely exhausted. I started the engine and drove without any specific target in mind. I passed the promenade, feeling the need to be alone. Just like I had when I learned about my first pregnancy. And just like last time, I needed to sit down and watch the ocean.

I parked by a beach and put on shades before walking to the shoreline. I plopped down on the sand and cried some more, watching the waves, thinking about death. How was I supposed to tell Nacho? He would never look at me the same way.

"Hey, kiddo." His warm voice startled me. "Let's talk."

"I don't feel like talking," I snapped, trying to get to my feet. He held me down. "And what are you doing here in the first place?"

"All our cars have trackers. And after you behaved like you did at home, I was concerned. I wanted to know if everything was fine. What did the doctor say?"

His voice broke a little. He must have known, or at least felt, what the answer would be.

"I'm having a procedure tomorrow," I muttered. "They're going to get rid of it."

"You're pregnant?" Nacho's voice was calm, full of tenderness.

"Please, talk to me, Laura," he added when I didn't respond. "Goddamn it! I'm your man, and I don't intend to watch on as you fight this alone!" he cried. "Let me help you."

I lifted my teary eyes to him. He took off my sunglasses. "Talk to me, bee, or I'll call the doctor and he'll say what I want to know."

"I am pregnant, Nacho." I felt more tears streaking down my cheeks. Another sob shook me. "But I swear I didn't want it. I'm so sorry."

Nacho sat me on his knees and embraced me. Held in his strong arms, I felt safe. I knew I didn't have to fear. He wouldn't leave me.

"I'll take care of it. I'll make it go away."

"*We* will take care of it," he corrected me, kissing my brow.

"Please let me do it alone. I don't want you there. I know how cruel it sounds, but it is what it is." I looked at him pleadingly. "I'm begging you. The more you're involved, the more guilty I'll feel. I just want it over with."

He nodded and hugged me closer. "As you wish, honey. Just please stop crying."

We returned home. I tried acting normally, but it was that easy. I hid and cried every so often. Truth be told, I wanted to curl up in bed and leave only when all my problems disappeared. The Canarian saw how difficult it was for me. He tried pretending it wasn't depressing him, too, but he wasn't as good an actor as he would like. Luckily, the day finally ended. The long walk I took with our dog helped a little.

———

The next day, I woke up very early, only to find out Nacho wasn't there. I had fallen asleep at his side, embraced and pressed against his wide torso, but I think we both felt uncomfortable. It was as if Massimo were lying between us, pushing us apart.

I took a shower and threw on the first thing I found in the wardrobe. Who cared how I looked? I didn't want to think or feel, only wake up in two days' time and breathe with relief. I packed a small bag with the barest necessities and went down to have breakfast. Nacho wasn't there, either. Neither were Amelia or the dog. I had told them I wanted to do this alone, hadn't I? Resigned, I sat at the long table. The sight of food only made me want to retch. I looked over the table, into the distance. I would rather starve out that innocent little being inside me than allow the results of the awful things I had suffered to destroy my life. I shivered. The sip of tea I had a moment later bubbled up my throat, and before I knew it, I was throwing up on the lawn. I wiped my mouth and looked at the puddle of my vomit.

"I don't think I want to drink anymore," I groaned.

With the last pregnancy, the vomiting had started a lot later. Or maybe I was just that susceptible to suggestion. Maybe the knowledge itself was making me nauseous. I shook my head and went back into the house.

An hour later, I was in the car, driving to the clinic. My phone was silent, but that didn't bother me. I didn't want to speak with Nacho anyway. I didn't need to ask where he was. There was no chance he was anywhere else but the beach house. Surfing, drinking beer, riding horses, and fuming. It was sad that he had to deal with all those emotions because of me, but I couldn't do anything to stop it. Amelia didn't know anything, but Olga . . . I completely forgot to call her. Quickly, I dialed my friend's number.

"At long fucking last!" she greeted me with her usual courtesy. "What's the news?"

"I'm going to get an abortion as we speak."

She sighed.

"It should be over by tomorrow."

"So this is how it's going to be," she said and sighed again. "I'm so sorry for you."

"Stop it," I whispered, my voice breaking. "Don't feel bad for me. And I don't want to talk about it. Tell me what you learned."

"Mario is fine. Massimo doesn't know he let you out of the house. Or at least that's what I think. So you don't have to worry about him. Someone broke Massimo's nose. Was that you? I heard you slammed him with a gun handle." She laughed. "Good for you. You should have kicked him in the nuts, too. Anyway, he doesn't seem keen on looking for you anymore. Domenico told him a head of a mob family shouldn't look desperate."

I breathed a sigh of relief. "But you know how he is. You never know what's in his head."

"That's at least one good thing, I guess," I said, parking the car. "I've got to go, Olga. Keep your fingers crossed. I hope you'll come so I can congratulate you properly. And how are you feeling, by the way?"

I felt guilty. I had focused on my own problems and ignored hers.

"Oh, just great. The sex is better than ever. Domenico loves me more than ever, too. Carries me around. I've lost weight, and my boobs are huge now." She sounded genuinely happy. "I'll come visit, but closer to your birthday, okay?"

"Oh, shit, the birthday," I groaned. "I got a dog."

"Another one?"

"Yeah, but this time it's a real dog instead of a rat crossed with a yarn ball. A bull terrier." She took a breath to say something, but I cut her off. "But I'm getting a present each day now. I got a go-kart and my own racing track, a surfboard, a helicopter piloting course. Listen, I really have to go now. I love you. We'll talk in two days."

"Love you, too," she said joylessly.

"Catch you later."

I pocketed the phone, took a deep breath, and tightened my grip on the handle of the bag. *Let's do it*, I thought.

———

The doctor performed an ultrasound, sticking something like a vibrator into my pussy. It wasn't pleasant at all, but I guess it had to be done. I didn't even look at the screen, afraid I'd start developing feelings for the thing inside me. Moving the cold pipe within me, the doctor said:

"All right, Laura. I'll give you the pill. It'll make you bleed. Then we'll see if the procedure is required. It's late for the pills to work on their own. Seven weeks. But I guess we'll just wait and see . . ."

I didn't listen too closely. I didn't care. But something caught my attention. I snapped out of my stupor.

"Wait, what did you say?" I asked, surprised. "How many weeks?"

"I'd say seven." He pressed a button, measuring something inside me.

"But . . . that's not possible . . . The man, he raped me around . . ."

That's when it hit me. The child wasn't Massimo's. It was Nacho's!

I kicked out with my leg on instinct and jumped to my feet so fast it made me dizzy. Confused, I sat back down. The doctor was looking at me without understanding.

"Doctor," I said, "are you sure the child isn't only three weeks old?"

His eyes widened, and he nodded. "Positive. The fetus is too large. And the blood tests show that your hormone levels are higher than . . ."

I stopped listening. It wasn't the tyrant's baby. It was Nacho's. The baby was Nacho's. My colorful boy would be a father. I smiled widely. The doctor was surprised.

"Thank you, Doctor, but I won't need the pill or the procedure after all. Is the baby all right?"

He nodded, confirming.

"Can I get a printout or something?"

I rushed out of the clinic and ran to the car, dialing Nacho's number before I even reached it. He didn't pick up. He must have been swimming. I started the engine and set the GPS to take me to our hideaway.

My mood took a one-eighty swing. Tears were flowing down my cheeks again, but these were tears of happiness. Was it a good time to have a baby? We barely knew each other . . . but it didn't matter. The little life inside me was his. I knew how much he loved Pablo. Now we were about to give the little boy a cousin. They would grow up together. And Olga's kid, too . . .

"Fuck! Olga!" I cried out and dialed her number. She picked up. "I'm pregnant!" I screamed gleefully. She fell silent.

"Wow, what the fuck? Are you okay, Laura?" she asked, not quite following. "They drug you again?"

"It's Nacho's! The baby!" Another silence, followed by a high-pitched screech. "Massimo didn't have a chance. I was already pregnant!"

"Oh, God, Laura," Olga sobbed. "We're going to be mothers."

"Yes!" I cried out, grinning. "And our kids are going to be the same age. How cool is that?"

"Does Nacho know?" she asked after we cried out in joy some more.

"I'm driving to see him now. I'll call you when I calm down a bit. Probably tomorrow."

I drove like a maniac, regretting that the car didn't have a tele-portation device on board.

I hit the brakes, the wheels throwing up great gusts of golden sand. Nacho's bike was parked by a palm tree. He was here. I didn't know how to tell him and stopped midstride. What if he didn't want the baby? What if I told him he was going to be a father and he told me to get an abortion anyway?

Then I recalled him saying that at his age, it was about time he had a kid. Back on Tagomago. That he wasn't afraid of me getting pregnant. I had asked him for contraceptives, and he'd just told me to change clothes and come for a swim with him. That thought spurred me on. I started to run.

I barged into the little house and saw him sitting on the floor with his back against a kitchen cabinet. He lifted his eyes and dropped the bottle of vodka he was holding. Suddenly terrified, I froze. Nacho pushed himself to his feet and swayed a little, grabbing the fridge to keep his balance.

"What are you doing here?" he asked, almost angrily. "What about the procedure?"

"I can't do it," I said, looking him in the eyes, shocked by the state he was in. "The child . . . ," I continued, but he staggered right at me.

"Fuck!" he yelled, cutting me off and smashing the bottle on the wall. "I can't take it, Laura." He stormed out of the house and rushed to the sea, so drunk his legs barely moved.

My eyes teared up. He'd drown if he went into the water.

"It's your baby!" I called out. "You're going to be a father, Nacho!"

———

Hot wind winnowed my hair as I drove my convertible down the promenade. Ariana Grande blared from the speakers. I couldn't think of a song more fitting for my current predicament than "Break Free." I nodded my head to each word. I cranked up the volume.

It was my birthday. I was getting older and should probably be feeling depressed, but the truth was that I felt more alive than ever.

As I stopped the car, waiting for the light to turn green, the chorus began. The bass boomed, and I couldn't feel happier. I sang along.

"This is the part when I say I don't want ya. I'm stronger than I've been before," I bawled with Ariana, waving my arms. A young man stopped his car next to mine. He sent me a flirtatious smile, tapping a hand on the steering wheel to the rhythm of the song. Aside from the loud music and my even louder exclamations, what must have caught his eye was my attire. Its scantiness, to be precise.

I wore a black bikini that perfectly complemented the color of my purple Plymouth Prowler. To be honest, there weren't many things that didn't correspond well with that car. It was perfect itself. The beautiful, rare car had been my birthday present. I suspected the gifts wouldn't stop coming anytime soon—that my man wouldn't quit—but I hoped against reason that this one had been the last.

It all began a month before. I got something new each day. My thirtieth birthday required something special, he had said, and thirty gifts would apparently do the trick. I rolled my eyes and stepped on the accelerator as soon as the light turned green.

A few moments later, I parked the car, grabbed my bag, and

headed to the beach. The weather was sweltering hot, and I intended to make the most of it. Reach my limits. Sunbathe until I'd had more than enough. Taking a sip of iced tea through a drinking straw, I plodded across the sandy expanse, relishing in the feeling of the hot sand on my feet.

"Happy birthday, old girl!" my man shouted. I turned around and a geyser of Moët Rosé exploded in my face.

"The hell do you think you're doing?!" I screamed through bouts of laughter, trying to escape the fizzy stream. Without effect. He chased me with the bottle spewing out its pressurized content. When it was empty, he threw himself at me and toppled me to the ground.

"Happy birthday," he whispered. "I love you."

His tongue slid between my lips and started its dance. I moaned, wrapping my arms around his neck and spreading my legs as he took his place between them, hips slowly twisting.

His hands locked around mine and pinned me down. He pulled away his head and held me with a stare. His lips twitched in a semblance of a smile.

"I have something for you." He wiggled his eyebrows and got up, pulling me with him.

"What do you know," I mumbled, rolling my eyes behind the dark barrier of my sunglasses. He reached out and took them off. His face grew serious.

"I-I'd like to . . . ," he stammered as I watched on. He took a deep breath and knelt before me, extending his hands cupped around a small box. "Marry me," said Nacho, his lips spreading in a wide grin. "I wanted to say something smart and romantic, but most of all I wanted to say something that would convince you."

I inhaled, but he raised his hand. I said nothing.

"Before you say anything, Laura, please consider. A proposal isn't marriage. And marriage doesn't have to be forever." He prodded me gently with the little box. "Remember, I don't want to make you do anything against your will. I'll never order you around. Say 'yes' only if you want it."

A silence descended on the both of us for a long while. He waited patiently for my reply. He got none. "If you refuse, though, I'll send Amelia after you."

I couldn't take my eyes off him. I was scared, worried, awestruck, and . . . happy.

"All right, I can see that didn't convince you, either." He looked over to the ocean and then turned his head back to me, looking at me with his big, emerald eyes. "Say 'yes' for him." He bent down and kissed my stomach, putting his brow against it. "Remember, a family needs at least three. At least. So I might not stop at this one baby." He lifted his eyes, smiled, and took my hand.

"I love you," I whispered. "And I wanted to say 'yes' from the start, but since you cut me off, I decided to let you have your moment."

His eyes sparked with joy.

"Yes, I will marry you!"

EPILOGUE

"**G**oddamn it, Luca!" Olga sprung up from the sunbed, and her sudden sprint focused everyone's attention.

"Come here, you little shit." Resigned, she sat on the sand. Her beautiful, black-eyed boy threw himself into my arms.

I wrapped him in a towel, set him down on my knees, and started drying his hair.

"He only pretends he doesn't know Polish," Olga grumbled, lying down and grabbing a bottle of water. "But as soon as I speak Italian, he gets everything, isn't that right?" She flicked the little angel on the nose.

"Don't get too angry. You're pregnant," I said with a laugh. "Go to Mommy," I told the boy, leaning in closer. He waddled straight to her.

Olga hugged and tickled him, and the boy laughed, trying to break free. Finally, she released him. Ignoring his mother's cries, the boy ran straight back into the water.

"He's just like Domenico. Never listens to what I say." Olga shook her head. "I can't believe he's grown so big. I remember how small he was . . ."

There was a sliver of nostalgia in her voice.

"Yeah . . . me too." I nodded, recalling her wild mood swings from right before the birth.

I couldn't be with her that day, even though I wanted nothing else. Olga had told Domenico to get me on a Zoom call. He had brought in a laptop and placed it behind Olga. That way I had assisted in her labor, though I had nearly died of fright. Olga had screamed her lungs out, punched Domenico, cursed him and the doctor, and finally cried. The childbirth hadn't taken long. Two or three hours and little Luca was with us. He was the most beautiful baby I had ever seen.

"That little brat is going to be the end of me." Olga sighed before calling out: "Luca!" Domenico's little clone was trying to waddle into the water again. "He's so spoiled, I can't cope with the little monster. And that's his godfather's fault." I glanced at her, squinting.

"Is Massimo getting under your skin?" I asked.

She shook her head.

"Try to understand him. He sees Luca as the son he never had."

"If he keeps fucking around, sooner or later he's going to get one. At least he doesn't visit too often." She sighed. "But when he's there, Luca gets a miniature Ferrari. He bought the kid his own racing track. Can you believe that? A four-year-old! He bought him a motorboat. He's even talked Domenico into teaching the boy four languages at the same time! And he has to play the piano now. And train in karate and tennis. 'Sport teaches you discipline' . . . What bullshit."

I shook my head. It had been five years since our divorce. And it hadn't been the easiest thing to get done, especially since Nacho and Massimo still hated each other's guts. The divorce itself had been easy enough—we had signed the documents and that was that—but the road to make it happen was a slog through hell.

On my birthday, Massimo had finally realized I would never get back with him. That had been exactly three hundred and sixty-five days since he had kidnapped me. I still don't know why, but on that day, he finally gave me a divorce.

Any normal human being would have sent the papers over through the mail. Not my ex-husband. He just had to show off. Four men with graying hair arrived on Tenerife, carrying a mountain of paperwork with them. They meticulously explained what was in the documents.

At first, I had told Massimo I didn't want anything from him, but for some reason the Man in Black had dug his heels in. It had been one of his conditions. He said that after everything I had gone through, I deserved—as he had put it—something to secure my future and a bit of recompense. What he really wanted was for me to never be financially reliant on Nacho.

So my ex had given me the company I had created with his money.

"Mommy!" The cry of a child broke me out of my reverie. I saw little outstretched hands.

"Daddy showed me a dolphin!" the girl said as I took her in my arms and hugged her.

"Did he, now?" I nodded my head as Stella launched herself to her feet and ran back into the sea. She was a very active little girl. She took after her father.

I wondered if I would ever grow bored of the view, as I looked at my husband, who was walking toward me with our daughter in his arms. The little blond girl wrapped her arms around his neck and kissed him time and time again. Nacho held his surfboard in one arm, while the other was wrapped around Stella. His wet tattooed skin glistened in the sun. He didn't look like a forty-year-old. Physical activity allowed him to retain his youthful vigor and beautifully toned muscles.

"I can't believe you allow her to surf," Olga said, pushing a piece of banana into Luca's mouth. "I would be too scared. He keeps sitting her up on that board, and she keeps on falling into the water. That's just too scary."

"She doesn't fall. She jumps. And who would have thought we'd be such different mothers." I laughed, keeping my eyes on my man. "If I remember correctly, I was supposed to be the panicky one. You were going to be the one to drink booze with them before they turned eighteen."

"Not a chance!" she cried out. "I'm still considering locking them all up in a basement until they grow up. Or till they're thirty. Just to be sure."

Suddenly, the sun vanished, and a pair of wet, salty lips pressed against my mouth. Keeping our daughter in his arms, Nacho leaned over my sunbed and kissed me once more.

"Stop it, you perverts," Olga said.

"Don't be jealous," Nacho retorted, grinning. "If Domenico would finally stop sulking and come here, you could have enjoyed a bit of loving, too."

"Oh, fuck off," she countered, not even looking his way. I was grateful our kids could speak several languages, but English wasn't one of them. "My husband is just true to his family." She shrugged.

"Yeah, right." Nacho snorted. He grabbed a towel and wrapped Stella in it. "So you're a bad mobster wife because you betray the family with Canarian gangsters?"

"With a charming Polish girl." She pulled her glasses lower, sending him a glance. "It's just a coincidence she's the wife of a Spanish gangster."

"Canarian," we both corrected her. Nacho smiled and stroked my chin, kissing me softly.

Seeing Stella was out of the water, Luca immediately ran up

to her and hugged her. He wasn't even five yet, but he was a great brother. He showed her seashells and small stones, and cared for her as best he could. Sometimes when I looked at him, he resembled Massimo more than Domenico. Those black eyes of his could sometimes get hard and cold . . . He was but a child, but I knew the Man in Black was rearing him to become his successor. Olga didn't want to hear it, but I knew why Massimo kept her, Domenico, and the boy in the residence.

The truth was that Domenico had become a very rich man. He could have afforded his own house. Unfortunately, he was still under Massimo's influence. And his older brother wouldn't let him leave. So he'd talked Olga into staying at the Sicilian mansion. It was, after all, the place where they had first met. Somehow, Olga had turned into a very romantic and compliant wife. She stayed without protest.

"Being a single mother is so hard," said Amelia, joining us. She put her expensive bag on the sunbed by my legs, flicking Nacho's wet towel to the sand.

I turned, looking with amusement at two burly bodyguards lugging a ton of toys, baskets filled with food and alcohol, yet another sunbed, and a beach umbrella. The "bare necessities."

"Sure. Especially with three nannies, a chef, housekeepers, a driver, and some damned idiot that keeps referring to himself as 'your man,'" Nacho said, putting a hat over Stella's head.

"Can't we just buy this beach?" Amelia asked, ignoring him. "I wouldn't have to carry all this stuff each time."

Nacho rolled his eyes and shook his head. He straddled my sunbed and lowered himself, crushing me. He kissed me, and I could imagine the women on both our sides glaring at us.

"We're making ourselves a son tonight," Nacho whispered. "We'll make love until you tell me you're pregnant." His green eyes were happy. He rubbed his crotch against my leg.

"Oh, no you don't!" Olga and Amelia cried out simultaneously. Amelia started throwing things at her brother.

"Pervs! There are kids around!" Olga cried.

"They aren't even looking," Nacho grumbled, getting up. He pointed at the three children, who were occupied with watching some bug half-buried in the sand. "And I told you before." He turned to Olga. "You find some way to bring that stubborn Sicilian here." Then he looked at Amelia.

"And you . . . start supplementing bromine. If it works on men, it might work on you."

He grabbed his surfboard and left us, jogging toward the sea.

"He still doesn't accept him?" I asked, and Amelia shook her head sadly.

"It's been two years now, and he still doesn't even shake his hand," she said.

"I thought that if he employed him at his company, they'd at least start talking, but no. Diego is one of the best lawyers in Spain. He's good, fair . . ."

"He works for the mob," Olga added sarcastically.

"He loves me," Amelia said. "He's even proposed!" She reached out with a hand. There was a large, beautiful, and expensive ring on it.

"Marcelo is going to kill him," Olga said.

"I'll talk to him," I promised. "Tonight. I think tonight it might work. Will you take Stella for the night?"

I sent Amelia a brief look, and she nodded.

"I don't get it. Why won't you get a babysitter? Without Maria I feel lost. Besides, picturing Luca barging in on Domenico and me fucking makes me want to scream in terror."

"I manage. And I work, too." I lifted my brows. "And speaking of work, I'm opening another boutique on Friday. On Gran Canaria this time. Want to come? We'll have a party. There are going to be lots of surfers." I wiggled my hips. "The surfing brand sells better than the Italian one." Who would have thought?

"Will Klara be there?" Olga tied her tunic and reached for a candy bar. "She always makes me feel like a teenager." I laughed and nodded.

Since I'd bought my parents their own house, I could enjoy their company whenever I wanted. They lived on Gran Canaria, only an hour from us by boat.

Dad had found himself a new passion—saltwater fishing. He was spending whole days out on the sea. And Mom? Well, her passion was making sure she always looked breathtaking. After turning sixty, she'd discovered she had a talent for the fine arts and started sculpting in glass. To my astonishment, her works were selling like hot cakes.

At first, I had considered moving them to Tenerife, but living so close to them was too risky—for me and for Nacho. Fortunately, he wasn't as well-known as Massimo had been, so buying my parents a house a hundred miles away was a safe solution.

"All right, enough chitchat. I'm going for a swim."

I reached over my head and grabbed a pink T-shirt that perfectly harmonized with the sporty swimsuit I had on. "I'm going in the water. Keep an eye on the kids, you two."

I took my surfboard and headed toward the shore.

"How come you still have a body like that?" Olga called after me. In her state, she had more in common with a whale than a human being.

"It's all about sports, babe." I pointed to my board and then to my man, who was zipping down a tall wave. "Sports!"

I kissed Stella on the head and went into the water.

My life was complete. I had everything and everyone I loved with me. I glanced at the snowy peak of Teide, then at the girls waving at me, and then, finally, at my colorful boy in the water. He was sitting astride his board, waiting for the perfect wave . . . waiting for me.

AUTHOR'S NOTE

If you haven't found the moral in my story, I'm in a hurry to explain. The 365 Days Trilogy does not glorify rape and Stockholm syndrome. Massimo, as you can see, is not perfect or flawless, and Laura is stupid. I'm sorry, but if you fell for the charm of the main character, you've probably done it more than once in real life. But remember! All that glitters is not gold, and money and the appearance of happiness do not bring true happiness. Freedom, independence, space, and partnership count, not dictatorship and expensive shoes. ☺

ACKNOWLEDGMENTS

Invariably and more and more, I thank my parents. Mom, Dad, you are my life's greatest support, and I love you very much. I would like to thank my friend and business partner Maciej Kawulski. Brother, thank you for believing in me, thank you for the opportunity, and thank you for producing my films with me. It's an honor to be able to call you "brother." Thanks to my manager, Agata Słowińska. Without you, there would be no me, no success, and no vacation every two months. I love you! Thank you, fans all over the world. It feels great to know that you are in love with my story. I hope my books are as good in your language as they were in mine. ☺